Ivy is a Weed.

IVY IS A WEED

Robert M. Roseth

ISBN 978-0-578-62246-0
Library of Congress Control Number:2020900005
Seattle, Washington

Visit the author's website at https://robertroseth.com.

To Kathy with love

...ivy is an opportunist that takes over ecological niches. Ivy adapts very well to a wide range of conditions. That adaptability is what makes it and other weeds dangerous.

Ivy has already created serious damage, not only in urban and suburban settings, but in the wild.

One of the worst pests around, this pesky creeper displaces native plants and harms host trees and shrubs. It also harbors rats and other rodents, not to mention slugs.

--*The Ann Lovejoy Handbook of Northwest Gardening*

CHAPTER ONE

I heard the ringing as I rose to the surface from a deep dive. At first I thought it was part of the dream. But by the third ring I was gently peeling back the covers so as not to disturb Andrea, although she was a sound sleeper. I put both feet on the floor, trying to keep my movements soundless, and gingerly grabbed my phone. Middle of the night calls are never a good thing.

"Hello," I croaked, lucky my voice was audible. Barely.

"This is Officer Symonds from the university police. Is this Mike Woodsen?"

"Hi, Phil. Yeah, 'sme. What's up?"

A longish pause. "Dispatch fielded a call, one hour and three minutes ago. The caller, with a voice characteristic of a young male, reported that he had sighted a body on campus. Not moving. Upon further questioning, he described the approximate location. Dispatch identified a cruiser in the vicinity and sent two officers to investigate. Upon reaching the aforementioned location they debarked from the cruiser and proceeded to investigate. The caller was at the scene and helped to direct officers to the precise location. A brief search revealed that a body was present. The officers responded to dispatch and per our protocol the chief was notified and we began the normal alert process."

I shook off the last of the grogginess, stretched to get my circulation going and grabbed a pen. I started scribbling on the first thing in front of me, some magazine renewal notice that had fallen onto

Andrea's dresser. Andrea moaned softly, a reminder to keep my voice down. "A body. What time is it now?"

"Three fifty-two."

"Uh-huh. Location?" I carefully printed *Body*.

"Near Main Central. To be precise, in a vegetated area adjoining the building."

Right near my office. Well, that got my attention. A body outside my office, in the center of campus. Another pause. I waited. And waited.

"Was the caller a student?"

"Do you want a name? It was a student. Said he was heading back from a late night in a lab."

"No names yet. Please continue."

"The officers performed a cursory hands-off examination, following normal procedure. The person appeared to be deceased. Additional authorities were notified, per our protocols for handling situations like this. Which includes notifying you as PIO." Short for Public Information Officer, who manages relations with the news media.

Fully awake, I wrote *Dead* in front of *Body*. A university is usually pretty quiet, especially after hours, except maybe during exam week, which this was not. We have our share of incidents. And people do die. Usually students and usually alcohol-related. And we've had our suicides too.

"Phil, any idea if it's a student?"

I could hear a deep breath.

"Don't want to speculate. We're still trying to get a positive ID. The Medical Examiner is on the scene now, as am I as the SOCO." Scene of Crime Officer. They loved their acronyms. "But he looks older. I see some gray hair visible. Could be an older student, or really anyone. At this point we don't know."

"Huh." I was writing on the renewal form: *Gray hair*. Near Main Central, 3 am. *Student?* When these things happen it's near the dorms or frats, or in apartments near campus. Someone drinks too much and falls. Over a balcony. Off a roof. Even out a window. Or a fire escape. But never before in the center of campus. At least not on my watch of little over a decade.

"Any media calling yet?" This was my job, helping the police with the reporters. Usually the cops would provide the details to the media directly from the official report, terse version, and that was that. But if things got hairy I'd help them out, shoulder part of the work. It wasn't spelled out anywhere exactly who would answer the questions in an incident like this, because they were so infrequent; we'd work it out on the fly. But I was inclined to do as much as I could. It was a way of staying in the cops' good graces, a deposit in the Favor Bank, should I ever need to make a withdrawal. You never know.

"No. But we've been using the scanner since before the first officers arrived on scene, so it's been broadcast pretty widely. And it's probably all over social media; I haven't had time to look."

"Right. I'll get dressed and be there in fifteen minutes. And we'll figure out what to say to reporters. Not much, given what we know."

I could almost hear him nodding. "Not much. See you soon."

I dressed quickly in Andrea's bathroom. My shirt was wrinkled but no one would care. If I spruced up people probably wouldn't recognize me. My anything-goes hair style was starting to obstruct my vision: time for my six-week barber visit, if I couldn't persuade Andrea to trim the fringe. I turned sideways and frowned at my slight paunch. I grabbed my keys and notebook and headed out.

From Andrea's apartment it was a quick drive to campus, even quieter than the rest of the city late at night. The air was supporting either heavy dew or light mist. Welcome to the moist days of early autumn in the Pacific Northwest.

Campus was empty. As I headed down the main drive, I noticed the few deciduous trees had begun turning fiery under the muted lighting. Some of the firs were already brown and had dropped their first needles. It was a campus with a mix of classic university architecture and relatively inoffensive modernist boxes. But the best natural features were the lush vegetation and signature meandering creek that rolled through the middle of campus, deeply set into a cleft that ran north-south, beloved by current and former students.

I pulled into the parking area in back of Main Central, where the chief administrators including the president worked. My office, the news office, was there, too — although they persistently threatened to move us out in favor of someone more important. And in the university hierarchy, we were regularly reminded, just about anyone was more important than we were.

I parked alongside the squad cars. I could hear chatter from the cruisers' radios, punctuated by beeps, hisses and the occasional growl.

I had been to a few death scenes as a daily newspaper reporter, mostly auto accidents, and never got used to them. Death, even the thought of it, made me sick to my stomach. Just observing a dead human body, even from a distance, gave me shivers.

Right outside my office.

A half-dozen officers, some from campus and a couple in city uniforms, were standing around in a semicircle on the asphalt sidewalk near some empty bike racks and a row of low bushes. A few students, probably alerted through social media, were lurking on the periphery, staring down at their phones or trying to find a clear path for a photo. I'm sure they'd be shooting selfies with the body if the cops would let them.

The body was visible just where the bushes surrounding the building ended and the grass began. It was still uncovered, as the Medical Examiner's team was continuing its work.

The surrounding area was dimly lit by the waist-level lamps focused on campus walking paths. I could see two or three people dressed in purple windbreakers kneeling around the body next to squarish briefcases. One of them was holding a portable floodlight that cast its too-white LED glare over the corpse. I could see a limp hand stretching in my direction. I imagined it reaching out, trying to grasp something. The body was prone, legs splayed at an unnatural angle. A sandy mop of hair, salt and peppered. The other arm straight out 90 degrees from the neck, also bent midway between wrist and elbow. The soles of both feet rested almost squarely on the grass, bending back the ankles. There was a gentle hum of half-whispers from the ME's team.

I'm no medical expert, but it looked to me like he had fallen from some great height. I looked up and saw the arched Gothic windows of Main Central, the likely place where his final descent began.

And I'm no Sherlock Holmes, but people generally don't just fall out of windows, unless they're drunk or intending suicide. Which would make this a crime scene.

I edged into the group of officers and found Phil Symonds.

"M.E. still doing his thing?"

Phil turned, giving me a look as if I had intruded on something, but when he recognized me his face softened. He was well over six feet, towering above me by a good five inches (more when I slouched, which was always) and had a nearly shaved head except for sideburns. Even when he relaxed I could see the outline of the rippling muscles under that uniform. He was absently slapping his oversized flashlight against his palm, waiting for something to happen.

"I think he's almost done. But no COD mentioned yet."

I figured that meant cause of death. "Any more news?"

Phil scratched his chin. "Not really. If we're lucky he'll give us an I.D. before taking away the DB."

Dead Body. This guy loved procedural acronyms, even ones he made up on the spur of the moment. "Not sure I'd call it lucky."

"Whadya mean?"

"Well, all other things being equal, I'd just as soon bounce the media to him. If we are told he's one of ours, which is likely, then I have to field the calls."

Phil chuckled. "You looking for an easy way out? I thought you got the big bucks just for times like this."

"Nah, I get paid the little bucks for touting what a great place this is for sending little Johnny or Sarah off to get an education, what great faculty they will have. That's what us PR types do. Not dealing with DBs. They don't pay me enough for that."

Phil kicked at a clod of weeds left behind by the gardeners. "Truth is, neither of us get enough for that. That's one of the reasons I left city law enforcement."

The only way I recognized the ME was that he was the only one wearing a suit. Not a pressed suit. He looked like he'd worn it to bed. He resembled an overworked, underslept, overfed bulldog. When he turned away from the body I decided to try acting official with him. I blocked his path.

"I'm the PIO here. Anything you can tell me?"

He looked me up and down and scowled. I heard a deep growl. "We don't release anything until we've examined the body in the lab."

"Can you at least tell me his name? I'm gonna get calls." As if on cue, over his shoulder I saw the first TV news crew pulling into the lot.

"Not until we confirm his identification. And try to contact next of kin." He turned away.

"That went well," I said to Phil.

"That's the drill." He yawned. "Call us about mid-morning and we'll probably have his ID for you."

I liked Phil and the other campus cops that I knew well. They had gravitated to law enforcement out of a desire to serve and protect, as the motto said, as well as lock up the bad guys, but the percentage of hot dogs and cowboys (to mix metaphors) here on campus was pretty low. Not enough juice for adrenalin junkies. They had opted for the relative peace of a college campus and enjoyed acting as mentors and occasional parent-substitutes. For the most part it was a sweet gig.

A couple of university cops were helping load the body onto a gurney. Some of the ME's techs were still examining the ground where the body had been, taking samples, but even if they found something it was obvious they weren't going to tell me.

"Any reason for me to hang around here?"

"Not unless you like watching paint dry." He sniffed. "This is my first death on campus. Just seems wrong to find a body in a place like this. Still, anything is possible."

"Who's going to call the shots?"

"I'm going to tell the chief that we should lead the investigation and not defer to the city cops. They have the technology, but this is our turf. And if there are people to interview, they'll probably be more comfortable talking to us."

"You going to issue some brief statement?"

"Suppose I should. Once the normal day begins, the social media will light up with speculation. Better to try and head off the worst of it. Yeah, I'll put something together, ultra-terse. We found a body. No ID. Investigation underway. News at 11. You wanna see it?"

"Nah, I trust you. But I'll call you mid-morning to see how it's going."

Phil looked around. "I'll handle that TV crew if you want. Go home and catch a few z's."

"Thanks."

As I headed to my car I snagged the TV reporter, told him the little we knew and advised him that at this point no one was likely to go on camera but pointed out Phil as the contact with the PD.

Calls from reporters started coming in while I was driving home. I figured there was no reason to disturb Andrea twice in the same night by going back to her apartment; at least one of us should get a good night's sleep.

Our intrepid local reporters were just filled with incisive questions, and I was ready with witty and complete responses:

No, we don't have identification.

No, we don't know cause of death.

No, we have no reports of a serial killer on or near campus.

No, we haven't alerted the students and are not on lockdown in the dorms.

Yes, you can go to the scene, but don't disturb the crime tape if there is any.

No, I won't go on camera to tell you we don't know anything yet.

The calls continued sporadically into the early morning. So much for trying to catch a little sleep. I came late to my windowless office in the bowels of Main Central. Fran, our receptionist, cocked a single eyebrow at my arrival.

"Late night?"

"You could say that. Cops called me about three."

"And?"

"A body. Right around the corner."

She perked up. It's amazing how death makes people pay attention.

"I heard some reports on the radio and saw a couple of mentions on social media. Anyone we know?"

"Speaking of which, where were you after midnight?"

"I have a long list of people I'd like to do in. Starting with...."

"Don't tell me, let me guess."

She pasted a mock-grimace on her face, her eyes dancing with mischief. "Only if I could do it slowly and painfully."

"Well, stay tuned and have hope. Maybe someone else beat you to it."

I checked my emails. They were of the same flavor as the calls: reporters jockeying for position, trying to claim I owed them favors, that they would do the best job if I called them first, that they had heard rumors that foul play was suspected.

As a university news office, we dealt mostly with faculty who make news through their research findings, which we announced through news releases and briefings. Second on the hit parade was the never-ending need in the media for experts to comment on a wide range of subjects, lending perspective and gravitas. Third was providing information on general campus events ranging from student demonstrations and the occasional scandal (often involving athletics) to megagifts and opulent new buildings. Crime was seldom serious enough for news coverage, thank goodness.

It was mid-morning by my reckoning. I called Phil.

"So, what can you tell me?"

"No COD yet. But the ME has said, not yet for public consumption, that there were no signs of injury other than what would've occurred when the body hit the ground."

"So, he fell?"

"That's the current theory."

"And that means... he was in the building? In Main Central?"

"Can't put anything over on you, can we?"

I began rummaging for a note pad and one of those fat pens that fit my stubby fingers. My desk was its usual mess.

"So, we're thinking this guy worked here or was a student?"

"Affirmative."

Geez, this was like pulling teeth. The phone made a scratchy noise rubbing against my indifferently shaved chin. "Do you have a positive ID?"

The phone seemed to go dead. Except Phil was a heavy breather.

"Phil? You still there?"

"The ME has confirmed his identity. But they don't want to release until they've notified family. And if possible, they'd like to nail down the COD."

"Well, I hope he decides quickly."

"I do, too. Otherwise there's going to be a shitstorm. A real shitstorm. People around here aren't patient when it's one of their own. And the shit always flows downhill, to us."

"Geez, Phil, what's going on?"

"Look, this is all off the record, OK?"

"Hey, the same person signs our paychecks."

"This guy was a big deal. A veep."

"OK."

"Do you know who Jeremy Ronson is? Or was?"

"Yeah. He does, or did, something with administrative systems for computing. Tech support for campus infrastructure. Something like that."

"If you say so. Right here it says, 'Vice President for Strategic Infrastructure Support and Vice Provost for Systems Design and Integration.'"

"Yeah, just what I said. We have a positive ID?"

"Seems so. But the ME wants to wait on releasing it. It's looking like an accident but they want to tie up some loose ends. And I suspect the chief wants to make calls to some of the leaders around here. So there are some wrinkles in releasing his name, some protocols we've never had to use before. This is one of those sensitive cases that almost never happens. So give us some time."

"How soon?"

"With luck, by the end of the day."

"That may seem soon for you, Phil, but for me it's going to be an eternity. Not only will the media be all over me for details. Those calls have started. But the campus rumor mill is already hard at work. I mean, if Ronson is the victim he's going to be missed. People will notice and they'll start to put the pieces together, even when they don't fit. Who knows what stories they'll come up with. If we don't get news out soon the rumors will be the story of the day, right or wrong. Once the false story gets broadcast, it's hard to put the toothpaste back in the tube."

I had a few stories of my own to account for Ronson's death that were starting to form themselves in my head: High-ranking administrator takes a header in the middle of the night out an office window from a building normally unoccupied at that time. What could be suspicious about that?

It was clear from Phil's radio silence that he was unimpressed with my situation.

"I guess I'll just hunker down between now and then. But do what you can to hurry this along, please. People, especially the media, are going to get suspicious if they think they're being played. And then we'll have a real shitstorm."

When I heard his click I put down the phone and went to talk with Fran.

"Be back in a few minutes," I told her. She got pissed when I left unannounced, not knowing to whom I'd bequeathed what we jokingly called "the football," in imitation of the Strategic Air Command launch codes. These were the urgent calls that no one else wanted to handle.

I headed for the spot where they'd found Ronson's body, now a patch of bare earth in the midst of the verdant lawn. I looked up. The building's Gothic-style windows, stretching up five floors, had tiny rectangular glass panes which occasionally came loose from their moorings, crashing to earth without notice. These tall windows opened outward with a simple handle. A fall from the fourth floor was surely enough to be fatal. Ronson's office was up there. It was nearly impossible for me to imagine someone just falling out of a window that high, that exposed, without some help.

And they're saying he just fell? Nonsense. If they asked me (which they never did), I'd suggest one obvious option.

Defenestration.

Technically, defenestration applies only when someone is forcibly ejected from a window. You could stretch it to include self-defenestration. But I wasn't buying this "accident" explanation that Phil had just offered. I imagined Ronson leaving the building, however he was propelled, and landing with a thud and low-frequency cracks. Geez. Ah, time to return to the office and answer the calls that surely were piling up.

I referred the steady stream of reporters to the ME's office, who kept bouncing them back to me. No one was happy. I knew that if I was still on the beat at a daily, I'd be unhappy, too. Fran was giving me The Look, meaning the callers were getting testy with her — but she always gave at least as good as she got. She also knew we could stiff-arm reporters for only so long when we actually had the goods. They'd start calling everyone they could, including our bosses, with inflammatory rumors and veiled threats.

Phone rings.

"You hidin' down there?" It was Rolf Trencher, my boss. The one Fran usually targeted in her fantasies. Of mayhem, that is.

"Just waiting for the other shoe to drop."

"Well, before it does, do you have a minute?"

"Be right up."

The offices got bigger as you rose in Main Central. And the titles grew longer. You could often measure the salary by the length of title. Ronson had one of those double-barreled titles suggesting handsome compensation. Trencher was up on the third floor, a little lower than the angels and fundraisers (as if there were a distinction).

In the wave of pseudo-business-speak that had swept through administrative offices like a plague in the past several years, it was no longer sufficient to describe what someone did. If you were sufficiently high-ranking you were blessed with an "aspirational" title, reflecting some airy, unachievable but nonetheless worthy goal. The people pushing this approach had read some crackpot article and convinced our president that such titles focused people's attention on what they should be doing. For a place that prided itself on careful research in its laboratories, it continued to amaze me that leaders were able to rationalize adopting new administrative strategies based on zero evidence.

Trencher's title used to be something like Associate Vice President for Public Affairs. Late one night, someone with a stencil kit defaced his door, which still bore:

Associate Vice Leader for Aural Excellence

Champion of The Golden Name

I knocked and entered. "Fun day we're going to have," I offered.

"Any word from the ME?"

He was still typing an email. Despite the fact that he was one of the higher-ranking execs, entitled to all sorts of luxurious appointments, he worked in a bare, utilitarian office, his perch behind a faux-wood metal desk. The room had a small table that looked like it had been lifted from a sidewalk cafe, piled high with thick reports. The only notable piece of furniture was the fine oak chair with a cushion in university colors in which I was sitting. The walls were covered with photos of academic celebrities, some of whom I recognized, but most to me were just old white men dressed in academic garb. One wall had a white board upon which Trencher had last written many months ago. In one corner was a large and very uncomfortable-looking rocking chair with the university's seal. And in another a seldom-used coat rack.

"Not yet. Hoping it's soon."

He pivoted from behind the computer and stood up. All five feet of him in suspiciously augmented shoes. He ran a hand through hair that was thinning beyond the point where the comb-over was a viable strategy, but apparently he wasn't quite ready to acknowledge that. He cracked his knuckles. How I hated that sound.

He was dressed in a flashy, expensive suit, cut in the severely tailored, form-fitting style usually associated with places like Milan. He also was wearing striped suspenders and cuff links. Trencher was what the Victorians would call a dandy.

"We should try to get this behind us as soon as we can."

"Kind of depends on the ME's pronouncement." The view from his windows gave the sweep of the campus and on a clear day (this wasn't one of them) the distant mountains, which now bore a light dusting of autumn snow, still too little for the ski slopes to open. His windows were tall, too. Big enough to accommodate a mid-sized individual without crouching; more than tall enough for Trencher to exit without bumping his head. Just sayin'.

"We're pretty sure it was an accident," he said. Trencher's power consisted of the things he knew, especially those gleaned from conversations with the campus elite, so he gave out information like it was coming from Scrooge's purse pre-Marley. But you could be reasonably sure he had his information from highly-placed sources.

"We?"

"What else could it be? Guy is found on the grass just below the windows to his office. Maybe he was drunk. But surely accidental.

Let's tie a bow on it quickly and ship out the news as soon as possible. Get it behind us."

He paused for dramatic effect. "And put your reporter's instinct in deep freeze for once. Mike, I want this one done quickly and without rancor. Is that clear?"

I gave Trencher a nod and a mock salute. I never found it productive to argue with him, although I was inexpert at concealing my opinions. He regarded conversation as a mixed martial arts event in which all arguments, logical or not, were weapons. I just wanted to gather information and reach conclusions through a frank exchange of views, but that almost never happened. Like dogs in a confined space, we had each marked our territory long ago.

"We'll know pretty soon, the cops tell me."

"Do you want help drafting a press statement?"

I tried to hide my revulsion. The word *prolix* (itself a hifalutin way of saying *verbose*) had his photo nearby in the dictionary. A tic left over from a too-long career on the academic side, where accomplishments could sometimes be measured in pounds of paper.

"We could use a quote from the president," I parried. "About the 'immeasurable loss to the institution.'"

Trencher snorted. "Some loss." The corners of his mouth sagged.

"He wasn't well regarded?"

"The guy was an asshole. Of the first rank. And incompetent. Things — decisions, responses, almost anything that required his input — would stop dead in his office for months. He was disinvited from cabinet meetings, the only time I've ever seen that happen. A royal PITA."

"Persona non grata."

"What?" He'd stopped listening to me. His mind had already dismissed our meeting and moved on to his next activity of the day.

"Not Mister Popularity."

Trencher resumed his work on the computer, signaling the end of our conversation.

"I'll get you a quote in the next hour. Let me see your statement before we send it out."

I closed the door behind me.

I was back for no more than ten minutes when the phone rang. Phil from campus police.

"ME's report came in."

"Let me guess. Natural causes."

"Not unless falling out a window is regarded as natural." A stab at constabulary humor.

"So he's saying Ronson's death was accidental?"

"The findings are that he was killed by the fall. Preliminary tox screen is negative. No alcohol, no drugs. No obvious signs of struggle. A broken neck. Dislocated shoulder. Busted femur. Broken arm. Dislocated joints. A couple of busted ribs. Based on these facts, and with our concurrence, the ME is calling this an accidental death. We have found no evidence that would call this a homicide or a suicide.'"

I began mentally drafting our statement as he talked. After ten years I could do this kind of thing in my sleep.

"Did you look in his office? Anything out of place?"

Phil laughed. "Hard to tell. The guy was a pack rat. There were piles of paper everywhere, on every surface. Looked like it hadn't been cleaned in at least a year. But we'll confer over here and issue a report soon. No obvious signs of foul play. No farewell note, either. So odds are the report will call his death accidental."

"What does the ME say about the time of death?"

"He just said late evening or early morning."

"Did Ronson usually work late? Did he have a reason for being here in the middle of the night?"

"Why are you asking me? I couldn't pick the guy out of a lineup."

"I thought you were in charge of the investigation."

"I am. Or I was. It's over. Except for tying up the findings and signing the report. The chief wants this over and done with. It looks pretty cut and dried."

"Case closed." I was thinking this was unusually fast. I thought of Trencher's instructions and could imagine Phil trying to tie a bow on the police report. Conclusion first, then write to fit it. Not a good plan for finding the truth.

"Yeah. Anything else?"

"No. You want to see my news release?"

"Probably not. I'll ask the chief and see if he has any interest. As long as it doesn't go beyond our findings."

"Probably won't even mention them beyond the ME's declaration."

I started to do my diligence and gather the necessary details to flesh out the statement. Like the police investigation, it was going to be short and sweet: I tried to suppress my uneasy feelings about this whole operation. What had caused this rush to judgment? I put the finishing touches on my news release.

University mourns the passing of top administrator

The body of Jeremy Ronson, 57, who had worked at the university for more than twenty years and headed the strategic infrastructure division, was found on campus by a passing student early this morning.

The Medical Examiner has determined that his death was accidental.

"Jeremy Ronson's untimely death has shocked us all," said President Marchand Yarmouth. "We celebrate his many contributions to this fine university as we grieve along with his many friends and colleagues."

A celebration of Ronson's life is being planned on campus but no date has been set.

Ronson, who had a doctoral degree in computer science from the University of California, Berkeley, had been at the university since 1991. He was in charge of the division that provides and maintains the computing infrastructure for most administrative functions. The division has an annual budget of $30 million and employs more than 300 people.

He had no family, or none that I could easily locate. The ME was trying to figure out where to send the remains, but we needed to issue the statement pronto. And none of the reporters really cared about survivors; he wasn't of the stature that would've merited a public obit, save for the nature of his demise. And even that was worth an inch or two at most these days.

After passing the release upstairs to Trencher for one last look, arranging for distribution to the usual media suspects and posting it online, I went outside again and looked up again at Ronson's window.

I was feeling itchy. The ME's conclusion struck me as too hasty and quite possibly wrong. I wanted to take a peek in Ronson's office. I needed first-hand convincing that he had simply fallen out the window.

In my experience, it was rare to complete any death investigation in a single day. My years as a reporter had nurtured my skepticism for so long that even now, immersed in university bureaucracy, I was always wary of the official story. And this story set off all kinds of warning signals for me.

The easiest thing was to head right up and try his door. I waited until the end of the day when the building was nearly empty. I was sure that officially I wasn't supposed to be there and I didn't want to cause any raised eyebrows. But there were no signs prohibiting entry, no crime tape. After all, the police had completed their work.

Door was locked. No surprises there.

My efforts frustrated, I decided to take another look at the scene from ground level. On my way out, I ran into Gina Gertsch, one of our staff writers and mistress of all things tech.

"Hey, Gina." She always had a mysterious inner glow that illuminated everything around her. Although she was the youngest person in the office, she had quickly acquired a reputation as a great writer and interpreter of faculty research. She had a knack for disarming reluctant faculty sources with her incisive responses and a laser-like focus on the essentials. Her previous jobs with computer industry publications were a terrific background for this work. It probably didn't hurt that her husband was a professor in the College of Engineering, which gave her instant credibility and social entree.

Her sharp features were accentuated by eyebrows that she had thinned to black lines. But she softened her appearance by wearing colorful ribbons around her neck. It was the only fashion touch she had acquired from her grandmother, who was born in Korea.

"End of a busy day," she offered, walking up the stairs to the building's south exit.

"Yeah. Who woulda thunk someone would take a header from the fourth floor of Main Central."

She stopped just inside the door. "Who indeed?" She paused and licked her lips, readjusting her small backpack and biking helmet. "Are they calling this an accident?"

I nodded.

"Do people fall just out of windows?"

I shrugged. "I've been wondering the same thing. Just about to take another look at the scene from the outside. And I tried to get into his office," I lowered my voice to a whisper, "but it was locked."

She raised her brows to an inverted V. "Should you be doing that?"

"Maybe not. But I figure if no one knows…"

"I don't need to warn you about the possible results of curiosity." She lowered her voice. "Just remember, you're not in a newsroom any more. No one around here is going to give you kudos for answering questions they didn't want asked."

"You're probably right, but someone died here, a dozen steps away from where we're standing."

"True, but excuse me for wondering who asked you. Really, Mike, I'm all for truth and justice, but if you carry this further the only result, that I can see for certain is big trouble, for you."

"I understand. And I appreciate your concern. But as they say in bridge, one peek is worth two finesses."

She shook her head slowly. "If you're determined to stick your neck out, let me know if I can help, as long as it doesn't involve breaking and entering. The guy had a faculty appointment in computer science, although I think it was just a courtesy. Who knows?"

I held the door for her and waved goodbye.

"Be careful out there," she shot over her shoulder.

I followed her out the door, stood on the bare spot below Ronson's window and looked up. I scratched my chin and pulled out my trusty notebook. Ronson would have fallen about 40 feet to the ground floor, maybe a bit more given the tall ceilings in Main Central. Just out of curiosity, I did a quick calculation of how long it would take an object to fall that far: less than two seconds. Not much time to review your life. The landing area was about four feet out from the building's edge. To my untrained eye it looked like there was some horizontal momentum to his last step on solid ground. I scribbled these observations, replete with question marks.

It was class break time, the last classes of the day for most students, and the background noise level around me rose. I walked slowly around the building's perimeter, hoping a new perspective would add something. I held my thumb in front of my face, trying to compare the height of the window with its width. Truth is, I didn't know what the hell I was doing.

"So, is this where it happened? The death, I mean?"

I turned around and saw this very tall blonde wearing a loose-fitting army fatigue jacket. She was carrying a backpack over one shoulder and had heavy-framed wide sunglasses that flared up at the corners, giving her a cat-like appearance. She had peach-colored lipstick and wore her hair up in a bun. The skin on her face looked mottled from an overdose of sun. Probably a grad student from California.

"Beg your pardon?"

She giggled and then quickly covered her mouth with her right hand. "Sorry, I shouldn't laugh. I mean, a guy died here. Didn't he?"

"Yes, but how did you know? The details haven't been released yet."

"Who cares about facts when you have social media? It's the top trending story on campus and probably in the state." She shifted the pack to her other shoulder and kept a tight grip on her phone.

"Well, to answer your question, this is where the body was found early this morning."

"Did he work in this building? Up there?"

I hesitated.

She nodded. "It's okay. I didn't mean to put you on the spot. I'm sure the information will be forthcoming momentarily." She waved her phone at me and grinned.

"I suppose." I found myself mildly annoyed at her breezy attitude as she turned and strode away at the pace of a speedwalker. I took one last look at the window. I shook my head. This was just too weird to believe. And I didn't.

I decided to take a look at social media and what was being said about Ronson's death. Other than noting that a death on campus was uncommon, and the lateness of the hour, it hadn't prompted much comment. To most university people and especially to students, Ronson was just another anonymous administrator whose high salary was another reason for the ever-increasing tuition.

Workday concluded, I headed back to Andrea's. She had picked up some deli and had laid out the fixings on the pass-through counter between the kitchen and dining area. She brushed my lips with a kiss and rushed off to the kitchen, asking me how my day was. I was still mulling over the locked door and whether I had a non-destructive way of getting in. I knew it needed to be soon, before it was cleaned.

"Earth to Mike! Come in please!"

"Huh?"

"I was asking how your day was."

"Well, a day that begins with me climbing out of bed around three to go meet the police at the site of a dead person who fell or was pushed from a fourth-floor window in the building where I work can't be all good."

Andrea stopped, turned around and walked back, rubbing my shoulders. "I'm so sorry. Was it someone you knew?"

"Not well. In fact, hardly at all. Still, it's a death. And the circumstances… well, they left me uneasy. The police are saying he fell, by himself, out of his office window."

"And…?"

"I dunno. Unless he'd been drinking, which they say he wasn't, I don't understand how someone just falls out a window. It doesn't add up."

"My advice is to spend the evening clearing your head. Think about something else for a while. Like what you want to do this weekend. I heard there's this terrific horror movie opening at the Regal. I know you don't like them much, but you know I do. The word is this director is going to be this generation's Wes Craven. He uses rookie actors, closes the set when shooting the scariest scenes..."

Andrea, a horror movie buff, quickly transitioned to talking about this director's art. She knew I couldn't care less about the horror genre, but she made a spirited effort at distracting me. Still, I kept trying to picture a body hurtling from a window, the victim suddenly realizing, too late, he had stepped off solid ground into nothing. The pieces refused to fit together.

But in my meanderings, I had at least figured out how I might get into Ronson's office.

CHAPTER TWO

E arly the next morning, I met with Stella, our office manager. I was trying to think of a plausible cover story I could manufacture for her benefit, but my mind went blank. I never played poker: couldn't bluff worth shit. The best course of action was to make her my confederate. That would save me the trouble of remembering any lame yarn I tried to spin. Stella could get me into Ronson's office, I was pretty sure: She bore the informal, unpaid title of building manager, which gave her access to just about any space in Main Central.

"You heard about Ronson?"

"Of course. Everyone has. Too bad."

I looked up at her. She was dressed, as usual, in an outfit of loose-fitting slacks, wrinkled blouse, oversized pink-framed glasses hanging from her neck by what looked like an old-fashioned lanyard, the kind we used to make in summer camp. She moved with a swagger that had only one interpretation: "Back OFF!"

We had never had an angry word between us. I respected her territory, her ability to manage our resources, to keep the computers and other systems running smoothly. She took it as a point of pride that she could cut deals with the campus tradesmen to give us discounts, the kinds of things that were supposed to be impossible in a rules-driven bureaucracy.

"Did you know him?"

She scratched her arm. "Hardly. I don't know anyone who did. He was pretty much a recluse. Never sighted in the halls or the elevator.

His AA was actually working in another building. Everyone would make up their favorite story about him, but no one had any juicy facts."

"You know the ME says he fell from that window."

She glanced at the door, which she had shut on her way in.

"That's the story I heard."

"And...?"

She put on her glasses and pulled on her earlobe. "I don't have any information that would suggest otherwise."

"Something strikes me as odd about this. A healthy man, apparently not under the influence, falls out a window by accident? I suppose it's possible. And people who investigate these kinds of things for a living have decided that's what happened..."

"But...?"

"The investigation was brief, too brief in my opinion, like maybe the police were operating under specific orders to expedite."

Stella shifted uncomfortably from foot to foot.

"Well, even if the story smells — and I can see why you might think it does — what can you do about it?"

"Probably not a lot. The police have already closed their investigation."

It was time for the big question.

"Stella, I'd like to get into Ronson's office. Can you help?"

"Is that all?" She laughed out loud. "Is that what this was leading up to? I thought you were going to stage a night raid on some secret files and needed some muscle."

"You think you can help me?"

"Shit, why do you think I keep that box of keys in my bottom desk drawer? Is there any crime tape around the office? Would we be breaking any laws?"

"I don't think so. But the door was locked."

"One condition. I want to go with you. I mean, if we're not crossing a police line we're just being ordinary snoops. Sounds like a fun operation."

"Agreed. We need to do this after 5. The sooner the better, before the office gets cleaned. Today, if possible."

"I can do that. Just what do you expect to find there?"

"No idea. Maybe something that could convince me it's really possible that he fell out of the window without help. Or maybe a clue pointing in another direction. I dunno. I just think there may be more to the story."

Stella twirled a bunch of keys around her finger. "Well, a lot of people around here think he was a little nuts. Without hardly knowing him, that is."

"You think anybody tells me the good gossip?" I laughed. "Who's dishing the dirt on Ronson?"

"Just talk to the people with inside knowledge around here — the secretaries, administrative assistants and..." she blew on her fingernails theatrically, "... office managers. We know where the bodies are buried, even when the body is still warm."

"Thanks, Stella. And this is just between us, right?"

"What is?"

To clear the decks I went through my morning emails. I got copied on all kinds of threads that were of no value to me except entertainment.

TO: All University Faculty and Staff
FROM: Content Approbation -- People, Promise, Programs and Purpose Enhancement
SUBJECT: Permitted use of colors and phone numbers
    Dear Gang:

We know you are busy, but we're all supposed to be on the same team here! Our job is to make this university shine, and you are the chamois cloth. In the spirit of buffing appropriately, we offer the following guidance.

Colors: the university's colors, as you know, are cobalt and amarillo. These colors have specific meaning and resonances. They are NOT just any "blue" or "yellow."

Please, in all your printed and web publications, use Pantone 16-4529 TCX, otherwise known as "cyan blue." And the amarillo is Pantone 14-0756 TCX, otherwise known as "empire yellow." If you use another version of either color, you can expect a nasty note from us. If this correction is not applied, we may shut down your website until the proper colors are deployed. And let's be clear, there will be other consequences. You don't want to know what those are.

Also, and we hate to be sticklers but that's the responsibility we've been granted by the President, when you have an email signature it is <u>required</u> that you separate the digits of the phone number by periods. Not dashes, not parentheses and certainly not commas, but periods:

555-297-3000 is not OK

555.297.3000 is correct

We have research, literally mountains of research, which shows that people think we are a friendlier institution if we use dots rather than dashes. And everyone knows we need all the friends we can get, right?

Remember, it's all in the interest of making us better liked, more respected, higher ranked, more sought after. And we have research that shows it works!

Thanks a ton,

Your colleagues

TO: Heidi Fellows, vice president for People, Promise, Programs and
    Purpose Enhancement
FROM: Margaret Hietflower, Provost
SUBJECT: Are dots friendlier?

Heidi, I received a number of queries from faculty asking for citations concerning your research on using dots in phone numbers rather than dashes. I know you are busy, but can you direct these people to a reliable source that will back you up?

TO: Provost Margaret Hietflower
FROM: Heidi Fellows
RE: Are dots friendlier?

Margaret, I'm surprised anyone has raised the issue of dots versus dashes. For years, throughout market-driven organizations around the country (and indeed overseas as well), it has been accepted wisdom that the dot is a clear symbol of informality, approachability and friendliness. I suppose I could contact some corporate marketing executives, but it would consume so much time and finally, are we willing to reopen this discussion? I know I'm not.

When I said we "literally" had mountains of research, I didn't mean to suggest I had actually assembled the research. I rely primarily on my network of colleagues and my sense of the consensus we have reached on this and other topics. Kind of like crowdsourcing.

On a personal note, coming from the private sector to the university has been quite an eye-opener for me. The word "research" takes on a hallowed meaning around here, as if there is something sacred about the concept. In my world, the idea of research was used to show which way of thinking was ascendant, what was catching the current spirit, the zeitgeist.

Please pass the specific questions from our esteemed faculty on to my assistant, Ryan Spike. We'll draft a suitable reply and keep the Doubting Thomases out of your hair!

There was a canyon separating the realm of the marketers and that of the faculty, most of whom would be outraged at the cavalier use of the term "research" by people who clearly had no understanding of what it meant to those who actually conducted research. There were many faculty who had deeply held beliefs that what marketing people did was a waste of resources. But right now, they were voices crying in the wilderness. Academia had bought hook, line and sinker into paying image consultants in an effort to gain the upper hand in the never-ending quest for better students, more donors, and, perhaps most important to many, a greater measure of respect from the general public. These goals were incongruously grafted on to an institution that was still medieval in many ways. Imagine Copernicus announcing his planetary theories on Twitter.

Higher education in the 21st century had many deep divisions — between the arts and the sciences, research and teaching, tenured faculty and the growing army of teachers employed on short-term contracts. They were breeding grounds for resentment, enmity, gossip and feuds.

I had a hole in my schedule, so I thought I'd begin to satisfy my curiosity about what kind of a guy Ronson was, to see if there was anything notable the police might have missed, just to test the waters on their hurried investigation.

The most logical place to start was with his administrative assistant, which the directory said was Anne Mayfield. Email was the preferred form of communication on campus, but for something like this a persuasive voice might help tip the balance in agreeing to be cross-examined.

She picked up on the first ring. Lucky. I was already mentally composing my voicemail so as to allay her anxieties.

"I wonder if we could meet. Today, if possible. I'm doing a little background information-gathering in the event that reporters decide Ronson's death, or life, is worth a story."

"Really?" Her voice escalated quickly in volume, pitch and velocity. "Let me tell you, he's not all that interesting. Maybe the most interesting thing about him is how he died."

"True. Anyhow, I can imagine something like his unusual death arousing a reporter's interest. Our conversation shouldn't take long."

"Well, OK, but I didn't know him all that well. And the police have already interviewed me. But if you think it will help you...."

An hour later I found myself in Anne's office, about a mile from Main Central in a low-slung building that used to be apartments. It was one of those fringe structures that universities accrued on their periphery, to the consternation and fear of neighbors and small nearby property owners. The fights and ill will engendered by such acquisitions seemed disproportionate to the value of the real estate, which was usually marginal.

Why would universities risk alienating neighbors and city fathers for the sake of a rundown apartment building? Their leaders seemed to think that expansion was their natural right, and that their land acquisition was synonymous with neighborhood betterment. In a previous decade, universities found themselves at forefront of what was then deemed the progressive fight for urban renewal, and many of them still carried the torch.

The battles between the university and its neighbors had become so fierce that cowed city council members had washed their hands and appointed mediation panels. To everyone's surprise, the panels had worked fairly well, with both sides giving some ground and treaties signed. The university nonetheless bitterly resented this "intrusion" in its growth plans. Even some longtime residents who signed the compacts were deeply suspicious that their outsized neighbor would be coming back in a few years for another bite of the apple.

As a result of the Korean-style stalemate, this office space, acquired nearly a decade ago, was being allowed to deteriorate. The tired buildings had clearly exceeded their useful life and looked anomalous, oddly cheek by jowl with eight-story modernist expressions that housed bleeding edge research projects. Eventually they'd be replaced but probably not until the neighbors were more concerned about public health than they were about university expansion.

Two squat, narrow structures were set back from the street fronted by a poorly-maintained plot of grass. The clapboard siding was split and peeling, stained from leaks in gutters or worse. I had heard that building occupants complained about rats and other vermin.

I knocked on the door, which responded by rattling in its frame. The large glass panel had lost its glazing and was held in place by wood trim and luck.

A woman came to the door, dressed in jeans and a blouse that contained an inordinate amount of glitter. She grinned weakly as she unlocked the door.

"Sorry, but we've been told by the cops to keep the door locked. They don't patrol here, because we're officially off campus and outside their protection zone, and we've had a few street people camping in our courtyard." She showed me to a chair that had seen better days: its plastic seat was scored and only three of its metal legs would make contact with the floor at any given time. The whole scene reminded me yet again that there is indeed a class structure at the university.

"What did you do to deserve this exile?"

She smiled. "Me? Hell if I know. One day I've got this cushy executive space in Main Central and next thing I know I'm packing up my boxes for Lower Slobovia, without an explanation and certainly no apology. I've been at the university a few years, and nothing really surprises me anymore, especially when it comes to space."

She looked over her shoulder at the tiny cubicles and uniform fluorescent overhead lighting which made the ceiling seem lower than it was. "It's not as bad as it looks. And the people here are fun to work with. More fun than I ever had with the 'central administration.'"

"So how long were you working for Ronson?"

"About three years. More than two of them I worked right next door to him."

"I didn't know him well. What was he like? As a boss and a person."

She grimaced. "He was so hard to figure. Very private guy. When I started there, I'd bring him coffee in the morning, not because he ever asked me or anything, but more as a gesture, something you'd do for a friend, colleague or coworker." She paused, pushing her brunette bangs away from her eyes. "I waited for him to say something. Anything. 'Thank you' would've been nice. He'd look up from his keyboard, nod in my direction and return to his computer. And he'd drink the coffee. Every day the same thing. After a couple of weeks of this I decided to stop with the coffee, figuring that might elicit some reaction. But he never said a single word. Not a one." She sipped at her water bottle, which bore the insignia of a recent 10k race.

"He was never rude or impolite. And I sensed that maybe he *wanted* to be friendly but just didn't know how."

"So an archetypal nerd."

She snorted. "Yeah, he fits the stereotype to a T. Or he *did* fit the stereotype. I guess high salary and a staff of dozens is no deterrent to nerd-like behavior. But he wasn't unlikable. He had a kind of charm. Well, maybe not charm exactly. He reminded me of my little brother. He wore his hair in this boyish, early-Beatles-style mop, even though he was well over 50. And he always dressed in jeans that were very well-worn. He must've bought multiple pairs at the same time." She paused, looked down at her own legs and grinned. "I'll bet it took him quite a while to cram himself into those jeans each morning. They were tight."

"Did you keep his schedule?"

"Not really." She tucked her hair behind an ear. "He kept it himself, on his computer, and I had access to it, in case I needed to get a meeting on his calendar and he was out of the office."

"Did he have frequent meetings with IT staff? Or whatever IT is called now? I can't tell the players without a scorecard anymore."

Anne crossed her legs and dangled a shoe with her toes. Her toenails were painted silver. "Well, when I first came there, he had a lot of meetings with staff. But then they seemed to tail off. Maybe he lost interest or delegated it to others."

"Did he meet with the provost or president?"

"Maybe once or twice. That I know about."

"Did you screen his calls? Just curious who would know him well on campus, who he talked with frequently."

She stared at her hands, spread out on the desk.

"I wish I knew. No, usually the calls went directly to him."

I was running out of questions.

"Do you know if he associated socially with the people in IT? Or maybe with some faculty?"

"He did seem to spend some time over in computer science, according to his calendar. Don't know who he was meeting with, though. And there was this guy who seemed to drop by at least once every few months. Never identified himself and blew right past me into Jeremy's office. Didn't even say hello. I never figured out exactly who he was, but I don't think he was on the faculty."

"Why not?"

"He dressed too well."

"Seriously?"

"Yeah, he always wore a suit, freshly laundered. And cologne. Enough you could smell him coming from the floor below."

"Huh. I wonder where he sat in that office."

Anne looked up at me, surprised. "So you've been in there?"

"No, but I've heard rumors that he wasn't exactly the most organized person in the world."

"Yeah, it was a great office, large with great views, but always a real mess. I offered to try and straighten it up, but he described the stacks of papers as his 'filing system,' without any irony. I figured he was just a pack rat." She swept her bangs out of her eyes. "It is kind of funny, though, for one of the major computer leaders of the campus to keep so much on paper."

I shifted in my chair as the split in the Naugahyde was beginning to chafe.

"He did seem to have one buddy from within the department. Someone who would drop in pretty often. I got the impression that they were friends." She opened her desk's bottom drawer and pulled out a stenographer's notebook and began flipping through pages at lightning speed. "I have his name here somewhere. I didn't get to know a lot of the people in the department because they were never introduced to me. It was a weird place in that respect. No social events. Not even a holiday party... OK, here it is. Arthur Kingston. I don't know what he does, but I don't think we was one of the computer nerds. He didn't look the part. They seemed to do lunch a lot." She snapped the book closed. "Anything else I can tell you?"

"I think that's all for now. Thanks for your time."

She got up to walk me to the door. "Sorry I couldn't tell you much. He is, or was, one of the strangest people I've met. Do you really think reporters will want to write about him?"

I scratched my head, pretending to think it through. "You never know. It's always better to be prepared."

I headed across the street, watching carefully for kids exceeding reasonable speeds on the bike path. I knew if I was to die on campus it would be under some maniac biker's or boarder's wheels. I noticed an enormous black SUV parked near the crosswalk. While vehicles on campus typically had leftish bumper stickers, or pictures of sports mascots, this one had a decal that I'd never seen before. It looked like a skull wearing goggles superimposed over crossed arrows. And north to south there was a saber. There was also a bumper sticker I didn't understand: "Check your six." And another: "Grunt by association." I had no idea what any of that meant.

Mayfield hadn't provided much help. But I had at least one new name, Arthur Kingston. I'd try to call him when I had a free moment. And maybe Gina could help me figure out what he was doing over in computer science.

But right now, I had to head upstairs for an obligatory meeting of what our vice president called the Executive Staff, but which for me was My Weekly Out of Body Experience. I never thought I'd be viewing my inert body from afar in a staff meeting, but detachment proved to be a highly effective strategy for coping with terminal boredom.

About a year ago, we had been gifted with a new vice president who came to the position with much fanfare. Roy Ganas had worked at several universities and had been a key staffer for a powerful state legislator. All his previous bosses, according to the search committee, had given him high marks. The committee allegedly was impressed with his command of the rhetoric of image promotion and reputation enhancement. The decision to offer him the position was unanimous among the search committee and the president's key advisers. Cynic that I was, unanimity made me suspicious that the appointment had been dictated by some person of great influence. I mean, no candidate was *that* good.

So it came as no surprise when, over the last few months, he had lost his mojo. Rumor had it that the president had expected more from him and was disappointed with his leadership as Vice President for Image Buttressing and Brand Incubation.

What President Marchand Yarmouth's expectations were exactly, no one knew. But when I walked past Roy's office on the third floor I often saw him pacing while talking rapidly on the phone, with an uncharacteristic clipped edge to his conversation. His public manner, once fluent and confident, had changed. He hesitated before he spoke, as if he was second-guessing his own thoughts.

I had felt sorry for him. Past tense, since he had taken his anxieties and dumped them on those around him, like his executive staff. It was one thing to demand results but quite another to change the rules of the game at halftime.. So we had lost confidence in him. Most of us were just going through the motions when we met with him, trying to keep as low a profile as possible in his presence.

At an exec meeting about a month ago, I had witnessed an emblematic exchange. It began with a brief presentation by a team that had been assigned to write the president's message in the alumni magazine. A month prior, we had sat in that very same room and batted around ideas. Suggestions ranged from touting the latest breakthroughs in medical research to how the university had become more sustainable by installing solar charging stations for its growing fleet of electric cars — the usual stuff with which presidents try to impress alums, big on flash and low on controversy.

After much discussion, it was agreed that the team would focus on how our students were changing the world. Changing the world had become one of the mantras you'd hear all over Main Central. We would use these examples of student projects to springboard to the idea that the university was one of the great change agents in society. It was never enough to say that we were good at what we do. Superlatives ruled. This was another hallmark of the growing emphasis on brand and reputation — adjective inflation.

The team sent around copies of their draft before the meeting. I read it over a few times. I thought it filled the bill for what had been requested.

But at the review meeting Ganas was just this side of livid. He glared at the team leader, Gerald Bransford.

"This isn't what we agreed upon. Not what I expected, and not what the president will approve."

Bransford, although taken aback by Ganas's vehemence, initially refused to give ground. "Three of us from my team were in the room for the discussion, and everyone agreed that this approach was the best. In any case, we're coming up on the deadline and need to regroup if you find this unsatisfactory."

"You certainly do," said Ganas, pushing his copy of the draft in Bransford's direction. He was sweating profusely, and there was a definite wheeze in his respiration. Rumor had it that he suffered from high blood pressure. I wondered who in the room might know CPR if it became necessary.

"This is unacceptable," he said, glaring at Bransford, who covered his embarrassment by adjusting his hand-tied bow tie. "It is poorly written, logically inconsistent and almost embarrassingly simplistic in its approach. I don't know where you found these students, but their quotes are insipid. This was not supposed to be an exercise in free expression for the students. You make it sound like the students did this work on their own, which we all know was far from the case. The absence of faculty from these profiles is ridiculous."

Bransford, looking puzzled, glanced across the table at Delores Sert, who I was pretty sure had drafted the piece. She was a fine writer, having produced numerous speeches and guest columns for a host of individuals on campus and as a ghostwriter for corporate celebrities when she had worked in a private public relations firm. She shrugged her shoulders imperceptibly, carefully guarding her facial expression.

Jerry had worked in large advertising firms, handled public relations for mid-size companies and worked with a bevy of professional and amateur editors. He exuded suave. "So is the problem that these students talked too much about the political milieu in which their work occurred, or something else?"

"We don't have time to go through all of that now. There's too much on our agenda today, and having the group edit your prose won't be fun for anyone." He was clearly exasperated. "But we can't go forward without a complete rewrite and new approach. This involves more than just tinkering."

We went on to other, less inflammatory topics, but Ganas never recovered his equilibrium. He didn't crack a smile for the entire hour and didn't catch his breath, huffing like a steam engine as he spoke. Our discussions, which back in the old days had been easygoing and allowed for a free exchange of ideas, were frequently tense and perfunctory, but this dispute was the most vicious and off-the-hook I had encountered.

I was curious what Bransford & Co. would do next. I waited a couple of days and called Jerry.

"So what the hell was that about?"

"Search me. Did you think our work was all that bad? Be honest."

"No. It seemed responsive to what we had agreed upon. And as with most of Delores's work, it was well-written."

"That's what I thought. We went over it pretty carefully, trying to weed out anything that might give our university leadership heartburn."

"So what have you heard from Ganas?"

"Nothing terribly helpful. He wants the students to be more effusive and less political. And more faculty, lots more faculty in there."

"That sure isn't the approach we arrived at in the exec meeting."

"Well, the wind shifts and we have to tack with it, or against it, I've never understood which. But I don't appreciate having my colleagues reamed out at a meeting when they've done exactly what was requested."

"What do you think is going on with Ganas? This isn't the first time we've been exposed to a side of him that a year ago we didn't even know existed."

"Rumor says he's on the outs with Yarmouth. I've done some back-channel snooping to figure out what's really going on. Apparently, some of the senior faculty had a private meeting with the prez and expressed disenchantment with Roy's approach. They suggested that the substance of the faculty's work was being ignored in favor of highlighting what they called 'bright, shiny objects.' They took issue with the emphasis on what they think are minor programs and were miffed that less prestigious faculty seem to be receiving disproportionate public attention, conferring on their work a status that, in professional circles, it really doesn't deserve. Typical academic fights over prestige.

"In fact, the story going around is that they left Yarmouth with a consensus list of the university's most distinguished academics and pretty much demanded that those individuals receive attention right away.

"So we're rewriting to focus on our stellar faculty and paint the students as wide-eyed acolytes worshiping at the feet of the Illuminati."

Next week, they circulated another draft. It read like Exodus 34:29, when Moses came down from Mt. Sinai with the Ten Commandments. An excerpt:

"Ashley Brooks's view of her future has been transformed by her work on developing efficient alternative energy strategies. She expects that finding a job upon graduation should be easier than if she had confined her work to the theoretical realm.

"'But I'd be nowhere, precisely nowhere, without the mentorship of Professor Hermione Beasley,' she said. 'Not only did she keep my energies focused on the big picture, but her expertise and depth of knowledge was a perpetual source of inspiration for me. I believe that the kinds of experiences I've had here may well be available nowhere else on the planet.

"'I feel so fortunate at the gift that has been given to me. Regardless of what the future may hold, I will be eternally grateful to Professor Beasley and her colleagues in the department for sharing their time and wisdom. They could be off in the private sector making tons of money, I'm sure, and developing patentable products that would set them up for life. But they chose to come here, to work with novices like me. There are no words to describe the generosity of their sacrifice and dedication.'"

Hard to imagine a student saying those things. I shot a note back to Bransford and Sert.

"Don't you think this is a wee bit over the top?"

"I do," responded Delores, by phone, presumably to avoid any paper trail. "But Jerry and I have a bet riding on this one. I told him it was all about satisfying Ganas's expectations, however inflated they might be, as communicated to him by the president and his minions. Which means placating the largest of large egos among faculty. Would you like a piece of the action? We're offering even odds."

"Sorry, I'd never bet against you."

When the next exec meeting was convened, Ganas began by commenting to Jerry, "Well, that's more like it! That's the kind of work I want to see from our teams. This is exactly what we want on projects for this president. Congratulations to you all. I have no doubt the president will love it."

Delores was looking down at her tablet, her straight black hair obscuring part of her face, but I could still see a tight grin. Jerry just looked relieved. I mouthed a silent "Congrats" when I caught Jerry's eye. But the incident left a mark on all of us. A reminder that when talking about faculty there is no such thing as hyperbole.

Today's meeting was about slogans. "Some of us think it's time for a new slogan for the university," Ganas began.

"I've always wondered why we need a slogan at all. Harvard doesn't have one, unless you think *Fiat Lux* qualifies. Stanford doesn't, and neither do most of the prestigious public universities." It was Kris Benefield, our lobbyist in DC. Although most people regarded her as a royal pain in the butt, and she was, I liked having her around because she'd say the kinds of things other people thought but were reluctant to say out loud.

Kris had deep circles under her eyes, which gave her a forever-weary look. She was always wearing pantsuits, which were mainstream for the halls of Congress but stood out in the less dressy environment here.

"The matter of whether the university will have a slogan is not really up for discussion here," Ganas replied. His tone had turned icy. He was absently stroking what he called a beard. He started growing it shortly after his arrival, to fit in better with the tweedy set, but it was still growing unevenly and was three shades lighter than the hair on his head and his forearms.

"Can we review some history, for my benefit, since I'm relatively new here?" asked Marilyn Marcuse, the state lobbyist. She'd joined the university in the past year after a long career as a nonpartisan staffer in the state legislature and a brief stint as an independent lobbyist. "I'd like to know how the slogan gets used, what its purpose is, and how we arrived at the current one... which is...?"

Ganas looked at Mark Stewart, the liaison with the People, Promise, Programs and Purpose Enhancement empire. Stewart had two bosses who really didn't talk with one another while jockeying for his time and presenting him with conflicting instructions. His job was to thread the needle and satisfy both of them — something for which he seemed ideally suited, as he remained blissfully unaware of any contradictions in his marching orders.

University leadership described these kinds of relationships as "dotted-line reporting," as displayed on a box-filled organizational chart, meaning that two roughly equal power lords (or ladies) were engaged in a protracted turf battle. Ganas had fought PPPPE to a stalemate, at least for now.

"About eight years ago," Stewart began, "during the nonpublic phase of the university's last capital campaign, we worked with a consultant to craft our current slogan. It was used on selected pieces of campaign literature and on some university banners scattered throughout the campus and displayed at public events. It appeared on the campaign website and in selected other university Web pages. We made every effort to get university officials to use it in speeches and other public remarks, and we worked to have it incorporated in the products of the admissions office, although candidly that effort was only moderately successful. And of course since the campaign ended it's fallen into disuse..."

Since I knew this silly history intimately, I zoned out during Mark's recitation and thought about what I would look for in Ronson's office. It had to be something subtle, since the cops had allegedly given it the once-over. But given the speed of the investigation, it's possible they overlooked something in plain sight. Should I bring a note pad to copy down my observations? Dare I remove anything from the room? I saw myself hefting a big magnifying glass and wearing a deerstalker hat. Then Mark's voice burst into my musings.

"Oh. And our current slogan is: 'The spirit. The challenge. The future.'"

"I remember now," added Marilyn. "I've even seen the related graffiti around campus. One was 'The few. The hungry. The horror.' I think that was influenced by some undergrad's reading of Joseph Conrad."

"Well, that was at a different time, under a different president and for a different purpose," Ganas continued. "The next fund-raising campaign won't start for at least three years, at least in its public phase. We have our officials giving speeches all the time, not just to the campus but to business and civic groups. Our leaders would be well-served by a single idea that can capture the essence of this university. So let's spend some time this morning just brainstorming."

"Wait a minute," said Trencher, shifting forward in his chair. "What are the parameters here? We're just going to throw it open and start coming up with slogans without first identifying the attributes we want to stress? We'll be all over the map."

"Fair enough," said Ganas, grabbing a dry marker and marching to the white board. "Let's begin by listing the things that make us distinctive."

"To whom?" It was Cal Weiner, the head of the alumni association. Although not officially part of Ganas's empire, he showed up from time to time just to... well, I didn't exactly know why he showed up. He was always dressed in a polo shirt with the university's colors and logo. His crew cut followed his receding hairline.

"President Yarmouth wasn't here during the previous iteration, so why don't we begin by imagining what kinds of messages he would feel comfortable delivering. After all, he's our most visible spokesperson and generally is the public face of the university. So, let's start there."

I was by no means an expert in sloganeering. In fact, I hated the whole idea, drawn from publicity for soap products, fast food and automobiles — products of low intrinsic value, not higher ed. But putting that aside, it seemed like it was a bad idea to create a public campaign to satisfy an audience of one. Speculating on what he might like to say seemed futile. I was beginning to understand why Ganas was no longer the fair-haired boy of the administration. The ready-fire-aim approach to public relations carried high risks.

As the discussion swirled around me, I thought back to Ronson. If he didn't die at his own hand, deliberately or accidentally, who might carry a grudge weighty enough to cause his death? How might I go about locating them? I started to flip through my mental address book.

"...we do want something future-oriented. Something that portrays this place as dynamic." It was Terri South, who worked with city government and the nearby neighborhoods. "Our main product, our students, are in the process of becoming. And so are we, especially when it comes to research."

"I think we should try and talk about the future without ever using the word," Trencher piped up. "Everyone who has slogans uses the word 'future.' We'll just seem to be one of the crowd."

Ganas was scribbling notes on the board, some of which were readable. No one seemed to notice that my attention had wandered except Delores. I had this weird sensation that she was trying to communicate with me telepathically; I saw flashing neon signs behind my eyes with the words "more hype." I blinked and stared at her, grabbing her attention for a couple of seconds until she retreated to her tablet, her right hand absently playing with the single thin purple braid she wore, terminating in a bright yellow bead.

"I think we need to own the future," I heard myself saying. Heads turned. Even I was surprised.

"What does that mean?" Kris asked.

"It's just that... if we try to position ourselves as *part* of the future, then we lose our uniqueness. I mean, everyone is part of the future, everyone who isn't already dead, and maybe even some of them, too. We want people to believe that, more than any other institution or company or group of individuals, we embody and make possible what is going to happen. If you want to know where the city, country or world is going... come to the campus."

There was silence. People were hoping for a cue from Ganas. He had written "We are the future" on the board and was staring at it.

He put a circle around it in red marker and erased everything else.

"Let's focus on this for a while and see where it takes us."

I nodded at Delores, silently thanking her for the inspiration. She licked her lips and stared down at her tablet. I think she was suppressing a giggle.

Back to my daydream. I found myself imagining that I was Jeremy Ronson. Working late, trying to grasp one big idea. Pacing the floor, erupting with half-digested thoughts and tossing them in the garbage. Rummaging through folders, looking for something. Becoming impatient. Opening the top button on my shirt. Opening the window to get a breath of cool, moist air. Resuming the pacing, engaged deep in thought and then, without recognizing it, stepping off into the abyss....

"...we have six candidates." Ganas. He was still writing on the board while erasing the discards.

"Watch what happens."

"Apologies to Michel Legrand," said Cal, surprising the assemblage with his knowledge of music trivia.

"Welcome to the next big thing."

"We're inventing tomorrow."

"Press play."

"Our greatest hopes become reality."

"Our spirit ignites a fire."

Ganas stepped back. "I think this is a good day's work. Let's not try to take it any further at this time. We surely will want to edit these and refine them. You can send me your edits, comments and suggestions. We'll wrap it up at next week's meeting, hopefully in just a few minutes. There were other things I wanted to discuss this week, but they'll have to wait. That's all."

As people shuffled toward the door I caught Delores's eye. We found a quiet corner nearby.

"Were you sending me messages telepathically? Something really strange was going on in that room. And I think you were involved."

She looked mock-shocked. "I have no idea what you're talking about."

"There was a voice in the back of my head that was keeping up a drumbeat. 'More hype. More hype.' Was that you? I have this feeling it was."

"Now why would I do that? And how?"

"You tell me."

"Well, whatever was happening, I think you took it to a different level. Whether that's a good thing…." She left, waving at me over her shoulder.

* * *

I was lucky that Stella was willing to let me in to Ronson's office, and doubly lucky she could do it so quickly.

While some faculty members teach evening classes or work late in their offices and labs, administrative buildings such as ours tend to shut at 5. Some people do burn the midnight oil, albeit in the privacy of their home. Outside doors got locked up close to 5.

So by 5:15 the building was quiet. Stella and I gave some lame excuses to the rest of the office about why we had to work late.

I walked over to her desk, notebook in hand.

"Ready?"

She rummaged in her file cabinet for the ring of keys. "You bet. Have you thought of what you'll say if we're spotted going in or out?"

"No. I tried to think of a plausible explanation for rummaging around in a dead man's office, but I couldn't think of one."

She stood stock still with her arms crossed. It was pretty clear she wasn't going to move until we had some kind of cover story.

"I propose that I lay this off on you. After all, you're the one with the keys and access to all offices."

"Thanks a ton. You'll come visit me after they haul me away, won't you?" She bent as if to return the key ring to the cabinet.

"No, wait. Just think for a minute. There's no way anyone is going to buy a story about why *I* had to go into that office. But you... you coordinate building services, don't you? You're the one who approves repairs, brings in guys to fix up offices after damage. I think cleaning out the office of the departed could fall under your duties to maintain the building, don't you?"

"I suppose."

"So who would normally figure out what was in there? What needed to be moved, what happens to the papers, what the cleaning needs are... stuff like that? Especially with his administrative assistant located somewhere else?"

She smiled up at me. "Very clever."

We headed up the narrow staircase to the fourth floor. The elevators were locked down and that was one thing to which Stella did not have a key. Main Central, built about 80 years ago, had that old building smell and feel. The wooden handrail was worn smooth, made black and slick by decades of sweaty-palmed administrators going to or from a dressing-down delivered by the boss, or attendance at meetings for which they were poorly prepared. The flop sweat smell seemed to overpower everything else.

"We should've found a way to take the elevator," Stella paused and panted. She was in lousy shape. It wasn't entirely her fault, as she'd been brought up near a coal mine by two parents who smoked.

"No hurry. In fact, the more time we take, the less likely it is that anyone will be around." I slowed my pace to match hers and paused frequently.

The fourth floor was quiet. The overhead fluorescents were still on, humming obliquely, awaiting the night cleaning crew. But given the budget cutbacks, which had reduced the custodial staff by nearly half, our chances of encountering them were pretty slim.

We approached the office with baby steps. Stella soundlessly pulled the key from her pocket and put it ever-so-slowly into the lock. With one quick glance over her shoulder she turned the key and opened the door.

We hurried inside and closed the door before turning on the light.

Either a tornado had hit the office, or it had been ransacked.

Upon further review, it corresponded to Phil Symonds's and Anne Mayfield's observations about the condition of things. People living in this maelstrom would insist they could find anything they needed, that they had a "system."

"Geez," Stella said. "I hope there's nothing living — or growing — underneath all this crap." She moved slowly and carefully among the files, reports, books, folios and forms, in stacks that climbed ziggurat-like to thigh level all over the room. Amidst the papers were CDs and DVDs, both in their cases and naked, as well as a smattering of thumb drives and other less common storage devices.

I stood frozen near the door. I tried to imagine Jeremy Ronson's daily routine, especially people coming into the office to meet with him. There were several chairs, but like every other horizontal surface they were suffocating under the written word.

This was a prized corner office, facing east toward the mountains and also south. The entire east wall was windows and there were two south-facing windows over six feet tall. The Collegiate Gothic style of the exterior had remained intact through dozens of remodels and interior reshapings, which was both good news and bad news. The stolid, solid, quasi-religious-appearing structure conveyed a sense of permanence.

The bad news for residents and sustainability mavens was that buildings like this were an energy conservation nightmare. The windows were single pane with metal frames that over the years had bent and deformed, leaving sizable gaps even when closed. Cold air filtered into the room no matter what. The draft was noticeable now, with the outdoor temperature dropping. People who thought academics dressed in tweed vests and sweaters because of style or affectation had never spent a day inside one of these monstrosities. A dank chill was settling over the room, despite the low hiss of the ancient radiators.

Stella broke my reverie. She was poised by one of those leaky windows. "Is this the one? Where he 'fell'?" she said with air quotes.

"I think so." I made my way carefully to the window and opened it. "This must be it. You can see where he landed."

The window began slightly above the floor level, on a brick ledge It was about 28 inches wide — in other words, very much like a door. You couldn't really just walk out into nothingness: you had to step up slightly to enter the void. Or trip over the sill.

I paused to examine the vista. Even at night I would describe it as lordly. A Realtor could wax eloquent about the territorial views. In the distance, I could see twinkles from tony suburbs, while the tallest downtown penthouses were visible over the low southern hills. This was what a ten-word title bought you at a university. I looked down. It wasn't far enough to induce vertigo, but it certainly was high enough to kill someone. I ran my hands around the frame, hoping to pick up something, anything — a piece of clothing, a drop of blood, a button. Nada. I looked back at the office. It was possible to discern a path for going, carefully, from his desk to the window, eluding the paper towers along the way.

I walked back to the desk and played my own game of Twister, trying to land on the squares of carpet visible among the debris. It was possible if you were dexterous. Possible but not easy. I looked back at my path to see if any of the nearby paper bore footprints or indentations, but I didn't see any.

"Well, have you seen enough?" Stella asked. "I'm getting hungry. I must admit I'm a little bummed. I was expecting something revealing. But I haven't seen anything that makes me think we are at a murder scene. Just one shithole of an office." She stood with her hands on her hips, shaking her head slowly.

"I'd like to stay a few minutes, if that's OK."

"Well, I'm heading out." She stepped gingerly back to the door. "Remember to turn off the light. The door will lock when you close it."

I was staring at the path from desk to window, losing myself in speculation. "Thanks again, Stella."

The room felt different when I was there by myself. It took on a living presence, odd considering the circumstances. There were secrets here, I felt, if only I was clever enough to discover them.

Something told me to drop down on all fours. From that level I felt myself in a forest of paper. Guessing that no one would know or care what I did in this room, I grabbed a few of the sheets and began reading them.

After a long day it was hard to keep my mind focused on their content, especially since I didn't know what I was looking for. Words, rivers of them, flowed before my eyes.

I picked up and discarded sheet after sheet, not sure what I should be doing, what I was looking for, what mattered. This wasn't going anywhere. As perplexing as it was, Jeremy Ronson appeared to have fallen from a fourth-floor window and killed himself.

I was sitting on the carpet, legs crossed, staring blankly at yet another boring memo about a contract renewal, this for a large, centralized server system. I remembered this particular contract because the trustees had raised questions, as they often do when a contract is big enough. Ultimately, as was usually the case, the administration had satisfied the trustees' concerns and gone ahead.

I read the memo again, without really focusing on it. But then something struck me. This was a memo regarding a *prior* renewal of the contract, from several years ago. In other words, ancient history. An antique memo.

I picked up a sheet nearby and scanned for the date. It was over two years old. I rummaged deeply in the stack beneath it and found a couple of memos from last month. So the most recent memos, that should have been on the top, were near the bottom, and vice versa.

At least one stack had been disturbed, maybe turned upside down. Maybe Ronson did it in the course of going through his "filing system." Or maybe not.

I crawled back toward the desk, following the direct route from the window, and sampled the correspondence. There was a sprinkling of recent memos in the top layers, but also a large number of older notes there, too. The deviation from normal sedimentary deposition was striking.

It was clear that the piles had been disturbed.

I looked outside the pathway and read samples. The memos and other papers generally conformed to the LIFO (last in first out) pattern. The only disturbance I found was on the route from Ronson's desk to the window. If this was a coincidence, it was a strange one. I had found my needle in Ronson's haystacks.

I tiptoed through the papers to the door, turning the knob slowly and soundlessly. As I opened it, I thought I saw movement down the hall in the doorway to another office. I stood stock still, waiting, for several minutes. My attention was focused and I realized how vulnerable I was, unprepared to explain my presence, especially without Stella. I waited a bit longer and decided it was nothing. I crept out of the room slowly, softening my steps. My hand shook slightly as I grabbed the handle to the door on the stairway entrance. I threw one final glance over my shoulder at the office. As I went downstairs, my legs felt slightly rubbery. Not sure I was cut out for stealth operations.

There was more to this. How much more, it was too early to tell. But even assholes (if I accepted Trencher's characterization) deserved an honest accounting of their final minutes. I started to consider names of people I knew who could shed light on Ronson's career, the good and more importantly the bad and especially the ugly.

Those stacks of paper. Maybe there's another explanation. It's possible that they just fell on their own and were stacked randomly. Maybe the cops altered them — but surely they would be careful not to do that. The only other explanation was some kind of struggle had preceded Ronson's fall. And either the police had ignored the evidence or didn't do much of an investigation.

I concluded, provisionally, Ronson was helped out that window.

I went back to my office and made some notes.

"Who would want Ronson dead?" The words stared back at me.

"Work related?"

I always liked an aphorism, attributed to Henry Kissinger, that "academic gossip is vicious because the stakes are so low." In fact, the stakes in academia usually *are* low. You can screw up in major ways, and nothing serious happens. It's hard to get fired or demoted. Unless you're a surgeon at our medical center, you screw up and no one dies. No company goes bankrupt. There are no angry shareholders to storm the castle. And the Board of Trustees, the official public overseers, are like most boards of directors — led around by the nose through the assiduous efforts of the president and his minions. Mistakes are buried.

It was hard to wreck your career through administrative incompetence. Not impossible, though. So, a grudge or insult or misstep that would lead to murder? Not very likely, based on my knowledge of higher education. I couldn't think of any set of circumstances, no matter how dire, that could cause someone at the university to take his life.

So?

"Robbery or other crime?"

Possible. Maybe a robbery gone wrong. Maybe he was just in the right place at the wrong time and observed something he shouldn't have. But circumstances argued against something like that: the building is locked tight at 5, with entry only by a special code or pass key. Nothing had been reported as missing by the police.

"Personal life? Vendetta? Love/sex? Drugs? Rage? Money?"

This would be the most obvious route: jealousy, avarice, disappointment, frustration, anger... all the biggies from the emotional/financial/domestic treasure chest. If someone had it in for Ronson, enough to force him out a fourth-floor window, it would be for something big, life-changing, deeply painful. Or maybe Ronson had a really huge debt, financial or otherwise, that the cops hadn't found in their cursory investigation.

I put a circle around "anger."

Ronson and I didn't travel in the same circles. But now that my curiosity about the contents of his office was satisfied, I wasn't sure I wanted to pursue this any further. It would be a lot easier and safer for me if I could convince the cops to reopen the case. They had the time and the resources to do this right. The most logical thing was to test those waters, gingerly.

I called Phil Symonds and lucked out. He was getting off his shift in a couple of hours and agreed to meet. I preferred that whatever we said was not overheard by anyone on campus, and that our meeting was not observed by anyone who might care.

We arranged to meet at a nearby coffee shop, mostly a student hangout. As faculty and administrators headed home or to higher-end establishments, we'd have the right kind of atmosphere for a private conversation.

I'd never met with Phil outside of work hours. We weren't exactly friends, but we'd worked together for several years now. Like most campus cops, Phil had worked in several municipal departments, mostly in suburban towns. In my experience, he was a straight arrow, by-the-book officer with no swagger. As the usual designated public information officer for the department, and my liaison, he had learned quickly how to handle reporters asking questions he didn't want to or couldn't answer in a manner that was deft: they never knew when they were being handled.

It was a cool evening and the cafe was full. I huddled over my hot chocolate, trying to keep my hands warm as careless students held the door open, letting in that early autumn cold, wet wind.

Phil came in, dressed in civilian garb. Out of uniform he was just another guy, except for being totally ripped. He was wearing a yellow parka and an old baseball cap. He ordered a cup and sat, blowing on the coffee before taking a gulp.

"Thanks for meeting with me."

"No problem. Why all the cloak-and-dagger?"

"It's not a big deal, but I didn't want to make things awkward for you. And for me. The campus is so full of gossip."

"I never worry about that stuff." Phil had crystal blue eyes that seemed to get colder when he was annoyed.

"I wanted to ask you about Jeremy Ronson."

"That case, as you know, is closed." He stared off into space, his eyes dropping several degrees and focused just above my head. I knew immediately where this conversation was likely to end. Nevertheless...

"Yes. I'm aware of that." I paused to sip my drink. "I wanted to understand a little better what happens after an incident like this. Just for my own background. This case was closed pretty quickly. Some reporter might come back later to ask me about that." I was making this up on the spot, hoping it would fly.

Phil looked skeptical. "You think so?"

"Maybe. You never know. But it's good for me to understand how this all went down, for future reference."

Phil stared down at his coffee.

"So you have the ME's official report with the cause of death."

"Right."

"And no drugs were found in his system."

"No."

"And there were no signs of any injuries other than those caused by the fall."

"Correct."

"Did the report say anything about his clothing?"

"What do you mean?"

"Was it torn? Missing any buttons? Things like that."

"The ME only deals with the corpse itself unless there's something that stands out. But I can tell you from my notes that everything was consistent with a fall. Clothing isn't much of an indicator of anything. He did have a couple of popped buttons on his shirt, and a tear in one sleeve, but hell, given how people dress around here he could have come to work like that."

"And from the accumulated evidence you decided he accidentally fell out the window."

His eyes took on that penetrating look, and his mouth narrowed into a thin line. I could almost hear him counting to ten, slowly, to lower his level of irritation. The irises were taking on an icy sheen. "You think otherwise?"

"I'm just trying to understand what happened, and the way I do that is to ask questions, some of which you may find stupid or even insulting. And I'm sorry if you think they're silly."

He nodded once. "So we concluded, based on the evidence from the ME and our own work, that he fell. The evidence was consistent with that explanation."

"In a case like this, do you consider other alternatives?"

"Such as?" he tensed slightly.

"Well, he could've been pushed. Or maybe he fell intentionally."

Phil smiled and raised his eyebrows. "You mean suicide?"

"Yeah, did you consider that?"

"Actually we did, briefly. But we had even less evidence for that." He held up one finger. "He didn't leave a note." Second finger. "None of his coworkers or friends saw evidence that he was distressed." Three fingers. "As far as we could determine, there had been no major changes in his life that typically precede such an action." Four. "We didn't see any contributory circumstances, such as diagnosis of a serious illness or accumulated debts or family problems, something that might cause psychological distress. Or evidence of alcoholism or drug abuse. Or really anything. So we decided that was less likely than an accident."

"And you were able to check all those boxes in one day?"

"We're good. We assigned a bunch of officers to this. We called dozens of people. We were thorough. And fast."

"And you did consider that he might have been forced out the window?" This was the $64 question and to mask my anxiety, I stared down at the table. It hadn't been cleaned well and bore numerous coffee stains. You'd think they'd have a table surface in a coffee house that was immune to coffee stains.

Phil took a deep breath and let it all out with a hissing sound. I think he regarded my question as foolish and was suppressing his impulse to just say that. "Of course, we looked into that. But there was no evidence to support that theory either, as I've told you. No abrasions. No sign of a struggle. We found no forced entry to either the building or to his office. Our key-card log for after hours building entry showed no unusual activity." He paused. "So that reminds me, where were *you* at about midnight last night?"

"Very funny, Phil. For the record I have an alibi and also no motive. But maybe he was forced out at gunpoint."

This caused a belly laugh. "Yeah. That happens all the time around here, we're a real gun-crazy campus. Seriously, I suppose it's possible. But there wasn't any evidence supporting that theory that we could pursue. We also didn't find evidence that this was a failed, misguided effort at human-powered flight, so we didn't look into that, either. You can't pursue a theory if you can't find evidence to support it."

"Did you examine his office?"

"We did."

"And?"

"It was a fucking mess, as I told you before. We didn't find any evidence that there had been a struggle. The chaos was organized, more or less."

I didn't want to let him know I'd been in there or what I'd found. I was sure that second-guessing his investigation would not go over well. And it might well end whatever trust existed between us, basically closing my account in the Favor Bank. I swallowed hard.

"Have you ever conducted a murder investigation?" I almost added "before."

"No, I haven't." It was clear he found the question insulting, as he seemed to spit out the words. "But that doesn't mean I'm unfamiliar with police procedure where we need to consider the possibility that a serious crime has been committed. That's part of our routine and our training. And I wasn't doing this alone. I worked under the close supervision of the chief, who by the way has experience with death investigations, including homicide."

"I wasn't suggesting… it's just that. Do people actually fall out of fourth floor windows? I know it has happened here to drunken students. But to middle aged administrators?"

Phil was fiddling with a stirring straw. "That's what I thought when I first came to the scene. But when you go through the alternatives, they're all unlikely, in a sense. Except falling is the least unlikely, as it turned out."

The least unlikely. "What would it take to reopen the investigation? What new information would raise serious doubts about the official determination that it was an accident?"

Phil chuckled. "We almost never open a closed investigation. We'd need substantial new evidence either of a crime or a suicide. Something tangible *that we missed*. When we close an investigation it's because we've pursued all the significant leads. In this case, we were lucky, it didn't take very long, and there really wasn't anything there. So it was quick, but also thorough. Trust me, Mike."

I wanted desperately to ask him about outside pressure to make this go away quickly but I knew that was a really bad idea. Tantamount to questioning his integrity. Besides, if the request to speed up the investigation came from above, from the chief, it probably would have been cloaked in things like a reminder of the department's limited resources and the need to get on with other pressing business. Do the work, but do it quickly. That's how it would have been described. Not as a deviation from normal procedure.

I pushed myself away from the table to bring our conversation to a close.

"You know how in those procedurals the cop or PI says something like 'This smells funny'? It's just that this smells funny to me. And I wanted to put my doubts to rest."

Phil pushed his chair back from the table. "My advice is to keep your smells to yourself and let me and my crew investigate possible crimes. We'll all sleep better."

I shrugged. "I suppose."

"Anything else?"

I hesitated. There was more but I knew at this point it was not going to lead anywhere productive. "No. Can't think of anything else. But thanks for your time, Phil."

He headed out the door. But the funny smell persisted. And I needed to figure out what I was willing to do to make it go away.

* * *

I needed to walk around and think things through. It was clear that I would need to dig much deeper into the Ronson case if I ever expected any help from the police. Once a case is closed it's like a steel trap. I needed to find something dramatic and unexpected, something important that they had missed. A stack of papers wasn't nearly enough,

I had reached an inflection point. Either I was going to let things go, or I was going to find a way to continue looking for an answer that satisfied me, without any official help or sanction.

It was an easy call: I was pretty sure there was more to this and I was going to do my damnedest to find out what it was.

It would require stepping outside my daily routine and embarking on a path that I knew officially was prohibited. If I was discovered or turned over the wrong stone, it could end up costing me my job, regardless of whether I found anything. It was risky with little or no tangible reward.

I had a sense of what I was signing on for; essentially, this would be a second job. I needed to make lists, keep careful records, devote a lot of brainpower if I was going to do it right. I had conducted investigations before when I was a reporter and had to check out something that had been deliberately kept out of public view. It could have its visceral rewards but for the most part the process involved mindless details.

The only physical clue I had, the disturbed papers, was about to be swept away in the office cleanup. Pretty much everything else I was going to do relied on my interviewing skills. I needed to learn as much as possible about Ronson and his campus activities. That meant talking to as many people as I could who worked with him, who could shed light on his character, activities, successes, failures and who he might have pissed off.

The way I conducted investigations like this when I was a reporter was akin to assembling a puzzle. Each person would provide a little piece if I was lucky. Taken in isolation they wouldn't amount to much. But each interview would lead to another person who could provide a bit more information and a different perspective. At this stage I wasn't looking for suspects, just people who could add to the picture of Ronson. Slowly, as evidence accumulated and possible motives emerged, the clues would suggest at least one pathway to follow. More likely, I'd have to pursue leads that pointed in multiple directions. Over time, the evidence might help me narrow my work down to the person or persons who most likely had helped usher Ronson out of this world. That was my dream scenario. In reality, an investigation is filled with false starts, uncooperative persons, missing documentation and clues that take you in the wrong direction. And frequently an unsatisfying conclusion. There's really a lot of wandering around inherent in this kind of work.

Still, I would have to accumulate an impressive portfolio of evidence that I could take to the police and let them have the glory of whipping out the handcuffs and frog-marching the perp.

In a sense, confronting the evildoer would be an anticlimax. In my work as a reporter, the real fun came in assembling facts, looking at them in different ways, figuring out how seemingly unrelated information could fit together, creating a narrative for a story that otherwise would have been left untold. That was the real work, the creative part. It required some smarts but mostly it required determination. I had been told that, as a Leo, I came by my stubbornness naturally. Not that I bought that astrological stuff. But it was true. I didn't like giving up.

When I arrived at Andrea's, she saw the worry lines in my forehead and reached out instinctively to smooth them away. I smiled weakly, told her I was beat, and we headed off to bed.

CHAPTER THREE

I felt Andrea's weight shift in bed. "I think you should let it go." Waves of pleasure continued to wash over me with a tidal pull. I sealed my eyes and tried to hold on to the moment, basking in the afterglow, while she was prepared to resume normal conversation. I was often a step behind her. And especially given the day's exertions, I was wiped out, physically and mentally.

I grunted in response, trying to prolong the body rushes a few seconds longer, staying in my low-earth orbit. Ever so gradually I felt myself come back together. With an effort of will I directed my breathing back to something resembling normal, my heartbeat slowing commensurately.

When I opened my eyes I could see the gentle curves of her torso, the swelling of her hips and the effortless extension of her legs. My hand brushed against her, following the arc. I kissed her just above her pelvis, running my hand along the smoothness of her glutes.

My importunities had no immediate effect on her desire for conversation. "I mean, what do you know about crime investigation? What makes you think you can do better than a police department? Even if you think someone offed him?" Her voice was muffled by the pillow. She rolled slowly onto her back, the black ringlets cascading in casual disarray across her neck and shoulders.

My hand pursued its own agenda, describing the line from her neck down to her shoulder, the always-tanned skin in which I could never detect a wrinkle. Andrea was no longer in the first flower of youth, but her body refused to acknowledge it. I lay in wonder, continually, and responded to her questions reluctantly.

"Can't say. I think there's more to this than the campus police will admit. They took the path of least resistance. They wanted it over and done with, as did the higher-ups."

"So you've decided they botched the investigation, or that they sold out?" She turned toward me, her head propped up, and began teasing my left nipple. From the very first time, six years ago, Andrea had known where all my buttons were located and she could choose to push any of them, or not, as the mood struck her. She read me fluently and frequently was able to anticipate what I was about to do and say.

"They just landed quickly on what they thought was the most likely theory, based on the evidence they looked at," I said. "They could be right. But what I saw in his office made me think there is more to this."

She puckered her lips and blew slowly across my chest. I shivered.

"So what are you gonna do now?"

I reached behind her neck and I drew her to me. "Not sure. I've never investigated a murder before."

She halted in mid-breath. "So you're calling it a murder?"

"I suppose I should call it a *possible* murder. I'm just a rookie at this kind of thing."

I felt a tongue in my ear. "It can wait."

I woke a couple of hours later, roused by dreams I couldn't remember. I was going to have a busy day tomorrow, what with the regular office stuff and my amateur sleuthing. I was excited, anxious and eager.

I slithered out of bed and carefully climbed into my clothes. Andrea's steady breathing continued uninterrupted. I usually didn't leave like this, but I wanted the peace of my own thoughts uninterrupted.

Given Andrea's high-definition intuition, my sudden departure to my own place and my own bed wouldn't surprise her one bit.

I slept poorly and arrived early at work. Most of the staff were gathered at the coffee pot, talking and laughing. I was uncomfortable shooting the shit with them. If the conversation headed in the direction of Ronson I was worried that my lack-of-poker-face would tip my hand. And I was nowhere near ready for that.

I tried to sweep past Fran without saying hello, but her scowl brought me to a dead stop.

"You've been a busy boy. Rushing in and out. No morning jokes And closing your office door. Buffing up your resume'?"

"Nah, I'm afraid you're stuck with me a while longer. Anything interesting on your watch?"

She looked down at the notes scattered on her desk. "Mostly same old. You did get a call from Shelley Strong." Strong was the longtime higher education reporter at the city's daily paper. "She said it wasn't urgent, but if you had a moment…"

"I'll get right on it."

Back in my office, I looked up Arthur Kingston in the directory. Turns out he was some budget person in IT. I could never tell from the titles what people really did, but the word "director" after his name suggested he was pretty highly ranked. I'd give him a call, right after talking to Shelley.

"Thanks for calling back so quickly."

"You never know, I figured you might be on deadline and need some help."

"Nah. Just fishing around for a story, something the editors might want for above the fold on a slow news day."

"Glad someone still worries about placement on paper in this digital age."

"Truth is, placement still matters, whether it's on paper or the Web."

"Well, we aren't expecting any celebrities on campus this week. And I'm fresh out of Watergate-type scandals for you."

She laughed. "I wasn't expecting anything really juicy. By the way, too bad about the guy who fell out the window."

I stiffened involuntarily. "Yeah, it's one of the more unusual things that's happened since I've been here. We have students get drunk and injure themselves, as you well know. But for a high-ranking administrator to fall. That's never happened before."

"From what I've been told — off the record, of course — this Ronson guy was a really odd duck and not very well liked. When I was at Trustees meetings and he was there, he'd always be standing off by himself. Administrators would breeze on past, never shaking hands or greeting him. You got the feeling he had become part of the wallpaper, that he was facing the academic equivalent of shunning. I probably shouldn't be talking like that as I hardly knew the guy. But he never returned my calls and I had to work around him for anything that seemed to fall in his area."

"That's why I never referred you to him, Shelley. That was his reputation, and he wasn't going to change his behavior because I asked him."

"Enough about dead guys. I'd still like some ideas in the way of feature stories, if not for today then ones I can track for the future."

"Hey, give me a minute." I fumbled through some papers on my desk and looked at notes from the last staff meeting. "We've got a professor, a woman, who is working on making a renewable energy source from slime. How about that?"

"Really? You mean my bathtub might be competition for the Bakken formation?"

"I don't want to comment on your domestic hygiene. But if nothing else, you have a great way to begin the story. It's serious research but the professor doing it has a sense of humor, so it should be a fun conversation. Let me know if you want to pursue it. We were going to send out something but I'll hold it for you if you're interested."

"I'll give it some thought and bounce it off a couple folks here. Thanks!"

I hung up and tried to reach Arthur Kingston but was shunted to voice mail. "This is Art. Sorry I missed your call. As of September first I'll no longer be working at the university. Should you need information about budgetary matters related to information technology, contact Olivia Deschang, who works out of the provost's office. Thanks."

Big help Mayfield was. I looked over the notes from our conversation. The only other lead she had provided, a thin one, was with his frequent visits to computer science. Maybe I'd wander over that way after lunch.

There was a knock at my door. It was Stella.

"Hey, boss." I waved my hand as if to wipe away the epithet. "Any news from the fourth floor?" she whispered.

I decided to low-key my discovery. "Nothing I could hang my hat on. But I'm still not convinced he took a header from the office window."

She shut the door carefully. She was bouncing up and down on her sneakered feet, clearly waiting for me to ask what was up.

"Well, you gonna make me guess?"

"It's kind of a long story. Mind if I sit?" She pointed to the sole chair in the office, which was buried under a collection of magazines, old news releases and thick reports. Welcome to the Paperless Office. I pushed them to the floor with a thud.

"You know that before I came to work here, I used to be a budget person in the College of Real Estate Leverage and Speculative Construction?"

"Is that its real name?"

"Close. That's what we used to call it during the boom. Or worse. We could've included Homelessness Promotion in the name, now that I think of it. Folks there spent a lot of time groveling and bowing to the slimiest people from the private sector that you could imagine." Stella wore her politics on her sleeve.

"Anyhow…" I prodded.

"Anyhow, while I was there I developed a web of contacts among the budget specialists all over campus. We used to have monthly workshops and occasional social evenings. And I've kept in touch with some of them."

"And?"

She stared at the floor for a moment, then looked up and pinched her nose. "It's just a rumor. I haven't been able to find anything definitive. But my sources — I love to say that, 'my sources' — they think there were some funny things going on in Ronson's empire."

"Interesting. What kinds of funny things?"

"When budget people use words like that, they usually mean something like phantom transactions, deficiencies in record-keeping. Sometimes outright mishandling of money or fraud. But no one I've talked to has the specifics."

"And what do you think it has to do with Ronson's demise?"

She chuckled. "Well, probably nothing. I mean, would he jump out the window because they found his fingers in the cookie jar, or because he was less than scrupulous in handling the state's money? I kinda doubt it."

"Thanks for the information. If you find out anything else, let me know."

"Sure thing." She stood up.

"Just one more thing," I stopped her. "Have you ever heard of a guy named Arthur Kingston?"

"Oh, sure. He was Ronson's go-to budget guy. If there was any wrongdoing you can be sure he was in it up to his armpits. Handled the entire budget for the office. First class jerk."

"What makes you say that?"

"Cuz he is. Always thought he was smarter than the 'girls' who handle most of the budgets around here. Sexist pig. You could see him and Ronson together in the hallway, cutting down anyone they saw. They had something snide to say about everyone, up to and including the prez. Immature schoolboys. But especially Kingston, who is also a huge suckup."

"Well, the suckup is gone, according to his voicemail."

"Nobody will miss him."

"Do you think there's a connection between your unverified rumor and his departure?"

"Wouldn't surprise me."

"Stella, please see what else you can learn. I'm still skeptical that there's a connecting thread, but you never know."

"Right, chief."

Kingston had moved to the A list of people I wanted to talk with — to build out the portrait of Ronson. I needed to find something solid to give me forward momentum in pursuit of the truth regarding Jeremy Ronson's demise. The only leads I had now included some unnamed people in computer science and Ronson's amigos who were still available on campus.

I decided to take Gina Gertsch up on her offer to help. Conferring with her was better than simply wandering the hallways in the Computer Science Building.

"Hey Gina." There was no place to knock in a cubie, so I tried not to startle her.

She swiveled easily in her chair, flashing that smile. "Hi. What's new?"

"Same old shit." I didn't want to start making up stories, and there was really nothing to tell her yet. "That was a great story about remote control of robots with thought waves over the Internet."

She laughed. "I only wish it were that dramatic. We're talking very small movements that are statistically significant but not exactly like having a psychic joystick." Her dark brown eyes danced with mischief. "That's the lead I would've used if I could have, though. But the researcher wasn't ready to go there and after talking to him, neither was I." She ran her hand through her short hair. "Maybe next time."

"Maybe. I need some help."

"Sure. What do you need?"

"I'm doing some background on Ronson. Just tying up some loose ends." This excuse was growing ever more stale; I was going to have to come up with a better one. "I hear he hung out with some computer science faculty. And you mentioned he had some kind of faculty appointment. Any idea who might've been his contacts over there?"

She spun back to the computer, doing a quick search. "I didn't know Ronson." She scrolled down a list of faculty. "But I'm guessing the kind of faculty who are involved in big hairy projects that require extra computing muscle would be a good place to start, since those are the natural crossover points between faculty research and the administration. Also maybe some of the more senior people who have been around a while, like he was."

"Seems right to me."

She stared me in the eye. It was pretty clear she had bought exactly zero of my cover story.

"Is there more to his death than people think? You know there's still a lot of buzz about it. Some pretty fantastic theories if you care to read about conspiracies. Not on work time, of course."

"I assume you learned about them by osmosis. The police have given their judgment on what happened, calling it an accident and officially that's the last official word." I swallowed and continued at a whisper. "I promise you if I find something you'll be among the first to know."

"If there is something else going on, I'm not sure I want to know. But thanks for the offer." She pulled out a yellow legal pad and began writing. "If I were you I'd try a couple of guys who have been around a while, are pretty well connected and have no compunction about dishing the latest gossip. If nothing else, talking with them will be entertaining. They have their fingers in lots of pies. Their names are at the top of the list."

"Thanks, I could use a little humor or at least some snark."

"Let me know if you need more help. Or more snark."

Gina was a rock. I called the first person on her list and Dave McDivitt, an eminence grise in computer science at the ripe old age of 50 and one of the legendary gossips on campus, picked up on the first ring. He agreed to meet later that morning. He had risen rapidly through the faculty ranks, accumulating awards, acolytes and offers of administrative positions, both at the university and across the country, all while he was still in his 30s.

But like a distance runner who suddenly hits the wall, his administrative ascent had come to a grinding halt about a decade ago. A popular rumor was he had gotten crossways with a high-ranking bureaucrat that the then-president regarded like an adopted son — but I'd never met anyone who had any actual evidence.

Another plausible theory, and one that I personally supported, was that he had just tired of institutional politics and returned to his first love, research, a familiar story in academe. Faculty thought the rules that applied to being a successful professor were also relevant to successful administration. They figured a background in searching for truth would be useful in university governance. This laid the groundwork for bitter disappointment.

When someone completed a study and submitted the results to a journal for publication, their work was subjected to critical review by their peers at other universities, and there were agreed-upon rules that governed those critiques. It was perfectly legitimate to question a colleague's theory, experimental design, results and interpretation of the results. Personal attacks, and attacking another researcher's motivation, were generally off-limits. It was pretty much obligatory that any discovery of note would have to satisfy objections, almost all of which occurred in the public arena. This is how academic research had been conducted for a long time.

Faculty members who became chairmen, associate deans, or directors and crossed over, at least temporarily, to administrative duties, encountered a sizable learning curve. Some made the change for what were very traditional, unselfish motives of "service" to the institution, seeing this work as a necessary evil and an obligation that was short term. Others took the job and title (and salary bump) in hopes of filling in missing parts of their resume in a march toward higher administrative leadership. Many of those individuals ended up being disappointed, overwhelmed by the contrast between working at the lab bench and the conference table.

A researcher who became an administrator might regard initiatives or new policies as similar to laboratory experiments: Results are hoped for but seldom can be guaranteed, so some kind of measurement must occur. In other words, you're testing an idea.

If this were an actual experiment and you were trying to determine what was true in a rigorous way, you might address such questions as:

- What would you hope to achieve?
- What evidence do you have that your experiment has a reasonable chance of success?
- Have you thought about any unintended consequences from your experiment?
- Do you have a plan to gather enough information to see if your experiment achieves the desired results?
- Have you given any thought to how you might revise your policies in light of the information that you gather?

Embedded in the consciousness of serious researchers is the principle that you learn more from a failed experiment than one which is completely successful. Failure opens the possibility for a deeper understanding of things, of questioning assumptions that may heretofore have had the status of received wisdom. Surprises of a negative nature are considered a gift.

But faculty who leap across the chasm from academic research to administration find themselves in an alien environment. Those questions considered obligatory in research are usually off the table when the discussion concerns a new administrative policy. Such indifference to what would be considered standard research procedure surprises and rankles administrative newbies. Many things are not measured, results may not be tracked, policies are seldom re-examined or fine-tuned. There is an absence of critical review and truth-telling, because the waters are muddied by towering egos and political divisions. For many researchers, this change causes intellectual whiplash. Such slogans as "failure is not an option" strike many of them as counterproductive nonsense.

Some adapt. But the vast majority eventually return to the classroom and lab, happy for the brief exposure to how things work on the Dark Side. And they unsurprisingly carry with them a career-long suspicion of administrators.

Such was the case, I surmised, with McDivitt. He knew that he usually was the smartest guy in the room. While maintaining decorum in academic debate, he had a reputation for not suffering fools gladly. I'd witnessed him in administrative confabs where his boundless energy and willingness to invite debate was put to the test by the button-down style of longtime university staffers. In particular, their aversion to risk visibly rankled him. In response to his challenge of "What's the worst that could happen?" they'd envision dark clouds gathering, torrential rains for days on end, and the gathering of animals in pairs to preserve some semblance of Life As We Know It. McDivitt would sigh, while suppressing an even deeper sigh, shake his head sadly, and mutter, "OK, have it your way." And you could almost see his lips form the words, "you little shit."

And then he'd return to his research.

Before my appointment with McDivitt I had a few hours for playing boss and exploring my inbox. The inbox was full of comments on the president's annual address to the campus, which was held last night. Although I had been urged to attend, along with my staff, in order to beef up the attendance, I had pleaded an important engagement. Exploring Ronson's office was way more interesting than anything the president might have said.

Following an obscure tradition, the idea of an annual speech was modeled loosely on the State of the Union address. For years the attendance had been predictably anemic, but Yarmouth tried to goose it with new tricks.

In a desperate attempt to incentivize faculty and staff, the administration tried to buy them off with gourmet-quality goodies in a post-speech reception. A couple hundred hungry and thirsty stalwarts would sit impassively in the cavernous auditorium, barely filling the first dozen rows, for twenty minutes and applaud lustily, no matter what was said. Some of them told me this was known as "singing for your supper."

This year's event was no exception. I had glanced at the speech on the internet between sips of coffee that morning. Yarmouth went on at length about the achievements of faculty and students and how well-regarded the university was within the academic community, and how its stature had risen recently. It's a wonder he didn't get a cramp from patting himself on the back. But he didn't follow the normal roadmap for a rousing address. He did not articulate a vision for the future; nor did he have any specific initiatives to announce. Despite efforts to spice it up with graphics and music, the result was dry and boring, according to the accounts I read .

Inevitably, the address attracted its critics.

TO: President Marchand Yarmouth
FROM: Aiko Fisher, sectional dean of the arts
SUBJECT: Your remarks to the university community

President Yarmouth, I know it is hard to please everyone and impossible to mention every program in a 20-minute speech, but your annual address was striking for the absence of a single reference to programs outside of the sciences, medicine and engineering.

I know that we are in an environment where we feel the need to prove that everything we do here translates into money — either feeding the maw of industry with the commercial equivalent of cannon fodder (i.e., our graduates) or turning research into products that can make a buck for someone (usually not for us; I've read the reports on what happens to our technology and it makes our laboratories look like farm teams for the corporate sector. Not that it matters to me, as a flautist. No one is going to be beating down my door with payments for my recent compositions, as well reviewed as they have been. But I digress…).

But here you are, speaking on campus to a room that should be filled with your best and brightest faculty (and that's another thing: why have this speech in an auditorium that holds more than a thousand and then fill just a handful of rows? Can't you offer people a reason to come? Can you advertise some special announcement to draw a crowd? And if you can't, well, maybe the age of speeches to the faculty has passed). You should be talking about the whole university, not selected short subjects that appeal to the most unsophisticated palate.

I realize we are not living in a golden age for the arts. Do you have any sense of how demoralized my colleagues are? They see all the attention and, yes, all the resources going to fields that seem more glamorous, and they feel like second-class citizens here. And I think that's unjustifiable. Just to keep things in perspective: every concert by our student symphonia has drawn a crowd bigger than your address. And that's without fancy canapes.

Can't you throw us a bone? I could write your lines for those richly deserved plaudits, it would be easy. Talk about how the arts make life worth living, appeal to humans' higher and better selves, open the mind to possibilities that cannot be reduced to ones and zeroes, express the inexpressible, tie us in a very real and fundamental way to all of humanity, past and present.

See, it wouldn't be that hard. And I assure you the remarks would put a spring in the step of every single person in the Music and Art buildings.

I have to end with kudos for your public declarations regarding the death of Jeremy Ronson. Everyone, and I mean everyone, around here knows there was no love lost between you two. Who gets banned from cabinet meetings? Not that you weren't justified in doing that, because you were. But when the chips were down and you could have taken the low road, you showed some real class. I know it must've been hard, given what he used to say about you and your people. But it was the right thing to do.

* * *

That afternoon, when I walked into the computer science building I was impressed by its airiness and quiet, modulated by the hum and buzz of small robots being tested by undergrads just outside the very busy main-floor cafe. It appeared they were having an informal competition to see if they could direct the robots via phone or tablet to pick up objects of various sizes and shapes, carry them across a field of obstacles, and deposit them in a waiting receptacle. The floor was littered with many machines literally spinning their wheels, with a few devices struggling up and down inclines, trying to bend under limbo bars or navigating across small ponds. Whatever the purpose, the students seemed to be enjoying themselves, and a few faculty had assumed postures of judgment, complete with clipboards, on the periphery of the field.

"It's a regular activity," said McDivitt, who had sidled up to me on cat's paws. He was tall and painfully thin, with the hollowed-out cheeks of someone on a long-term starvation diet, but his eyes were dark and glowed like coals.

"It began a few months ago as a demonstration from the student robotics club. But then people just walking by started asking things like, 'Can it climb a ladder? Can it go up and down steps? What kinds of objects can it pick up — do the objects need handles or can you make one pick up a sphere, and what about something hotdog-shaped?' So the students in the club got energized, they recruited more students and even got a few faculty to let them bring some of their more challenging problems into a couple of classes. We're thinking a few of these experiments are going to result in special-purpose devices that have commercial value. But mostly it's for fun."

We found a cafe table somewhat removed from the others and from the proving ground.

"I've been told you are a fount of useful information about people and personalities in the department and related areas."

"Please cut the bullshit. I've been here a long time, that's all. I know where most of the bodies are buried and the spots reserved for cadavers-in-waiting." He flicked a crumb from his jeans and put both hands on his knees, leaning forward. "What did you want to talk about?"

"Jeremy Ronson."

He whistled. "I'd been waiting for someone to ask. A top administrator and prime scumbag like Ronson 'falls' out a window and no one has any questions? Give me a fuckin' break."

"Just so you know, anything you tell me is completely off the record, not for attribution."

"Do I care? I'm tenured. I don't have any special knowledge of Ronson. Just the conventional wisdom and information that makes the rounds."

"Well, give me an example."

McDivitt leaned back and crossed his legs.

"In an institution with an indifferent record in managing its resources, Jeremy Ronson set the standard for profligate spending and disregard of standard money-handling practices. He treated his budget as if it were his private discretionary account, picking favorites in both people and projects and penalizing those who fell out of favor. Because he worked in a technical area, he managed to hide his total incompetence with glossy reports and glowing anecdotes prepared for people with as slippery a command of truth and ethics as he had.

Namely his counterparts in the rest of the administration who languidly exercised their responsibility for oversight of the fraud."

McDivitt had a booming voice and I could see heads turn briefly at surrounding tables. When they saw who it was they returned to their macchiatos with a shrug.

"Ronson essentially was running his office like a Ponzi scheme. Or more accurately, like Wimpy. 'I'll gladly pay you Tuesday for a hamburger today.'" McDivitt snorted. "He'd start projects with no source of funding and assume that somehow, if he waved the flag enthusiastically enough, he'd get bailed out. It's a measure of the incompetence of successive generations of university leadership that he managed to get away with this for so long. But sooner or later it was inevitable that the chickens would come home to roost."

"So what happened?"

"Quite simply, the bubble burst." McDivitt uncrossed his legs and sat up. "His ever-growing budget requests finally came up against the reality of limited resources. And the story I heard was — how do they phrase this in film noir? — someone 'dropped a dime' on his operation with the auditors. Then the shit hit the fan."

"When was this?" I was tempted to take notes but realized this might inhibit the flow, even for someone as outspoken as McDivitt.

"Not sure. Some time ago, actually. Maybe two years."

"And he was allowed to stay?"

"When was the last time you heard of someone being fired around here? Especially someone making a salary in six figures. Simply doesn't happen. You could be banging undergrads and they'd find a way to send you off with a neutral recommendation and no paper trail." He dropped his voice to a stage whisper. "I could give you chapter and verse on those cases, if you're interested."

I ignored his offer and pushed on. "So there was an audit report?"

"That's what I heard. Never saw it. But if it contained one-tenth of what I know that Ronson tried to pull off, they could've shown him the door by sunset, had they been so inclined." McDivitt chuckled. "Some think he must've had a dossier on the president or some of the trustees that prevented them from canning his ass."

"So nothing happened? Nothing at all?"

"As is common in cases like this, the miscreants get off scot-free. But there was still a Day of the Long Knives. In order to bring the budget back in balance about fifty people were given three hours to get out of Dodge. It was quite a scene.

"They brought in a bunch of security guards and took people into a conference room where they were told they'd be given a couple of weeks' severance pay. But they couldn't return to work. After all, these guys ran systems like the personnel database, payroll and grant accounting. They literally had the keys to the kingdom, and it would be pretty easy to cause mayhem with just a few lines of code. So they were escorted from the conference room to their desks, where they were provided with cardboard cartons to pack up their belongings and personal effects. The security guys escorted them out of the building, which had been locked down."

"What happened after that?"

"Now *that's* a real interesting question. Near as I can figure Ronson's entire empire was put into receivership. Someone took over temporarily-permanently. I suspect the president had to tell the trustees about it, because the cumulative impact of Ronson's shenanigans must've been in the millions. So we can safely assume orders to paper it over and keep quiet came from the top."

McDivitt looked over at the student competition. One powerful robot's master had decided to turn the event into a demolition derby and was shoving other machines off the course to a chorus of muffled cheers and protests. A few people were documenting the competition with photos. One, a girl in a hoodie across the cafe from McDivitt and me, even had a camera with a long lens.

"I can imagine the people who were let go without warning were pretty angry."

McDivitt nodded. "For sure. They didn't do anything wrong, yet they were out on the street. If I were them I would've blown the whistle on this schmuck publicly, at the very least. I started to get calls from some of them, looking for work. I did what I could to help." He shrugged.

"Yeah. I wonder why I hadn't caught wind of this before."

"Maybe if we had a newspaper that wasn't more interested in clickbait than doing actual news gathering, this would've become public by now. I dunno. That's your area, not mine."

"So let me get this right. The audit finds what you'd typically call malfeasance. Ronson isn't fired but a bunch of other people are. He's forced to relinquish his day-to-day responsibilities. Does he get to keep his title and salary after all that?"

"You sound surprised. Never heard of the rubber room? It's a common practice in situations where you can't or won't fire an individual because they have tenure or something. You take away their authority. Put them in an office by themselves. Remove them from all decision-making bodies and even advisory groups. If someone asks, you say they're assigned to 'special projects' or maybe 'planning,' a catchall for people who have flamed out from responsible positions. And you just hope that after a decent interval they go away."

"But Ronson didn't go away."

McDivitt abruptly stood up, our conversation clearly at an end. "No, he didn't."

McDivitt's insights opened new avenues of investigation. It was simply a question of which ideas to pursue first. The implosion of Ronson's empire had occurred under the radar, as far as most of us were concerned. But it shouldn't be hard to track down both victims and participants in the fiasco. On the one side, we had the people who rode the up escalator with him, those people who rose to positions of prominence and influence on his coattails, like Art Kingston. But there was that other group, tossed over the side as his empire collapsed. And of course, there were the ubiquitous administrators trying to cover their tracks and bury their mistakes.

CHAPTER FOUR

I was feeling guilty about the amount of time I already was sinking into amateur sleuthing. At this early stage of my investigation, I was becoming disengaged from day-to-day office duties. We were a small, cohesive team and relied pretty heavily on one another. Although I was the boss, I knew others would resent my absence from the group if I wasn't careful, and loss of trust was hard to regain. Maybe I was reading too much into inflected remarks and raised eyebrows, but I sensed that my withdrawal from office life was already not going unnoticed.

I carefully closed my door. I had an hour, maybe two, of quiet time. Enough to catch up on one of my regular responsibilities that, if I shirked them, folks were likely to resent.

I was the office editor-of-choice, assuring that our news stories made sense, explained things well and were stylistically consistent. The staff, composed of recovering journalists, was religious about deadlines. So I concentrated on editing a few stories for which my response was urgently needed. This would at least fulfill my minimum responsibilities to the team.

When I had moved from newspapering to the world of public relations, I had done so without considering how things might be different. Given a relatively free hand, I hired people with whom I was comfortable — in other words, people like me, news people. The office, unsurprisingly, had the feel of a newsroom. That meant respect for language and dedication to getting the story right — not just right, but clear and understandable.

Our approach put us at odds with the bread-and-circuses crowd on campus, who thought that a flashy show with greater hype resulted in bigger media buzz than actual news. They regarded the news business as part of some demimonde inhabited creatures less exalted than themselves. Something that they would wipe their shoes on. And to them, we were part of that netherworld, too.

In fact, the news business had changed in ways to make the bread and circus strategy plausible. If news media were becoming obsessed with clicks and likes, how could I argue that real stories, the kinds of developments happening in laboratories across campus, still mattered?

Ever since moving from the news business to universities, I had begun seeing the challenges facing higher education echoing those that had confronted the news business. Both industries had the feel of a monopoly, a system that really wasn't a system at all, fractured ever more acutely into the haves and have-nots, the shortcomings papered over by a steady revenue stream for the stars and the also-rans.

Universities faced a host of challenges: aging faculty immune from mandatory retirement, the growth of online education and alternate certification schemes, a funding model based largely on student debt, a growing skepticism about the value of higher education for the average student, and a growing partisan division on what should be the future of America's higher education "system." These challenges were faced by institutions wrapped in bureaucratic straitjackets that could strangle the most ardent innovators. Like newspapers, change didn't come easily if at all.

Meanwhile, universities as a group persistently ignored vast underserved populations, dominated by the poor and people of color, whose absence constituted higher education's greatest shame. Instead, institutions battled one another over issues of privilege, status and primacy, all pretty much beside the point when it comes to social justice.

My choice to move to higher education from journalism had been motivated in part by the desire to become part of an institution that was dedicated to improving the human condition. I wasn't so much an idealist as a pragmatist with a values fetish. But when I saw the time and resources being frittered away on political infighting while crucial issues were neglected, I wondered if I had made the right decision.

Enough! I dove into the stack of documents that awaited my TLC.

The staff's writing cheered me. It was crisp, to the point, and on occasion even exciting. I made precious few edits, raised a few questions, and sent the documents back to their authors. It was absurdly quick and easy. I felt like the whole operation could exist on autopilot without my intervention.

Which was good, because I could pursue my other interest without fear of the office going off the rails. It was about noon when I finished my editing chores. I hoped to spend time soon tracing whatever scraps of information about Ronson that existed in our office files, university archives and on my own computer, just filling in the gaps in the public record.

I took a spin around the office, checking to see what was up with my people and just saying hello so they didn't forget I was still there. Then I returned to my desk and the never-ending flow of emails.

I had no idea why I was copied on so many emails that had nothing to do with my work. Some people had the annoying habit of including just about everyone that they knew on almost everything, perhaps in the hope that their kudos/complaint/observation would strike a chord with someone. But at least it kept me up to date on campus gossip and some under-the-radar events and controversies.

Anyhow, today's crop contained the following gems.

TO: President Marchand Yarmouth
FROM: Trudy Blockwright, assistant vice president of corporate and
     foundational engagement and encouragement
SUBJECT: Football seating

President Yarmouth, I know we are in the midst of the football season (one that many of us would prefer to forget), but it is not too early to begin discussion on what we can do to improve the leverage exercised by the allocation of prime seating in the area of the stadium that has become known colloquially as "Yarmouth's Select Few."

As you know, every major college football program such as ours tries to use the luxury seating strategically. They use the section to reward key donors but also to attract future supporters. It's one of those key opportunities to create a social networking environment that is highly desirable, with you at the very center.

Remember that last year we agreed to give 20 percent of seating space to our esteemed colleagues in the Office of State Accountability and Public Propinquity. So what did our elected representatives provide during the most recent legislative session in the way of institutional support? The words "Diddly" and "Squat" come quickly to mind.

One of my rules at work is that I should not reward bad actions. I think it is time to "send a message" to our elected officials by limiting their access to one of the great entertainment values in the city (even with a losing team) and make some hard choices about who really deserves this kind of gift.

One other issue: the behavior of some of our guests makes me wonder if we need a new policy regarding alcohol in the section. There was more than one incident involving people who are prominent on the political scene. If knowledge of their private behavior (and it may be stretching the definition of private in this case) was known to their constituents, I suspect the wrath of the voters would be visited upon them during the next election cycle, if not sooner. We're running a significant risk here, in my opinion.

Without appearing to be "piling on," which I'm told can bring a 15-yard penalty, I suspect some of our female VIPs would be much more receptive to future invitations if they knew that the authors of some crude and inappropriate remarks would no longer be welcome. With the rise of women in local business, we need to be more sensitive to these issues, especially since these women ultimately will represent a potential source of philanthropy that will rival the persistently paltry contributions from our state government.

I suggest that attendance in the Select Few by our political leaders be reduced, at least temporarily, until we have officials more sympathetic and more "couth," if that is a word. We have reached the point where for me going to the games is a high stress experience, if only due to fear of some untoward event for which I will need to apologize.

TO: Trudy Blockwright
FROM: Aaron Thyme, assistant director of State Accountability and
      Public Propinquity
RE: Football seating

Trudy, I am dismayed that you involved President Yarmouth in a discussion of who should, and should not, be allowed in "Yarmouth's Select Few." As you know, the allocation of a specific number of seats for the discretion of my office has been a long-standing practice, stretching back decades if not longer. It is an essential part of the continuum of contacts we have with elected officials. For some of them it is a symbol of their importance and connection with the university. For you to insert yourself in a process that is not under your purview is inappropriate.

Given the charges you have leveled, I suppose I should respond. But I'm not sure that it serves either of our respective units to continue airing dirty linen when it is clear that the slime will get on everyone. Not to put too fine a point on it, I could cite chapter and verse over the years, and so could you, of incidents involving people other than legislators who embarrassed themselves and/or others.

As you well know, probably the most celebrated incident in the president's area — and I still marvel that it never made its way into the papers — involved one of "yours." The fact that we had to carry someone through the indoor suite, unconscious but moaning loudly, and down the stairs to a waiting ambulance in full view of fans on the north side stairways, leaving the ladies' restroom in a condition that could only be described as deplorable, is something that I will not soon forget, nor will the hundreds who witnessed this.

Pot, meet kettle.

TO: Aaron
FROM: Trudy

Well, touché! I was thinking you might dredge up that incident (whose protagonist, by the way, claims to this day that her problems were caused not by alcohol but by food poisoning). But it's hard for me to view repeated boorish, harassing behavior in the same way as an incident involving the ill health of a single individual.

I have talked with several prominent female donors and friends who expressed discomfort at what has transpired recently. I don't know how we get public officials to clean up their act. Maybe we should eliminate alcohol at these functions? Or give our bartenders some discretion or training in when to say no?

All I know is, the present situation is untenable. As the university's deputy chief fundraising officer, I never thought I'd be spending so much time as the equivalent of grade school hall monitor. Really, I think the situation is close to getting out of hand. We've clamped down on the boozing at tailgating. If people become rowdy drunk in the stands they get cited and tossed out. But we're still allowing this in the president's suite?

TO: Trudy

FROM: Aaron

Trudy, as long as the goose and the gander are equally sauced (or in this case, de-sauced) then I will support a change in policy. We just can't pick favorites based on either donation level or clout. But the first time one of our young, sweet bartenders refuses to refill, and we hear a booming (or shrill) voice announcing incredulously, "Do you know who I am?" are you pledging to intervene? Am I?

This isn't as easy as it seems.

I think we should discuss this privately, probably over drinks. (Just kidding. Sorta.) And at the same time, we can toast the untimely departure of our least favorite geek.

TO: Aaron

FROM: Trudy

That's truly the most tasteless remark I've read all week. But I accept your invitation.

Public universities such as ours rely heavily on donor allegiance and legislative influence. The loss of support of either group certainly would spell doom for any administration. So whatever sins its members might commit in private, they were pretty much washed clean by whatever public gestures of respect and admiration could be extracted from them.

The email exchange also caused me to wonder how many other people around campus were covertly celebrating Ronson's departure. Why was a thinly veiled reference to him popping up in emails between a fundraiser and lobbyist discussing the president's box?

I figured the most direct path was to call one of them and ask. I knew Trudy slightly better than Aaron.

"Trudy, it's Mike Woodsen. Thanks for copying me on your discussion with Aaron over the use of the president's box. I was just calling to ask if any of the miscreants included media executives. You know, publishers, executive editors or editorial page people."

"Hey, Mike. Truth is, I've been so anxious at those events that I didn't even notice your people. I don't think I've ever heard a complaint about their behavior."

"Some journalists drink a lot, but they usually know how to hold it in public. At least that's the conventional wisdom."

"I guess so."

"So, one more question while I have you. Why are you and Aaron so... how should I put this? Not gleeful, exactly, but I guess it's safe to assume you aren't mourning the passing of Jeremy."

"Awkward. The death of anyone, especially in such circumstances, is a tragedy, of course. But, to be honest, I must say my recent interactions with him were odd. Off-putting. A couple of months ago, in fact, Aaron and I finally felt compelled to go to Yarmouth and get him banned from the box. The first and only time we've done that."

"Geez, what did he do?"

"As I said, it was odd. He was a standard invite for years. And he'd show up maybe once or twice a season. Kept to himself, grabbed some food, chatted only a little. I wondered why he was on the list but it was never a big deal. Then, in the past year or two, something changed. He interacted more with people, showed up more. But he seemed devoid of impulse control. He always had a sarcastic edge to him, as you know, but he started letting it show more in conversations with total strangers. And given who the guests in the box were, this became a problem.

"What finally did it for me was when he insulted the wife of a major donor. They were just chatting. I was nearby. He started ridiculing her for purchasing a particular model of smart phone. He even called her technologically illiterate. She tried to laugh it off, but I could see that inside she was seething.

"A few days later, I learned from Aaron that at that same game he had cornered a legislator and berated her for over-regulating the university's purchasing authority for major computing systems. Maybe he was on firmer ground there, but according to Aaron, Jeremy went way over the line. He told the legislator that since state government had made such a mess of its own computer systems they were hardly in a position to comment intelligently on the university's decisions; he also predicted that if the state systems experienced any major outages, they would be 'up shit creek without a paddle,' his words, because their backup systems were so weak."

"Had he been drinking when he did this?"

"He didn't appear to be visibly drunk. I think it was just his usual obnoxiousness finally gaining the upper hand. But it was enough for us to get him relieved of further invitations."

"Did anyone hear from him after he was banned? Do you know if they notified him or just stopped inviting him?"

"I think it was the latter. But as far as I know, he never made an issue out of it. He was such a snide little shit. I can't help but think he came there deciding to test the limits of what outrageous behavior we would tolerate, knowing eventually he'd get banned. But I have no evidence to support that except that it fit with my overall view of his personality. I don't want to speak ill of the dead, although I guess that's exactly what I'm doing. I never liked him. I don't say this often, but he was not a nice person."

I quickly combed through the remainder of my accumulated email sludge, triaging messages into obvious deletions, forward to an office colleague, or respond. I found myself wondering how I had missed this announcement:

To the university community:

I wish you all to know about a reorganization that is taking place in our academic and administrative computing division.

Sylvia Plumer, who has been the interim/acting vice president for academic and research computing resources, is assuming the new position of Vice President for Seamless User Interfaces and Excellence in Data Distribution, which encompasses all of the work that is done by our computing team to manage and improve the resources available to faculty, administration and students.

Her office will also assume all ongoing responsibilities for Strategic Infrastructure Planning and Systems Design and Integration.

I want to publicly compliment Dr. Plumer for excellent work under what can only be described as difficult circumstances.

If you have any questions about how this change might affect ongoing projects or support for emerging ventures, please don't hesitate to contact my office or Dr. Plumer directly.

Sincerely,
Marchand Yarmouth
President

If you didn't keep a scorecard you might not understand the import of this message. All the authority formerly delegated to Ronson was being transferred to a successor who, fortuitously, was waiting in the wings. The announcement of the reorganization came hard upon Ronson's death.

My calendar noted that I was scheduled that afternoon to attend a "command performance" about the launch in the next phase of the image campaign that President Yarmouth had embarked upon about a year ago.

I had received an "invitation" marked **Urgent.** It bore all the earmarks of an order. It came from the President and the Provost, although it seemed like the event was in the hands of the Vice President for People, Promise, Programs and Purpose Enhancement. It read, in part:

> These are perilous times for the university. While private support continues to grow, our state government support has declined markedly over the past two decades. This compromises our ability to compete for the best faculty, to continue to receive the research funding on which so many units rely, and longer term could even compromise our ability to attract the best students.
>
> Indeed, many of the top state students do not perceive us as their most attractive option, a perception we need to correct if our national and international standing is to be maintained.
>
> When we look around, we see an environment full of threats, but one in which those threats could easily be transformed into opportunities. For example, we face a growing threat from online institutions that purport to offer high-quality instruction for a lower price, and also offer great flexibility for students, potentially limiting our ability to attract older adults to our daytime and evening continuing education programs. While we know their claims are greatly exaggerated, a vulnerable and ill-informed public looking for bargains could

be swayed into thinking that both the discounts and quality are for real. Thus the threat from online schools can be viewed as a chance to reassert the high quality of our education, much higher than any electronic college.

We can't help but think that the current challenges with which we are faced arise in part from a misapprehension among potential supporters about the crucial contributions that this university makes to our state and our nation. If the university's essential role were properly understood and appreciated, we are certain that adequate resources would be forthcoming.

Accordingly, we are pursuing a path pioneered by the corporate entities in America which have achieved iconic status by stressing their unique strengths and essential role in our way of life. While some may regard this choice as risky, we believe the risk of doing nothing far exceeds the relatively small investment in a grand plan to raise this institution's profile.

We would like to invite you to a preliminary gathering with the consulting firm of McGarvey, McCandless, Scarbuff and Glanz, renowned for their insight into the special qualities that have made icons of many Fortune 500 firms as well as a growing list of highly-respected nonprofit entities. The principals for this firm will outline their plans for the coming years and how they can tap your expertise for the greater good.

Please know that your participation is essential to the success of this most crucial venture, especially at its inception.

From previous experience I knew that invitations of this type means attendance was "highly recommended," that is, if you valued future employment. And it was set for this afternoon.

* * *

The presentation was to take place in a former hydraulics laboratory that had been converted into a banquet facility. It still bore the exposed plumbing and brick walls of its historic use.

This meeting was intended to be inclusive, which in university parlance meant that academic leaders below the level of dean, as well as people like me, were invited. As I arrived, a crowd of maybe one hundred was busy grabbing coffee and pastries. I nodded to a few people I recognized and took a seat near the back.

"You know, they're taking names and you won't be able to sneak out early."

It was Don Glanville, professor of finance and sometime leader of the Faculty Senate. He wore his sardonic grin as a permanent mask, but it did not succeed in drawing attention away from his very poor hair transplant. You could see individual, identical strands standing in rows like a farmer's meticulously planted corn field. It was impolite to stare but it was hard to avoid.

"They really must've cast a broad net if they invited you, Don."

"Oh, I'm here as a sub. They somehow planned this on a day when current senate leadership was unavailable. I promised to come and give them an unvarnished report on what transpired."

"Right. You can sit here as long as you didn't bring any tomatoes."

He feigned shock. "Moi? The latest trend, as you probably know, is tossing shoes, not tomatoes. But I came unarmed except for what's in my verbal quiver. About which I make no promises." Don thought very well of himself and his rhetorical skills. Most regarded him as a loudmouth.

We settled in and the lights dimmed. Up front was a temporary stage and large projection screen. The video began with a helicopter view of campus and the university's fight song. A booming voice rose above the song.

"This is a great university. A treasure not just for the state, but for the nation and world. It is part of an elite group that makes tomorrow's discoveries, educates tomorrow's leaders, and in a very real sense actually creates our tomorrow."

I was having tinges of deja-vu. Hadn't I said something at a staff meeting about "owning the future?" Maybe it was in the water.

The scene shifted to ground level shots in black and white. And the music became a somber violin chorus with a clear, plaintive oboe.

"But tomorrow is changing from hope to just a faint wish. Our state has decided not to invest in its own future. If it weren't for our generous friends, neighbors and fellow citizens, the doors of opportunity would be slamming shut."

We see the doors of the library closing and the lights inside flicking off. A student runs up the entrance to the library and shakes the locked doors, a look of worry on her face. We flash to a colorful sunrise and a heavy back beat.

"Today begins a renaissance for our great university. Think of the turnaround at Apple." We see a split screen of the original Mac and today's iPad.

"Ford." A mustang of yesteryear, a pinto, and today's Focus. "And Caterpillar." Farmers driving a CAT circa 1920 and alongside a bright modern green machine with heavy treads and a big scoop.

Glanville pushed his elbow against my ribs. "If their pitch goes on in this vein much longer, they'll need a bigger shovel." The film's omniscient voice continued.

"Leave your doubts at the door. This is a new age with new ideas. With a positive attitude and a great plan, we can succeed beyond our wildest dreams. For those of you with doubts, we're about to convert you from being Eeyores... to Tiggers." The images of A.A. Milne's characters exploded onto the screen and then faded away.

"I say pooh on all of this," Glanville stage-whispered. A person behind us shushed.

The university's mascot, the legendary Spirit Snake, known colloquially as Slinky, filled the entire screen, startling the people in the front row. The fight song reached a crescendo and the screen went black.

The crowd was silent. A man appearing to be in his mid-thirties wearing a three-piece suit, a neon tie and pastel running shoes bounded onto the stage.

"Thank you all for coming. I'm Miles McCandless. I hope that inspired you, gave you an inkling of where we're going with this. We come from the corporate world, but like you we understand the value of good research. We're going to tell you what we've learned in talking to your neighbors, fellow citizens and voters, and where we think that should lead us. We'll allow time for questions and we're eager to hear your ideas."

He began a PowerPoint that interspersed the results of his company's research with pictures of happy students, concerned faculty, supportive parents, and the occasional touchdown celebration.

That was the windup, and here was the pitch: "You are the best kept secret in the state and beyond. Everyone knows you, but what they actually know about you could occupy the space inside a thimble. People are favorably disposed, but their knowledge is less than what they know about an instant celebrity or a minor sports star. That is to say, next to nothing.

"You're fighting for mindshare," he said, waving his laser pointer at the crowd. I hoped he had switched it off. "People have only so much brain-space, and you're either in or out. It doesn't matter how good you are, how valuable you are or the great contributions you make to improving the quality of life for people *if they don't recognize it.*

"If they don't recognize it they won't talk about or act upon it." He bounded across the temporary stage in three long strides and pivoted to face us. "And if they don't act, you're just like any other claimant at the public trough, and your outlook will be poor."

He pointed at us and gestured emphatically. "You need to generate customer enthusiasm and loyalty that moves people to action. People need to clamor for your services. You need to increase demand to the point where you are perceived, correctly, as a highly valuable commodity."

He paused dramatically and looked out over the crowd with a sweeping gesture. "The citizens of this state, led, I should add, by the people in this room, need to have loyalty to your school colors, your name, your logo, your mascot. And that's just the beginning. We want to bring that message to the country and beyond, to make you as beloved and familiar as these brands. Our branding initiative will be supported by an extensive, national recruiting campaign for the best and brightest undergrads." He flashed familiar symbols across the screen: Coca Cola, McDonalds, Apple, followed by those of the elite institutions, Harvard, Stanford and others. Some of the recent discussions and priorities alluded to by Ganas at exec meetings were making a bit more sense.

"Why isn't your university's name up there, with those icons? Can anyone tell me?" he asked rhetorically.

"Maybe because we're not Harvard or Stanford," Glanville piped up.

McCandless looked surprised by the interjection, although he had invited comments.

"Obviously that's true. But it's only part of the answer. These icons have cultivated and nurtured their image over a long period of time. They have penetrated the consciousness of the American public. As a result, they enjoy success beyond their founders' bold ambitions." He beamed at the audience. "And that's where we'd like to take you."

"But don't you have it backward?" Glanville again.

"How's that? I'm not sure I understand your point." In a mock-salute, McCandless shielded his eyes from the stage lights, trying to identify his critic.

Don stood up. "Look, I don't want to disrupt your presentation. And if I'm the only one with questions... well, I can just ask them later."

"No no no. We really want to hear what you think. You're the ground troops, the foot soldiers. Without your wholehearted acceptance, we have maybe half a plan. So, please...?"

"It's just that.... Let me be blunt. We're not Harvard. We're not Stanford. Imagine if some other computer company pretended they were Apple, if some local burger franchise decided to behave as if they were McDonalds. It's a little silly."

Heads turned as Glanville continued.

"There's an argument being made here. This is not about achieving excellence in what we do, whether it's teaching or research. This line of reasoning, if you can call it that, assumes we're already there, at the pinnacle, and that people just don't know it yet.

"Now, I wish this were true. I wish our faculty in the political science department was commuting daily to the nation's capital as consultants with our country's leaders. I wish our business school students were being recruited routinely by Wall Street headhunters. I wish our engineers were causing a renaissance in corporate startups that would come to dominate our regional economy. I have lots more wishes for many more of our esteemed faculty and their work. But let's face it: we're not there yet. Not by any means. And saying we are isn't going to make it so. This approach is borderline delusional."

A few heads were nodding in agreement. But there were a lot more blank faces. I looked up at the front and spied President Yarmouth, who looked as if he had just swallowed a very sour pickle. If this were a cartoon, smoke would be puffing from his ears. If he could secretly stick a shiv into Glanville I had a feeling he might be up for it.

The speaker's smile had been reduced to a thin line. "Thank you for your comments, professor. But I'm afraid you're misunderstanding the context for our approach. This entire strategy is based upon the aspirational reality for this university." He punched the words "aspirational reality" as much as he could.

"In simple language, we believe you will become what you behold. This is an ancient concept and has been found in many traditional belief systems for millennia, and it is a basic psychological principle as well. We're simply adapting it to the current context. We believe it can work — on the people in this room, on the greater university community, and on society at large. I hope that addresses your concerns?"

Glanville shifted his feet uneasily. "Not entirely. I don't believe reality can be manipulated in the way that you suggest."

"We're not manipulating reality," McCandless said. "Just people's perception of reality."

Granville continued shaking his head. "I'm sorry. I still disagree. But I don't want to make my skepticism a show-stopper." He sat down. There was some scattered applause.

The presentation continued but I sensed a shift in mood. The faculty, particularly, were a tough crowd regardless of circumstances. Those who had risen through the ranks were certain that they had seen it all. Tenure gave them a sure sense of their own future. They weren't about to change the way they did things, or thought about things, based upon an outsider's PowerPoint vision of the future, aspirational or not.

It was time for the wrap-up from Yarmouth. He conferred briefly with the consultant before taking the stage. He was tense and even from my remote observation post I could see moisture forming on his upper lip.

His voice began weakly and haltingly but quickly acquired its pace. "First, I'd like to thank you all for taking time from your busy schedule to attend this meeting. We are kicking off something that I believe will change the trajectory of this great institution for the better.

"When I arrived here just over two years ago, I was amazed, simply amazed, by the quality of the work that went on here, in the classrooms and laboratories and with community partners. Then I was greeted with what I'll charitably describe as an indifferent reaction when I went to the state capitol. I attended national meetings with leaders of higher education and found that this university, despite its excellence, is not held in very high regard there either. Frankly, I was aghast. And while our numbers for private fundraising are climbing, I know we could do better if only people recognized what a treasure this place is."

He paused, moistened his lips and swallowed. I noticed how large his Adam's apple was. "Consider today's presentation as the first discussion of a long-range strategy to heighten this institution's image among key constituencies. The ultimate aim, of course, is to raise our level of support across the board. That means, for example, you'll see our name and logo and key messages displayed more prominently throughout the city — on billboards, in advertising on television, radio and the Web, and anywhere else we might deem opportune. We're going to arm our alumni with talking points, video packages and PowerPoints. And we will begin developing a vigorous national campaign in the media and by meeting with thought leaders. In basketball terminology, what I'm calling for is a full-court press.

"We're employing proven strategies from the corporate world that only now are being adopted by the public and nonprofit sectors. I am confident that within a year or two we'll be asking ourselves, 'Why didn't we do this sooner?'

"New ideas, new ways of doing things, always need to survive a hail of skepticism and naysaying. But the naysayers and skeptics are typically deficient in articulating alternative strategies. They rely on a misreading of history to say, 'We tried this a number of years ago and it didn't work.' Well, no one has tried this here before, and after a careful review, my administrative team concluded that this approach has the best chance of bringing us the kind of success that we all want to achieve.

"I'll conclude by asking those of you with concerns to suspend your disbelief and simply give this a chance. And again, thank you for coming."

There was scattered applause as people rose and quickly dispersed.

"Remind me not to sit next to you again. You're going to get me in trouble," I said to Glanville, who just grinned.

"Hey, that was pretty mild compared to what I could've said. And since when is it frowned upon for a faculty member, especially a tenured faculty member, to call bullshit on something… that's actually bullshit?"

"You mean you didn't get the memo? The one about not calling bullshit?"

"Speaking of memos, did you have any hand in creating that invitation to this fiasco from Yarmouth and Hietflower? What a piece of crap that was."

"Can't say that I had the pleasure. I happen to live in the wrong silo for that kind of work."

"Lucky you. So, what else is keeping you busy?"

"Nothing too exciting. Trying to satisfy some of my curiosity about Jeremy Ronson's demise."

Glanville ran his hand through the man-made crop on his head, which stood stiffly away from his scalp. "I think that Ronson was the limiting case of what happens when weak leaders, and by that I mean our esteemed presidents both past and current, refuse to face up to their responsibility. He should have been gone years ago. And by 'gone,' of course I mean fired and not dead."

"Well, he wasn't the first beneficiary of noble privileges and I'm sure he won't be the last. We could probably count some of your tenured colleagues in that group, I suspect."

Glanville ignored the barb. "I think deep down he always knew he was a second-rate intellect. Maybe that's why he insisted that the administration agree to an employment contract when they hired him."

"I thought only coaches had contracts."

"And of course the president. But I've heard rumors of a few others. Ronson among them."

"So you've never seen it?"

"Hell no. You think anyone would show that to me, given my big mouth? And how would you go about asking for something like that?"

"True. But it is a public document. Probably."

"If you want to file a public records request, go right ahead. Just make sure you provide the postal service with your forwarding address and the police with names of your next of kin. Names will be taken and consequences will be doled out."

Sometimes, tips come from the most unexpected people. I silently thanked Doug Glanville for having such a big mouth.

I began wondering who might know about employment contracts at the university and would be unafraid of a candid conversation. I knew it had to be someone who was resistant to normal bureaucratic timidity. That narrowed the list considerably.

* * *

"There's something distinctly odd about your workplace. I'm not quite able to put my finger on it."

Andrea was standing in front of her closet, picking out her work outfit. In addition to her job as a licensed massage therapist, she was working occasional shifts as a waitress in one of the city's trendier restaurants, specializing in small, cheffy plates that resembled women's hats from the Jazz Age. The boss loved her and would have been happy to employ her full time, but she liked the independence that self-employment afforded her, while she loved the fabulous tips from the well-heeled.

Working mostly in client-focused occupations, Andrea had become a keen observer of the human species. I wouldn't call her eye jaundiced, but she was acutely sensitive to the comedy of everyday life.

When I'd met Andrea, I wasn't looking for a relationship. I had bounced around the country, back when there was still a somewhat vibrant newspaper industry. I'd worked in towns large and small, covering everything from schools to pets. I regarded all the jobs as temporary; there was so little room for advancement, the rewards were scant, and writing about the same thing day after day quickly got old for me.

Finally, after more than a decade as a nomadic writer, I'd opted for the security of the public-sector bureaucracy. I had started to see the handwriting on the wall for my chosen profession. I tried to find an organization that didn't offend my sense of values. Higher education came about as close as anything. Or so I had thought at the time.

Still, I figured this gig was as temporary as all those preceding it, which suggested that socially I'd engage in yet more drive-by relationships. I hadn't realized how little I knew about myself and my needs at this point in my life.

I met Andrea when she was working as an independent massage therapist in a local spa. It was one of the many careers she had pursued. She had come highly recommended. A good treatment for my chronic backaches.

Andrea's dark features, long hair and ready smile were stunning. I was sure that every single fellow who entered her studio harbored lascivious fantasies. As for me, I was too intimidated by her presence — she made it clear from the opening bell, in the tone of her voice and her body language, that she was very much in charge. I was hesitant to even move without her permission. So I lay inert under her hands for most of the hour. Near the end she blurted out, "Can you tell me what the deal is with you? Did I do something wrong?"

"What do you mean?"

"I seldom have a client who just lays there, silent. Not even any social banter. Most try to make casual conversation. Some even try to put the moves on me. But from you, nothing. Did I do something to piss you off? Or are you normally so standoffish?"

I shrugged as I moved off the table. "Not in the least. That was probably the best massage I've ever had. Your hands have a wonderful intuition, going right to the spots that needed care."

"So, what's the deal?" She stood there with her hands on her hips, almost daring me to answer.

"Truth?"

"Truth."

"First, I'm terrible at small talk. My mind just goes blank. But in addition, you made it clear at the outset that this is your studio, your show. I was intimidated. I figured that if I stepped out of line you could introduce pain and discomfort to your arsenal at a moment's notice. So my silence was part fear, part self-preservation, part shyness. Maybe I over-interpreted the ground rules. If so, I apologize."

Andrea laughed loud and long. "You know, you're right. Although pain is a last resort and I've only had to do it a couple of times. How come you're so smart?" She began cleaning up the studio and turned her back to me.

The massage had relaxed me more than I had anticipated. It also loosened my tongue. "I figured a woman like you has heard every conceivable line and come-on. So the only strategy left to me was absolute silence," I deadpanned. "The mystery of the man who says nothing can be very alluring, I've been told."

She gave me a business card, and I noticed it had an extra phone number written across the bottom.

"Gotta hand it to you. I mean, literally, I *have* to hand you this card. With my home phone number. I promise no violence or pain. Unless you really want that. It turns out that respect is a huge turn-on for me. Who knew?"

And the rest was history.

As a single parent with grown children, Andrea Bell had not had an easy path. Higher education was not a tradition in her family, and having two small children and a failed marriage when she was just out of high school complicated the picture. But she was a survivor, doing whatever it took to keep a roof over their heads and food on the table. She had risen above the threat of poverty and had overcome addiction. She had an acute moral compass, but also a healthy dose of practicality. We'd hit it off almost immediately, in ways both gratifying and mysterious.

We had discussed moving in together, but for now we were happy with our separate residences — mine in a tiny house, hers in a snug apartment. We were both moody, in our own ways, and occasionally needed time alone. But we also treasured our time together. I was thinking of raising the subject of living together again but was just looking for the right moment.

No one at my work knew anything about Andrea. I had decided to keep my private life private. My colleagues knew I was in a relationship, but that was as much as I was willing to tell them. There were some things about who I was that I was unwilling to share with them.

I appreciated Andrea at many levels. In the current circumstances, she was the only one with whom I could share the details of my investigation, my thoughts about who might have done what to whom and why.

She suspended her judgment, took in what I said, and waited until I was ready to hear her views. Even if they included disparaging comments about my workplace.

"What makes you think my place of work is so strange?" I responded.

"Well, by your account, management skills appear to be almost nonexistent. Not only that, but there appears to be no accountability.

In a lot of places I've worked, bad managers at least live with the threat of being fired. But that seems a low-order risk at the university.

"Also, your workplace seems to thrive on excessively high drama, given that you're not dealing with matters of life and death. The gossip seems vicious. And many of the people there have such a strange view of the world outside the university, like they haven't seen much of life. They don't seem to have a great deal of respect or regard for how most of us earn a living or the challenges faced by the average Joe or Jane. I'd say they behave as if they were in a different class from common folk."

"They do think well of themselves. Often without justification. That much I'll grant you."

"I hear all this bluster and tough talk, this posturing in private meetings with really vicious attacks on people who oppose them, but when it comes to action they freeze."

She threw a hanger with a tasteful black skirt onto the bed, followed by a demure white blouse. "And you're still thinking that one of them might have offed a vice president? I have serious doubts about that. Who would have the balls? Seriously, have you met anyone who you think is capable of committing that kind of crime?"

"Not yet. The people I've met, they're way too cautious, and timid, to let their emotions take over and run rampant. But people get crazy and do things they wouldn't normally do. I would say it's not likely that one of the people I've met is capable of murder. But neither is it likely that some guy just fell out a window."

"But please tell me, where did you get the idea that it should be your job to find the truth? What makes you so all-fired interested in this? From what you've told me, the world is free of one asshole and no one else gives a shit. Why should you?"

I paused and shrugged.

"I dunno. I suppose to a degree I've been taking the university's proclaimed virtues at face value. They claim that one important goal of a university education is to value critical thinking, looking at facts honestly and logically to reach the right conclusion. All I'm doing is applying that kind of approach to this situation. I just think the story they're peddling is incomplete, with too many lose threads."

Andrea found a pair of black dressy shoes that had the soft contours of an athletic sneaker. "I still think that this isn't the best idea you've ever had. But if you want to waste your time, that's entirely up to you, sonny. You know, you've permanently warped my view of higher education."

"How so?"

She laughed. "I used to be so awed by the whole idea. People who spend their lives getting paid for thinking, like the scarecrow in the Wizard of Oz. It sounded so exotic, so elevated. Passing knowledge along from one generation to the next, selfless and high-minded. The solemn rituals, the graduation gowns, the mortar board hats. An ancient tradition."

She shook her head slowly. "Now, I just don't know. After hearing how it plays out day to day, a lot of that life sounds… well, it sounds silly, so petty. The talk about lofty aspirations seems to be reserved for speeches and PR for the masses, not everyday decisions.

"It's like a magic incantation, but from what you tell me I'm not sure anyone believes it any more, if they ever did. All the same, the people who work there live a lot like I do day to day. But to hear you tell it, in casual conversation many regard what they do as something better, more refined. A higher calling, like the priesthood."

I grabbed her shoulders from behind and gave her a squeeze. "See, they've lived off that special status for centuries, in many ways just like a priestly class. Of course they aren't special. Still, the high-minded stuff exists side by side with the petty, day to day bullshit.

Those lofty goals and aspirations historically were at the core of why universities existed. Within the laboratories and classrooms there are things going on that truly can change our lives.

"But for me, the hilarious thing about universities is when the people working there deny the silly stuff goes on. They need to believe that they behave logically and rationally. It's an article of faith. I work in the temple of rationality."

She picked up an emery board and began filing her nails. "I don't know. Part of me wishes that they really were temples of knowledge rather than what they actually are."

I gave Andrea a hug and nuzzled her neck, that hollow just next to the clavicle. "That tickles," she said, squirming in my grasp.

"Thanks for listening to all my crazy ideas. Without you, I'm not sure where I'd go for my reality check."

She pushed herself away and gave me a look. "We're all a little crazy, I think. You just need to hang around more with a better class of crazies."

CHAPTER FIVE

The next day began with a pretty clear agenda: get hold of someone who could clue me in about the details of what Dave McDivitt had called the Day of the Long Knives. And look for an expert on employment contracts.

One of the good things about working in a news office was that we had contact with people all over campus. I did a morgue scan of articles we had written about the search process for recently filled high-profile positions where employment contracts were likely involved. I came across a few likely suspects, but I focused on one in particular.

His name was Dean Forbush, a professor of English. I recalled a rumor that his parents chose his name as part of an unsubtle attempt to direct him to this particular career, themselves being middling professors at a middling university in the Middle West.

Since receiving one of the major endowed professorships available to humanists, Forbush had become quite active in academic politics, as well as participating in many high-level searches.

I picked up the phone. After some hesitation on his part, I was reduced to shameless flattery, which often had a magical effect with faculty. He chuckled, said he could rearrange some less-pressing business, and agreed to meet that very afternoon.

Meanwhile, I looked through our morgue of stories emanating from IT and came across a familiar name. Harry Joyce was a team leader for administrative systems, at least the last time we quoted him.

He had been around forever, leading a group that helped to create the university's first Web pages eons ago. He was normally a person of few words, but when loosened up he could be quite a good source.

According to the online directory, he had not been a casualty of the epic budget fail.

I told him I had a project that required his special expertise and I wanted to talk with him as soon as I could. I figured if I told him on the phone the details of what I was doing it would be all too easy for him to gracefully decline. I kept my intent secret but offered to buy him coffee at one of the dozen or so locations on campus, and even a scone if he was good. I tried to embellish my cover story, making it sound somewhat important. I was on a mission from the Board of Trustees, I bluffed, knowing he would have trouble refuting the claim. He agreed, reluctantly, to meet me in a coffee shop in the architecture building around mid-morning.

I mused about what McDivitt had told me concerning the precipitate layoffs in IT. If I were a computer programmer, or any employee, and I was called into a conference room without warning and told to clean out my desk *right now*, that I was out of a job effective immediately, with no explanation — I'd be mighty pissed. It wouldn't take long to figure out the layoffs occurred not because they had done anything wrong, but because someone who was untouchable had screwed the pooch.

I couldn't believe the police missed this. I felt like calling Phil. So I did.

"Did you know that Ronson had been responsible for fifty people losing their jobs a few years ago?"

"Are you still chewing over that old bone? Boy, you don't give up easily, do you? Earth to Mike Woodsen: the investigation is closed. Nothing more to find. Finito. But to answer your question: yes, we'd heard that there had been some layoffs in his area, but I didn't know the number."

"And that the layoffs took place in a few hours, with no warning, and the former employees were ushered off campus, carrying all the belongings from their desks, watched by security guards?"

"We didn't have all those details. But I'm not sure it matters."

Now I was getting annoyed. "Why not?"

"If we don't have a crime, then we don't investigate who had a possible motive. It's that simple. And as I said before we didn't find anything at the scene which suggested that he was forced out that window."

"But if you had, your next step would have been to look at the fifty as possible... perps."

Phil sighed. Then he laughed. "Yes, we'd look at them as potential suspects. If we had a determination from the ME of foul play. Which we didn't. And besides, these layoffs were quite a while ago."

"Thanks, Phil." I tried to say this without sarcasm. Gotta keep all your bridges intact.

I wasn't convinced. I'd really like to talk with some of the people who were let go, to take their temperature.

When I entered the coffee shop, Harry was already there. As promised I bought refreshments and brought them to the rickety cafe table. We were in the building's atrium, surrounded by student projects of various shapes and flavors. There were artists' renderings on easels, scale models on display tables, and videos on continuous loops. Some of the classes were experimenting with crowdsourcing the project grades, one of the truly bad ideas spreading around campus, so there was a steady stream of students circling the display area, their smartphones fully loaded and at the ready.

"So, for what information am I the unique and special source?" Harry asked without ceremony. He stretched his longs legs under the table, careful not to disturb its precarious balance. He dressed better than your average IT guy — although his sense of color coordination didn't do much for me, a much-used maroon sport jacket over a deep purple dress shirt. His jeans looked like they'd been pressed.

He extended a hand and we shook.

"It turns out that my office missed a big news story."

"Really?" He pushed his John Lennon-style glasses back up his nose. I'd known Harry since he had hair, but now he had shaved his head. It gave him a stark and aggressive aspect, although I'd never seen him in anything but a highly reserved mode.

"It's nothing recent. But it was so big I'm surprised I never heard about it."

"Yes?"

"Someone called it The Day of the Long Knives. The story I was told was that an auditor found a big hole in the IT budget. Action needed to be taken right away. So overnight, roughly fifty people lost their jobs. True?"

Harry sat back in his chair and briefly scanned the room for possible eavesdroppers. He nodded. "More or less."

"I wonder why I never heard about it."

"You know, of course, it wasn't my job to bring such information to the news office. I suppose the folks in power had their reasons for not bringing you into the loop."

"I'm not suggesting that you should've called me. But this was big enough, you'd think someone might've let me know. Or mentioned something in passing. You'd think there would be a buzz around Main Central about it. Pretty striking to let fifty go in one fell swoop."

"I'm not in a position… to second guess who should or should not be told certain kinds of information." It was beginning to look like this would be a short conversation.

"I'm not insulted, just curious."

"Really."

"Really. Do you have any insight into how they decided who was going to get the axe? Were any particular units targeted, or any special category of employee?"

Harry removed his glasses and pinched his nose. "This is very old news and I do wonder why you are stirring the pot just now."

I fiddled with my coffee cup. "It was a request from one of the Trustees." I looked up at Harry but couldn't read his expression. "Apropos of Mr. Ronson's, uh, demise, one of the long-serving Trustees remembered receiving a briefing on the precipitate cutbacks necessitated by a major budget shortfall. But he couldn't remember the details and he asked the president. So, by some circuitous route the request filtered down to me. I think the assumption was that I had something at the ready in a file, something to release on request from that time. A reasonable guess, since we try to anticipate stories that could become news. But I didn't, of course."

"I don't know if I'm the right one to ask about this." Long pause. I'm sunk. "But given the turnover in IT, I'm one of the more senior people now. And while I certainly was not involved in the bloodletting, I did have a bird's-eye view."

I gave Harry time to organize his thoughts without hectoring him. I figured I was better off letting him proceed at his own pace if he was to proceed at all. Silence often brought its own pressure, like a vacuum to be filled.

"You must understand, those of us who remained were scarred by what happened. Within a few hours, we lost valued colleagues and friends without any warning or explanation. For months after that, it was like we were holding an extended wake. There were all these empty spaces, some still with nameplates and personal objects left behind. We had worked alongside these people, some for many years, and then they were gone."

Harry sat back and sipped his coffee, settling in. I saw him take a deep breath and let it out slowly. And another. And a third. Fully composed, he began.

"A number of us had been wondering about Jeremy's profligate approach to financial management for some time. There was no single thing but an accumulation of strange decisions. For one, he'd stage these technology extravaganzas for key administrative leaders, diverting significant talent and money to projects that probably wouldn't be revenue generators for many years, if ever. In those days, for example, he staged an Internet video conference call before there were things such as Skype. It was technically interesting, but of course no one had the necessary equipment to do that kind of thing routinely — and by the time they did, whatever product we might've developed was supplanted by cheap consumer goods. He was very proud of using technology that was invented here, and for the engineers it was a heady time.

"But the institution paid a heavy price for such self-indulgence. It meant that when things broke, they really broke, with little or no backup and certainly no contractors who could come in 24/7 to produce a fix. There were only our technicians to find the problem, working from software that was often pretty buggy, as we'd fall chronically behind schedule in development and then had to proceed headlong into launching it without adequate testing. We were deploying what in effect was version 1.0 of products across campus, which invited criticism, especially from the faculty, when it failed, which was inevitable."

Harry was warming to the subject. He removed his constantly-sliding glasses and put them on the table. "Administratively, our division was a mess. It was hard to even call it a structure. We had people in different units working on the same issues, independently and without any interchange of information. Some work that should have been farmed out to contractors with enforceable deadlines languished forever in the development stage, inviting what we call 'feature creep' and thereby delaying rollout even longer. We had real trouble finishing work and getting it out the door. The bad PR grew.

"Jeremy's pet projects received significant subsidies. Ever wonder why the university's home pages contained all those different live shots of various locations? That was his idea, or one that someone convinced him was worthwhile."

"So? Cameras are pretty much ubiquitous anyhow."

"Quite true now. But at the point he deployed them the technology was largely undeveloped and untested, which required a major investment in time and infrastructure. And for what? A toy."

Harry fiddled with his frames, twirling them between two fingers. "If that had been the only time he squandered resources no one would've noticed or cared. But there was a pattern."

"Didn't anyone ever complain? In the unit or from outside?"

Harry laughed and looked up to see if anyone noticed, although the students couldn't be bothered. "Jeremy never wanted bad news. If there were criticisms, they seldom would make their way to his desk, and I'm sure when they did he just brushed them off. He had a pretty low opinion of the brainpower around here, aside from his own and a few trusted… I was going to say lackeys, but let's just say colleagues. I wasn't going to raise questions, and the people who really knew the situation…"

"You mean like Art Kingston?"

Harry looked up, surprised.

"So you've talked with Kingston?"

"Not yet. I tried to reach him but…"

"He bailed about two months ago."

"You know where I might find him? It would help a lot. With my report."

"We were not close friends. In fact, his only friend around here as far as I know was Jeremy. I have no idea where to find him. Anyhow, the culture was one of unstinting praise for favored projects, even for crazy ideas that had no future. Criticism was not encouraged. In fact, it was suppressed."

"So you think the whistle was blown from inside, by people who had no avenue for registering complaints?"

"That's the inference I drew. As time went on and the budget situation worsened, Jeremy stopped calling senior staff meetings and was hardly present to most of the people in the unit. He would transmit instructions through intermediaries and was very slow to make decisions. He just froze in place. And the things he had set in motion earlier remained in motion. In a manner." Harry sipped his coffee. "Then there was the day of the Great Unraveling."

I nodded. "I've already heard about that. Ugly."

"I'd rather not go into that again. I can't imagine one of the Trustees would like that level of gory detail."

"No. But could you discern the rhyme or reason to the layoffs?"

"No explanation from management was forthcoming. All I could do was piece together what had occurred and draw some conclusions, which may or may not have corresponded to reality.

"One thing for certain: none of the directors lost their jobs. They were among the highest-paid people but as far as I know not one of them was shown the door, and we had several dozens of them. It seemed like there were a lot of programmers and engineers let go. The telecommunications unit was decimated. Most of the people who did training and customer service just disappeared."

"I went to a few of your classes, when we were rolling out some of that invented-here software. The training was always excellent. But I can't remember the names of my instructors. There was a young woman, quite tall with long frizzy hair."

"You must be referring to Liz Bacon. Great teacher. Single parent. I hear she's got some part-time work at the community college."

"And telecom used to send out people to help us program the new phones, which were impossible to understand."

"That was either Randi Marshall or Mark Alberts. Both laid off. You're on your own now, unless you're friends with one of the few remaining technicians, who usually don't make house calls. We have some online help files, and I use the word help loosely."

"Have you kept in touch with any of the people who were laid off?"

"Is this for the report?"

"No. But I was curious. There must have been considerable anger."

"There was white-hot fury. When people found out the scope of the layoffs, and pieced together the reason, they were livid. If they had learned what I found out, the back story, it would have been even worse. The initial proposal, emanating allegedly from the university's budget office, was to lay these people off with no benefits, just the option of purchasing health care at the usual exorbitant market rate. It was a shittier, more mean-spirited deal than any of us thought was possible at this university. But it came within an eyelash of happening. Or so I was led to believe."

"How did you find out about this?"

Harry smirked. "I have my sources, and in this case my source is unimpeachable but also insists on anonymity. My source also tells me that the decision about how to handle these people went all the way to the president's office. He vetoed the initial proposal, apparently approved by Human Resources, and decreed that all laid off people would be given ninety days of health care at the university's expense. Plus any outplacement counseling they wanted."

"It probably saved his office from being stormed by an angry mob."

"Indeed."

"So people didn't focus their wrath particularly on Ronson?"

"There was plenty to go around, at least initially. As for the edict that resulted in the layoffs, we knew originated from outside IT. But why was our budget allowed to deteriorate so drastically? If mismanagement in IT came as a surprise to anyone in the administration, then they just hadn't been paying attention for a very long time. Jeremy's errors in judgment, his unchecked spending, his sweetheart contracts and self-aggrandizing, wasteful projects were all hidden in plain sight. We were amazed he got away with it as long as he did. We chalked it up to poor leadership and outright cowardice at the very top that allowed him to keep his job."

"I would think there would have been more of a public fuss about this from at least a couple of disgruntled former employees. I'm surprised they went so quietly."

"There was some talk about getting even, and not just among those who were cashiered. We were all angry and looking for some avenue, some way to make our voices heard. But there was nowhere to go within the university. And we concluded that going public could make our former colleagues appear to be troublemakers, clouding their prospects for future employment. So we swallowed our anger." Harry began looking around again, as his voice had grown louder when he recalled the debacle.

"And how about now?"

"I only kept in touch with a handful of people, and they've done pretty well. In fact for some the ugly incident contained a silver lining, since they now are paid a market wage in the private sector. For some reason the university has always operated as if it should be a privilege to work here — and that people should pay for that privilege by accepting a discount on their salary." He wadded up his coffee cup and turned to throw it in a recycling bin.

"But a number of people weren't so lucky. They saw their health care run out while they were looking for work. I'd get calls from some of them looking for anything, freelance or part time, just to cover expenses. I wish I could've helped them, but I wasn't in a position to make any hiring decisions at that point."

"Anyone in particular stand out?"

"You're getting awfully nosy!"

"It's what people in my job do."

"I've lost touch with them now. But I do remember that Danny Slidell, who had been working on the much-stalled payroll system overhaul, called and emailed me a number of times. And Ellen... what was her last name? Ellen Trachtenberg, I think it was. I know she had a baby girl at that point, and she was getting desperate. Hope she's doing OK. If you manage to get hold of either of them, do send my regards."

* * *

I wondered if it was possible that someone had waited nearly two years for revenge. Maybe a former employee had reached a point of desperation and decided that Ronson could still help, but that things went horribly wrong when they met. Or maybe the simmering anger had been stored for a long time and finally boiled over. There's no expiration date on hate. So I suddenly went from having no suspects to fifty or more, counting spouses.

I scribbled down the names Harry had given me:

Liz Bacon

Randi Marshall

Mark Alberts

And just below them:
Danny Slidell
Ellen Trachtenberg
Just out of curiosity, I entered Ellen's name in various online directories. No luck. But Danny seemed to have landed on his feet. Or maybe on his knees: the directory said he was a staff assistant, a much less responsible and less well-paid position than programmer, in the department of anthropology. I dialed his number and he answered.

I explained that I was engaged in assembling a kind of history of IT on campus and was trying to contact as many former employees as possible to gain some perspective. It sounded lame to me, but I needed some pretext.

"I dunno. It was a while ago, and my memories are not entirely pleasant."

I explained I had talked to Harry and was aware of the circumstances of his departure.

"There's no reason to be defensive," I told him. "I understand that what happened had nothing to do with you. I'm just trying to learn a bit more about the organizational culture, at least as it was. Your perspective will be very helpful."

"Look, I've tried to forget that period of my life. It took me a long time and a lot of heartache to recover from that blow. In many ways, I'm still recovering. I'm working outside of my field now because it was all I could find, after an interminable search. People who I used to think were friends stopped returning my calls. I haven't told a lot of people, but I sought medical help for clinical depression. It is not something I want to relive."

"I understand, and I certainly don't want to drag up unpleasant feelings. But just tell me, when you found out the cause of the layoffs, what was your reaction?"

"Are you kidding? When I found out that it was all due to incompetence at the top? I was livid. But by then I was gone and what could I do? I can tell you, it made me very cynical. Those with positions of power apparently can do no wrong in the eyes of top leadership here."

"I assume you mean Ronson."

"Most of the good work in that organization occurred despite his leadership. We would've done better with no one at the top. Rather than firing all of us, if they had canned his ass and appointed someone moderately competent, we could've turned things around in a matter of months. There were so many bright, dedicated people there who... just went away that day. It still makes me sad."

"After that day, did you keep in touch with any of your colleagues who met the same fate? I'm thinking you might've formed a de facto support group or something like that."

"Kind of. We had online chats and some of us met once or twice in person. Mostly there was a lot of venting. We became creative in expressing our anger. One of our favorite games was, 'What I would do to Jeremy Ronson if I could be guaranteed immunity from prosecution?' We were able to come up with a long list of horrific tortures. None of us wanted to see him die quickly. The things we came up with were positively wicked."

"Did any of you consider more...?

"What? No, we were angry but not crazy. The key part of our hypothetical was the guarantee of immunity, clearly impossible in the real world. Most of us had families, or debts, or both. We were just trying to get past what had happened, and gallows humor, even recognizing that we had a prime candidate for the gallows, was as far as it went. At least among the people I know."

"I see."

"We all had grudges. But it ended with pure fantasy. I doubt that even one of us will mourn his passing. But no one I know would have taken it any farther. We're all decent people, not in to criminal behavior, even when pushed to the limit.

"That's really all I have to say about my glorious career in IT. It was a good gig while it lasted. But it feels like it was in a previous life."

"What were your assignments there?"

"I was assigned to the payroll project. We could never get the attention of the people at the top to make a decision, so all we could do was build small demonstration modules. I thought we were being dishonest with our clients, because there were quite respectable products available in the retail market. But they all carried the NIH stamp."

"NIH?"

"Not Invented Here. We were very big on being original. This was OK when the Internet was a shiny new toy and only a handful of experts knew how it worked. But as times changed, we really fell behind and spun our wheels. In fact, some of our risk-welcoming colleagues who left voluntarily in that era ended up founding companies whose products would've worked very well to solve some of our problems, if leadership hadn't been so pigheaded."

"Danny, I'm not promising anything, but would you send me your resumé and some examples of projects you worked on? You never know."

"Hey, thanks. That's generous of you. I have kept my programming skills up to date. The anthropology department has given me pretty much a free hand in designing digital tools for teaching and occasionally for research, so long as I complete the drudge work. That helps to fill out the more recent parts of my resumé.

"You've told me more than I had reason to expect when we began. Thanks for your time."

I decided I'd try to reach the other people Harry Joyce had mentioned. I couldn't find anything on Randi Marshall or Mark Alberts.

Harry had mentioned that Liz Bacon had latched on with a community college. Her named popped up in an online search at one of the city's most urban facilities, right in downtown. I called their computer science department and left a message for her.

While waiting for her return call, I perused the odd messages that had come my way. Today's oddest came from Stella.

Stella had a fine appreciation for the absurd and a proper disdain for unnecessary rules, and she used those traits effectively to navigate the university bureaucracy, as this exchange suggested. She copied me on this coup de maitre.

TO: Stella Maris
FROM: Clementine Lynch, Photographic services
SUBJECT: Paper towels

Stella, I hate to bother you with trivia but we can't get a regular supply of paper towels from the custodians. We use them a lot for cleaning up around the office and especially for our green room when we're doing portraits. People come in here to prepare themselves, sometimes applying makeup, so the towels are pretty much an essential. I don't know why I'm explaining this to you. You've been over here enough and know what we do.

So, one night I was staying late when one of the custodians came by. Her English wasn't too good, but I got across the idea about the towels. She looked really uncomfortable, shook her head no, and suggested I talk with her boss.

I don't know her boss, but you seem to know everyone who works in building maintenance, so could you check and see what the story is? I really don't want to make a fuss. Still.

TO: Enrique Bones, sector supervisor, custodial services
FROM: Stella Maris

SUBJECT: Paper towels

Hey Enrique sorry to bother you. But could you have one of your people drop off a roll of paper towels in our photography office in the lower level of Abelmerk Hall? They go through a lot of them, it seems. Thanks, pal.

TO: Stella
FROM: Enrique
RE: Paper towels

Sorry, no can do.

Here's the deal. Photography has a sink but it doesn't have a paper towel dispenser. Not even a tube holder. We have a new rule, to keep costs down, of only filling dispensers. That means no replacing of paper towels except in designated locations. Sorry.

TO: Enrique
FROM: Stella

Seriously? You're trying to save money by scrimping on paper towels? You know we have all sorts of VIPs over there for pictures. Are they supposed to wipe their hands on their thousand-dollar suits? Or should I have them call you personally to explain your new policy? Who makes up these brilliant ideas anyhow? I'm sure if you tell me, the president's office will submit it for a national award, right after they get the dirt out of his pinstripes.

TO: Stella
FROM: Your friend Enrique

We've had some real budget problems over here, Stella. The policy was made above my level, that's for sure. And no one consulted me before it was announced.

I can't provide an official solution or workaround. But, you might be interested in knowing that our paper towel dispensers, the ones we fill regularly, are showing up empty more frequently since we adopted this policy. It could be just a coincidence, but maybe not. We have no idea where those towels are ending up, and we're not about to spend time investigating the mystery.

I thought you might find that information useful.

TO: Enrique
FROM: Stella

Interesting and useful. I'll be sure to drop you a note if we find where those missing paper towels have ended up.

* * *

About an hour later, Liz Bacon called and told me she'd be delighted to meet. "Sure, I'd love to talk about that little turd," she said. "When I heard he'd died I cracked open an expensive bottle of Malbec. The world is well rid of people like him. You want to listen to me vent? I'll meet with you anywhere and give you a few thousand well-chosen words."

We agreed that I would swing by her college office on my way home that evening. But first I had a meeting with Dean Forbush. I pored through our office files before going to visit Dean Forbush and conferred with a faculty member in the English department whom I knew well, just to get some background on the guy.

Forbush had fulfilled his parents' ambitions for him, to a large degree. He had been an English major at one of the Ivies and gravitated to the study of Formalism. While the movement had been overtaken by trendier topics, such as gender studies, pop music and even television as a literary form, Forbush had assumed an ever more prominent position among the shrinking group of Formalist scholars.

Forbush was recognized as one of the department's most eminent faculty in a field that almost none of his colleagues had dabbled in since their undergraduate years, which gave him a free hand for frequent condescension, a skill he practiced as if he had been born with it. He wore an air of diffidence and mystery, keeping most of his colleagues at a disrespectful distance.

I'd attended one of his lectures — I don't recall why — and his presentation gave me nightmares. He was freakishly tall with a creaky, squeaky voice. He spoke like a rusty machine gun — rapid-fire followed by long, pregnant pauses. His skeletal hands formed odd, disturbing, almost sculptural shapes as he spoke. It tended to stay with you, for better or ill.

He had served in the leadership of the Faculty Senate for a number of years and was appointed to numerous high-level task forces and search committees. Many of his colleagues had declined to be the "token humanist" for initiatives that ended up being ways of boosting funding for the sciences, but Forbush was known as a vigorous debater, articulate defender of the arcane, and reasoned critic of educational ventures that seemed to disregard or debase the traditional areas of liberal knowledge. So his colleagues were delighted to have him fight the good fight on their behalf.

Forbush's office was on the top floor of one of the great architectural failures on campus, Damien Wilson Hall, named for a past university president whose reputation, according to campus historians, was just a bit better than James Buchanan — a rare case of a building receiving an appropriate name by complete accident. You'd walk into buildings like this, and your first thought would be, "What were they thinking?"

Although not all that large, Wilson Hall had three separate front entrances, leading to three separate lobbies with three separate elevators. For many purposes, Wilson was three separate buildings, but they were connected on floors two and four. The interior space consisted of short hallways broken up by abrupt turns. For some reason, Wilson, now about forty years old, had hallways so narrow that it was hard for two people to pass without care. The interior consisted of exposed brickwork, making it almost impossible to hang anything without an impact hammer. The rare bulges in hallways were invariably made into tiny staff work spaces with precious little privacy and no sound insulation.

The building housed faculty offices in the humanities, languages and literature. Offices were shoebox shaped with casement windows that tried to echo the Collegiate Gothic theme on much of the campus. But the low bidder had done a poor job of attaching the windows, which rattled in their frames, had bent and rusted over time, and seemed to siphon rain into the offices. Hence the mildewy smell throughout. People with chemical sensitivity were now being housed in a "temporary" trailer nearby, with no prospect for better permanent space.

And some people wondered why morale in the humanities was so poor.

Forbush answered quickly when I knocked and directed me to the only chair in front of his desk. Everything was stacked neatly and books were arranged in sections — hardbacks, anthologies, references and paperbacks all in separate areas, and I was sure if I looked closely I'd see that they were alphabetized, too. The papers on his desk were arranged as if on a grid. He crossed his remarkable hands in front of him on what looked like an old-fashioned blotter and peered out over half-frame glasses.

"What can I do for you?" he creaked.

"Professor Forbush, I was trying to learn a bit more about hiring procedures for top-level administrators, and everyone I talked to told me I should start with you."

"Well, that's both flattering and misleading." He uncrossed his hands, seeming to stroke the blotter as he reached for a pen — not your average ballpoint but what looked like a real honest-to-God fountain pen. He took off its top and reached for an unlined sheet of paper as he continued. "It is true, I have been involved in many searches and have even participated in negotiations for a number of people we've brought from the outside over the years. But the real experts are elsewhere, in the personnel offices and sometimes on the legal team." He began drawing perfect concentric circles, dipping the pen occasionally in a small well that appeared to be sunk into the desk.

"That may be true, but I'm trying to have conversations that are somewhat unofficial, and in my experience the moment you begin to question the people who run those offices they assume the verbal equivalent of a defensive crouch."

Forbush stopped drawing and chuckled. Actually, it was high-pitched and closely resembled a cackle. "I suppose you're right. I'll be happy to answer your questions to the best of my a-bil-i-ty." He resumed his drawing, this time of overlapping squares.

"Thank you. In your experience, after a decision is made to hire someone, especially for a top administrative post, who handles the negotiation?"

"It varies greatly. Naturally, the person who will be supervising that individual is deeply involved and usually is the focal point for communication with the top candidate. But in the case of top-ranked administrators there can be a whole team. In addition to the offices I mentioned earlier, you might even have the fundraising people consulted if there is contemplated use of an endowment or some special request for private funds. The finance people might be brought in. As I said, it could be a fairly large team."

"Is a contract involved?"

"Sometimes. Faculty members usually sign a letter agreeing to their appointment under a pretty standard set of conditions. For people who don't hold faculty appointments, there is a letter of appointment with all the nuts and bolts — title, salary, benefits — plus a section that includes 'special conditions' such as a short job description, reporting relationship plus anything else that has been agreed to in the negotiations. Such documents have been found legally binding when taken to court."

"Have you ever been involved in a negotiation where the candidate had some specific conditions that he or she insisted be part of the contract?"

Forbush began connecting the boxes in what looked like a random pattern of crisscrossing lines, but he seemed to be connecting them with some overall design in mind, hesitating before drawing each line, his brows contracting. "It happens. You can imagine each circumstance is unique. Some people come here with spouses who they'd like to receive consideration for appointments. Typically, our response has been to do those kinds of things informally and not include in the contract because they really aren't in our control. But there are other matters such as discretionary funds, laboratory startup expenses, special space needs. The list does go on... is any of this helpful to you? I'm sorry my answers are so vague, but the circumstances can vary a lot."

"No, this is helpful. When people enter into negotiations, are they usually doing this themselves?"

"Not sure I understand. The conversations officially are between the hiring unit and the candidate."

"Of course. But does the candidate bring advisers into the room?"

Forbush laughed. "The football coaches always do. They have agents. And not just the head football coach. And in other sports, too. After all, we're talking about real money there, often more than faculty are paid. Of course, they are in a situation of much greater risk and can be fired almost without notice. So there are a lot more moving parts and contingencies to be considered, and naturally a smart person would want to bring in experts for the best deal possible. It's only natural."

"But outside of sports…?"

"Well, among other employees, our lecturers, whom I do not consider regular faculty, have contracts. That's standard because they are hired for a specific period of time, and the ability to negotiate changes is severely limited. But in all the cases I know they have represented themselves."

"What about administrators?"

"The president, of course, has a contract. I've never been involved at that level, but I've read about it in the papers. I assume a presidential candidate would have a legal adviser and probably a financial consultant. Whether they end up in the room, I have no idea."

"What about other administrators? Is there anything that comes to mind as unusual?"

Forbush put down his pen. His face colored slightly. "Can you tell me precisely what information interests you, rather than this vague fishing expedition? We could have saved each other a lot of time if you had just come out and asked me what you needed when you walked in the door. Are we talking about any administrator in particular?"

"I'm sorry, I was trying to gain a little context, since I know virtually nothing about this subject. Yes, I did have someone in mind. Jeremy Ronson."

"You mean the one who fell out a window?"

"Yes."

Forbush pushed himself back from the desk and locked his absurdly long fingers behind his head. "Sorry, but they didn't involve me in Ronson's hiring. Indeed, that was before the time I was considered for search committees."

"But surely you know that Ronson had an employment contract." I decided I couldn't go wrong appealing to his vanity.

"It was common knowledge. At least in *some* circles." He began a gentle rocking motion. I sensed there was a bit more to squeeze from this lemon.

"Were the provisions of his contract common knowledge too?"

Forbush grinned. "You're not very experienced at this, are you?"

I blinked. "At what, exactly?"

"Oh, at getting information from slightly cooperative sources. Trying to gain confidence and then springing the trap." His eyes widened. He enjoyed the game of rhetorical fencing.

"I figure either you're going to tell me what you know or you won't. I can't offer you any incentives for talking to me, and there certainly aren't any penalties for tossing me out on my ear."

"True."

The silence went beyond the point of calling it a pause. Clearly, Forbush could be more patient than I.

"Well?"

"I was just thinking." He let out a deep sigh. "I wonder if my colleagues in computer science feel like they dodged a bullet." He looked at me with his eyebrows raised in a note of conspiracy.

"Why should they feel that way?"

He stared up at the ceiling with its popcorn texture, the cheapest way to conceal a poor drywall job. "Well, the rumor I heard was that Ronson had a special clause in his contract. It stipulated that, if his administrative position was eliminated, he would automatically revert to a tenured faculty position. In computer science."

"Have you ever heard of any other arrangement like that?"

"We've brought in administrators and after a thorough departmental review," he peered at me meaningfully over the tops of his reading glasses, "we've given them a courtesy appointment — tenured, of course. The administrator typically never taught a course or attended a departmental meeting. If he or she was dismissed, as happened in a few cases, there is not a single instance of which I'm aware in which the individual invoked the right to become a faculty member with those perks and responsibilities. Oh, there were cases where the academic department provided a landing space for at most a year. But then the people moved on." He paused. "Again, it's just a rumor, but I've heard Ronson was in the midst of exploring his academic options."

"So who was running the university when Ronson was hired?"

Forbush scratched his head. "I honestly don't know. It was, what, twenty years ago?"

"And presumably the president would have needed to get the approval of at least the chair of computer science?"

"At least. If I were the chair I'd insist on a vote of the executive committee, if not all the faculty. Granting tenure sight unseen, even as a contingency, is unheard of. Many people would say that the decision to recommend the granting of tenure is the most important decision that a department makes. You always want to offer positions to a person of the highest caliber. You are potentially obligating a position financially that you can't use for any other purpose, effectively locking it in, and who knows how future bean counters will measure that?"

"Professor Forbush, you've been extremely helpful. Thank you for your time."

He chuckled. "All I've done is pass along common knowledge and unsubstantiated rumors. I hardly regard that as a singular service. You didn't see a sign over my desk identifying me as an oracle, did you?"

I pushed myself up from the chair and headed to the door. As I looked out one of the tiny vertical windows in the hallway, I saw that it was raining like hell. Just rounding the corner and disappearing out of sight, I thought I saw a large, black SUV that reminded me of something.

I needed some time to digest what Forbush had told me. It was interesting, juicy. But it was unclear that it moved me any closer to figuring out what had befallen Ronson.

Still, it was a lead of sorts. Ronson's contract was on file somewhere. One copy might be among the papers of the president who had negotiated it. Another perhaps in that labyrinth known as Academic Human Resources. Surely one among Ronson's personal papers, wherever those might be. And maybe one somewhere in computer science.

Asking in any of those places directly wasn't going to get me anywhere. Or more precisely, it was going to get me somewhere I wasn't prepared to go, career-wise. If the wrong people found out they would demand my head on a platter.

* * *

With the rainstorm on a Friday afternoon came titanic traffic jams, so I left for my meeting with Liz Bacon a little early. Indeed, all getaways from the university were clogged. This was one of those Northwest autumn downpours. In other parts of the country where I had lived, cloudbursts like this would be over quickly. But here they could go on for hours. Sometimes even days. And out on the northwest

Pacific Coast, an entire season or two was devoted to storms. Out there they called it weather.

I tried to breathe slowly and deeply as the traffic inched along. The region had grown fast, too fast for the road system. Downtown was a mess of one-way streets and torn-up blocks as new high-rises appeared to sprout like bamboo. As I approached the campus of the community college downtown, I realized street parking was going to be an impossibility and I pulled into a below-ground lot.

Liz Bacon's office was in the main building of the community college complex, which was constructed entirely of bricks and mortar, very un-college-like for this part of the country. As for the student body, I think if I had the piercing and tattoo concession near campus I could've parlayed that into an early retirement. I was all but invisible to the students, except for the one who held a door open for me. I needed to work out more.

The corridors echoed with conversation, shouts and laughter. In fact, the surfaces were all so hard that even whispers produced echoes. I found Bacon's office and was greeted by a lively young woman with a thick mane of red hair — not ginger but a dyed, more-fiery version of her natural color, which showed at the roots. She seemed to blend right in to the college atmosphere, with frayed, patched jeans and a wide metal-studded belt. A much-used peasant blouse with a scoop neck completed the ensemble.

"I'm surprised after my rant that you bothered to follow up." She gestured to a superannuated office couch with one crippled leg, the only other piece of furniture in the room. It gave a squeak and whoosh as I sat.

"Maybe you'll tell me something useful after you get done venting."

"Could be." She removed her sandals and began massaging her calves. "Excuse me, but standing up all day is doing a number on my hips, legs and back."

"Harry Joyce recalled that at the time of the layoffs you were raising a child on your own."

Liz scratched absently at the inside of her thigh. I noticed her nails were fuchsia and very long. "Harry has one hell of a memory. All that time at the university seems so long ago. Yes, Sophie was about a year and a half when the ax fell. I was worried I was going to have to admit failure and move home to my parents in Montana. But when I found out that the whole sad affair was a product of executive mismanagement, I was determined to fight back and take charge of my future. Sophie and I have become a great pair through the struggles. I'm a good mom. The only thing keeping me from being with her at this precise moment is you." Her eyes, a kind of jade with gold flecks I'd never seen before. I could imagine them shooting death rays.

"I'll try to keep this short."

"It's OK. Sophie relishes her me-time, which she calls any time that I'm not there. I sometimes think I may be a little too much for her, but that's a good problem to grow up with. Much better than the opposite."

"Anyhow… you seem to have landed on your feet." Her feet, by the way, had toenails with an exotic shade that looked like pinkish brown. With glitter.

"Eventually. It was a rough time. If it hadn't been for the extended health insurance benefits, I would've been forced to move home for sure. But I was lucky enough to land a part-time gig here the next semester. And slowly, I built up experience and accumulated a course load. The courses weren't all here initially — they were scattered throughout the community college system encompassing the greater metro area. I became part of group of 'road warriors,' as we called ourselves. The proletariat of higher education instruction. No wonder there's been agitation for union representation.

"We're a vagabond army with advanced degrees, filling the gaps in the system with our undercompensated labor. Talk about exploitation! No benefits, not even an office for most of us, at least not for several years. Starbucks was where I held office hours, any Starbucks near whatever campus I was at. I gained more class consciousness in a year of hand-to-mouth existence than I did in all the political science courses I took. I've become a big fan of organized labor."

She was rubbing her feet and colorful toes throughout her diatribe. She saw me staring and threw a glance my way. "I considered a career in interior design or in fashion consulting when I got laid off. I love to experiment with color. My students exhibit remarkable palates in their clothing, accented by great imagination in their tats. You hang around with them long enough and it starts to influence you. But Sophie has insisted I draw the line at piercings."

"It's not surprising that you harbor ill will toward Ronson."

She slapped a sandal on the desk. "Ill will? I hated the guy's guts. He put me and my little girl at risk, for what?"

I think she brushed away a stray tear.

"But my anger was nothing compared to Cody's. My boyfriend at the time. He was obsessed. Finally, it poisoned the atmosphere between us. He became weird, really unstable, and that scared me. So we parted ways."

Liz laughed nervously. "He'd talk about what he would do if he encountered Ronson alone. Most times it involved methods of torture which grew more baroque over time. He'd say it all so offhandedly, as if it were a joke. But he also went through a period where he created scenarios about how he could do away with Ronson and never get caught. I concluded that Cody was inherently unbalanced and my experience had just lit the fuse." Her eyebrows crinkled. "I'm sure his threats were mostly macho bluster, but I didn't want that kind of bluster around my daughter. I told him he had to leave."

"Did you have any contact with him since then?"

"Not of my doing. He admitted he had gone off the deep end with his animus for Ronson and claimed it was a passing thing. But I saw a side to Cody that I didn't like at all. I tolerated some of his calls while making it clear we couldn't go back to the way things had been. He was upset, really upset, unwilling to accept my decision. Finally, I had to stop answering his calls and responding to his emails. I felt sorry for him, but sorry is not a good basis for a relationship. His calls and emails have continued sporadically. He says he's past his obsession but I'm not buying it." Liz was visibly agitated, running her hands through her hair, crossing and uncrossing her legs.

"A couple of weeks before Ronson's death I got another email from him after a long lapse. The email ended with strange stuff. It had a rant about justice and moral law, a thread I really didn't follow. Then he said, 'We need to act as if humanity is an end in itself, not a means.' I didn't know what to make of that."

Liz had gotten out of her chair and was gently rearranging her small store of personal objects in the room — mostly Sophie's artwork. She paused and locked her hands behind her back. "When I read that, I knew I made the right decision about ending it. The guy is just too weird to be around us."

"I'd like to talk with Cody, if you'd be willing to share his contact information."

"No problem. The guy is all over social media and some weird sites. He's really into those alternate reality scenarios and a lot of stuff that both bores and scares me. It's not like he protects his own privacy." She scribbled down an email and handed it to me.

"In return I'll ask one favor. If he mentions us, tell him to leave me and Sophie the fuck alone."

CHAPTER SIX

E arly Monday morning my phone rang. It was Anne Mayfield, Ronson's final administrative assistant.

"I came across something that I thought might interest you. It's about the fancy dresser who used to come by and visit with Jeremy. Maybe."

"Did you find out who he was?"

"Not exactly. But Telecom sent me a list of Jeremy's out-of-area calls for his last month. I never pay attention to them. I'd just ask Jeremy if he made any personal calls over the university system, because those he'd have to pay for himself. Anyhow, there's a number he called a lot. Where is area code 415?"

"Bay Area."

"That's what I thought. Jeremy might have family down there or something. I think that's where he went to school."

"But you also think it might be connected to the guy in the suit?"

"Maybe. I don't know. I was just jumping to a conclusion. But maybe it's just family."

"I know the medical examiner tried to track down family and didn't succeed, and I know they checked in the Bay Area. Well, there's one way to find out for sure who he called."

"Yeah, I know. Call the number."

"Yeah."

I thought the line had gone dead. "Does that make you uncomfortable?"

"Yes. First, I'm not sure whether that information is confidential or not. Second, even if it isn't, what do I say to whoever might answer the phone?"

"I understand." My brain was spinning. I was trying to say anything to keep her on the line until I could figure out how to get hold of her information. "What makes you think the guy in the suit might be connected to a number in the Bay Area?"

"My memory isn't the greatest, but when I was looking down this list of calls I swear I remember Jeremy saying 'Have a nice flight' to the sharp dresser. At least once, maybe more often. I am not certain about that, but I think he said it. I could be wrong though. And he could have been flying anywhere. I'm not a fashion hound, but when I think back on how he dressed, I think maybe San Francisco. I have no idea why."

"I know you don't want to violate anyone's privacy. But just calling a number, I don't see how that could be a problem. Even if the person on the other end was curious, you could just say you're doing your job — your financial diligence, to see if these were legitimate calls on university-related business, something for which the university should be charged. And there's no other way to check that."

"I suppose you're right. Still…"

"How about this? I'll be your witness. We'll both be on the line, and I can swear to the whole conversation if need be. Which is really unlikely, but if it makes you feel better. If Ronson were alive you'd be going through a similar process, right?"

"I suppose. Tabulating those calls was part of my job."

"Right. So let me know and I'll come down there."

"Does your office have a door?"

"Sure."

"Can we do it there? I have no privacy here, and the fewer people that know about this the better I like it."

"I understand. Why don't you come by early this afternoon? If we do it in the middle of the day we may have a better chance of someone picking up."

When I turned to my computer, I encountered a flurry of messages regarding an event, held over the weekend, that I had made a point of forgetting about. It was billed as a campus-wide "Spirit Rally," organized by People, Promise, Programs and Purpose Enhancement. The event, intended for faculty and staff as well as students, included, according to the invitation, "speeches by Claire Yarmouth, the First Lady of the university, and a keynote by Sgt. Clem Farnsworth (Ret.), who survived incarceration in a POW cell in North Korea for three years."

Oh, and that wasn't all: "The first five thousand attendees will be given a choice of a free spirit T-shirt or a President Yarmouth bobble-head doll."

I wasn't big on spirit as a college student and didn't intend to change in middle age. Judging from the responses on which I had been copied, I had made a wise choice.

TO: Team PPPPE
FROM: Prof. Jack Spence, Department of Political Science
SUBJECT: Spirit rally

I suppose I should be upbeat about this and wish you well, even though I will not attend your rally. Actually, I am urging my colleagues and even total strangers to avoid this and similar boondoggles like the plague.

Ventures like this cost money, money we can ill afford for what amounts to an empty gesture. More importantly, you can imagine what legislators will think of this gigantic waste of time. I'm sure our lobbyists are already trying to invent explanations that will placate them:

e.g., We're not using state money, attendance is voluntary, it's a way to enhance performance by raising morale, etc.

Piffle! You may fool them, but you can't fool me. In the months that this new "campaign" has existed, under President Yarmouth's aegis, you have succeeded in turning him into a source of derision on this campus and elsewhere in the country. What's next? Tricorn hats, fifes and drums in celebration of the university's founding, with spurious connections to the Founding Fathers? I can hardly wait!

Oh, and I have ideas what you can do with any of the leftover Yarmouth bobbleheads, but this is not the kind of suggestion I would put in a written message.

TO: Team PPPPE
FROM: Susan Dilan, director, Women Studies
SUBJECT: The "spirit rally"

I just have one question for your team: Did no one ask to read Claire Yarmouth's speech before she delivered it? Is she immune from the vetting that should occur whenever a high-ranking university official makes public remarks?

I'm referring, of course, to her referring to her husband publicly as "Pookie Bear." She's entitled to call him whatever she wants in private. But I don't care to know their familiar names. People in the audience were afraid to look at one another when she said that, but at the conclusion it was the only thing that people were talking about.

Whatever you hoped to accomplish with the event was undercut by her bad judgment. I hope you've learned a lesson. And if Claire Yarmouth needs to be read the riot act by someone other than you, please give her my phone number.

TO: Team PPPPE

FROM: LTC Clay Mountblank (US Army ROTC), Col. Kelvin Masterson (US Air Force ROTC), Capt. Bryce Wheeler (US Navy ROTC)

SUBJECT: "Sgt." Clem Farnsworth

As the chief representatives on campus of America's armed services, we felt compelled to write and ask Team PPPPE what you thought you were doing by including the alleged representative of the US military at your "spirit rally."

Let's begin with "Sgt." Farnsworth's remarks. I don't know if you had an opportunity to discuss his presentation in advance, but we wonder why someone's experience allegedly penned in a 6'-by-6' cell, allegedly for as long as three years, should be relevant to university employees. Are we attempting to draw some parallels here? Because if so we don't see them. Work is work and prison is prison.

His calls for what amounts to passive resistance and living an interior life to the exclusion of the "real" world also seemed similarly inappropriate, although it might help an individual survive in extreme circumstances such as a POW camp. In general, this seems like poor advice for anyone on a college campus or in most work environments. Couldn't you have found a speaker, from the military or elsewhere, who focused on the values of community solidarity and accountability?

We thought his mimicking of his cell by pacing back and forth across the stage was perplexing at best. Maybe this kind of theater works in some settings with particular audiences, but the people we talked with had trouble determining if this was intended as some kind of re-enactment of his experience or what, exactly.

Finally, and most importantly, you should have checked this fellow's credentials. His official military records, which we have obtained, indicate that he spent a total of three months in (South) Korea, most of that time as a cook. There is no record of his being captured.

Indeed, his post-military career has been as a motivational speaker, bolstered by an ever-inflating story of his personal travails while in service.

The trail begins about four years ago with small companies and Rotaries in the Phoenix-Tucson region, where he talked about the great leaders he encountered as an "aide to some of the top-ranking military leaders in the U.S. Army while stationed in Korea." There's no evidence in his record that he served as an aide to anyone.

He went on from there to Colorado, New Mexico and Nebraska, to talk about the challenges of overcoming a lifetime of drug addiction (we could not verify if this was true or not, although there were no criminal violations we could track down) through the discipline and inspiration of the Army, culminating in him winning multiple medals in various kinds of athletic competitions (to the best of our knowledge he never did receive such awards).

About a year ago he began talking about his alleged incarceration, traveling in a much wider circle throughout the country (we believe he may have adopted an expanded itinerary as part of an effort to stay ahead of law enforcement).

Perhaps it is just a footnote, but he never rose to the rank of Sergeant. Private Farnsworth served his time and did receive an honorable discharge. His post-military career, from our perspective, has been much less than honorable. We are disappointed with your choice of him as a speaker for your event and hope in the future you will exercise better judgment.

TO: Team PPPPE
FROM: Marchand Yarmouth
SUBJECT: Pep rally

Well, that was fun! Thank you all for your hard work on this event. I know we had hoped to fill the stadium, but remember that even our football team doesn't do that, especially this season. My wife and I were very pleased with the reception of the "Yarmouth-head." Some people actually believe it is better than the original....

I believe Sgt. Farnsworth's remarks gave us all something to think about, putting our petty problems in perspective. It's sobering to know my bathroom in the presidential residence is about the same size as his "home" for nearly three years.

And a special thanks to all of you for giving Claire an opportunity to speak to the community. As you know, she's not a very public person and this was a good way for her to "ease in" to a higher profile, which certainly will be essential as our campaign moves along. My own biased opinion is that she is our secret weapon.

* * *

I decided that my next task on the Ronson matter was to track down Liz's former boyfriend, Cody. She was right: it was easy to find his posts all over the place. He commented frequently on sites appealing to mythology enthusiasts — sites where people got deeply into the philosophy, morality and application of various mythologies to everyday life. Enthusiasts created whole cyberworlds operating in parallel to our own based on a particular theology, class structure and pantheon. To some of the participants, I gathered, these were not simply games but an effort to create a kind of digital utopia.

Cody and I exchanged a bunch of emails. I was surprised he agreed to meet, even though I decided I couldn't use his prior relationship with Liz as an entry card. I told him I was planning to submit an article on mythology and digital realities to a startup fanzine. I told him that I thought his views of a parallel moral universe might help me in my research.

We arranged to meet that night at a combination pub and gaming club.

Anne Mayfield was at my office door promptly at 1:30; I had told Fran to expect her and send her back. She was nervous.

"Tell me again why I should be doing this?"

"Anne, this is part of your job."

"Right. Then why do I feel so uneasy?"

"Because your boss is dead, that's why."

Anne deposited herself in the chair next to mine and brushed her bangs out of her eyes. From her purse she pulled out a list from telecom containing the number in question.

"How many times did he call the number?"

She scanned the page. "During his last month about ten times. It doesn't add up to a whole lot of money."

"We can use my speaker phone. Do you want me to dial the number?"

"No, I've come this far, I'll do it."

I pushed the phone over to her.

"What do I say if someone answers?"

"The truth. You work at the university and are checking on calls that your supervisor made, to see if they were for official business."

She began dialing, pausing every few seconds, rechecking the number and sighing. I pushed the speaker button and heard the signal. Then it connected.

"McGilvray, Simmons and Walker. May I help you?"

Startled, Anne's voice came out in sputters. "Yes, this is Anne Mayfield. I'm checking on some calls made by my supervisor to this number. We work, that is, Jeremy, Mr. Ronson, worked at a public university, and it's my job to make sure the calls made on the state telephone system were for state business. So I'm calling to check.

Since Mr. Ronson is no longer available." Anne made a face at me and stuck out her tongue. Beads of sweat stood out on her forehead.

"Let me put you through to Mr. Walker's secretary. I believe that Mr. Ronson is a client of his."

Anne exhaled loudly. "A law firm," she mouthed, and I nodded my head. "Should I hang up?" I shook my head no.

"This is Kimba. Can I help you?"

"Uh, yes. This is Anne Mayfield. I am, I was, Jeremy Ronson's assistant."

"Yes?"

"Well, it's my job to check on calls made from university telephones, to see if the nature of the call was private or if it was university business."

"Yes?"

"Well, since I'm unable to ask Mr. Ronson, I'm calling you. To find out if the calls were on university business."

"Can you hold for a second?"

"Of course."

About thirty seconds later she came back on the line. "I'm sorry, but I checked with Mr. Walker. And attorney-client privilege still applies here. We can't discuss the nature of the calls between Mr. Ronson and Mr. Walker."

"I see. But is it true that Mr. Ronson called Mr. Walker a number of times over the past month?"

"Yes, but beyond that..."

"I understand. Thank you for your time."

"Yes. And we want to take this opportunity to express our condolences on behalf of Mr. Walker and the entire firm. Jeremy's death came as a shock to us."

Anne hung up. "Well, that was fairly useless."

"Not entirely. We know he called a law firm. That's something."

"Huh. I still don't know if it was personal or university business."

"Well, actually you do. If it had been university business, they wouldn't have invoked privileged client communication." I was escorting her to the door.

"What should I do with the charges?"

"That's up to you. You could contact someone in the attorney general's branch office here and let them decide, since technically it's a legal issue."

"That's a good idea. If I decided the calls were personal, to whom would I send the bill?"

"I think you did the right thing by calling, no matter what the AG decides."

I'd squeezed Anne Mayfield as hard as I could to get what I wanted. I felt a little bad about it, but nothing she had done was inappropriate.

I was guessing that the conversations and meetings had to do with provisions in Ronson's employment contract.

Now was the time to figure out how to gather specific information about Ronson's employment contract.

* * *

I re-read my own news release about Ronson's death, which noted that he had started working as a vice president at the university in 1992, twenty years ago. Our office had extensive historical files that were pretty easy to comb through. It didn't take a lot of research to find out that the university had had a series of temporary leaders in that period.

Those were tough times and the newspapers were filled with ugly headlines. There were a series of sports scandals involving not just the football team, a perennial ethical cesspool, but virtually every other high-profile sport. Even normally clean activities, like rowing, had labored under a cloud of suspicion involving allegations of improper recruiting, although nothing was ever proved. Coaches lost their jobs, star athletes changed schools. Legislators, normally eager to pontificate on moral issues and to bring arrogant higher education leaders down a peg, were notably silent. I suspected it was because the booster community as a whole was pretty well connected politically, and there was no percentage in it for a legislator to kick a hornet's nest.

In the midst of these sports scandals the administrative side of the institution wasn't doing so well, either. When a long-serving president decided to retire, a series of bad decisions and some bad luck plagued the search for a successor.

As I pored over news articles I realized that such intensive coverage of a presidential search process appeared quaint by today's standards. The scandals would've gotten their share of ink, but hiring a president was unlikely to merit much of a reporter's time now.

The presidential search process resembled a soap opera. Several times the search committee seemed about to name a new leader only to have the deal fall through. The explanations were various. The individual's current institution offered to rewrite his contract. The finalist was brought to campus and then there was silence for months. Poor impression? Failed negotiations? Once, a president was even announced and then, inexplicably, the announcement was rescinded. Exaggeration on the resumé? Spousal veto? Pick your own explanation.

The incumbent president had announced his firm intention to retire by the end of the school year in 1991. There were photos of the Board of Trustees, sitting around the table, the men with their ties off and their shirt collars open, women yawning and trying to readjust their hair. The longer the delay, the more the institution acquired a stigma, justified or not, in the circles where up and coming leaders were prospecting for their next gig.

For a brief period, the provost assumed the title of president, delegating much of the provostian academic work to his phalanx of vice provosts, making this one of the few times in university history where having so many high-ranking individuals was a virtue. When it was clear that the interim period was not going to be short, the provost went to the trustees and asked them to appoint someone else as interim.

An obvious choice, the dean of the university's largest college, the College of Letters and Vanities (as it's called now), agreed to take the job for six months. It was clear he had an interesting ride. There had been a state revenue shortfall and legislators threatened the university with sizable budget cuts. The interim leader, used to being plain-spoken in deliberations on campus, was publicly quoted calling the proposed cuts "stupid and short-sighted." He went on to say that legislators would be condemning the state's sons and daughters to menial service jobs within the growing technology economy, and that this approach would decimate the chances for closing achievement and income gaps for minority students. Legislators accused of a racist and classist approach to budgeting responded with even more threats and questioned the wisdom of the trustees' decision to offer the interim position to someone who spoke so bluntly.

After the dean went back to his cushier position out of the limelight, he was succeeded by the ultimate caretaker. George Pennybaker, who had led the university in what were increasingly referred to as its "glory years," was drafted out of retirement to accept what he hoped was a very temporary reappointment. Now pushing eighty, he appeared in the photos still with a shock of his trademark white hair and a face miraculously unlined. Known for his sunny disposition and impatience with fools, Pennybaker clearly was brought back as a symbol of historic stability and perhaps also out of hope for some magic. He served for one year and two months. Happiness reigned in the kingdom, according to the news clips.

The odds were that Jeremy Ronson's contract was signed by Pennybaker.

Good news but also bad news. University presidents from across the country and legislative leaders, including the current and past three governors, had attended Pennybaker's funeral in 1999. One direct path to finding the contract's contents was closed, with Pennybaker's passing, and others were dicey. If I marched right into the personnel office and asked for a copy of the agreement, the minions were likely to refuse, leaving me with my final recourse, filing a public records request. This was not a direction I wanted to take unless I was desperate and willing to face very unpleasant consequences. But I hadn't been at the university for so long without establishing a network of knowledgeable people at all levels of the organization. Especially with administrative assistants, the front-line people in offices and departments. When policies were crafted, they often were the first to know. They had demonstrated their value to me many times. Almost all information flowed through them at one point or another.

I flipped through my mental rolodex. I needed someone with a really long administrative career working with top leaders. There was really only one choice. Leigh Lambert.

Leigh had worked just about everywhere as a key staffer, from the president's office to those of various deans and even with the financial people. Whatever network I had accumulated was dwarfed by Leigh's intimate knowledge of the institution. She had a reputation for a sharp tongue but also total circumspection, which meant she probably knew more secrets than anyone else I might call.

"Leigh, I need your help."

Laughter. "I figured you'd get around to me sooner or later. For the record, I didn't push Jeremy Ronson out his office window, but I'd be happy to give a medal to the person who did."

"What was your beef with him?"

Sigh. "He was your typical over-paid, snide, arrogant boy who never grew up. He was like the kid in third grade in the back of the room making rude comments about all the girls, as well as the teacher, and would play little, embarrassing tricks on them for which he was almost never punished. You could hear his mother remarking on how cute he is, and how he just had the Devil in him and she didn't know what to do about it. And that's how you end up with Jeremy Ronson."

"Leigh, this is completely confidential."

"Do we ever have any other kind of conversation? Do I want you passing on my observations about the quality of leadership in our great university, for starters?"

"I'm trying to find out about an alleged employment contract that Ronson would have negotiated when he was hired."

"I'd heard rumors. The only other reason he hadn't lost his lofty position despite his incompetence would've been blackmail. But the boring lives of most administrators scarcely support that theory."

"I'm guessing it would've been signed during the second Pennybaker administration."

"Sounds about right. I remember he came here with much fanfare when we lured him from California. He set a tone from the get-go by refusing to wear anything but jeans, even to high-level meetings. We had the impression that his authority came not just from his title but from some kind of special, exalted status he'd been granted. Wooing him was one of Pennybaker's proudest accomplishments during his second regime."

"So who would know what's in the agreement? I don't want to go public with this. I'm looking for someone who would remember the contents but wouldn't feel a need to run my request up the administrative food chain."

"You'd want someone who is out of the line of fire now but still has all their faculties. Have you thought of Harriet Bauskas?"

"Sorry, I don't know that name."

"Before your time, I guess. Harriet worked in the executive suite for maybe a decade, with various titles. She was chief administrator, office manager, personal secretary, administrative secretary, scheduler. Those are just the jobs I remember off the top of my head. Back when everything was on paper, she maintained the office filing system for the president and provost. So every piece of paper came across her desk."

"Is she still around?"

"She retired, oh, about ten years ago. I've heard she's still in town. Let me do some checking and get back to you."

"Leigh, I owe you one."

"Nah, just let me in on the juicy stuff. That's all I want."

*   *   *

After work I set out for my meeting with Cody. His choice was a bar that was a hangout for serious gamers. About half the people there were so scrubbed, clean-cut and cheerful I could imagine them buttonholing me on the street to hawk the Book of Mormon. The other half wore a pallor suggesting they hadn't been exposed to sunlight in many months, and a twitchy manner that reminded me of butterflies, flitting from one attractive object to the next.

Cody fit into the latter group. He was dressed entirely in black and wore an odd little beret along with a pencil-thin moustache. His fingers, thin and bent, reminded me of talons, complete with the fingernails decorated with stars or something (I couldn't tell without staring). His eyes, hooded by heavy black lashes that I swore were enhanced with mascara, darted around the room, unable to focus on me even as we introduced ourselves.

His handshake was limp and chilly. I ordered beers for both of us and he muttered a thanks. As we talked, his head swiveled at conversations or movements at other tables. He was a poster boy for the downside of multitasking. I plunged ahead.

"As I said in my email, I'm doing research for an article on the moral basis of world-building activities online and the crossover between imagined universes and ours." I had prepared for the interview by doing some quick research, enough to make a plausible case. "What I'm interested in is how people like you, who spend a lot of time living in those digital societies, are influenced in their daily lives by the values of those other worlds. I picked you because, among those posting on the sites I visited, your vision seemed among the most articulate and impassioned."

Cody glanced at our wooden table, which had placemats with themes drawn from astronomy, astrology and legends about the constellations. Mine bore information about black holes, specifically about how they often functioned as portals to another dimension in science fiction. Cody's was themed on dark matter and the seeming paradox that most of what existed in the universe was invisible. As a reporter, I learned to read upside-down.

He shifted uneasily. "Uh, I'm far from an expert on these things. Sure, they interest me and I have fun debating the ideas. But I don't pretend to have any particular insight. And I separate digital worlds from this one. I'm not delusional." He sipped his beer while looking everywhere but at me.

"No, of course not. But I've observed that there is a strong moral code in many of these worlds, including ones where you are active. This code interests me. I read your posts, and I thought your observations were pretty interesting. I'm curious about what you think comes first: whether especially moral people are attracted to these sites, or whether the sites end up making its participants more conscious of moral imperatives as they begin to interact in those worlds."

He looked up at me with a crooked smile. "This sounds like a pretty dumb idea for an article. I hope the publisher of the fanzine is a friend of yours. Because if it were my publication I would have rejected the premise entirely."

"Maybe you're right. It's a kind of chicken-and-egg thing, which doesn't lead anywhere. But what about you? What draws you to worlds that are based on codes which often come from mythology?"

He looked annoyed with my question. "I'm not sure how to answer that. I enjoy world building. I suppose it gives me an element of control that people lack in their daily lives. I've always been interested in questions of morality, so in these activities I tend to focus on the moral aspect." He blinked and returned to the placemat.

"Do you think your moral focus was tied to your upbringing? Or was it a later development?"

Cody snickered. "I don't go in much for psychoanalyzing my own actions. But for this evening I'll humor you. I don't know if there's a connection between how I was raised and my choice of hobbies. That's pretty far-fetched.

"I can tell you this: I was brought up in a religious home. But as a teen I rejected all of that. A psychologist might say that despite my efforts I still haven't escaped my upbringing. I think that's bullshit. I've pretty much chosen my own path in the world.

"From an early age I was interested in moral principles quite apart from religion. I was drawn by the idea of Immanuel Kant's categorical imperative — that you do something not because it's convenient or even because it's a good idea, but because that action is required for a human being. A moral sense is what defines us as humans. Those who don't operate by moral principles, even if they have opposable thumbs, are actually animals."

"I see. The way you explain it sounds so simple and logical."

He flashed a gap-toothed grin. "Of course it isn't, really. Doing the right thing is often ferociously hard. And humans have the freedom not to do the right thing. But for order to exist in the universe, we need to take action.

"The digital societies we have constructed are founded on that principle. For me, spending time there is like leaving the city for the country. The air is fresher. The experience is bracing. There are fewer roads but they are very clearly delineated. There's right and there's wrong. In those worlds you get to exercise your moral muscles in a clearly defined environment."

"So after you spend time in that atmosphere, how does it feel to return to reality?"

He raised his eyebrows, pursed his lips and shook his head. "We are building this world, the real one, every day with the choices we make," he droned with a patronizing tone. "So, there's no reason that feeling of rectitude can't carry over into this world.

"My digital persona, of course, is very different from my physical one." He chuckled. "I'm able to create and maintain an image there that pleases me. In my online persona I can live the idealized life I want and not just talk about it. Say things I wouldn't say to you sitting here. Do things, or suggest things, that would be hard for the me you see in front of you to do."

"Such as?" I sipped my beer, trying to keep the flow going.

"Online I can afford to take risks. Be outrageous. Be dangerous." The last word came out slowly and rounded. He smiled. "The moral code is primary. It trumps everything.

"Some might find that threatening. Even in other worlds some people have found my persona more than they could handle and got me kicked out of their space. I've been banned from some timid sites because they reject that kind of honesty. But I'm proud of that person. In many ways, he is my better, purer self. He's the one who can get things done, regardless of perceived limitations."

"Do you see yourself as a kind of avenging angel, righting wrongs and restoring a sense of morality? Is that your role there?"

He responded slowly, haltingly. "Nearly everyone in these online worlds adopts characters that are somewhat idealized. That's one of the reasons to participate, to clarify and stress what's important. I'm comfortable with my role as a kind of moral policeman."

"What about in this world?"

He stared at his placemat and took a sip from the mug. "I'm just trying to get by without getting caught in the web of evil. Which in itself is no small task. I regard my online activities as a kind of safety valve for nobler impulses."

"But with such a strong sense of morality, how do you feel when you encounter evil? In this world, I mean."

Cody tapped absently on the table. "Sometimes it's not easy. You call out a person. You tell the truth. You tip others to bad actors. You try to gum up the works of the Evil Empire." He grinned and shook his head. "But you always wish you could do more."

"Yeah, many of us feel that way at times. But your sense of outrage — and tell me if I'm overstating the case — it seems almost palpable, something that is with you pretty much all the time."

Cody snorted loudly. "Well, I don't walk around in a state of constant fury. Justice is by far the most important characteristic of civilization, in my opinion. And when it doesn't operate, I feel the need, at a minimum, to speak up."

"So this is completely off the record, not for the fanzine or anything else. Just because I'm curious. Have you ever considered righting a wrong by taking direct action that some might consider beyond the bounds of propriety, or even technically illegal? Because the circumstances seemed to demand action? For someone like you, that must be a real temptation."

He looked up with a quizzical expression and opened his mouth. But he thought better of saying something, yawned and scratched his chin. "You know, I've confronted only a few moments where that seemed like an option, and it was tempting. I've done what was in my power to stifle evil. And it felt good, I have to admit. Whether it crossed boundaries... I don't know if I'm comfortable saying more than that."

"I understand. But you must have thought about that moment when extraordinary actions are necessary and justified. At least theoretically."

He nodded emphatically. "Some people anesthetize themselves by believing that it all evens out, the good are rewarded and the evil are punished. That the arc of the universe inevitably bends toward justice, regardless of individual decisions. So they can wash their hands and walk away without doing anything. But if everyone sits back and waits, how do they think that actually happens? Sometimes I wish I had blind faith. Then the choices wouldn't weigh so heavily."

"The weight of inaction..."

"It can be suffocating. I actually have felt it physically."

"And...?"

He shook his head. "I... I..." His voice cracked. "I'm sorry." He made a palms up gesture of what-more-can-I-say.

I gave Cody some breathing space, hoping I hadn't spooked him. I looked around the room. It was pretty full for a weekday. Most of the guys, and it was predominantly male, had laptops or game consoles in front of them, although a number were playing on their phones. Most were dyads, but several tables had as many as a half-dozen participants. There was a low-level buzz in the room, with the occasional exclamation or exhortation delivered in half-whispers or as snarky laughs.

I decided to venture into the deep end. "Cody, I've got to come clean. I didn't find you randomly. It was Liz Bacon who suggested I contact you. I had a long talk with her, and your name came up when I told her about my project." He looked angry at first, then his jaw softened. "She's a remarkable woman. Brave and determined," I added.

Cody brightened. "I know. I keep hoping that I didn't shut down all future possibilities with her. It's good to know that at least she still keeps me in mind. I know I'm on the outs now, but... I'm trying to convince her that I've always held her life, and Sophie's, above my own. And that I can be relied upon in the future." There was a softness to his expression, but at the same time he had balled up his hands into fists and his knuckles were white.

"She described how angry you were at what happened to her at the university. The layoff without notice."

"That was a horrible thing, senseless. She's managed to salvage her life, but how much easier and better it could have been for her and Sophie without that sonofabitch."

"You mean Ronson?"

Cody snorted. "Ronson is Exhibit A for how evil often runs rough-shod in this godforsaken world. So wrong."

"Was."

"What?"

"You said *Ronson is* when in fact he *is* no more."

Cody laughed. "Right." He looked off into the distance. "Laughter at someone's death may not seem appropriate, but in his case an exception is justified. I... saw a story about his death somewhere. Can't say it brought me anything other than joy. Some major wrong was finally righted. A categorical imperative has been addressed. Kudos is merited."

"The police ruled his death was accidental."

Cody shrugged. "Whatever. The arc of the universe."

"Did you ever meet Ronson?"

He hesitated, licking his lips and gritting his teeth. "Can't say that I had the... what's the right word? Not the opposite of pleasure. Maybe disgust. Nausea. Something like that. But nnn... no."

"He was a bad actor, from what Liz told me."

He looked at me and winked awkwardly, a studied gesture. "Chalk one up for the good guys. The universe may be indifferent, amoral, but I still don't believe in pure chance. His death was not a pure accident. As long as there are humans that are willing to act." He suddenly appeared more intense, staring at me in a way that was unnerving. I felt a kind of gravitational pull as I edged into the border of his universe and worldview and I turned away in discomfort. I'm sure he thought Ronson's death was intentional, but I was also sure he'd said about as much on that subject as he was likely to. I broke the pregnant pause.

"Cody, it's getting late and I have to get up early. Thank you for your time and insight."

"Yeah. I'm enough of an introvert to dread any conversation, but this almost qualified as fun. I'm more comfortable in the world of ideas than I am in this funky room." He swept his arms wide to encompass the entire bar.

"If you see her, say hello to Liz, will you? I know she won't answer my messages, at least for now, but she's still very much in my thoughts. And I'd do anything..." He let his voice trail off as we waved good-bye.

As I walked to my car I couldn't help but wonder what he meant by anything. His ongoing efforts to woo Liz back suggested a long memory for love, and probably also for hate. In his own personal hall of mirrors, might he have decided to lay Ronson's demise at the feet of his love, much as my cat used to bring me a dead bird as a kind of tribute?

I put Cody's name in the suspect list. For now, the only name in that category.

As I drove home, still thinking about Cody, I noticed the car behind me was following closely, so close as to be a traffic hazard. Instinctively I slowed down and pulled slightly to the right on the two-lane road, hoping he'd pass. It was dark and misty and I wasn't going to drive any faster than I felt like.

I looked in the mirror and noticed the other car had slowed down, too, creeping up on my bumper. I honked, figuring maybe he was high or dozing off. He responded by flashing his brights in my eyes, a couple of seconds too long to serve as a simple acknowledgment. More like a challenge.

Against my better judgment I sped up. So did he. When I slowed down again, he followed suit. I didn't know what game we were playing but I didn't like it.

I made an abrupt left turn without slowing down, my tires scraping on some gravel. The other car followed, creeping up on me again. Another right, with the same result.

It was late enough that traffic had been had thinned out considerably. My house was maybe fifteen minutes from here, but I didn't want to lead this nutso to my doorstep.

I slammed on the brakes at the next corner, bracing for a possible rear-ender, but the other driver just barely stopped short, although I thought I felt the lightest touch from behind. I tried to glance inside the other car but could only see vague shapes.

I waited a full half-minute, then I stomped on the accelerator, my wheels spinning in the damp. I turned right at the first opportunity and headed for the limited access highway. It wasn't anywhere near my direct route home, but I figured it would put a stop to these shenanigans. I merged into the steady traffic and could no longer spy my unwanted companion. I had gone considerably out of my way, so it was another ten minutes to the closest turnoff to my house. I took a deep breath and turned on some jazz.

Just after the turnoff I spotted the brights in my mirror. This was getting old. I parked three blocks from my house, got out of the car and prepared to confront this idiot. I was pretty sure I had a lug wrench in my trunk. I popped the lid and found the wrench loose on top. I grabbed it and stood in back with my arms crossed.

My follower flashed his brights on and off, slowing down. He remained motionless for a few seconds, then gunned the engine and sped by me just a few inches away. He honked but it sounded more like an air horn, which made me jump, the echo ringing in my ears. He was out of sight before I could even swear at him.

It took me an hour and several beers to stop shaking. That night I dreamed of car chases straight out of *Smokey and the Bandit.*

CHAPTER SEVEN

Next morning, when I climbed into my car, there was something blocking my view tucked under the wiper. Probably a flyer for the latest neighborhood takeout place.

But scrawled in red marker was this:

You think a lug wrench can protect you? Think again. Nice digs. Fireproof?

I did a once-over around and under the car, looking for any obvious signs of tampering. Nothing. I thought about grabbing a bus but the stubborn streak in me asserted itself. I turned the key slowly, as if that would make any difference. The engine turned over as normal. I touched the brakes, felt their reassuring grip, and headed to work. I kept checking my mirror. I parked in a busy area near campus, hoping that might offer my vehicle some protection.

Leigh Lambert called right after I sat down with information about Harriet Bauskas's whereabouts.

"She's in a retirement center not far from campus. It's called Paragon House."

"Did you talk with her?"

"No, I just did some sleuthing. I don't know her very well."

"This will be a big help, I hope. Thanks, Leigh."

"Just keep me in the loop when you figure out whodunit. Or as they say in academia, whodidit."

"Right."

It was easy to get hold of Harriet and she agreed to meet me late that afternoon.

Paragon House was a retirement center built with university faculty and staff as its target market. It offered university-affiliated individuals a number of discounts and special deals. The building was decorated simply but comfortably, with plush couches and Victorian-style draperies. Gold and red were the dominant colors and it had an Old World feel to it.

The front desk called Harriet and she came down in a few minutes. She was perhaps eighty, a bit stooped but moving quickly and with a firm handshake, her snow-white hair in perfect order. We sat in a small lounge on the second floor. The first thing I noticed about her was her sweet perfume. She was wearing a lot of deep red lipstick and the blush on her cheeks was from a bit of rouge. The ensemble made me think of screen actors from years gone by. She sat with her hands folded on her lap.

"Thank you for agreeing to meet with me. I didn't give you much of an explanation on the phone because it's kind of a long story."

"Take as much time as you need. Dinner isn't for another hour and a half and I have no other engagements. I'll be whatever help I can, but my relationship with the university did end a number of years ago."

"That's all right. I'm looking for information concerning something that may have occurred in the second Pennybaker administration."

She sighed. "Oh dear. Those were awful times. You can't imagine what it was like working with leadership in those days. You might have described those people, the leaders, as paranoid, but the truth is that some people really were out to get them. At least that's how we saw it. We joked that administrators should start wearing jerseys with numbers and names on them, because you couldn't tell the players without a scorecard, the turnover was so rapid.

"I've never seen leaders come and go as quickly as happened then, with one scandal coming on the heels of another. I'd get up in the morning and scan the headlines to see what could possibly go wrong that day. There were many bad days, and there were days that were even worse than bad. Much as I might like to forget what happened, I can't put that experience aside. It probably shortened my working life by quite a few years."

As she talked, I could see the strain in her face as she endured the echoes of those tough times. But she also had a flinty quality that told me I'd want to be in her lifeboat if it came to that.

"And you worked as a personal assistant to President Pennybaker when he returned."

At this she brightened. "I did. He was a wonderful man. Generous to a fault, courteous, with a wicked a sense of humor. I have never met a kinder man or better leader. He was the best person to pilot the university through those rough waters. We were lucky to have him waiting in the wings."

"I've heard many great things about him. I'm trying to find out about one of his appointments. He hired the first person to head the university's computer systems. His name was Jeremy Ronson."

"I recall that name, but only vaguely. You say he became the head for computing?"

"Yes, I think his title was vice president."

"I'm sorry, but, you know, it's been so long, a lot of the names moosh together." Her mouth was a thin line and her words came more slowly.

"Well... maybe if I described him physically, do you think that might help jog your memory?"

"If you could. You never know."

"He wasn't very tall. He had a round face and wore his hair in what I'd call a bowl cut. Kind of like the early Beatles. He was clean-shaven and never wore anything except blue jeans."

Harriet brightened visibly and broke out a thousand-watt grin. "Oh HIM! I'll never forget the first day he came into the office. You'd think he could've chosen a shirt that wasn't so wrinkled even if he insisted on wearing those horrid jeans! I'd never let my children leave the house like that, let alone go to a job interview with the president dressed so sloppily."

"Ah, so you did meet him."

"Several times. Usually, the hiring committee makes a decision based on one interview and whatever negotiations occur are usually concluded over the phone in a few days or at most a few weeks. Of course, there are always exceptions. I wasn't privy to what was going on, not the gory details, but this fellow — Ronson, you say — he must've come back to meet with Dr. Pennybaker a half-dozen times. I remember Dr. Pennybaker leaving those meetings shaking his head. He'd say, 'I don't know how good an administrator he is, but if he's half as good at administration as he is tough as a negotiator, he'll be one hell of a leader.' I remember the president's words very well, because he wasn't given to swearing, at least not with me."

"Did you ever talk to Ronson?"

"Not really. It seemed all he could muster was hello. His attorney was much more pleasant and affable."

"Attorney? Was it common for people to bring an attorney to meetings like this?"

"Well, there really were very few 'meetings like this,' so there wasn't much precedent. Face-to-face negotiations with an attorney present — it may have happened before, but I'd never seen it."

"And this went on for weeks?"

"Actually, it stretched over several months. Dr. Pennybaker had other things to handle, as you can well imagine."

Time for the $64 question. "Did you handle Dr. Pennybaker's correspondence when it came to things like employment agreements?"

"Sometimes I would take the draft that he'd pound out on his typewriter — he wasn't up on technology — and get the final version of agreements to him for his signature." Harriet had a curious expression on her face, wondering where all this was leading.

"Did you handle Jeremy Ronson's agreement?"

She shook her head. "I'm sorry, but no I didn't. Is that why you came to talk to me?"

"Yes, it is, Harriet. But even without that you've been very helpful."

"Is Jeremy Ronson in some kind of trouble?"

"Actually, he died recently."

"So sorry. He must have been quite young. I remember that behind his back people in Main Central used to refer to him as 'boy wonder,' you know, like out of Batman?"

"If you didn't help with the agreement, is there someone else who was likely to have assisted President Pennybaker?"

"It was always either me or Pensativa. We were the only ones available for things like that."

"Pensativa?"

"Excuse me. *Doctor* Pensativa Becker. I think her title was special assistant."

"So she was likely to have helped?"

"I'm sure she did, if I wasn't involved."

"Do you know where she is now?"

Harriet wrung her fingers. She was concentrating hard, trying to dredge up memories from two decades ago. "I knew it once. When she left... I think she became president of a community college.

Somewhere in Oregon, maybe. But we didn't keep in touch after that. She was an odd person, truly odd."

Harriet paused and licked her lips. "I've never been much of a gossip, but that woman used to make me so angry. She made it very clear that she considered that job beneath her, that it was just a small stepping stone as part of her march toward a prestigious position. And the rest of us... we were just part of the furniture, as far as she was concerned. The way she'd treat the other staff was shameful. I feel sorry for the people who work for her now. I don't usually say things like this, but she was hell on wheels."

"Harriet, I don't want to take any more of your time. Can I call you if I have any more questions?"

"Of course you can. Of course you can. I'm happy to have helped, if only a little."

*   *   *

There weren't a lot of ways I knew to locate George Pennybaker's special assistant. My one hope was that she hadn't changed her name. At least not her first name. I rolled the dice and typed into my search engine.

There was one Pensativa Becker and just a handful of hits. The most recent one, from just last year, had her as president of a small college in Nevada. From the accumulated stories it appeared she had gone as dean at one community college to president of another to this school in Nevada, one that was in the state college system but in a small town.

I punched her number, trying to form a rough plan of attack in my mind while doing so.

I managed to get through her secretary with a story about how I was from one of her old institutions and we were looking for a piece of information not in any of our files that she might just remember. Anyhow, I had her on the phone.

After we got through the introductions I cut to the chase.

"I talked with Harriet Bauskas recently."

"How is Harriet? She was the only person in that administration, including Pennybaker, who had any class. In fact, she outclassed most people I've met before or since. Lovely woman."

I bit my lip. "She's doing very well. Living in a facility not far from campus. She appeared in good health and good humor when I saw her. And she said you might be able to help me with a... situation that began when you were here."

"Uh-oh."

"Excuse me?"

"There were so many sticky situations from that era. It was like a sausage grinder that continuously turned out scandals, seemingly without end. If it wasn't accusations from the feds that a researcher had misspent grant money, it was a member of the football team taking gifts under the table from a sports agent.

"Every time this happened, poor Penny would have to give the same tired statement: 'We're truly sorry this happened, the miscreants have been fired or otherwise disciplined, and we've taken steps to prevent it from happening in the future.'

"When he was saying that, he knew — we all knew — that there was no easy way to prevent those kinds of ethical lapses from happening again. We were whistling past the graveyard. Now that I've been in a leadership position, I wake up each morning and consider it a good day when nothing goes horribly wrong. I've found there are some questions I just don't want to ask, because if I get the wrong answer I don't know what I'd do about it. Being a top administrator in higher education is like trying to manage a goat rodeo."

"Actually, this is not about one of the scandals. It concerns Jeremy Ronson, who I believe was hired as vice president for computing while you served as special assistant."

There was a pause and when she responded there was a catch in her voice. "I was thinking I might get a call like this. I was surprised, after Ronson's death, that no one bothered to check with me. I thought eventually they'd get around to asking me how this sad business started, figuring out who might've done it and why."

"You know his death was ruled accidental."

"If you believe that I'd like to interest you in a degree program from an esteemed institution in the desert which claims it offers an education every bit as good as Princeton's. Are people buying that bullshit?"

"The police closed the case and no one else is officially investigating it."

"Sounds like they didn't want to turn over many rocks. I haven't lived in the area for more than a decade but I could name a handful of people who swore out loud that they would like to see the fellow disappear from the face of the earth."

"And how many of them would actually lift a muscle to make it happen? Or, if they had the means, would think about paying someone to make it happen?"

She coughed right into the receiver. "Well, you've got me there. People at universities enjoy displaying their feathers like proud peacocks, but that's usually where it ends."

"Why did people want him… to disappear?"

"I can give you several reasons. He was a disaster as an administrator. His staff mostly hated him. He was disruptive in high-level meetings, when he deigned to attend, which was infrequently. He was an arrogant sonofabitch. He made very expensive wrong decisions, repeatedly. And worst of all, in the eyes of some of the top leadership of the university, he could do no wrong, so he was immune from criticism, not to mention punishment. All this was, however, predictable from his interviews and references. Should I go on?"

"That's enough. So you helped Pennybaker negotiate the employment agreement with Ronson?"

"Helped?" Her voice rose several octaves. "I was the one that had to meet with that simpering slob and his slimy attorney. Penny would show up when we reached an impasse or when his long lunches ended early."

"Was the attorney named Walker?"

"That was the turd's name. It was like talking to a stone. I had to repeat everything three times and in three different ways to get him to understand. It may have been an act, but he had me convinced from day one that he was hopelessly stupid."

"Do you remember any of the key elements of the agreement?"

"Hey, aren't you supposed to have that on file for at least as long as he lives?"

"Yes, well, that was in the pre-electronic days. And you know the systems at human resources. I'm sure there's a copy somewhere, but frankly it was easier to pick up the phone and ask you."

"Well, I didn't keep a copy. And even though he's dead, I'm not sure I should be talking about the details of his employment agreement over the phone. Can't you submit some kind of official request in writing?"

"Look, I'm going to be completely honest with you. There's only one investigation underway regarding Ronson's death and I'm doing it. It's completely unofficial. I think something bad happened, but I'm not sure what. Because I work here, I can't go through official channels to pursue this — I'd be out on my ear in a minute. I have to do this quietly, *sub rosa*."

"That's all well and good, but you're putting me in an awkward position." There was a long pause. "I admire your spunk. You may be on to something. Maybe some other bastards... made that bastard disappear."

"That's what I've been thinking, or at least trying to investigate to quell my own suspicions."

"I'd love to help. I really would. But what you're asking... I don't want to be drawn into anything."

"Nothing you say will ever be attributed to you. And ultimately, if anything comes of what I'm investigating, it will need to be corroborated officially with the actual employment agreement. So you're completely off the hook."

"Ronson was an asshole. I think the world is well rid of him. But that doesn't necessarily justify... what might've happened. Someone should be brought to justice if a crime was committed. But, well, I still don't know."

"How about this? You think about it overnight and I'll call back tomorrow. I don't want to pressure you. Well, actually I do. This investigation may go nowhere without your help."

"OK. Call me mid-morning. It will give me time to assemble my recollections and figure out if I want to be pulled into this. You know that was a chapter of my life I'd prefer to forget."

"If I had any other way of getting this information I would've used it already. Expect a call tomorrow."

A glorious end to the work day. I still had a job. My investigation was plodding along. I was a little dizzy from being whipsawed between the job for which I was being paid and the one that had grabbed my passion. Not to mention the lingering effects of the car chase and warning note. I was grateful to find my car undamaged and without additional love notes.

* * *

I needed some serious R&R.

"Are you sure you know what you're doing?" I said from what might be termed a compromising position.

"Of course I do. Trust is a very important part of BDSM experience, especially for a beginner like you. Just tell me, who do you trust more than me? You should have no reason to doubt that I have your best interests in mind. Even as I gently torture you."

I felt like a trussed turkey. If that turkey was about to experience a degree of torture and pleasure described in famous erotica.

I was spread-eagled on the bed, each extremity tied to a corner by bits of cloth. Tight but not painful. I was able to lift my head enough for Andrea to put on a blindfold. There was what I call yoga music playing in the background — tuneless, with instruments I didn't know and a structure I couldn't grasp.

"I promise that you will like this. And remember, you specifically requested 'something different.'"

"I must tell you, I'm a little nervous. Not that I don't trust you."

She blew in my ear. I was startled. I hadn't felt her move to the side of the bed. She whispered in my ear. "Relax. You're in good hands."

"My nose itches."

She waved a feather over my face, gently stroking my cheeks, lips and nose.

"Better?"

"Now I feel like sneezing."

She kissed and licked the tip of my nose, sucking on it briefly.

"Now?" she whispered.

"Better," I gasped. I had discovered a new erogenous zone.

With her feather, she moved down across my chest. Then I felt her tongue on my nipples as she sucked briefly. She held one with her teeth and squeezed. The sensation was not unpleasant.

I felt her lips reach across my stomach to my abdomen. "Want me to go further?"

"Very much."

"I'm sorry, but I can't do that. At least not yet. Are you comfortable?"

"Not so much. But I still have circulation in my hands and feet."

"How about here?"

"Yes. But you can see that."

She was back up near my ear, her tongue flicking at the lobe. "I think they call that greatly engorged. I'll play with it later."

"I wish you would."

"Shhhhhh…" She sucked on my lobe and her tongue described an arc extending all the way in to the drum. Her breath and mine became synchronized. I could hear oceans.

Her mouth was hovering just above my lips. I reached out with my tongue but could barely touch her. She recoiled.

"Not yet, lover, not yet." From her breath I could guess her position poised above me, and I felt her shift until her body was just over mine. She began a horizontal dance, gently rubbing her skin against my chest, her legs spread wide.

"Oh yes. Do you like that?"

I moaned approval. My senses were on a hair trigger. She unfastened her hair and dragged it across my face, wrapping me in a sensuous tent. Her lower body took over the rhythms of the dance and I could feel her wetness against me.

"You'd like to come inside, wouldn't you?"

I grunted yes.

"Sorry, but you're not permitted. Not yet." She grabbed my erection. "Do you think I want that thing inside of me now? Do you? I have some better ideas."

She climbed off the bed and began riffling through drawers. "Ah, here's what I'm looking for." I heard a sound like an electric razor, loud and metallic.

"You'll like this. And even if you don't, I know I will."

I felt a buzzing sensation in and around my genitals. The buzzing traveled through my lower body, bringing me closer to the brink. Then it was withdrawn. She repeated this pattern more times than I could count, eliciting involuntary moans and gyrations. She had found my On button. Just as I thought I was going to lose it, she shut off the device. There was a catch in my throat and an exquisite anticipation all over. "No no no. It's my turn now."

The buzzing was modulated by Andrea's heavy breathing. "I'll bet you'd like to see this, wouldn't you? Well, that's not happening." Her breath came in gasps now, punctuated by the usual affirmative exclamations in a rhythm that started slowly and gained tempo, reaching a crescendo in just a few minutes.

"Just because you're deprived doesn't mean I have to be," Andrea said as the buzzing stopped and her breathing became deeper and more regular.

"How long are we going to do this?" This was testing my endurance and self-control.

"How long do you have? There's a rhythm to these things. We're tapping into ancient traditions here, you can read all about it later if you want. Postponing pleasure is an early step on the road to wisdom, some philosophers say." She was stroking me gently with her tongue, pausing to suck the area on the shaft below the glans and moving down to my scrotum. I moaned again and strained upward.

"You'd like that. But no, you need to be patient." Andrea positioned herself kneeling just over my mouth. I could reach up with my tongue and feel her, taste her sweetness. "That's very nice," she said. "Keep up the good work and you'll be rewarded." She rocked gently forward to back and side to side. I felt her inner thigh muscles clench involuntarily in spasm.

"You're really very good at this. But I'm sure you've heard that before." I felt her bear down on me, inviting deeper penetration, her juices flowing into my mouth and down my throat. And then, with short gasps and one long, shuddering climax, she was done and pulled away.

"I need to lower the temperature a little. The room temperature, I mean." She moved to away and I heard a fan starting. "That's better." She was at the foot of the bed, apparently with a piece of wispy cloth. "By the way, this is called tease and denial, in case you want to look it up." I felt her tickling the bottom of my feet and running her long fingernails slowly up the top and inside of my legs. The area was less erogenous than other parts of my body, it seemed, and I felt almost normal except for the restraints.

Her fingers did a dance up to my hips, up my sides all the way to my armpits. I felt her nibbling at the area near my clavicle. "Mmmmm, I like you there." Her breasts brushed my chest as she moved down to my sternum. "And there." She kissed the area just below my solar plexus while pressing down on my chest with both hands and squeezing. Her tongue described a circular path around my navel and gently flicked the interior. "And there," she said, barely audible.

"But mostly there," as her mouth engulfed me completely. A charge went through me. I felt I had grown to proportions well beyond normal. She massaged me with her lips, moistened with a combination of her juices and my own. Then she withdrew.

"My, you are excitable. Who would've guessed?" I heard her rum- maging through drawers again. "This is the kind of torture I just love administering." I felt myself drawn back from the brink but still at a wholly new plateau.

I heard a bottle being squeezed and warm liquid flowed onto my penis. "I promise this next part won't hurt a bit." Her mouth encircled me again and she worked the shaft repeatedly. Then her body covered mine, her left nipple against my lips, then her right. I heard her breath exhaled in jagged streams. "It's time, lover. And I promise it will be like no other."

As I felt the rage rising within me, I knew Andrea had gifted me with a profound truth. My brain was in orbit, leaving behind the shell of my convulsing, exploding body, extending beyond my reach. For just a moment I had traveled beyond sanity, into a realm beyond de- scription.

CHAPTER EIGHT

At the office the next morning I handled some routine work while marking time until calling Pensativa. If she decided not to cooperate, I had a few more options for exploring Ronson's demise, none of them very promising.

The phone rang. I was hoping it was Pensativa, calling because she just couldn't wait. Instead it was Trencher.

"Can you come up for a few minutes?" He seldom told me why.

I closed his door. "This is about the president's initiative."

I let out an involuntary groan, prompting a sharp glance.

"You have a problem with that?"

"Would it matter if I did?"

"Not really."

"Then I guess I don't."

"Good." He pulled out a sheaf of papers. "We have to be part of this. If we're not perceived as team players… well, you can imagine the consequences."

"Like getting tossed from an office window?"

"Very funny. Actually, not funny at all." He was flipping through the papers. "So, it seems they'll be taking another look at the branding marks the university uses, to update them and make sure everyone conforms to the new standards."

"I suppose that means I should take the dashes out of my phone number."

He looked up. "You're kidding, right?"

"Not in the least. You mean you missed the memo? The brand-lords say periods are friendlier than dashes."

"OK." He didn't even crack a smile. "Our work is to convince parents and students that this place is a good alternative to the Ivies. That our faculty are just as prominent and can teach them just as well. That the diploma they get here will be just as valuable as one with Veritas on it."

For a split second I wondered how many milligrams of actual veritas were going to be in Yarmouth's initiative. "How much time do we have to come up with some ideas?" After all, inventing a line of reasoning that is palpably untrue but plausible could take a while.

"Maybe two months."

"Not enough to conduct any research."

"These guys don't want research, they want implementation. Tactics, slogans, things that can be bolted on to current projects. We have to capitalize on things we're already doing, reshape them, bring them in conformance with the new themes."

"So, this is about making our language align with the new branding strategy, not necessarily finding what will resonate."

"Are you trying to be difficult? Our consultant already has staked out the approach to re-positioning." He scowled at me and raised his voice. "This branding group was hired at great cost to develop a new approach, to deal with some fundamental challenges facing the institution, to bring the very best ideas from the corporate world to bear on our challenges."

He had apparently inhaled the Gatorade powder. Inhalation gets it to the bloodstream faster, and in powder form it crosses the blood-brain barrier more easily. "We're just one little piece in a very large puzzle. If all the pieces are brought together, the entire picture will change. Get it?"

I opened my mouth to object further but closed it quickly. There are times in the world of work when you are being asked your opinion. Then there are other times when you are being asked exclusively for your approval, which you cannot withhold without lasting consequences. This was one of those latter instances.

"Got it. So what does that mean for us?"

Trencher sat back with the dirty soles of his shoes facing me over the top of his desk, a frequent if obnoxious posture. "First, we need to dig out rankings and comparisons that show us at or near the Ivies. We're going to create a web page that touts those benchmarks."

"That's easy enough." There were only a couple of instances where this university might have been included with the major privates. In some cases the source of the information was suspect and in others it was a pretty narrow set of criteria. But if I could find a straw I'm gonna grasp it.

"Next, we need to locate students who considered us and the Ivies, or places like Stanford, and were admitted to both but chose to come here."

"Are we sure such people exist?"

"I don't know. Use your contacts in admissions and in The Excellent, Engaging Undergraduate Experience to explore this question."

"What else?"

"We're going to help the consultants prepare a series of commercials that go with our admissions counselors when they tour the state. The theme, and this is not to leave this room, will be 'As good as or better than Harvard.'

"The spots will focus on faculty and their achievements. A couple will highlight alumni. Your job, your office's job, is to find suitable faculty — ones with degrees from the right schools combined with prominence in their field."

I mused about the expression "cherry picking." It comes from the practice of culling the fruit in order to harvest only the finest, ripest cherries. The expression derives from the erroneous conclusion that someone might draw from just examining the selective harvest: that all the cherries on the tree are as ripe and perfect as the ones in the basket.

"If they are Harvard quality faculty, why are they here and not at Harvard?"

"Do I need to say this again? Because we're just as good as Harvard. That's the aspirational fact. End of story."

I'd never heard the phrase "aspirational fact" before, but I realized we were operating now in aspirational reality. "Anything else for now?"

Trencher spun in his chair and began to read emails.

"That's it."

"And the consultant believes this is going to move the dial with students and parents?"

"That and some other things."

"Do we know what those other things are?"

"Not yet. Film at 11."

As I walked down the stairs to my office, I tried to figure out what to say to the staff that wouldn't result in an LOL-fest. Or ROFLMAO. Or worse. I came up empty. My group had many excellent qualities but listening to nonsense with a straight face wasn't one of them. The whole plan, if you could call it that, struck me as the shallowest and least effective response that could come from presumably intelligent people.

*   *   *

When I returned to the office I decided it was time to call Pensativa. I held my breath as I dialed the number. I was put through by her secretary.

"So are we going to do this?"

"I thought long and hard. I had a few more questions."

"Go ahead."

"What's your plan, moving forward?"

"I've been playing this pretty much by ear. What I have now is a basket of surmises and a couple of educated guesses. Given the tenor of my last conversation with the campus police, they're not about to re-open this case unless I bring them something of substance."

"So that's where you're headed? To get enough evidence to prompt a real investigation."

"I'm an amateur. At some point the pros in law enforcement need to take over, and I see my role as making that happen."

"So, you're putting me on the side of aiding justice."

"That's a good way to look at it."

Dead air. And there was a catch in her voice when the conversation resumed.

"OK. I'm in."

I let out a deep breath. "Good. Give me a minute while I put on my headset. I'm going to take notes, if that's OK. And just to reiterate, everything you say is completely confidential, just between us, and nothing will ever be attributed to you, or even point vaguely in your direction."

"Fine."

"So let's begin with the search process."

"The vice president for computing was a brand-new position back then. We'd had a few geeks promoted from within, with limited authority, but it was clear no one on campus had the scope of knowledge necessary to head what was becoming a very important department.

So we looked outside and created a high-level committee, mostly of faculty, to screen applicants. I staffed the committee.

"The pickings were pretty slim. There weren't many applicants with significant experience of the kind we wanted. When push came to shove, we had three people worth bringing to campus.

"One of them made a laughable presentation to the faculty. He clearly thought he was going to preside over a well-oiled machine and wouldn't have to do much work. About an hour after his presentation, which was followed by a faculty grilling, he withdrew.

"The second candidate was only a little more impressive. He had worked at a smaller school, so he had been very hands-on. But he didn't realize we were expecting this individual to create a plan to leapfrog ahead of other institutions. He simply didn't have the intellectual muscle and I think he knew it, although he stayed in the pool.

"Then there was Jeremy. Despite his towering arrogance, he clearly knew his stuff. He was already working at a powerhouse university, so he understood and was unfazed by the politics. It was clear he knew where he wanted to go. It was also clear he wasn't going to listen very much to others, regardless of the length of their title or the weight of their resumé. But the committee realized it was Ronson or no one. Committees like that don't admit failure. So we presented the findings to Pennybaker and characterized Ronson as the Anointed One. Pennybaker got the message and negotiations ensued."

"Tell me a little about the negotiations."

"This was a long time ago, and I spent part of the weekend trying to recall some of the details. You can ask me questions and that may prompt my memory. But there is one significant thing that I remember quite clearly, because it was the subject of much discussion and it delayed the agreement by several months."

"Yes?"

"Ronson wanted a golden parachute. Not all that unusual for academics who become top administrators, but pretty unusual in his case, because he had never held a faculty position in his life.

"But he absolutely insisted and made it clear he would never come to the university unless he was granted a faculty position. What he wanted was a clause in his agreement which stated that, should he ever lose his administrative position *for whatever reason*, and he emphasized those three words, he would automatically acquire a tenured slot in the department of computer science."

"Had you ever participated in a negotiation like that before?"

"We would hire faculty members as administrators who had a long list of publications in scholarly journals, whose research was every bit as creditable as the people we hired to teach and do research. Granting them a faculty position was appropriate and in some sense an honor for us. Some of them occasionally taught classes or participated in research projects.

"But this guy was cut out of different cloth. He had never conducted research. Never seen the inside of a classroom. Based on his conduct in our meetings, I would have advised keeping him as far away from students as possible. Not because he was creepy. Well, he *was* creepy. It was just hard to imagine him trying to convey ideas to a group of young people. He didn't explain himself well. He didn't have any patience — clearly regarding me and my colleagues as fools. And in no discussion did he ever indicate a desire to actually teach or engage in research.

"That made his request odd. But it was clear he wanted a sinecure.

"I talked with our attorneys, and they pointed out that we could dismiss him from both positions, but that might involve two separate processes. And to fire a tenured faculty member is way harder than dismissing an administrator. Not impossible, but very hard. So we might as well conclude we were offering him a job for life.

"When we fired administrators who had faculty appointments they typically left in short order. With Ronson, I was all but certain that if the situation arose, he had no intention of leaving.

"But Penny insisted we go for it. It was going to be the cornerstone of his second legacy. George kept saying to me, 'Make it happen! Make it happen!' and it was pretty clear he wasn't worried about the cost or consequences."

"So you agreed to his conditions?"

"It wasn't that easy. The academic department needed to grant him a tenured position. The first part, the easy part, was to give them an additional slot that didn't count against the actual number of working faculty they were allotted.

"The hard part was that the faculty had to agree formally to grant this guy tenure. And according to their normal rules, he wasn't even in the ballpark."

"So how did it happen?"

"First we called in the chairman. He was an affable fellow, very reasonable. But he was scared of his faculty, whom he knew well, having served there for over a decade. There were a number of outspoken characters and he knew they would make trouble if he called a departmental meeting. We decided there was only one way that this might succeed.

"Penny himself had to go to a secret meeting of the department's faculty. We actually moved it off campus to make sure there were no leaks. Even then we knew it was risky. But the chairman and I became convinced it was the only way."

"That must have been an interesting meeting."

"You might say that. Penny made it clear what the stakes were. To him, this was a crucial hire that would position the university as a research powerhouse now and in the future by enabling the creation of a computing infrastructure that would allow faculty, including those in the room, to do research they had only dreamed about. Ronson was uniquely qualified to make that happen. If Ronson turned them down, an elaborate search would begin again, with results that were uncertain at best.

"And as for the faculty position, in the unlikely event that Ronson was dismissed from his administrative job he would probably choose to leave for greener pastures, as had other administrators. At least, that's what George told them. So it was, in essence, a courtesy appointment."

"What was the faculty response?"

"Skeptical would be an understatement. They didn't like the department to be a 'dumping ground'— their words — for failed administrators, even if only in principle. There could be no guarantee that Ronson would leave if he lost his cushy chair in Main Central. And everyone knew Pennybaker was a short-timer, so any assurances he made would be void by the time his successor had unpacked his suitcase. Faculty kept coming back to how unqualified Ronson was for a faculty position, and the department's rules were clear in stating that they had to vote on the merits of the individual. They didn't like the precedent, they didn't like the optics. If a third option, other than a yes or no vote, had been available, to simply leave the room without saying anything, that choice would've carried the day.

"Penny was insistent. He made it clear that if they did not grant Ronson a tenured position, he wasn't going to let them off the hook. He would describe their obstructionism, as he termed it, to the search committee, to the rest of the faculty and to Ronson himself, saying that they had blackballed his appointment. Moreover, he made a thinly-veiled threat about how future departmental budget requests might be handled."

"In other words, he was playing hardball."

"And he had the hardest balls of anyone in the room, as it turned out. He was adamant, even belligerent. I had never seen a leader drop all pretense of collegiality as Pennybaker did. And this from a man who publicly was as genteel as they come, soft-spoken and self-effacing. It was an eye-opening experience. On the one hand, it's important to have a bottom line, to have some decisions that are so important that you're willing to go all-in. But it's quite another to twist arms to the breaking point. When Pennybaker launched into his 'or else' remarks, you could see jaws drop around the room.

"It prompted some pushback. There were mavericks who took his threats as a challenge, pretty much daring the president to try and follow through on them, at which point they opined that they might go public with the whole sordid mess, ratcheting up the stakes. But it was clear that his threats had moved the consensus.

"Penny and I had to leave the room for the vote. We could hear raised voices, interruptions, the rumble of discontent. George was nervous but never lost his air of supreme self-confidence. One thing you could say for ol' George, he looked every bit like a university president. And he knew it. The mane of white hair, the steely gaze, the world-weariness that suggested a kind of wisdom. He had it all.

"About thirty minutes later the door opened and the chairman announced that they had voted — reluctantly, he emphasized — to grant Pennybaker the freedom to offer Ronson a tenured position in computer science as a contingency. The wording was an effort to save face. There was still not a clear majority for granting Ronson tenure outright, but they were willing to leave the decision in Pennybaker's hands. They felt that this removed their fingerprints from what they saw as a poor choice."

"Pennybaker was aware of his narrow escape and didn't stand around to gloat. He shook the chairman's hand, thanked the faculty, and we left.

"On the way out, he said to me, 'Truth be told, I've never tried to stare down a group of faculty like that before. I hope to hell I did the right thing.' Then he stopped in his tracks and grinned. 'Of course, if I'm wrong it will be my successor who will pay the price, the poor bastard.'"

Pensativa had perhaps told me more than she intended, but once the words started tumbling out there was no stopping her even if I had wanted to.

I had no reason to doubt her explanation but still needed to figure out what it meant to my investigation. Were there people on campus aware of this key clause in the agreement, and what would they have done to prevent the department from becoming Ronson's new home?

If there had been discussion of removing Ronson from his administrative post after the budget mess was uncovered, which was likely, then the next move would have been to talk with the leadership in computer science, at least let the chair know what was being contemplated. I would have liked to have been a fly on the wall when that meeting took place.

If I was going to get to the bottom of this, I needed to do more than just imagine. I knew the chairman, Mark Chabeaux, only slightly. I doubted he would tell me anything if I just made an appointment to see him. My best chance was to talk to McDivitt again. Maybe he could grease the skids for me.

We chatted by email. He said his schedule was packed. I pleaded, saying I needed just a few minutes, and that I was following up on our earlier conversation. He said he could squeeze me in to a coffee break that afternoon.

* * *

But first was another executive staff meeting.

You never knew what would happen at one of Ganas's meetings. Literally. We were never sent agendas in advance, never had white papers to digest, never were posed questions to ponder before the meeting. It was like having a pop quiz for which it was impossible to study. And like flummoxed students, we learned to take these gatherings less seriously over time.

When we arrived today, we were presented with color copies of something titled "Extending the University's Media Presence." Its author was something called Gazoom.

"What's Gazoom?" I asked.

"You'll find out soon enough," said Trencher, wearing a tight-lipped half smile.

I began flipping through the PowerPoint, trying to gather the gist in a few seconds.

Ganas breezed into the room. "Sorry I'm late. I've just come from a meeting where we've been reviewing the proposal from Gazoom. So far, reaction has been very favorable, but I wanted this group to go through it carefully before we take it to the president.

"As you can see, this company is social media and search-engine based. In my view, for too long we've neglected what happens when people just type our name into searches. Or searches for our key leaders, especially the president. Or searches on subjects, especially fields of research, for which we should be well known. Sure, we know that our home page will be at the top when people type our name, but all kinds of random things show up on the first couple of pages after that. Some of them not especially flattering.

"And in the past we've assumed that there was nothing we could do about this. We've been abdicating responsibility for managing one of the institution's key assets, an element of its reputation that is growing in importance.

"Our leaders will not look kindly on us if we continue to ignore how the university's image can be enhanced, or damaged, by what transpires in the electronic town square."

I was pretty sure that he was giving us the condensed version of the sales pitch he had recently witnessed. Like many condensed things, it seemed canned. I felt my attention wandering to my upcoming meeting with McDivitt. I wasn't going to have much time but knew his support was essential to get a favorable reception from the department chair on the sensitive subject of Jeremy Ronson.

I was brought back to the present when Ganas clicked on the PowerPoint from his laptop and displayed it on the screen in back of him.

"I'm not going to lead you through every element of Gazoom's presentation. But let me just say we've conducted a quick survey of the state of the art in this industry and this group is, by consensus, a thought leader in both the nonprofit and for-profit sectors."

I wondered how good a job Ronson had done managing his reputation with his possible future colleagues in computer science. Maybe he had learned from his missteps in Main Central and was about to rebrand himself. Yeah, right.

Ganas began to click through the images at breakneck speed.

"A lot of this is just background about how important reputation is, how much time our target audiences spend with these media, and how the aggregation of the impressions they gain is a close approximation of our public image."

I looked around the room. Everyone was looking down at the copy of the presentation deck. Displayed on the screen in back of Ganas was a slide titled "A La Carte Reputation Management."

"Gazoom doesn't offer a single solution for all organizations. They recognize that everyone has their own concerns and their own approach to gaining prominence. For example, we are very interested in how parents of prospective students, and the students themselves, look at us. Drilling down on these groups, we know that a growing slice of prospective students and parents have progressive views on matters of social justice. Our analysis suggests they lean towards grass roots movements or crowdsourced social initiatives. This has strategic implications, in terms of future academic concentrations we should offer, as well as providing food for thought about where to deploy our messaging."

"Can you explain how they propose to manipulate the university's online image?" I asked. I felt it was a good strategy to let Ganas know I was still in the room mentally, at least part of the time.

"I was just getting to that. Gazoom has serious talent in its stable. What they propose is to create high-quality content that they will place on highly trafficked sites by employing their exclusive network of key contacts at public-facing media." He was reading this directly from one of their slides.

"What exactly does that mean?" Delores Sert, chief writer on the Image Brand and Cultivation team, was sitting with her arms crossed, the closest I'd seen to her displaying open skepticism. Her braid was a different color today, a forest green, with that same yellow bead at the end.

Ganas mopped his brow with a handkerchief, his face florid with exertion.

"This is based on the strategy of having Gazoom create news features and op-eds, then placing them on popular websites. This is a quality-not-quantity approach." He blasted through a few more slides, coming to one with what looked like about a hundred Bartlebys in front of laptops spewing forth cornucopias of words. I suppressed a snicker and sneezed instead.

"So." It was Trencher. "We'd be hiring a cadre of writers, what the presentation calls content specialists, to increase the output of good news stories about the university, with the value-add being that they have contacts at key websites where they can get the content placed prominently. We've done some checking and they appear to have an excellent track record."

"Pardon me for asking, but what about results, in terms of reputation enhancement?" asked Jerry Bransford who, as Image and Brand Cultivation team leader, perhaps wondered about how this outsourcing would affect his unit, which did similar work. I was wondering about its effect on my folks, too.

"These things are very hard to quantify and especially hard to benchmark. We didn't want to rely on metrics provided by Gazoom. So we went directly to some of their clients, ones they suggested and ones we found without their help."

Ganas pushed up the sleeves of his white shirt, exposing his stubby, hairy arms. "We did a quick survey of those clients and found they were uniformly satisfied with the company. We focused not on relationships — anyone can be pleasant when it's in their financial interest — but on the results."

"Perceived results," piped up Bransford.

"Well, this is *all* about perception," said Ganas, sounding a lot like the presenter at the public strategy unveiling, while also confusing ends and means. "Anyhow, the clients we contacted were highly satisfied. We searched hard for negative impressions and really couldn't find any. We've had some preliminary discussions with university leadership and they seem favorably disposed."

That was that. We all knew the code. The decision was a lock. Nothing we could say in this room, even if our views were unanimous in opposition, would influence the outcome.

I realized what the game was and kept to myself. I caught Delores's eye at one point and she shrugged. Bransford was doodling on his tablet; from my angle it looked like Words with Friends. Trencher was scrolling on his phone, smirking at something he'd probably located on Facebook. Kris, our federal lobbyist, wore a blank face and was likely thinking of the grass that needed cutting on her DC residence's front lawn. Marilyn, state lobbyist, had a bubble above her head: "How much will this cost and will the Speaker of the House hold it against us when he finds out?" Cal, alumni honcho, seemed completely in the room, but I'd learned that he was probably the most competent actor in the group. Mark, our liaison with the moneybags, was focused exclusively on Ganas, knowing he was going to be called on to explain and defend the contract to his other bosses.

"Well, there we are," said Ganas, flipping through the last slide. "Gazoom is going to generate their wish list of hot topics that will play well in digital media. They propose to vet these ideas with focus groups of donors and other influentials. Then the real work will begin."

Marilyn woke up. "I hope we'll confine this discussion to a hand-picked, confidential, inside group for as long as possible. Cranky legislators are likely to look askance at even the best-intentioned efforts. The don't take kindly to state agencies spending significant money on public relations campaigns."

Ganas looked nonplussed. I read frustration on Marilyn's face.

"You mentioned at the outset that the company also promises success in social media," I asked. "Is there a specific strategy for that?"

Ganas nodded. "Gazoom thinks the university's presence in social media should be strengthened. We don't want more Facebook and Twitter accounts, but we need to use those we already have more effectively to tell people what's going on around here and, to be blunt, how good we are. So that means more posts about this university's successes and accomplishments, its place in rankings and the major national and international news coming from this place."

Trencher broke away from his Wall. "And if or when reporters find out about the initiative?"

"I'll handle the media."

"If you'd like help with any talking points, just let me know," I piped up, just to signal that I was at least minimally on board. Ganas would never ask for talking points. He held media in fairly low regard and was certain he could dance faster than they could follow.

"Thanks." Ganas picked up his slide deck, laptop and left.

* * *

The Gazoom pitch struck me as too simple and too shallow. I felt a need for a reality check. Harry Joyce was surprised by my call. "I don't hear from you for what, three years, and then twice within a couple of weeks? I hope you don't want any more information on the bloodletting of years past."

"Not at all. And thanks again for that information. I was interested more in the technical side of your work. So you can relax and lower your guard."

"OK. How can I help?"

"I'm going to present you with a hypothetical. Suppose you were in charge of managing the reputation for an entity, an institution that already has some prominence. It doesn't matter what it is except that for this organization its public profile is critical to its success."

"We're not talking about any specific organization?"

"The question is, what's the best way to enhance an organization's public profile, its perception as measured through metrics drawn especially from the digital world?"

"Do you want the correct answer, or would you prefer something that satisfies many institutions' desire to control everything?" Harry had returned to his own smart, snarky self.

"Excellent question. Let's try the correct answer."

"I don't know how familiar you are with investment concepts, but do you know about efficient market theory?"

"A little. It means that the value of a stock reflects every common fact available. It suggests that all information gets digested by the market and incorporated into the stock's price."

"Close enough for our purposes. My opinion, and it is shared by many, is that over time an organization will pretty much get the reputation it deserves in the digital world, which in some ways resembles a market environment. Sooner or later, all relevant information about it is public, and that will determine the institution's reputation. Many would argue, with some merit, that the information market is not completely efficient, just relatively efficient. Nonetheless, people who try to game the system are likely to achieve unimpressive results over the long run, unless they have unlimited resources or are major celebrities getting constant attention. In other words, you can fool some of the people some of the time, but not over the long term."

"But let's say someone comes to your organization and promises to place good news stories in various locations on the Web, some reasonably prominent. They say they have a track record of success in these placements. And they further claim that having a large number of stories read widely will change the organization's reputation and also will influence related search results. Is there any truth behind this approach?"

"Part of the answer to this question depends on your expertise, not mine. Is it possible for any firm, especially one that exists for the sole purpose of reputation enhancement, to be taken seriously by information purveyors who attract large audiences and have high credibility? Are the so-called mainstream media, which still draw huge audiences on the web, going to pay any attention to material offered by a firm like this? Because getting placements in obscure locations, even a good number of them, is not likely to achieve the kinds of results that are intended. Going for mass quantities of questionable sites is a variation of a strategy called a link farm, developed near the beginning of the millennium.

"It was built around the idea that major search algorithms at that time could be tricked by the pure quantity of links mentioning an organization — even if those links contained no information at all. In other words, you can flood the Internet with information of dubious quality, with the result that your popularity in searches, and your connection to ideas of value, would be enhanced.

"Such things worked for a while. But search engines have continued to evolve and now take into account strategies that are, to put it politely, less than genuine. Companies with questionable ethics, out for a quick buck, continue to take advantage of gullible institutions that are looking for quick fixes to their reputation.

"The simple truth is, once the people programming search engines find out what scam is being perpetrated, they tweak their algorithms to prevent link farms or kindred approaches from achieving their desired ends. These companies are smart and client-focused, and the clients — the people using the search engine — want reasonably honest, useful results when they type in a search term.

"Even somewhat more sophisticated versions of the link farm concept have been addressed by the developers of most major search engines. The results of such activities are likely to be marginal in terms of overall impact on a company's public profile."

"And there aren't any new tricks that an enterprising firm can employ to trick a search engine?"

"Not really. Again, it's a lot like efficient markets. If something begins to work, and it violates the intent of the search engines to be what I would call 'honest brokers,' you can bet that any success will be short-lived."

"Good to know. One more question, about social media."

"It's something I only dabble in. There are better people. But go ahead and ask and maybe I can refer you to the proper source."

"What about a strategy that uses social media as essentially a digital broadcast source? In other words, you take the same information that you'd normally send to people who requested it, usually by email but also on your website, and you post it on social media such as Facebook and Twitter."

"You should check with my colleagues who specialize in social media if you're really interested in this subject. I can send you some names. But I can give you a couple of points of conventional wisdom regarding social media. The first is they work best when you recognize that social media... are social."

"Well, that's clear. But what do you mean?"

"They were intended to be used for two-way communication. Actually, for multi-way communication. Think of them as forming digital communities. Among real, live people."

"OK. So...?

"So that means in theory you should have authentic, living individuals sending the messages and, most important, encouraging responses. If you want to use the media effectively, that is. By which I mean building an audience and getting people to trust you and perhaps do things on your behalf."

"I see."

"Having said that, a huge percentage of what gets posted on social media is done by robots. In general, I regard this as a desperate effort by traditional businesses to take the old mass media approaches and apply them to social media. They aren't totally ineffective. Just comparatively weak strategies. Increasingly, social media have become a one-to-many means of conveying information, but the source loses a lot of credibility when it's clear that it's not an actual living and breathing person."

"Thanks, Harry. You are a font of wisdom."

"Conventional wisdom is more like it."

As I returned the phone to its cradle, I thought of how desperate Ganas must be feeling to get in bed with a company like Gazoom.

* * *

I wrestled with how to approach my next meeting with McDivitt. He was nobody's fool. I'd already gotten away with one lie and a second was probably pushing my luck. I had a few explanations at the ready but little confidence they would mollify him.

This time, we met "for coffee" in his office, a top-floor location in the computer science building. He had a wonderful view of greenery, lakes and mountains. It was such a clear day that I could see houses climbing precariously up the expensive hillsides in the distant suburbs.

"Do you actually want coffee?" McDivitt asked. "Truth is, our departmental coffee is pretty weak. I keep lobbying for an espresso machine but everyone else just laughs."

I wondered if it would be possible for him to look even more caffeinated than now, with his slightly bug-eyed aspect, his jerky movements and rapid-fire speech.

"Thanks anyway, but I'll pass. What I'd really like to know, though, is how do you get an office like this?"

McDivitt laughed. "Pay your dues, son. Bring in millions of dollars in federal research. Help to hire the best young faculty on the West Coast. Establish close personal friendships with some of the most dynamic corporate leaders in your field. And most important, keep your nose out of institutional politics except in your own self-interest. That last lesson I had to learn the hard way." He sat back in his chair behind one of the biggest desks I'd ever seen, a deep mahogany with a jumble of papers in the exact center. "What's up now? I assume it's related to Ronson."

"Yes. Have you heard rumors that maybe Ronson's fall wasn't exactly an accident?"

"Now why would one of the most reviled administrators who dies unexpectedly by *falling out a window* be the subject of rumors? I'm shocked, just plain shocked."

"OK, stupid question. Next question: Ronson used to spend a lot of time over here. Any idea why, or who he was meeting with?"

McDivitt cocked an eyebrow. "You've done your homework. I'd see Ronson around here pretty often, recently. I had the impression that he was spending time with hard-core researchers, to what end I can only speculate. Maybe he had a vision for using some of our research in developing the campus computing infrastructure. He may have actually had some friends here, although the faculty I know have higher standards than that."

"Well, who might have more details about his visits?"

"Before I answer your question, you have to answer one from me. Why are you so interested in this?"

I took a deep breath.

"I didn't know Ronson well. But everyone I've talked with, including you, describes him in a way... well, he was somewhat shady. Cut corners. Didn't always play by the rules. He pissed off people, yet he never was called to account. I keep wondering why not."

McDivitt shook his head. "True. But he's dead. What does it matter?"

"In my business it's always better to prepare for the worst. For the other shoe to drop. That means finding out the deepest, darkest secret that could ever come to light. Doing that kind of digging is like insurance. Or inoculating yourself against a virus. I figure whatever I learn about him is likely to be worse than what any random person, including most reporters, will unearth."

McDivitt snickered and shook his head. "I hope that story works on some people, but I'm not buying it. Just remember that whatever your reasons, if you learn too much you could turn yourself into a marked man, which could have consequences for your career." He sat back and stretched both his arms and legs with a grunt. "But given the way things work around here you might land a big payday from people who were willing to buy you off.

"I'm not interested in giving you the third degree. But I didn't just fall off the turnip truck. In fact, early in my career I actually drove the turnip truck." He looked at me meaningfully. I had no idea what he was talking about.

"I'm sure you have good reasons for delving into Ronson's sordid past. But you're likely to get yourself in serious hot water. One thing I've learned from my years in the salt mines here is that nothing is secret. Most of the time, the ears have walls, and other times, the walls have ears. So my unsolicited advice to you is simply this: watch your back."

"Thanks. But I really do need your help if I'm to pursue this thread. If Ronson's visits were more than just social, would Mark Chabeaux be the right person to ask? Would he be willing to have a candid conversation with me?"

"Well, it's worth a try. If it was something official, it would end up on Mark's desk sooner or later."

"Do you think he'd be willing to talk with me?"

"The only way he'd cooperate would be if I paved the way. He's pretty honest with his buds, and that includes me. But he's deeply suspicious of the people who live in Main Central, and rightly so. They have kept promising us more goodies and then at the last moment find reasons not to allocate money, sort of like Charlie Brown and Lucy with the football. I've told him he should try an end run and make friends with a few legislators, but he's reluctant to play that game. If I explain that you're a good guy, not out to screw him, maybe he'll be willing to talk with you. Stranger things have happened."

"I really appreciate it."

"Give me a day or two."

* * *

I had gotten into the habit of checking my email every time I returned to the office. But this time, the screen was blank. I pushed all the keys but the screen remained dark. I turned the computer off and waited a minute.

But when I turned it on, the screen was blue. After about a minute a single line of text crawled across the middle. "We know what you're up to," it said. I sat there, stunned. Whoever had hacked my computer apparently had knowledge of my recent activities. Probably the same person who followed me and left a note on my car.

If I needed confirmation that I was onto something, this was it. That was the good news. The bad news was the increasingly intrusive nature of the threats. If the message's intent had been to warn me off the case, it had just had the opposite effect.

A second reboot produced no further messages but the blank screen persisted. I called out to Stella. A day without electronic tools in a job like mine was a day pretty much lost. Before I could begin cursing, Stella was at my door.

"What's the trouble, boss?"

I just pointed to the computer.

"Huh. Blue screen of death. Haven't seen one of those in a while." She took off her glasses. "Mind if I fiddle with it a bit? Who knows, I might get lucky."

I stood up and gave her my chair. "Suit yourself."

She fiddled with some controls on the monitor. Then she started pressing keys and moving the mouse around.

"Well, it's dead. Luckily, most of our stuff is backed up to the Great Server in the Sky. So you probably didn't lose much, if anything. Let me call one of the techs. The bad news is, attacks — and that's what it looks like to me, but what do I know — usually aren't isolated events. If it's happened to you, it's likely that it happened to others, maybe hundreds. So it could take the IT staff a while to figure out what's up and to find a solution."

"Well, whatever you can do to make it happen soon, I'd be much obliged."

Stella steamed up her glasses and cleaned them with her flannel shirt tail. "I'll see what I can do. Sometimes, they come quicker if they think it's a challenging technical issue. The prestige of working in Main Central carries some extra juice, although when I tell them it's in the basement that tends to cool their ardor. I'll get on the horn and see what's possible."

"Thanks, Stella."

I looked around the office, wondering if there was any possibility that I was being watched. I had to assume that my surveillance didn't end with the computer.

I began to make a list, on lined paper with a pen, of possible leads to investigate after meeting with Chabeaux. I still thought I needed to see a copy of the actual employment contract. Who knew what else it might contain? There were plenty more layoff victims, but they had a lower priority in my current thinking. I didn't think there was more information that Cody would share, but I needed to keep him in mind, too.

Stella poked her head in to say a tech would be coming by later today. "They said they hadn't had reports of widespread attacks. Yours appears to be a one-off. So we went to the top of the queue. They thought they could have you up and running in a couple of hours or by the end of the day at the latest. They were really interested in doing some forensic work to see if they can figure out where the attack originated, although that's always dicey."

"Thanks."

This gave me an excuse to cut out early. I owed Andrea a dinner and thought my three-alarm chili would fill the bill. I stopped on the way home for some chuck steak, beans, and of course beer. Andrea loved it when I took over in the kitchen. I texted her with a warning to bring her appetite. She probably had already guessed the menu, as this was my go-to meal.

Over dinner, I told her laughingly about the computer hack but decided not to mention the two automobile encounters. She was less than amused.

"You better watch your step," she warned. "If they can get into your office, your computer, who knows where else they'll go? Your payroll file, your bank account, sending bogus information to law enforcement?"

"Let's not go off the deep end," I responded. "It's just one message. They wanted to scare me."

"Well, it worked. On me."

"You, scared? Now that's something I'd pay to see."

She backed off a little. "Well, maybe that's not the right word. More like concerned. Just watch your step, please?" She waved her spoon in my direction while chugging a beer. "And stop trying to weaponize your chili, would you?"

CHAPTER NINE

When I walked into the office the next morning Fran told me that Marilyn Marcuse, the state lobbyist, had already called three times. I checked my phone and discovered that she had texted me while I was driving to work. I called and she picked up on the first ring.

"Hey, what's up?"

"Do you have any idea how details about the new branding campaign might have made their way to the legislature?"

"This isn't exactly a confidential matter, Marilyn. Yarmouth presided over that big rollout which had more than a hundred attendees. There have been a series of emails to the campus. We've had some other events where it was mentioned. And of course the trustees have been briefed."

"Well, the legislator who called me heard one side of the story: vast resources allocated for a project with fuzzy and self-serving goals. Poor fiscal controls. A bad decision in light of the financial restrictions in the state. How parents and students will react when they find out that money is spent in this way rather than on improving the quality of education."

I could see Glanville's fingerprints on this one.

"Are you surprised with any of this?" I asked.

"Only with the speed at which the news has spread."

"So what happens now?"

"I know that if I take this to the staff meeting, the response will be — from some quarters at least — that this isn't something that should concern the legislature. We didn't use state-allocated funds for the project. So it's not like the money was taken from classroom use. And while it may look like a big amount..."

"How much is it?" I had a vague idea but was curious about Marilyn's information.

"The rumor I've heard is a couple of million. And if that's the right order of magnitude, even if you took every penny and put it into raising faculty salaries, for example, it wouldn't amount to much."

"And you're not happy with that explanation?"

"You can't tell a legislator it's none of his damn business. When it comes to higher education, every legislator wants to be perceived by the voting public as a champion for the common folk, the underdogs, against the big, powerful and indifferent university, something we feed into when we respond dismissively.

"Any defensive response from us is likely to prompt the legislator to turn this into a cause célèbre. I can imagine one of our electeds saying, 'I understand, but my constituents aren't going to like this. They're going to ask me to look into it.' It could take the form of an official request to the president demanding a full public accounting and maybe participation in a public hearing. Or, worse, they could appoint a special legislative commission to look into the broad issue of non-essential spending of public funds. No matter where the money comes from, once it ends up in our accounts, many legislators regard that as public money.

"The legislator who called me is very interested in raising his public profile in preparation for running for higher office. And we don't need that kind of PR. There's no way it will come out sounding good. And I haven't even mentioned the media coverage that could result."

"I see. With the cat already out of the bag, what are our options?"

"There isn't any real possibility of the legislature actually inter-fering with the plan, but they can certainly gum up the works in other ways. Public attitudes, even when they are stage-managed by a legis-lator with an ax to grind, ultimately can affect budget discussions, and you don't want anything out there that can serve as a pretext for cutting our budget. So I want to find some way to head this off at the pass."

"You think you can do that without involving Yarmouth?"

"I hope. Ultimately, he may have to defend this. But this wasn't his idea. It was those guys in PPPPE. They never discuss this stuff with me beforehand, just spring it on us by getting the president to sign off."

I heard her exhale, whistling through pursed lips. "In theory I could brief Yarmouth and trot him off to meet with the legislator. But there's so many ways that could go wrong. Yarmouth is hypersensitive when it comes to what he thinks is the gap between the public's per-ception of the university and reality. The likelihood of him becoming defensive on the one hand, or stumbling into an insult to the legislator on the other, is pretty big. I'd prefer not to take that risk."

"So, you gonna handle this yourself?"

"I can do that, but you wanna be my wingman?"

"Dunno. I'm probably as critical of this branding project as whom-ever contacted the legislator. Not sure I would help."

"Truth be told, so am I. It's a pretty stupid way of trying to get more money into this place. The connection between what people call image and dollars on the table is weak. So we'd both be going to this fellow's office with our tongues firmly planted in our cheeks."

"That sounds almost as risky as sending Yarmouth."

"Trust me. I've done this before. I'll rough out a script. The reason I want you there is the same reason a sports broadcast has a 'color man.' It just flows better and is more persuasive with two of us. And this legislator may react better to a man than a woman. Ugly to say, but welcome to my world. So, are you in?"

"I can never say no to you, Marilyn. What happens next?"

"You just sit tight. I'll send you a script and we'll confer, then set an appointment. I think we'll do OK as a team."

"It's your show. I'm just there for comic relief."

A few minutes later McDivitt called. Chabeaux had agreed to talk with me that afternoon. This good news was followed by a knock at my door. Stella.

"Any news about Ronson?" she whispered.

"Nah."

"Did you track down Kingston?"

"No. I put that on hold. He's not listed in the local white pages and I don't know who he hangs with. There may be good ways to reach him but I don't know what they are."

She shut the door and her face assumed a Cheshire grin. "What would you give for his contact information?"

I sat up straight. "Are you kidding? Do you have it?"

"Almost." She reached into her back pocket and pulled out a small notebook. "I've been following the daisy chain, beginning with people I know really well, and moving on to their friends and associates. I've reached about five degrees of separation without the chain falling apart. I have a few more calls to make, a few more favors to call in. I think I'm getting really close.

"This much I do know: after his abrupt departure, ol' Art set off on a long trip. Some people think it was a combination vacation and job search.

"Some claiming inside knowledge say he was pressured steadily by Ronson over a period of years to make things look better financially than they were. These people say that when the wrongdoing was discovered he slowly self-destructed. According to them, he left seeking R&R, or maybe he went into rehab.

"The trail gets sketchy after that. But I'm optimistic that my *confidential sources,*" she really relished rolling out those words to me, "are going to come through. Real soon now, I hope."

"Stella, that would be wonderful. I think Kingston has an important piece of the puzzle. From what I've gathered he and Ronson were really tight."

Stella nodded. "Joined at the cranium."

"And in answer to your question about a reward, pick your favorite brand of Scotch, aged as long as you want."

She made to leave, but turned back one last time. "If you crack this we'll kill the bottle together. Oh, and by the way, you might be the recipient of some blowback from my interactions with the juveniles upstairs. Check your email."

With some trepidation I opened up my newly-restored computer.

Stella's responsibilities as building steward included general health and safety issues. Another case of "additional duties as assigned" with no additional compensation.

TO: Inhabitants of second floor of Main Central
FROM: Stella Maris, building steward
SUBJECT: Your refrigerator

I have been receiving reports with an alarming frequency about the contents of the refrigerator in your Break Room. I went up there today and checked for myself and agree that it is a HEALTH HAZARD! Please do not put your food in the refrigerator and leave it for weeks! Please think of the others on the floor who may want to use it, but not alongside moldy sandwiches and furry cheese! I know that it's easy to forget but if you put food into the fridge it is your responsibility to monitor and remove it when necessary. Remember, there is just one refrigerator for Image Buttressing and Incubation and the folks in Brand Development. Please learn to cooperate. Thank you.

TO: Stella Maris
FROM: Stacy Coughlin, assistant to the vice president of Brand Development
SUBJECT: Refrigerator

Stella, just so you know. My boss received a copy of your memo regarding the contents of the refrigerator and was greatly offended. She had me check with every single employee of our unit and now we know, without a doubt, that none of them have been responsible for leaving food in the refrigerator for excessive amounts of time. That means it must be our colleagues in Image Buttressing and Incubation (IBI). I suggest in the future that you focus your ire on them and leave our employees alone!

TO: Stacy
FROM: Stella
SUBJECT: Refrigerator

Stacy, I know there's bad blood between the people in your unit and those in IBI since the Great Realignment shifted more than 100 people from one unit to the other. But please, don't try and draw me in to your petty disputes. I don't know who is responsible for the mess in the fridge, and lobbing charges at one another (the IBI folks claim BD is responsible) isn't helping to clean things up. The only reason I ended up writing a note to everyone, as you well know, was that communication between the two staffs has become testy to the point of outright nastiness. If the people in IBI hadn't flat-out refused my request to talk to you folks, I wouldn't have become involved at all. If I didn't regard the current situation as a genuine health risk, I would have much preferred to stay out of it.

I suggest that you find ways of opening the lines of communication with your colleagues. You should know that people elsewhere in the building, aware of the second-floor civil war, are starting to refer to your area as The Korean Peninsula.

I hope someone can assume the role of adult and mediate this silly dispute.

TO: Stella Maris
FROM: Ashley von Winkle, assistant vice president for Brand Development
SUBJECT: Your exchange with Stacy Coughlin

I must say I'm astounded at the groundless accusations leveled against my staff! Can't you conduct a simple investigation, identify the do-er of misdeeds, and ban that individual from using the refrigerator? Is that too much to ask for our building steward?

Please, in the future, refrain from tarring everyone with the same brush until you have gathered your facts. I would bring this to the attention of your vice president, but unfortunately, he no longer responds to any of the memos I send him. What is it with you people?

TO: Assistant Vice President Von Winkle
FROM: Stella Maris
SUBJECT: Refrigerator

If communication between two campus units has broken down to the extent that even vice presidents cannot carry on a civil exchange, who am I to try and bring a modicum of decorum to the situation? I will turn this matter over to the campus sanitarian, who unfortunately does not have access to rooms in a sanitarium, which I'm sure he would find useful in this case.

My only recommendation is that one of the units purchase an additional refrigerator to eliminate one source of friction. But the problems certainly go deeper than mold and mildew.

It seems like all of you might benefit from a cooling-off period, but the skills to bring that about are beyond my pay grade. I promise, no more memos. Geez.

* * *

Mark Chabeaux's office was at the back and the executive suite on a lower floor of the building. There was an impressive array of support staff positioned in cubies on either side of the aisle leading to his office.

Chabeaux, dressed in jeans and a plaid flannel shirt, greeted me with a firm grip. He appeared to be in his mid-thirties, with thin, stringy hair. He wore an ancient pair of horn-rimmed glasses, and below his jeans were well-worn hiking boots. I looked quickly around the office and saw a variety of outdoorsy photos: Chabeaux and friends on a mountain peak, on cross-country skis, at a footrace. I could see a family photo on the corner of the desk. When I looked closely at his face, I noticed what looked like permanent red spots on his nose and cheeks, probably a result of overexposure to sun at high altitudes.

"So…" he started. For some reason, every conversation I had with anyone in computer science always began with them saying, "So."

"Dave told me a little about what you wanted to know. I agreed to see you, mostly because Dave asked as a favor, but I don't know how much I can tell you." He grinned, revealing uneven rows of teeth that stretched to both ears.

"This is all for background. It's likely that nothing you tell me will ever see the light of day. And I guarantee you anonymity. I'd just prefer to have this information in my back pocket in case someone from the outside starts asking."

He emitted a grunt that sounded like, "Uh huh."

"If you don't mind, I'll ask you a few questions."

He nodded slightly.

"How well did you know Ronson?"

His eyes went up to the ceiling. I followed his glance and realized that only half the fluorescent bulbs were functional.

"I should really get that fixed," he said. And I waited.

"I certainly wouldn't call him a friend. Or even a close associate. Maybe the most accurate description would be an occasional associate." Chabeaux looked at me, his face full of expectation, trying to be completely accurate but essentially noncommittal.

"It's funny, a lot of people say something like that. I haven't met anyone who says they knew him well or regarded him as a close friend. I know that Ronson spent quite a bit of time visiting over here. Do you know why?"

Chabeaux frowned as if passing a stone. "I'm not sure I want to get into that."

"Well, let me ask this: was he exploring his options, career-wise?"

Chabeaux seemed relieved. "So you know about his contract?"

"Yes. At least about the provision that if he was forced out of his administrative job he became a tenured faculty member here."

"That agreement was signed long before my time. And I was unaware of it until Ronson told me, and if anyone else in the department knew about it they've kept it to themselves. He said there were people in the administration who were gunning for him, and he was looking for a suitable landing place."

"That's one interpretation."

Chabeaux shook his head. "In any case, he was looking at what he might do as a faculty member here."

"I'm curious what you told him."

"I asked around in the department, confidentially, with some people who knew him better than I did. They were candid, which I appreciated given the circumstances. But their evaluations did not exactly constitute ringing endorsements. When I asked him about his work with students he talked about the computing services his shop provided, so I had the clear impression that he had spent no time in the classroom and really had no desire to go there.

"He had a few publications in the general area of computing technology, but it wasn't the kind of work that is a focus for the department. And frankly, it wasn't the cutting-edge work for which we've become somewhat famous. His publications consisted of short reviews or notes in secondary or tertiary journals."

"Let me ask you a hypothetical. If someone with his credentials had submitted a resumé for an open faculty position, would you have recommended he be interviewed?"

"No way. And that was the problem. We inherited someone else's commitment, someone else's mistake. I kept putting him off, hoping the situation in Main Central would be resolved in a way that gave him other options. As time went on that appeared increasingly unlikely, and Jeremy made it clear that he wanted out of his current job.

"I kept trying to present him with alternatives other than a faculty position. We actually talked about administrative jobs at other universities, and I offered to put out feelers for him. But he was unwilling to go that route."

The seven-figure deficits and mismanagement were not likely to make him a viable candidate for positions elsewhere. If he fudged on his resumé and managed to extort lukewarm recommendations from his current bosses, he was running the risk that his new employers would nonetheless find out what had happened. If this occurred after he was hired he'd be fired without a second thought.

"I talked to our dean, and we both met with the provost. She was clearly frustrated by the situation, of which she was not aware until we brought it to her attention. She talked to Yarmouth, and they actually consulted with the attorneys to see if there was any escape clause in his employment agreement." Chabeaux sucked on his lips.

"But they gave us bad news. The entire agreement read as if it had been constructed specifically to protect Ronson against losing his job if he was forced to relinquish administrative responsibilities. I even got a sympathy call from Yarmouth, who assured me he had looked for any way out of the contract and had discussed other options with Ronson, who was immovable. To add insult to injury, the agreement required the university to continue to pay him at his final administrative salary. I was amazed, really amazed, at how much they were paying him."

"Again, hypothetically, what might you have done with him had he been forced upon you?"

Chabeaux shook his head. "Honestly, I don't know. I tried to make it clear to him that there wasn't a good fit. Even though the administration had agreed to make us whole regarding money and faculty lines, there was a serious question of morale. It would've been bad news for the department, and I lost a lot of sleep thinking about alternatives, but I never did come up with any that appeared workable."

"Of course, that's all moot now," I offered.

Chabeaux started to respond but then thought better of it.

"Would any individuals in the department have suffered especially if Ronson had ended up here?"

"I would," he said, raising his hand. "Faculty members often think that department chairs have extraordinary power. I had quietly begun to lay the groundwork for Ronson's arrival here, should it have been necessary. But I'm sure there would have been lots of water cooler gossip about how ineffective I was. I know, because in the past I would've been part of that gossip circle."

"That's too bad. You didn't do anything wrong and were pretty much powerless to remedy the situation."

"I think I would've been collateral damage. The real wrath would've been directed at the dean, the provost and the president. We have some extremely assertive faculty members. I could envision them making a stink with university leadership, the trustees, maybe even legislators and the media. Who knows?" he said with a palms-up gesture, shrugging his shoulders. "And some of these people have access to the movers and shakers in the city. The university could have had a big black eye. The fallout might have been substantial."

"Maybe we all dodged a bullet."

Chabeaux nodded. "I gotta tell you, the more time I spent with Jeremy Ronson, the more amazed I was that he rose to such a position within this university. And when I began to hear the stories of what he'd done and how long he'd gotten away with it…"

"I know. Would the department have suffered in any tangible way, had the deal gone through?"

"Probably not. Although I didn't have it in writing, the provost agreed to make us whole financially. So junior faculty wouldn't be deprived of upward mobility. I wasn't about to put him in a classroom, so our students wouldn't have suffered. No, the damage would have been psychological and political."

Chabeaux looked up again at the failed ceiling bulb and then out the window.

"This was a very sad case for all of us."

* * *

"So how is your investigation going?" Andrea had taken my efforts in the kitchen as a challenge, this time offering something hot (picante) and rich.

"Well, there are two directions I've identified. One is the people who were laid off and their friends. If there were a murder, Cody would be a suspect." I opened two Modelos Negras. "He has motive. And he's at least a little off. He believes he is a modern knight-errant in a world without morals."

"But didn't you say he struck you as kind of a wimp? The kind of guy who lives through his boldest fantasies online. Could you see him as a man of action? And physically, would he even be capable of shoving someone out a window?" Andrea stirred the pot of food while also stirring the pot in the drama I had concocted. She was wearing a cooking apron over shorts. Her stacked heels looked dangerous, for her and anyone who came near.

"True," I said, taking a swig of beer.

She turned to face me, hands on hips. "And another thing: how would he get into a secure building after hours?"

"OK, fair enough. But is it just a coincidence that, according to Liz Bacon, Cody raised the subject of Ronson in an email a few weeks ago, just before the murder? He clearly had an obsession. Maybe he had an inside confederate who worked with him to actually do the deed, or to let him in and provide assistance.

"Then there's Direction Two: the damage that the computer science department would suffer, and actually what the whole university might share, if Ronson had to be given a position in the department. Quite a number of people were unhappy with that idea. So they may have had some motive for wanting him to go away. Whether they wanted it badly enough to make it permanent… I don't think I've met anyone yet who would take direct action. That doesn't mean they aren't out there somewhere."

Andrea kept stirring. "Hun, I don't think you've found yet what you had hoped for. Certainly not enough to get the cops to reopen the case."

"Maybe so."

"I still think you need some real evidence, dear."

"Well, thanks for throwing a cold bucket of reality on my theories."

"You're entirely welcome. So, what comes next?"

"Dunno. In the old B-movies they might bring Cody or Kingston in and sweat a confession out of one of them. Or some gumshoe would unearth evidence of a contract killing, by person or persons unknown. Failing that, I think I'll just keep on keepin' on, gathering info and see what happens."

I could hear the chicken sizzling in the pan and watched as other ingredients made their way into the mix: garlic, tomato, olives and raisins or currants. They were joined by an onion and teaspoon of red pepper bubbling in the oil. "And to change the subject, what prompted the explosion of culinary activity?"

"Hey, you've never seen me get creative in the kitchen?" She turned and flipped a wooden spoon, her other hand holding a beer. "I come from a long line of excellent cooks. Although I usually was too bratty to appreciate it, I grew up in a household with great food, especially when my tias or abuelitas came over. This happens to be my mother's recipe, which she claims was passed down for generations, for a Cuban-style chicken stew. Always served with rice. I loved the way my mother made it, but I felt it lacked... something. We'll see if you can guess my secret ingredient."

"I'm beginning to think some secrets are meant to stay secret."

"Did you really think this investigation was going to be easy, that all the pieces would just fall into place? You should be eager to track down other leads, even if the process is slow. Aren't there a few stones you haven't overturned?"

The aroma of the stew wasn't helping me think through my next moves. My taste buds were standing at attention.

"One thing I'd still like to have is a copy of Ronson's contract. I got some details from Pensativa, and a little from the chair of computer science. But I have no idea what else it might contain. It's just not the same as having the actual written agreement in front of me."

"But can't you find someone who would have the contract and would give you a peek?" The stew was boiling vigorously, sending a plume of fragrant steam up into the fan and throughout the kitchen.

"It doesn't work that way, babe. If I say directly what I'm doing to just about anyone at the university, I am pretty sure I'll be ordered to shut it down or look for work elsewhere. I've run out of people who might recall what was in the agreement. Remember, it was more than twenty years ago."

I watched Andrea pour the rice into a saucepan and add water. She stuck her index finger in the pan. "My mother always told me to measure the water up to the knuckle on my index finger and it would come out perfectly." She smacked her lips.

In a few minutes the rice began boiling. She turned down the heat and covered the pan. Meanwhile, the stew had reached the consistency she wanted, and it too was consigned to a simmer. She wiped her hands on her apron and moved to grab another Modelo. "Glad you saved me some," she said, noting that I was well into my third.

I shrugged. "Must've been thirsty."

"So, if you weren't worried about your job, how would you go about retrieving the employment agreement? Is there one place you can go and find someone who would let you in to browse?"

"There are archives in the library, especially for the papers of former university leaders. But sensitive things, including budget documents and employment contracts, are supposed to be retained in the originating office for as long as they are deemed relevant."

"And if you knew where that office was, could you just call them or write them and make a request?"

"It's actually simpler than that. If the contract is legally a public document, and most things in a public agency are, then all you have to do is file a request with the public records office. Under law, every state agency has to have a person whose job it is to respond to requests like that, to locate the documents in question, determine if they are legally public, and even to black out protected portions of documents whose content otherwise is public. When this whole fiasco began, my first thought was to go ahead and file a request. But my second thought was how this was a particularly quick way to end my university employment."

"Interesting."

Andrea was tapping her spoon on the cutting board, turning it over from head to tail, again and again. "But you don't have to be an employee there to use this office — what did you call it?"

"Public records. No, anyone can use it. Reporters use it a lot. And you don't need to explain why you're making the request. That's the law."

"Hun, how would you like it if I did you a huge favor?" The smile lit up her face.

And it came to me, too.

"Yes, you could do that. I'd help you fill out the paperwork. It's not hard. But you could file a request for Ronson's contract."

Andrea did a little dance. "This sounds like fun. An assistant amateur sleuth."

I gave her a big hug, spun her around and planted a kiss on her partly opened mouth. "We're going to make one hell of a team. The form is really easy to complete. The most important thing, of course, is never mention my name."

"Hey, I'm almost a detective now. I know better than that. All I need is a gun, a fifth of scotch in my desk, a voice like a grinder and a few ex-husbands to complete the profile!"

CHAPTER TEN

Very early the next day, with a fine-tuned script in hand, Marilyn Marcuse and I headed off to our meeting in the capitol. On the two-hour drive, she briefed me on our interlocutor.

Representative Michael Stanwick had been serving about a decade and recently became chair of the higher education committee. He hailed from a small town in a farming region, where the family business provided general supplies for farmers and ranchers. He was elected shortly after he returned from a stint overseas with the Army, where he served in logistics support. Like most rural representatives, he was a Republican, but generally regarded as a moderate.

Stanwick had attended a nearby community college and had an associate degree. His wife, who was staying at home with their two children, had been out of the work force since they married. The children were home schooled.

Since assuming the chairmanship, Stanwick had focused on creating incentives for greater efficiencies in public higher education. He had crossed swords with leaders of the four-year universities, wondering why they couldn't educate students for the same cost as a community college.

"The idea that there are different labor markets for different institutions is one that hasn't really made its way into his consciousness," Marilyn said. "Tenured faculty are simply more expensive than a community college's part-time instructors. But he's convinced that our greater costs are a product of poor management. He draws from his experience as a small business owner and is always talking about 'tightening our belts.' He wants more of the state's young people to participate in higher education but says his constituents are content to have their children at community college. He sees us as part of an urban elite with not much to offer the people who vote for him."

Our job, Marilyn explained, wasn't to change any of his bedrock beliefs. We wanted to convince him that the university was spending the money wisely and that, ultimately, it would have a positive effect on higher education as a whole.

Stanwick, dressed in an open-neck checked shirt and khakis, greeted us with a firm handshake. He was beefy with a shock of sandy hair and wide brown, almost black, eyes.

"Representative, we're happy that you were able to make time in your busy schedule for us," Marilyn said.

"Marilyn, I always have time for you and the university you represent. When I received this information, it alarmed me. You know how protective I am of higher education. But it seems that your leadership is tone deaf to the concerns of many citizens, including the people I represent." My first impression was that we were dealing with a fellow who affected an aw-shucks manner but would have sharp elbows under the boards.

"So let me describe why we decided to undertake this initiative and why we think it's important to the citizens of our state."

Stanwick was taking notes on a yellow pad as Marilyn launched into a brief explanation. We knew we had about twenty minutes to make the case. The nub of the argument we chose to make was that if people realized what a great university they had in their back yard, they would be more likely to believe their tax dollars should support it, even if their sons and daughters didn't go there. The university would create jobs, industries if it were funded properly — that was one of the pillars of the campaign. Ultimately, we were supporting Stanwick's efforts to have higher education grow and thrive.

Marilyn stopped there and waited for his response.

"I'm sure that your initiative is well intentioned," Stanwick was drawing circles around some words on his yellow pad and underlining others. "But a big PR effort isn't going to go over well with the voters in my district."

I cleared my throat. "But the farmers and ranchers in your district, through their trade associations, agree to tax themselves to support marketing efforts for their products around the country and overseas. In a way, that's what we're doing, too. Good efforts alone, without effective promotion, are not going to achieve the results we all want."

Marilyn nodded appreciatively.

Stanwick looked up from his pad. "I see where you're going and I'm not entirely unsupportive. But what my constituents see as a legitimate marketing effort for a private business is not something they are used to seeing in the public sector."

Marilyn piped up. "We put a lot of thought into this. The impetus is coming from our alumni, who supplied the funding. They are mostly businessmen who saw this as a worthwhile investment on behalf of the young people of our state. As the university gains respect and admiration, it's easier to draw resources that will supplement state funding across the board for all institutions. As we move forward, we're hoping to build a grassroots campaign with this initiative as its cornerstone, something that could support you and other legislators concerned about our state's future." Marilyn was just riffing here, I was pretty sure.

"Good luck with that." He drew his hands across his thighs. "I know most of my constituents are stretched pretty thin. Which is why expenditures of this sort would bother them. But I'm not going to make a public issue out of this. I'm not sure I would've made the same decision that President Yarmouth has made, but in this case I'm not going to second-guess him. I can see some merit in doing this, especially since it's your alumni that are carrying the water." Stanwick rose, shook hands, and sent us on our way.

In the parking lot, Marilyn exhaled deeply. "Well, we dodged that bullet. That argument about farmers' marketing cooperatives played pretty well. Glad we were able to come up with that."

"And that stuff about alumni pushing the effort? And a grassroots campaign?"

"Well, it's slightly true. Some of our biggest donors share the administration's view that the university is underappreciated, and that this lack of recognition leads to funding problems. They're footing the bill. As for the grassroots, well, our ad campaign will carry a link for additional information. So it's true at least in principle. Of course, Representative Stanwick knows our leadership has never been successful with building grassroots campaigns."

"So would you declare the fire under control at this point?"

"With this legislator at this time. But stay tuned. There could be others."

* * *

First thing back I called Don Glanville.

"Guess where I was? Meeting with one of our esteemed legislators. He had received a call from someone, he wouldn't say who, complaining about the waste of money on the university's re-branding effort. You wouldn't know anything about that, would you?"

If you can hear a smirk, I heard one. "Now why on earth would I do that? Am I the kind of guy who wants to air dirty linen in public?"

"Is that a rhetorical question?"

"My dear friend, I enjoy stirring the pot, vigorously. But the idea I would take my complaints outside, well, that's just shocking."

I tried not to laugh. "I'm not going on a witch hunt. Even when I'm pretty sure there is a witch. By now so many people know about the project it's a fool's errand."

"While I wasn't involved I can't say I'm sorry to see it happen, despite the heartburn it may have caused you and the university leadership."

"While we're on the subject, have you and your fellow-travelers figured out a course of action with your complaints against Yarmouth?"

"Actually, I was going to call you about that. Do you think any reporters would be interested if the faculty took a vote of no confidence?"

"Only if it passed. Is this tied to the branding project?"

"Of course. If Yarmouth wants to waste his own time, and that of his lackeys, that's one thing. But he wants us to be, what did they call us, oh yeah, his 'foot soldiers'. It's simply unconscionable to waste resources on these stupid projects. The rollout was bad enough. But to follow that with the fiasco in the stadium. He must have a screw loose. Seriously, we should all be a little scared of what might come next."

"So you're going to bring the motion to the senate?"

"I can't, because I'm not a senator, but there's a growing group of unhappy people. Mostly senior faculty who have watched their compensation fall consistently behind our peer universities. A bunch of them are hopping mad."

The last few years had been rough for the state economy, and it wasn't unusual for salaries of all state employees to lag when that happened. It's likely they would never catch up with the market. Such was life in the public sector.

Faculty, more than any other group I had encountered in my career, carried a deep sense of outrage over what they perceived as a great injustice. But to most people not at a university, faculty salaries were still lofty almost beyond belief, comparisons to professors elsewhere notwithstanding.

I helped Don play out the scenario.

"Do you think you can get a majority of senators?"

"Hard to say. We haven't done a nose count. But the number who are unhappy is growing."

I took that as a no.

"Has anyone talked with the trustees? Even if you have a majority in the senate, it won't mean much by itself. The trustees don't usually follow the actions of the senate closely if at all. Just shipping them your resolution isn't going to make much of an impression."

"Oh, we'll make sure that they're aware. They didn't get to where they are by ignoring incompetence and sanctioning waste. They're in a position of public trust and they know it."

Stella had knocked softly on the door, saw that I was on the phone and held up both hands in an "I'm sorry" gesture. I mimed that I'd come to see her when the call was over.

"Don, that's all well and good. But remember that it was this board, these very people, who selected Yarmouth. They talk with him just about every day, and he usually consults them on important initiatives before they are launched, and that includes the branding campaign. Unless he's done something egregious, they aren't going to vote to remove him. Unless you can get the support of an overwhelming majority of the senate, you haven't even earned their consideration."

"I never took you as an apologist for this administration. I must say I'm disappointed."

"Don, I have no opinion on whether Yarmouth is doing a great job or not. But assuming you and your colleagues have sufficient evidence to call for his ouster, I was merely suggesting the course of action, the steps that might lead to the outcome you desire. Or not."

I heard a low hum through the phone. People like Glanville enjoy kicking up dust without worrying about the outcome. They tend not to like it when you point out how empty their actions are likely to be.

"But that wasn't the question you asked when we started our conversation. You were asking about media coverage of the senate vote. I let reporters know of issues that are coming before the senate. So if this is on the agenda, I'll inform them. And if they're interested in a story should I direct them to you?"

"Let me think about that a bit. Nothing like becoming a target for the wrath of the administration if we're unsuccessful. Not that I'm able to keep my mouth shut anyhow. I'll confer with some of my partners in crime and let you know. What do you think the chances are that we'll get some interest?"

"Right now? I'd say one in three. Maybe less. There's been no previous evidence that Yarmouth's tenure is meeting with disfavor, so this doesn't fit in to any existing narrative. We haven't had a major scandal on his watch. From what I've seen at the trustee meetings he seems to have them charmed. So something like this comes out of the blue. I don't think reporters will be interested. And if they are, you might not like their angle."

"How so?"

"Oh, I could imagine a story that began with a lead stating that a small group of disaffected faculty is mounting a vague effort to have Yarmouth removed. When it comes to actionable behavior, they can only say it comes down to money — money that they would choose to have spent in what they regard as better ways. Such as on them."

"You think the story would take that approach?"

"Don, knowing what I know about the media, I'd say it's pretty likely that the story will follow that line. Either that or the man-bites-dog theme, where the normally docile faculty turn on the people who butter their bread."

"Well, that won't do our cause any good. Maybe we don't want news coverage of our motion."

"Maybe not. But remember, your senate meetings are public and several reporters have a standing request for copies of the agenda. So there's no real way to hide this from them if you want to. If I were you, I'd hope that they ignored it."

"I'd forgotten how infrequently senate actions get attention. When I was chair, I'd call or drop notes to reporters whenever we were doing something interesting and I never received a nibble."

"You forget. There was that story when the students demonstrated over the creation of a new distribution requirement. They sat in and barricaded the entrance. You had to move to an alternate location. That got plenty of notoriety. I think I remember seeing you interviewed on television."

"I'd blocked out that debacle. It was hard to try and explain what we were doing in a way the public might understand. In retrospect, I did a piss-poor job. And I don't relish finding myself in that kind of situation again."

"I think you and your friends need to figure out if you are more interested in expressing yourselves than actually bringing about change."

"I suppose I should thank you. But this wasn't the conversation I was expecting."

"I assumed you'd prefer candor. You're welcome nonetheless."

Stella was waiting for me at her desk. "This is too public," she cautioned, leading me back to my office and shutting the door.

"This is about Art Kingston."

"Have you tracked him down?"

"I've been working with people who actually know him and with whom he still has a level of trust. Both of them."

"And?"

"He might. Might. Be willing to talk with you."

"That's great. Thank you so much."

"Don't go thanking me yet." She pulled a sheet of paper from her pocket. "He has certain conditions that you'll have to meet before he agrees to an interview."

"Such as?"

"First: no recording and no photos."

"Fine."

"Everything he says is completely off the record, not for attribution. It's all completely on background."

"I can live with that."

"Even the import of the discussion cannot be communicated to law enforcement, internal or external auditors, any state government employee or to anyone in the news media."

"He really is concerned about legal action, isn't he? Makes me wonder what he was involved with that we don't know about. I'm not in a position to bargain, so OK."

"You can't make him part of a daisy chain, what in legal circles they call 'fruit of poisoned tree.' If what he says leads you to contact someone else, you can't disclose, even in code, about how you came to contact this individual."

"I think that's already covered in other stipulations, but I don't have a problem with that."

"The interview cannot occur in any public place where it can be overheard or where the meeting can be witnessed by third parties. It cannot occur in the private home of either of the participants. Kingston's preference is a rented meeting room or a motel. If a room must be rented, it should be paid for in cash so there is no credit card paper trail."

"Geez, is this guy giving me secrets about the theft of the Vermeer from the Gardner Museum? Or the shooter on the Grassy Knoll?"

"Yeah, he gives paranoids a bad name. But he did not indicate a willingness to negotiate."

"Stella, do you have any instincts here? Is it worth all this bullshit just to talk with him?"

She folded up the paper. "I'll put this through the shredder. I don't know what to advise. How bad you want to talk to this guy? Every-thing that went wrong financially went through his hands. He and Ron-son talked every day, or so I've been told, and Kingston knows more about the finances of IT than anyone alive. He may know even more about Ronson than we could guess. How likely is it that he'll tell you something you don't already know? How likely is it that he'll be tell-ing you the whole truth? Those are questions for you to answer, not me."

"If I agree to all the conditions, what's the next step?"

"I get back to his people with suggestions for a day, time and lo-cation."

I thought for a few seconds. "All right, I'm in. I'm thinking a mo-tel is best, one of those cheapos on the edge of the city. They always strike me as kinda sketchy, but I doubt they're monitoring guests' comings and goings."

I looked on the Web and found the Wayfarer's Inn, suitably cheap and nondescript. Some reviews suggested that guests had an unsafe feeling, and the showers were frequently broken. But the price was right. I told Stella I was willing to meet Kingston there late tomorrow afternoon, a Saturday. I'd arrive a few minutes early, pay for the room in cash, and wait for his text.

At the end of the day she heard back via third parties. The meeting was set. I thought carefully about what I might ask him.

*   *   *

The Wayfarer's Inn was everything the reviews had promised and less. Located on a busy thoroughfare a few blocks from the city limits, it was a stubborn, down-at-the heels holdout in a neighborhood about to become overrun with destination shopping. I pulled into the lot around back, paid at the front desk under an assumed name and got the key. The desk clerk, a dispirited young man perhaps of South Asian origin, scarcely looked away from ESPN as he told me checkout time was noon.

The room was moderately clean with interior furnishings that had seen better days. There was a double bed, dresser, television and a single chair. There was really only one place for the chair, just to the left of the door and a few feet from the bed. I figured I should claim the bed and give Kingston the comfort of Corinthian plastic.

A few minutes later my phone buzzed. Two word text: "Kingston here."

I responded with the room number and pulled out my note pad.

Ten minutes later there was a knock. I opened the door to a short, rotund, hirsute, bug-eyed gnome. He was dressed in a flannel shirt whose pattern appeared to have bled, shaggy jeans, and western boots with a tooled leather pattern.

I extended a hand, but he just shrugged and walked into the room, closing the door.

"Good location," he wheezed. "Off the beaten track. Anonymous." He looked around the room. "You aren't recording this?"

"No, per the agreement, all I brought was this notepad."

I offered him the room's only chair and he slumped into it, mopping his brow with a shredded tissue, leaving flecks on his forehead and pants.

"You aren't the easiest guy to track down."

"After what I've been through, you wouldn't be either. I've been blamed for everything short of murdering Nicole Brown Simpson. Living under constant threat of having my employment terminated without notice. Not to mention the physical threats. And that was before Jeremy croaked." He paused to catch his breath. Kingston was a wreck. His face was a pasty white and the hanging flesh on his neck vibrated when he gestured.

"Well, I appreciate your willingness to talk to me. But I'm curious, after dodging everyone else, why you agreed to this meeting."

"The fiasco over which Jeremy presided brought down a number of careers, including my own. I hung on for a while, looking for a soft landing place, first inside and lately outside the university. But the rumor mill is stronger than whatever equity remained in my reputation. Anonymous charges of fraud, mismanagement and corruption are impossible to refute; it's like whack-a-mole. They preceded or followed every letter of introduction I wrote, every job application I completed. I'm not even sure that moving to a different city will help, but that's probably my next option. Given that, I resolved to take modest steps to correct the record, so someone eventually knows what actually happened."

The oration left Kingston gasping for breath. He saw me looking at him with concern. "Don't worry. I may look like a wreck. Well, actually I *am* a wreck. But my condition is not as bad as it looks. Still, that also is playing a part in my decision to talk with you. At this point, all I have is shreds of what used to be an excellent reputation. I don't want my legacy to be shaped entirely by those with an ax to grind. I don't want the evil that I allegedly did to live after me and allow the good, and there was a lot of that, to be interred along with my bones. Not if I can help it.

"I know that whatever I tell you, it's going to sound self-serving, especially with Jeremy gone, so I wasn't ready to do this publicly. There's no one left who is willing to corroborate most of what I say, and even if Jeremy were still alive I'm not sure he'd be willing to vouch for me. I'm just hoping that, longer term, my comments make their way into a more accurate version of what happened in the IT department. Talking with you is the best offer I've received. The only one that didn't come from a party with a vested interest in a certain outcome. And that includes the media.

"In the short term, I know I'm fucked. But I realized that in giving you a truthful version of what happened, I had nothing to lose." He mopped his brow. Some color had returned to his face, but it was still blotchy.

The logic of his explanation escaped me but I moved ahead. "How long did you work for Jeremy? I heard that you may have been his best friend at the university."

Kingston shrugged. "I met him shortly after he arrived here and it's true, we did hit it off. I'm a numbers guy and Jeremy focused on the big picture, so our partnership — and I'd call it that, not a friendship, as I'll explain — appeared to be a match made in heaven. He'd come up with ideas, creative plans, in some cases visionary projects, and his question to me was, 'How can we make this happen?' And I'd find a way, push money around in different accounts — really, standard budgeting things. Nothing underhanded or even questionable. In the early days, when we had major audits, they always went through clean as a whistle.

"Those were heady times. Jeremy had been handpicked to lead the computing revolution on campus. He cut a sweet deal which promised what seemed like a limitless flow of resources to finance modernization. In those early years, the faculty loved us. Especially the guys in the sciences and engineering, who were early to recognize that this was a new era and that to keep up in their field they were going to need a nimble infrastructure that allowed massive computing at speeds that couldn't have been imagined a few years ago. Jeremy had enough foresight to hire very bright people and give them the freedom to follow what at times appeared to be crazy notions. But it all seemed to work."

Kingston paused to catch his breath. "And it worked for quite a while because of Jeremy's experimental approach. If we didn't fail fairly often, it meant we weren't pushing the limits. That was Jeremy's philosophy. And more times than not, Jeremy's approach was vindicated, although sometimes later rather than sooner.

"We were getting calls from IT departments at universities all over the country and even from abroad. They were asking how we did what we did. We didn't have much to offer them beyond our very generous funding model and an unprecedented free hand. We were always presenting at conferences in front of standing room only crowds.

"We thought it was going to go on forever." Kingston looked at me and then down at his boots, covered with red mud.

"What happened?"

Kingston patted his breast pocket and looked up. "Nervous habit. Doc made me give up smoking six months ago but it's still a reflex." He paused and breathed deeply. "I've had a lot of time to think about how it all turned sour. Depending on how I feel, each day I have a different take on it.

"Today, I'd say the basic lesson is that vision can take you only so far in the absence of sound management. People create wealth in the private sector by identifying the Next Big Thing, but how many of them are able to correctly identify the Next Big Thing after that? I'd say very few. Maybe we were a couple of standard deviations above the mean with our vision. But we had the hubris to believe we could continue on that path forever.

"I should have known that things were leaving the tracks when, confronted by a challenge or conflicting bit of information, we responded by trotting out one of our slogans rather than thinking critically about situations. We came down with a terminal case of wildly overoptimistic groupthink. Not every problem is an opportunity; sometimes, it's simply a problem. You can't address every challenge by creating another set of 'Big Hairy Audacious Goals.'

"We had been so successful with our own inventions that we thought we had cornered the market on creativity. We completely missed the big shift in the private sector's ability not just to generate highly flexible consumer technology, which everyone could see, but also the 'pro-sumer' stuff: technology a bit closer to the edge, designed for power users both within the academy and elsewhere. Some smart guys realized they could make big bucks with higher margins by serving a small group of top-end users. Those companies had research capabilities we couldn't even dream about. In the early years the stuff we developed was widely copied and, in some cases, actually licensed by other universities, but the tide went out and we were left on an island pretty much by ourselves." Kingston rubbed his boots together and the red mud fell on the carpet in big chunks.

"How does this relate to the unit's growing budget problems?"

Kingston shifted uneasily in the chair. "We always had a complex budget. We were funded by a mix of allocations from the administration, revenue from campus clients, some grant money and partnerships with other institutions that were using our inventions. So there was always some fancy dancing in trying to make the numbers come out right. But overall, we were running a pretty tight operation. In fact, there were some years where we had more revenue than expenses.

"As with many crises, it was a convergence of things that all came to a head in a short period of time. Just about all our revenue sources began to shrink. Our ability to innovate seemed to slow down. A lot of our partnerships fell away. The favored position we had achieved with major grantors just evaporated.

"But most important, the budget czars in the central administration who came on board a few years ago had a different view of IT. They saw our operation as a service that needed to carry its own weight without a subsidy. Our core allocations were reduced and we were supposed to make it up with 'novel sources of revenue,' whatever those were."

"How did Ronson react to his loss of favored status?"

"At first he argued. Jeremy never minced words, and calling his colleagues idiots didn't win him any style points. Despite all the years he'd spent in bureaucracies, he behaved as if he were an entrepreneur who was entitled to call all the shots.

"He appealed all the way up the food chain, including to the president's office. When they refused to reconsider, he went into denial. We'd go over the numbers and the reality was the budget couldn't be made to balance unless there were a different kind of organization in place, one that was smaller, provided fewer services and narrowed its scope of operations to areas where you could imagine generating revenue. I presented this to Jeremy in the plainest way I could. He knew precisely what this meant for his empire."

"So what did he do?"

For the first time in our conversation, Art Kingston smiled. "Nothing. He did nothing."

"How's that?"

"He made a conscious decision, when they wouldn't listen to him, to let the entire operation go to hell financially. His attitude was 'I'll show them.' And so we continued to operate as we always had, except that now our revenue came nowhere close to equaling expenses."

"That must've put you in an awkward situation."

He shook his head. "I had faith in Jeremy. He wasn't into seppuku or any other form of self-sacrifice, at least that hadn't been his MO. I assumed that he was playing a calculated game of chicken, that he was calling their bluff. Except it didn't happen."

"So what did you do?"

Kingston emitted a noise that sounded like half-sigh, half-wheeze. He paused for a long time; I sat still, waiting. "I did what budget people do. Keeping track of accounts, making sure bills were paid, even after the numbers turned red. It never dawned on me that there would be no follow-up, that we'd be allowed to operate pretty much as if nothing had changed, that there was no 'come to Jesus' meeting with the moneybags.

"Our budgets started to look weird. To a guy like me, anyhow. Like Enron at the turn of the last century, I expect, in its final days. I kept waiting for the phone to ring announcing that they — the central administration budget people — were calling in our loan, our overdraft.

"As time went on and our deficits accumulated, it became obvious that a number of people outside of IT were in denial. It was inconceivable that no one in the rest of the university had noticed our growing fiscal imbalance. It was starting to be big money. De facto, the administration was bankrolling us, making a large and growing loan with no discussion about repayment or restructuring. I was flabbergasted." Kingston had taken out another tissue, trying to stanch the dripping from his forehead and nose.

"How long did this go on?"

"Years."

"Years?"

He shook his head. "Crazy. We had all pretty much adjusted to the new status quo. Only a handful of us were aware of the details of our situation, although there was a high degree of suspicion among our senior managers.

"Then one day, seemingly out of the blue, the Sword of Damocles fell. To this day I don't know what triggered it. If Jeremy knew, he didn't tell anyone. Maybe they just reached their limit with being a sugar daddy. Maybe Jeremy hurled the wrong insult at the wrong people.

"Anyhow, Jeremy and I were called into a meeting with no notice. Sitting around the room were Dave Judd, the university's CFO; Francis Nickerson, from internal audit; and Denise Twitchel, the executive vice provost.

"They proceeded to read us the riot act, albeit in hushed and measured tones, for about twenty minutes. Several times I looked over at Jeremy, trying to get a read on his reaction. The word that came to mind was 'bemused.'"

"He wasn't upset? Embarrassed? Angry? Maybe even a little scared?"

"Far from it. He stared at the ceiling, stretched his legs, looked out the window, even cleaned his fingernails. All this time I'm expecting him to say something, even something snarky. But he didn't respond. At all.

"When the peroration was done, Judd began to outline the course of action. Essentially, IT was going to be put in receivership. Jeremy and I were going to be stripped of authority. New leadership would be given a 'decent interval' to begin turning things around and repaying the debt. But they also would be expected to slow the bleeding immediately. Which I was sure meant massive, precipitate layoffs across the organization. And the meeting ended.

"I expected we'd be given our walking papers, or at least a deadline to find another job. So I asked Jeremy about it. He began singing a song from *Willy Wonka*. 'I have a golden ticket,' it went. I thought he had popped a gear."

Kingston sat up in the chair, clearly approaching the end of his narrative. "We went our separate ways. We'd have lunch after that from time to time, but he seemed to be reacting to his changed circumstances with equanimity."

Kingston reached again for his phantom cigarettes. "It was months later that I learned, via the grapevine, about Jeremy's employment contract. No wonder he was so sanguine." He paused and looked me in the eye for the first time. "I assume you know about his contract?"

"I do."

Kingston nodded and continued. "New leadership was appointed the next day. The day after that the layoffs began. It was ugly, really ugly. I don't know how many people tried to call Jeremy directly for an explanation, but I must've had fifty calls. I set my phone to go direct to voicemail; I didn't know what to say to people. They were angry. Several of them made threats."

"Any that you recall?"

"Oh, they were all over the map. Lots of swearing. People telling me I'd never work in this city again, that they'd track down any future employers and give them all the dirt. Not far from the truth, it turned out. Some threatened me, or Jeremy and me, with physical harm customarily including exquisite tortures in front of applauding crowds."

"Did the people identify themselves? Did you recognize voices?"

Kingston laughed. "These were smart people. If they actually intended mayhem they weren't going to give me material for a court order. I thought there were a few voices I recognized. At first I didn't take the threats seriously, but the sheer volume did change my

behavior. I'd double lock my door. Take circuitous routes to run er-
rands. Didn't walk any place where I'd be alone on the street."

"What about Jeremy?"

"He was a hard guy to read. He let me know he was consulting
with his attorney and I assumed it was to hold the university to the
letter of his contract. He went on his shambling way. I never could
figure out what occupied his time after that. Officially he was given
some kind of job description having to do with long-term planning,
but insiders knew this was a fig leaf.

"I had taken my cue from Jeremy for so long I thought that maybe
he'd find a soft landing spot and take me with him. I still thought the
guy was brilliant. I figured he'd learn from his mistakes and still would
go on to do great things. He had a kind of reverse charisma, with a
personality so off-putting that it was compelling. I had hitched my
wagon to his star for so long that it seemed a good idea to let the situation play itself out.

"But we had never been really close in the way that actual friends
are, and he wasn't about to confide in me now. He agreed to have
lunch periodically but the conversation was perfunctory. I couldn't get
a read on what he planned to do next.

"I began looking for work elsewhere while I still had a job. I
wasn't sure why they had kept me around. Maybe they hoped to flip
me and use whatever information I had to break Jeremy's contract.
But over the following months I came to realize that my situation was
untenable and there was no hope of future employment on campus.

"Finally, I looked at the nest egg I had accumulated, calculated
how long it might last and decided to resign. The situation was just too
awkward. I couldn't figure out to whom I should send the resignation
letter: was it Jeremy or the new interim head of IT? I didn't want to
call and ask, so I just addressed it to both of them." Lines of stress ran

deeply in his face. He was pretty well spent by his debriefing. But I had a couple more questions.

"Did you keep in touch with anyone after you left?"

"I'm afraid all those bridges had been torched."

"When you heard about Jeremy's death, what did you think?"

"My reaction was mixed. I still admired a lot of what he had accomplished. He brought the university into the twenty-first century in computing and in many ways was a trailblazer. But his decline and fall resembled a Greek tragedy."

"The police, with the concurrence of the medical examiner, ruled his death an accident," I said. "They found no evidence of violence on his body, no evidence of a fight. No drugs or alcohol. And no note. What do you think?"

Kingston tore his tissue into shreds and tossed it in the nearby trash can. "What the hell do I know? If the police think it was an accident, who am I to second guess them? Who knows what went on inside that complex, weird brain of his? I suppose anything is possible."

"I suppose so. But just between us, I can't get past the notion that with so many people bearing him ill he could have been the victim of a clever criminal."

Kingston's eyes narrowed. He threw his arms out to his sides. "Who cares? The guy is gone. The how, what does it really matter? I prefer to look at the arc of his life, and I see his death as a fulfillment of his fate. Preordained in a way, the seeds of his own destruction carried in his very nature. By whose hands? In the end, does it really matter? Not to me. His story is complete."

"And yours?"

He shrugged. "I still want to have a life. I figure a numbers guy, even with a besmirched reputation, can always find employment. I'll probably have to take a pay cut and a step down in responsibility. And almost for sure I will have to pick up stakes and move. But I have a decade or more left before going out to pasture, if I manage to hang on to my health. I'll rebuild my reputation. I still think that the top leadership of the university bears a major responsibility for what happened, although I'm sure if confronted with the facts they'd find a way to weasel out."

* * *

Driving back to Andrea's, I replayed my conversation with Kingston.

I wasn't entirely convinced that he had been truthful. Kingston had presented a self-serving version of events and his relationship with Ronson, but their actual relationship had to be more complicated. Surely he must harbor some resentment for having his career and his health devastated by Ronson's actions. He struck me as being cold-blooded enough to develop a plan that would accelerate the arc of Ronson's life with a well-placed shove. I wouldn't trust the guy as far as I could throw him.

Despite his physical condition I listed him in the suspect category.

Kingston's version did reveal a level of indifference and incompetence among people in key leadership positions that took my breath away, and that part I found very convincing, based on my own experience and the gossip I heard. Even by those standards this was an extreme case. To permit deficits in the millions to accumulate for years, without any effort to intervene, seemed inexplicable. There was lots of culpability to toss around. It did make me wonder who else had been extended such friendly loan terms, and ultimately who was picking up the bill. There may have been a host of other scandals ripe for unveiling, ones I might just stumble across if I opened the right door. Or the wrong one.

That evening I helped Andrea fill out the Request for Public Records form. It was absurdly simple. Just her name, address, phone and email, and the records she was seeking. I told her to put in the following information:

"I am seeking the employment contract between the university and Jeremy Ronson, the former Vice President for Strategic Infrastructure Support and Vice Provost for Systems Design. The document should date from the occasion of his initial employment by the university. It should bear the signature of the university president at that time, which should be Acting President George Pennybaker. I am requesting this document and any modifications or amendments that may have occurred subsequent to his employment.

"I would also like copies of any performance reviews conducted of Mr. Ronson in his time at the university."

I also decided that I'd have Andrea file a second, separate request, for the sake of completeness:

"I am seeking any correspondence (including email) to or from Mr. Ronson, or involving anyone in the Office of the President, Office of the Provost, Division of Human Potential and Worker Actualization (Human Resources), University Attorney, College of Technology and Building the Future (Engineering), or the Department of Societal Improvement Through Digital Design (Computer Science) that refers to his employment contract or, more broadly, to issues surrounding Mr. Ronson's continued employment at the university."

"That should do it," I told her. "If they call with any questions, rather than responding immediately, tell them you want to think carefully about your answer and will get back to them. Then we can figure out what to say. And ultimately, any response to them should be in writing, in case they start getting sticky."

"No problem. How quickly do you think we'll get the contract?"

"It shouldn't be hard to locate, so it should be a matter of a few days if we're lucky. The second request is more of a fishing expedition and could take months. It probably won't have anything useful, but you never know."

In truth, I didn't know what I was looking for even in the contract. I was hoping that some language there would point in a direction that would help solve the mystery. Or at least provide additional leads.

Andrea turned to me. "Hey, you know, this is fun. I've never gotten involved in private investigator work. If this pans out, I might consider it for my next career."

"If this pans out, I might be forced to join you."

CHAPTER ELEVEN

The next morning, I noticed a long scratch on the side of my car. Looking closer, I realized it wasn't just a long gouge but a series of x's and vertical scratches as well as a deep horizontal line, right down to the metal. Although I distinctly remembered locking the car, a handwritten note was on the driver's seat:

Trust me, we can do a lot worse. And if you don't care about your own big nose, think about your girlfriend.

I ran back in the apartment and shook Andrea awake. Normally she wouldn't have to get up for several hours and reacted in groggy anger.

"What the fuck?"

Still shaking her shoulders, I showed her the note.

"If you don't want to be part of this, I'll understand. I don't know how serious these people are, whether they're just trying to scare me off or are willing to do something more."

Andrea was fully awake now. "What the fuck?"

"I'd suggest, to be safe, that you don't drive your car to work. Try not to be by yourself. Be aware of where you are and who is around you."

"Now you're scaring me!"

"I'm just suggesting that you take prudent precautions."

"And what about your investigation?"

I paused and held her hands. "If you want me to stop, it's done. If you feel unsafe, then it's over."

Andrea looked around. "Where is that form we need to send to the university to request the contract? I want to mail it myself, right now. I'm not foolish, but I also don't respond well to threats."

I kissed her on the forehead. "I was hoping you'd say that. But if at any point you change your mind…"

She shook her head. "Ain't gonna happen. But you be careful. If they want to harm anyone, it would be you, not me. You take care."

I felt I owed Stella some details so I called her into my office first thing Monday morning. She entered, shut the door and sat down.

"So you saw Art Kingston?"

"Indeed I did."

"What did you learn?"

"A number of things. First, Kingston regards Ronson's demise as a kind of Greek tragedy: Someone with prodigious gifts also possesses one enormous flaw, which causes his world to unravel."

"Huh. Well, if I forget about half of what I've heard about Ronson I could see how he might come to that conclusion. Real hero worship stuff?"

"Exactly, if you take what Kingston said at face value. Probably the thing that surprised me most was how long a leash Ronson was allowed. IT had been accumulating deficits for a long time before the administration pulled the plug. Lots of people knew the budget was circling the drain but no one intervened."

"You'd love the gossip when the budget people get together," Stella said. "Chasing the money is a time-honored game. In some cases it actually works. You have to show you can't operate on the money you've been allotted. When they call you in to complain about the red ink, you ask them which part of the operation they'd like to eliminate. If you're doing a good job and they like you, then you have a good chance of having your budget boosted. If not…."

"…They show you the door."

"Precisely. But there are many cases where it's almost the only way to get your budget adjusted." Stella looked down on her fingernails and blew in their general direction. "Not that I would ever stoop to such trickery."

"Of course not. But Ronson and Kingston must have set a record for abusing that leeway."

"From what I hear, that unit still is carrying a sizable debt. They've tried to impose a use tax on the entire campus for the services they provide, but there's been huge pushback."

"I don't understand about how our central budget people could look at a deficit that grows and grows and ignore it for so long. Why would they do that?"

"I can only speculate," Stella said, adjusting her glasses. "Maybe they figured that Ronson and company would eventually lose their nerve and curtail their overspending voluntarily. Maybe they lacked the authority for a crackdown. Maybe the number had to reach a certain size before intervention could occur."

Stella shifted in the chair. "So, does Kingston's tale bring you any closer to figuring out what happened to Ronson?"

"I don't know what to think. I know a lot more about Ronson and his sleazy empire than I ever cared to know. But I'm not sure I'm a lot closer to answering the 64-dollar question."

"Let me know if I can help any more. I love a mystery."

"And let me know about that Scotch. I owe you."

In light of my conversations with Kingston and Cody, as well as what I'd learned from Mark Chabeaux and Pensativa, not to mention the threats, I thought it was time to test the waters with the campus police.

* * *

I figured my best shot was another discreet conversation with Phil Symonds. I thought he would take what I had found seriously and give me an honest reaction.

Symonds was either very busy or deliberately trying to dodge me. But I hadn't been a journalist for nothing. After waiting a day for him to return calls made to his desk phone, I dialed his private cell.

"Officer Symonds."

"Hey Phil. You're a hard guy to get ahold of. I was beginning to think that it was something I said."

"No no no. Not at all. Just had a lot of paperwork. We're having another reorg over here and they've kicked me upstairs a bit. Lots of forms and training. That kind of thing."

"I should probably congratulate you on your promotion. At the risk of wearing out my welcome, I'd like to revisit the topic of the conversation we had a while ago."

"If you remember…"

"I know, you told me to leave police matters to the police. I must admit I didn't do that. But what I've found has left me with some questions I need to bounce off someone, and I think that someone should be you."

"This is dicey territory, Mike. I shouldn't need to tell you that. Once an investigation is closed it's pretty much off limits. We're not allowed to spend time on it. And this one, because of the personage involved, is especially sensitive."

"I know that. I've tried to be careful with what I've done so as not to arouse anyone's suspicions about what I was doing. But there's an accumulation, a lot of strange circumstances. Look, if we talk much longer I'm going to need to veer away from generalities. Why don't we just meet after work in a suitably obscure location. I promise it will be brief."

There was a long pause. "Just remember, this conversation never happened. And the meeting, that didn't happen, either."

Phil suggested an old tavern in a changing neighborhood still populated by modest bungalows and craftsman homes. But many of the older houses had given way to multi-story luxury condos with stunning views of the mountains and occasional peek-a-boos of the water. It was a popular neighborhood with the city's nouveau riche, especially from the tech community.

The tavern had survived by moving upscale with a definite foodie twist to its menu. Lots of locally sourced meat and vegetables, and an entire page devoted to gluten-free options. They had a large bar with many varieties of microbrews and "heirloom" distilled spirits.

We ordered craft beers on tap and found a vacant corner table.

"Phil, thanks for agreeing to meet with me. I know this is outside your ordinary duties. It's outside my ordinary duties. But I just needed to talk with a professional, to get a reality check."

Phil kept glancing around sidelong and over his shoulder. His legs were squarely on the floor under the table, a posture from which he could jump up and leave at a moment's notice. His expression was somber, even a bit sour. He wore a flight jacket bunched up at the collar, and his head seemed pulled in like a turtle trying to get back into a too-small shell.

"I keep wondering why I'm here."

"Because you're a good guy and agreed to do me a favor, that's why. And I appreciate it."

"Let's keep the preamble short. Tell me what's on your mind."

"When we met last time, I told you I thought there was something funny about the circumstances of Ronson's death."

"And I know that you remember what I told you."

"Yes. But I felt something was missing. So I did a little research. Talked to a few people."

Symonds showed no surprise. He was staring into his beer, taking occasional sips. "I guess that's what people like you do. Former journalists, I mean."

"I found that a lot of people hated Ronson. Not just disliked him, but really loathed him. Many held grudges that wouldn't go away, for good reason. There are powerful people within the university who would have liked him to disappear. In addition, there is a group of maybe fifty former employees, a number of whom felt he had ruined their careers, maybe even their lives. I met one fellow who still bore his anger as if the layoffs had happened yesterday. The idea of revenge was still very much alive to him. He had even developed scenarios involving ways of punishing Ronson."

I caught my breath, hoping that this summary would trigger some reaction. But Phil hadn't moved, except for continuing to sip the beer. I plunged on.

"I know the police think his death was accidental. But when I looked in his office…"

"You did what?" Phil's face was stony, and he spit out his words. Color rushed to his cheeks.

"I went into his office before it was cleaned up. This was well after your team was there. If you didn't want anyone to go there, you should've put crime tape across the door. I didn't disturb anything. The next day the custodial staff came in and cleaned the place out, and no one stopped them."

"Still, you shouldn't have been in there."

"OK. I had no authorization to go in the office. We can deal with that later, if necessary. But I looked closely at the stacks of papers."

"His office was a shithole," Phil appeared to relax a bit, which was good for me. I needed an ally, not an inquisitor.

I nodded. "I hadn't expected to see so much paper there. But the curious thing was that, while a few of the piles were pretty well organized in reverse chronological order, as you might expect, some weren't."

"So what? The guy was obviously not very anal about how he kept his so-called files. I've met his type before. They claim they know where everything is, until they actually need to find something."

"But. The only stacks that weren't in order were on a path leading from near his desk to the window. All the other piles, and there were plenty, were in order."

"So? Maybe those were just the stacks he'd been working through. Looking for something. Maybe those were his 'active' files and were being kept in some order other than chronological. There are easier explanations than saying someone else was in there and disturbed the papers while dragging him to the window."

"But just look at the facts. A bunch of former employees who hated his guts, seeing him getting off scot-free while their lives were upended. A group of university leaders who did everything short of firing to make this guy into an un-person..."

"Yeah, what about that?" Phil asked, his voice rising. "If he was such a loser, why didn't they just fire his ass?"

"He had a solid employment contract that precluded his firing for anything short of a felony."

For the first time, Phil looked genuinely surprised.

"Really? Where did you find that?"

"Hey, remember I used to be a journalist. I have my ways of getting information."

"Have you seen the contract?"

"No, but my information comes from what in the trade we would call an 'unimpeachable source.'"

"Interesting. But that falls far short of convincing evidence."

I nodded. "So, Phil, here's how I look at it. One, some of the stacks in his office may have been disturbed."

"Of course," he interrupted, "that's speculation. We can't go back and look at them now. The office has been cleaned up, the files moved out."

"All right, so just maybe we have a suspicious coincidence involving the files leading from his desk to the window. The only ones that appear to be disturbed."

"Maybe."

"Two, some of the people who lost their jobs, and close friends of theirs, hold Ronson responsible. Either individually or collectively they might have plotted revenge."

Phil shook his head emphatically. "Very, very few people ever act on revenge. People who are the most outspoken end up being the least likely to do something. And probably every person who reaches a position of authority has a long list of enemies. And the mass firing was how long ago? Two years? Why now? Whatever anger people might have had has likely cooled."

"Without talking to more of those people, it's hard to know for sure. It could be that something happened in their lives that rekindled that resentment." Phil was wearing his "color me very skeptical" look.

"Three, there are people in the administration who would have liked to see this fellow go away, but they couldn't fire him. There was a lot of pent-up frustration and anger surrounding him. There was some concern that having him receive a princely salary without doing anything would be a cause for public embarrassment or worse — maybe touching off a scandal that went well beyond Ronson's contract."

Phil laughed and shook his head. "Talk about wild speculation!"

"Phil, I'm just adding up all the information that I've uncovered without going far afield. I'm sure there's more that I haven't found yet. When you put it all together, I thought it might constitute grounds for reopening the case. I'm willing to bet your team would locate stuff that I haven't even thought about. What do you think?"

Phil pushed himself back from the table with a loud squeak from his chair. He uncrossed his legs. His face had darkened and he was taking a few deep, calming breaths.

"Mike, in all the time we've worked together, I've never criticized how you do your job. Even if I disagreed with your approach, I didn't think it was my place to do that. It would damage our relationship and probably wouldn't accomplish much, anyhow."

Uh-oh.

"I was hoping you would extend the same courtesy to me and my colleagues. What you've done... is amateurish. Unprofessional. It doesn't stand up to scrutiny. The 'facts' that you allege, taken all together, don't amount to shit. There isn't one thing in there, except maybe the contract (which, by the way, doesn't point in the direction of a crime), that isn't easy to dispute or dismiss entirely. So, what you have is really nothing."

I nodded. I guess I should be grateful he wasn't cursing me out. Yet.

"Even if we had known during our investigation everything you're telling me now, we would have determined the death was accidental. I say that with absolute certainty. There is simply *no physical evidence* suggesting a crime has been committed. Even if we had known in detail about the people who attribute their firing to Ronson's actions, we're not likely to go out and interview more than fifty individuals in the hope that one of them might confess. That's just not how it's done. And as for administrators wanting him to disappear, well, if you believe gossip then he's far from the only person in that dubious category. Frankly, I think you've been wasting your time. And now you're wasting my time." He rose from the table.

"Is that all you have?" he said.

I hesitated. "Well, there is one more thing." I gulped hard.

"What is it?"

I told Phil about the car shadowing me, the vandalism with the notes, and the computer hack. His expression changed from anger to surprise to concern. He sat back down and took a long drink.

"I'm sorry to hear about that, Mike, I really am. It could throw things in a different light. Now, it still doesn't give me enough to re-open the investigation. I gotta tell you, just between us, there was a lot of talk about how we needed to close the case as soon as we could. I can't tell you from whom, and I don't know their motivation, but it was from way above my level. Even your harassment may not give us much to go on, except that someone doesn't like what you've been doing. It could conceivably be that you were close to digging up other dirt, unrelated to Ronson, just by accident. There's no real way to know unless someone looks into it."

He paused and put his hands on the table, pressing them flat until the tips of his fingers under his nails turned white. "I'll tell you what we can do. If you're willing to file a complaint with the city, I'll use my contacts there to see if we can turn it into a joint investigation, and delegate myself to pursue it. I can't promise anything. But we'll follow the trail and see if we can turn up something. How does that sound?"

This was the best outcome I could hope for, considering. "That sounds good, Phil. And I really didn't want to step on your guys' toes. But there just seemed to be so many unanswered questions…"

He just shook his head. "Everyone watches mysteries and thinks it's easy, that you can just become an investigator and solve crimes. The truth is, we don't solve crimes the way they do in the movies or in novels. There aren't that many murders where the likely suspects don't jump right out at you. It doesn't require far-fetched theories to solve most crimes. It's nice to have your fantasies. But confusing fantasy and reality can be a waste of time and on occasion even dangerous. Imagine you found that someone was looking into your background, and how you might react. You're lucky."

"I'll try to remember that in the future. Sorry to be a pain."

"It's all right, I guess. You didn't break any laws, didn't level public charges against anyone." He adjusted his jacket in preparation to leave. "But it does look like you've pissed off someone. So if you do go ahead and file that complaint, I'll probably want to follow up and interview the people that you contacted. We might want to look at your notes. But fresh interviews will undoubtedly be necessary."

I blanched. As a reporter I didn't burn sources, which means never revealing who they are and absolutely never turning my notes over to anyone else. But I was not working as a reporter in this case. Still, the idea rankled. I needed to mull this over more before deciding my next move. I nodded slowly, an equivocal response.

Phil stood up. "I have to admit you did turn over some stones that we didn't even see. You may not have done things the way we would have, but for an amateur you did OK."

That was the closest he was going to come to a compliment. "Thanks, Phil."

He gave me a stiff nod and marched out the door.

I finished that first beer and had another, tossing it off in a few large gulps. And another.

What would Phil do with this dog's breakfast of facts, opinions and guesses I had assembled? Was he likely to find the person who keyed my car and connect that individual to Jeremy Ronson? Maybe in my dreams. To quote Phil, it didn't amount to shit.

If I gave Phil my notes and names of my sources, I might as well look for another job. I had promised people anonymity. In retrospect, maybe that was a bad idea, but it was the only way they would talk with me. I could imagine going back to my sources and asking for permission to turn their names over to the police, trying to explain how

I was being targeted by someone for undertaking my investigation. And then the calls would come to Trencher and probably Ganas too, complaining about my behavior. Once they learned what I had been doing, I was a goner.

I had painted myself into a corner. Shit. My only hope was that I could identify the killer myself and present the complete investigation to law enforcement authorities on a platter. I didn't like my odds.

I had a couple of more beers before heading home, driving as slowly as I could. Fortunately, there was no traffic. I didn't feel so great.

I tossed and turned that night. I knew I couldn't turn over my files to the police, even to a good guy like Phil. And he had made it clear, in his understated way, that there was very little chance of them ever reopening the investigation.

CHAPTER TWELVE

I got up late, feeling hung over, sick to my stomach and generally out of sorts. When it came to alcohol I was a lightweight. Lack of sleep and loss of confidence contributed to my bad attitude.

I shaved haphazardly and put on the only moderately clean shirt hanging in the closet without looking at it. I cursed every driver who crossed my path during the commute, as well as those annoying, oblivious student pedestrians with their heads down while gaming/texting/Instagramming/Snapchatting as they ambled across the street. Damn them all.

Fran gave me a long and disdainful up-and-down review when I arrived.

"Rough night?"

"Guess you could say that." I scratched one of the many fuzzy spots on my chin that I had missed and stared off into space. I hadn't even had a morning coffee.

"I'm not even going to ask." She backhanded-waved me on to my office.

Stella knocked lightly, a sheaf of papers requiring signatures in her hand.

"You look like hell."

I looked up and realized I couldn't form my mouth into a smile even when I tried. "I'd just as soon not talk about it."

Stella ignored my plea. "What happened?"

I didn't invite her to sit, not wanting to relive last night in any detail.

"Let's just say that someone pointed out to me that all my hypothetical scenarios about what might have happened to Ronson are just that — hypothetical. Not enough to trigger reopening the investigation by law enforcement. And not nearly enough to solve the crime myself. I'm so far from solving this I can't even see the end of the tunnel.

"There's something fishy about Ronson's death, for sure. I'm close enough that someone wants me to stop looking into it. I mean, that computer hack didn't occur by accident. Or some other things. But I'm nowhere close enough to figure out what happened."

Stella nodded, her mouth a thin line. "Geez. Let me know if there's any way I can help."

I felt my stomach rising and needed to cut this short. "Thanks. I'm gonna play out my hand, but right now I'm not feeling very good."

Shortly after Stella left, my phone rang. I was summoned upstairs by Trencher.

As usual, he was seated behind his ultra-clean desk, pecking away at his keyboard with two fingers. Despite a long academic career he had never learned how to touch type. He was dressed in his sartorial best, a navy pinstripe suit with vest and subtle repp tie, the kind with the diagonal stripes, and of course the braces. He continued typing, leaving me to stare off into space.

"So how have you been?" he asked, spinning a quick quarter-turn. It was an uncharacteristically personal inquiry, and I suspect after he looked at me he regretted it. He seemed slightly alarmed by my deshabille, raising a single eyebrow quizzically.

"Not terrible. Can't complain, and no one would listen if I did."

"Huh," he snorted, nonplussed, shrugging his shoulders. He shuffled through a stack of paper. "Can you guess why someone would want a copy of Jeremy Ronson's employment contract? We have a public records request, but it doesn't look like it came from anyone in the media."

I was ready for this. I knew most public records requests ended up on his desk. "Not a clue. I had several conversations with Shelley Strong and it was clear she wasn't going to pursue a story. Not a peep from any other reporter. Maybe it's a family member digging for gold. Or some former employee wondering why Ronson wasn't given the heave-ho when there were massive layoffs in IT a couple of years ago. Or someone who needs new reading material and doesn't have a life."

"I guess it doesn't matter. But the existence of that contract wasn't widely broadcast. Anyhow, we'll be turning it over to... Andrea Bell, the moment the folks in the president's office locate it. I'm pretty sure it's in an 'active' file. Maybe even being reviewed on someone's desk."

"Why is that?"

"Whatever Ronson touched, it was sure to become contentious. For a seemingly easygoing guy, he was one of the most disputatious individuals I've ever encountered. We're still hearing from his attorney who claims to be tying up loose ends."

Trencher pushed aside the papers and leaned forward, shifting gears.

"On another matter, have you heard any gossip about this branding strategy and reactions on or off campus?"

I wasn't going to tell him about my junket to the legislature, figuring he'd learn about it in good time, when I was better prepared for a private flogging for freelancing, as it was known in the bureaucracy. "Other than the usual faculty whining, nothing specific. What have you heard?"

"Oh, just snippets. A lot of people are whispering about the story behind the initiative. The gossip making the rounds is that Yarmouth was forced into this branding project and specifically into hiring McGarvey, McCandless, Scarbuff and Glanz."

This paralleled what my colleague Jerry Bransford had told me. "Who forced him?"

"The gossip claims that a phalanx of VPs marched into his office and demanded this. They were led by the fundraisers, but supported by the folks in student enrollment, the student experience and international programs, all of whom apparently decided they had a dog in this hunt. Allegedly, even the budget and facilities people were roped in. And, of course, our own VP.

"The theory they came armed with was that, in order to survive financially in the coming decades, this university needs to raise its standing among megadonors and also with the next generation of college-ready students, particularly those whose parents can pay full freight — not a growing portion of the population.

"People who look at demographic and financial projections say universities will be forced to engage in increasingly cutthroat competition for private money and gilt-edged students. They also see a gradual chipping away of the market from new competitors, including high-quality online programs, which are edging into the certification business. They say in the future the competition will be fierce, with many losers and a small number of winners."

"Seems plausible to me."

"For a public university, this means walking a tightrope, because if you become a school only for the elites then the average citizen and legislator will be reluctant about supporting an institution that is closed to most students.

"The people who advocate an aggressive re-branding effort think that positioning the university in the public mind as a top-flight place, like an Ivy, is essential to its survival.

"There's a struggle underway throughout the Yarmouth administration over this whole question. The way I heard it, he took office without any strong opinions on the subject and has been buffeted by various forces that see re-branding as crucial to future success. In addition to a growing number of top administrative leaders, that group includes a majority of the trustees, making them pretty much an irresistible force.

"He's also received unsolicited rebuttals from some faculty members who see branding as a gigantic waste of resources, completely devoid of validation from research and also offensive to traditional values."

As Trencher talked, I felt my hangover getting worse. The inside of my mouth had the texture of worn carpeting. I tried hard to maintain some focus.

"Some faculty have broadcast their concerns through a blog." He spun back to his computer. "It's something called the Faculty Dissident Blog. You might want to check it out, if you haven't already.

"Here's one faculty member's view of the re-branding effort: 'Apparently, cynical members of this administration, and some misguided members of our board of trustees, have noted the hegemony of popular culture in our society, to the exclusion of other frames of reference, and concluded that every major institution, including ours, needs to have a strong and sustained presence in the never-ending trivia stream of the Twittersphere, the blogosphere, social media and other forms of digital chatter. They see the inane grasping for attention among corporate players and individuals and wonder why our university is content to sit on the sidelines, outside of the spectacle. It is quite clear to me they are asking the wrong question.'"

"Interesting." A mixture of academic defensiveness and rehashed 1960s-style political sloganeering, with just a soupcon of anticapitalism. Trencher continued.

"His post goes on in that vein. I'm not sure anyone in authority actually cares what they think. Most faculty I know have pretty much checked out of academic politics, so this is probably the work of a tiny, vocal minority.

"Anyhow, if you get wind of any activity on this score do let me know. When faculty get organized, which doesn't happen often, they have the power to become a veto group, or at least dig some major divots in the road." Trencher had already swung back to his work, throwing the last remark at me over his shoulder.

I was curious about what else the faculty dissident had to say. When I returned to my desk, I continued reading:

"It's easy to get caught up in the whirl of trivia that characterizes 'pop culture,' an oxymoronic phrase to be sure. But for an institution with standing, with longevity, and with gravity it would be a serious mistake. One thing that is true about this country and increasingly true worldwide is that societal values are dominated by commodities. They are America's secular religion. Because they are, by definition, unimportant and insubstantial, the only way to maintain a semblance of interest in them among the gaping populace is by increasing the velocity of what passes for change. The things we are urged to buy must exhibit a freshness, an improvement, a difference from yesterday's objects that somehow is supposed to make them appealing enough to stimulate desire. The goal of market seduction is to define people by what they have, not who they are.

"Universities should be manning the battlements against this 'philosophy,' which I can't dignify to describe as such without quotation marks. If any remaining creditable societal institution enshrines eternal values and attempts to transmit them to the next generation it is higher education. To become involved in the prurient business of 'marketing,' with its pseudo-scientific trappings and fundamental emptiness, should be regarded as an abomination by anyone who harbors hope for the future.

"It will enmesh us in a continual search for ever-newer Bright, Shiny Objects. It will trivialize our mission and put our institution on a path to extinction: once we lose our special place in the psychological firmament, we will never be able to regain it. Once we become fully 'commoditized,' we have conceded we are just another bauble on the consumer merry-go-round. Our future will be determined by market share, mind share, likes and 'hits,' and the lowest-common-denominator strategies that must be employed to win them.

"The race to the bottom is not the kind of race an institution of learning should want to win. We will be drawn into a game where we can't possibly compete unless we distort our fundamental purpose into something unrecognizable to our forebears. My plea is that our leaders think long and hard about heading down this road. Once embarked upon, there is no turning back, the path is ever downward, and the results will be calamitous."

Quite a bouillabaisse of ideas.

These were deep thoughts, and even on my good days, of which this was not one, I'd have trouble grappling with them. So I returned to the daily grind.

Near the top of my inbox was an invitation:

"You are cordially invited to the premiere of a series of commercials produced expressly for the newly-launched branding campaign. Conceived by the team of McGarvey, McCandless, Scarbuff and Glanz, produced and directed by Dancing Delight, Inc. With a cast of thousands (well, maybe a few dozen)."

It was today at noon. This was one of those events for which attendance was not required, but given the buzz surrounding the branding initiative and Trencher's comments about a possibly growing controversy, I had every intention of being there. Cheap, good entertainment is always hard to come by.

*   *   *

The premiere was set in a small auditorium normally used for lectures in geography. Up front I saw about a dozen men with suits and also a number of women dressed too formally to be university employees. There was also a fellow in a blue jumpsuit and shades who I assumed was the director.

About ten minutes after the appointed hour one of the suits brought the crowd of one hundred to attention.

"Hi there. I'm Andy McGarvey, and I'm pleased to welcome you to the first public showing of a series of commercials designed to literally knock your socks off. We've shown these to focus groups — general public and university affiliated — and the response was enthusiastic. But we wanted you, our 'A Team' here at the university, to get a look at these before you started hearing about them from friends and neighbors.

"Although ultimately the content was approved by university officials, the creative essence and the details we chose to include are entirely ours. That's the way it needs to be if you're going to break new ground, capture the audience's attention and stand out among the daily clutter of information. It's what we call breakthrough thinking.

"To some of you, our approach may seem out of character for a university, but please trust us. We've done this before and have produced results for all our clients, including some of your competing institutions, and we know we can achieve similar results for you. So, I would ask only that you suspend your judgment for now.

"Please remember these are commercials, not public service announcements. So they need to have a style that is in keeping with how advertising looks to our audiences. In other words, we're selling something, and there's no reason to try and conceal that fact. Back in the old days, television stations gave away free air time to nonprofits as part of their federal licensing. But that has pretty much disappeared. All air time is purchased, and the commercials will be slotted to show when the station's audience most closely resembles our target demographics.

"I'd like to introduce our director. He has a list of credits too long to read here, but his awards for creativity and impact over the course of his career have been legion. We were lucky enough to snare him between major projects, so he did this almost as a hobby for us. Trust me, if we told you his regular fee your response would be, 'We can't afford that,' and you'd be right! Ladies and gentlemen, Bradley Goforth, principal director and the inspiration behind Dancing Delight!"

The guy in the jumpsuit came out. He wore his bleached hair in a mohawk and had huge rings on several fingers, one with a ruby the size of an almond.

"Thank you." He had a deep voice that sounded like it emanated from a cement mixer, and diction that seemed to trail off somewhere in mid-sentence. "It's been a pleasure to work on this project with my old friend Andy. I can't tell you the number of times we partied together in college, but that's a story for another time. I tried to do these spots with a light touch, so as to hold people's attention but not beat them over the head with the message. I hope you like what you're about to see."

He left the stage and the lights dimmed.

A student walks across campus. He's a stunningly handsome young man, dressed casually but tastefully in a button-down shirt and pressed khakis. He takes off his backpack, stops and stares at the camera, theatrically brushing the hair from his forehead. Behind him students are chatting, playing Frisbee, texting and walking to class. The tulips wave in a breeze. He stares into the camera.

"When it came time to go to college, I had my pick. I could've gone to Harvard or elsewhere among the elite private universities. But I chose to stay right here, in my home town. People ask me why. I tell them I did my research. I found that everything I wanted – great teachers, great programs, terrific social life, great sports teams and excellent job prospects — it was all here. Yeah, I could've gone to Harvard. But I believe coming here was the right choice. In fact, it was the only choice. No contest."

The university logo appears with a few bars of the alma mater.

Around me, there was whispering and people shifting in their chairs. After about thirty seconds, a new image came on the screen.

The scene is the football stadium. A large crowd is on the field. It has people of all ages, shapes and sizes, and they are grinning ear to ear, jumping up and down, shaking hands, excited. They are dressed in the school colors — t-shirts, sweat pants, shorts, modified sports uniforms, hats, jackets… A loud backbeat begins. What follows is a hip-hop remix borrowing some words, notes and rhythms from the soul tune "I Thank You" by Sam & Dave. The crowd jumps, dances, sings, shouts, and gyrates to the beat.

Loudspeaker voice: "I want everyone to get up out on the field and put your hands together and your arms together. And sing loud!

"You didn't need to teach me like you did oh so well, but you did… and I think it's so kewl.

"You didn't have to thrill me with those catches at the game… but you did, oh you did and I think it's so kewl and off the chain.

"If I'd gone to college anywhere else, I wouldn't know what it meant to learn from the cream, from the s$%@. You've made me feel so high with learning, so very ready, so happy I am here.

"Without those great profs, I'd be left in the dust. Every day here is something new. A great place to try new things, to shape my life. I'm so proud and happy for what I've done. And it's all so awesomely kewl."

The spot continued, repeating a chorus about how kewl it was to be here as the crowd danced more and more wildly. There was even some tossing of bodies among groups on the field. The spot ends with a huge cheer and whoop.

There was scattered laughter in the auditorium and a brief pause before the next video.

We hear a very traditional march. I recognize it as one of those bombastic ceremonial tunes all too common at universities on formal occasions. On screen there's a flyover of the city, highlighting skyscrapers, water vistas and mountains. An omniscient announcer:

"What makes a great city and a great city? Some would say it's the people. Others would say it's the vistas, the natural resources. Some might tout the food or weather or even the sports teams. But we think it's a great university. Where would we be today without our university?

Scene shifts to an anonymous stadium with a generic marching band, still playing the same march, doing figure eights on the playing field. Mechanically, without emotion, but technically perfect.

"Where would we be without a great place to educate our young people, to act as an incubator for the inventions that change our lives, and with those sports teams that we love to cheer? Where would we be without a great university? [pause] Probably marching around in circles."

The band halts in mid-stride with its members staring at the camera in mock-horror. The screen fades to black.

A bit more laughter in the audience. People look over their shoulder to see if they're being watched. The screen brightens again and elegiac violin music fills the room.

A misty sunrise with water in the foreground, mountains in the background. Voiceover:

"It's morning again in the Great Northwest. (Double-time scenes of commuting by car in a drizzle, people walking at lightning speed with briefcases, nodding to one another as they pass, like a video game.)

"It's a work day, and thanks to our great university, more people have good jobs here than ever before. (Shift to aerial panoramas of the campus with a blue sky, ground level shots of students, inside labs and classrooms of students working together and with faculty)

"We've weathered the financial storms because of our intellectual resilience. We have a vibrant economy and limitless potential here. Our educated workforce, thanks largely to the university, produces goods and services sought around the world. The discoveries in our labs ensure that our economy will remain competitive, and that we will be the home to exciting new businesses. So we can see a bright future for our children, too.

"We are not just a regional treasure. Our ideas will transform the nation and the planet. Such is the quality and impact of the work taking place here, the kinds of people who are attracted to this extraordinary institution, and the kinds of people who receive degrees."

Switch to ground-level campus shot "At the university, though, it's just another day. Business as usual. It's simply what we do."

After a few seconds of silence, the lights come up. I hear scattered golf applause. Andy McGarvey resumes his pose center stage. "Well, that's all for today. Please recognize there will be several more productions following up on these themes. Tell your friends and colleagues to look for these spots soon on broadcast and cable outlets, and they will be re-edited for use on radio. Also, you can expect a series of posters and print ads following up on the themes. Oh, and you'll find them popping up in surprising ways on social media, too. Stay tuned. I want to thank you all for coming."

He walked off the stage and shook hands with the director. On the way out, I heard several people remark that the hosts didn't ask for any feedback, to which one replied, "This is a done deal. You don't ask for opinions after you completed the work and cashed the cheque."

* * *

I wondered what my friends at the Faculty Dissident Blog would have to say about the show. I didn't have to wait long. About an hour later, the blog contained a brief entry.

> "We are living in an asylum. There is no other possible explanation for what just occurred in the Geography Auditorium, except that our administration and what passes for leadership among the Board of Trustees have all clearly lost their minds. Their version of reality bears no relationship to mine and I trust to yours. We are living in very strange times, when allegedly responsible individuals can spend what is likely a king's ransom on producing trite, shallow and wholly misleading views of this university, which they have pledged to use to saturate the media with noxious ideas and forgettable messages. I will comment further on this as soon as I have time and gain command of the fury that now engulfs me. But suffice it to say that this is a very sad day. It appears we are on a runaway stagecoach. How are we going to get hold of the reins and bring this to a halt???"

I noticed that in a short period of time the blog entry had already attracted several hundred likes. Made me wonder how widespread the dissatisfaction was.

Then I realized I didn't have to wait long to find the answer. The Faculty Senate was meeting late that afternoon. And it typically began with a report from the president.

I arrived early, scanning the audience for media, my excuse for attending. If anyone was likely to come it would be Shelley Strong, as the sole higher ed reporter from one of the surviving but diminished newspapers; there was no chance that anyone from a broadcast organization would be willing to sit through the interminable and obscure discussions that were the meat and potatoes of a faculty senate meeting. Moreover, the printed agenda gave little clue about what was going to transpire.

I didn't see Shelley but had planned to stay around nonetheless. After the roll was called, President Yarmouth stood at the front of the room, normally the location for moot court in the law school.

His remarks were brief. He talked about the prospects for budget increases in the legislature (poor), and the fundraising picture for the year thus far (superb). The acceptance letters had just been sent to prospective freshmen, so he described the profile of admitted students. Competition was stiff, so grade point averages and test scores continued to rise.

This was both good news and bad news: Good news because many of the major national rankings used the student profile in their "quality" measures. But the bad news about rising standards was significant. Fewer and fewer highly qualified students from within the state could gain admission.

This would be a badge of honor for a private university, but for a school that depended on state support it was a cause for concern. If a way above-average student couldn't get in, what did this say about the university's commitment to educate the sons and daughters of state residents? In a state with a profound populist streak, this argument was tricky, Yarmouth explained, and one he hoped to avoid.

Yarmouth finished his brief slide show on admissions, the screen went dark, and he uttered the two words I had been waiting for, "Any questions?"

Immediately, a half-dozen hands shot up. Yarmouth pointed to an older looking gent with a full beard and thick glasses.

"President Yarmouth, I was hoping you'd take this opportunity to explain what is going on with this series of commercials that were previewed today. Since you didn't spend time on this subject in your report, can I ask you a few questions?"

"Of course," he smiled. "That's why I'm here."

"Can you describe briefly why you and presumably others in the administration think this is money well-spent? I'm sure that the production was expensive, and then you have to pay to have these shown on various stations. You haven't released any figures on the cost, but these things don't come cheaply. What do you hope to accomplish?"

"I'm glad you asked me that." Yarmouth began pacing across the elevated platform. "I don't have time to go into great detail, but let me just outline our thinking.

"This university wants to be the best. But being the best doesn't mean much if you aren't *perceived* as being among the best. So the intent of our commercials, and the entire re-branding project, is to raise the university's public profile, to re-position the university in people's minds…"

"Excuse me for interrupting, but you just announced the impressive statistical profile of the students who have been accepted for next year. And you also noted the extraordinary amount of private funds we have raised. It seems to me like we're already in an enviable competitive situation. So what are we actually trying to achieve with this project that we don't already have?"

"You know, when people came to me — and many did — to propose this venture, I wondered about that initially, too. After extended discussion and deliberation, I concluded that we can't rest on what we've accomplished thus far, impressive as it is. Standing still is tantamount to losing ground in this business. If we don't continue to move ahead we run the risk of falling behind. Winning in such a competitive market requires constant vigilance and the continual development of new strategies. It's a little like the arms race, not that I'm fond of that comparison. We're in a kind of arms race with other universities, where the prize isn't territory but students and support of various kinds. As long as other universities try to gain market share, we need to protect ours. Does that answer your question?"

"About the money," someone shouted out.

"Yes." Yarmouth paused for a moment and looked down at his shoes. "First, you should know this re-branding effort did not divert a dime from our core missions, education and research. And of course there is no state money involved at all. We've received generous private donations for the entire project."

"How much is this all going to cost?" asked the same interlocutor.

"I can't give you a figure at this time. We're still developing the plan and haven't yet signed some of the key media contracts." There were a few groans at his evasion.

"Look, I know that we live in a time of constraints. We're going over every proposed expenditure with a fine-toothed comb. After all, in the final analysis it's always someone else's money we're spending, whether state money or what we raise privately, so we need to act as wise stewards. I'll come back to you later with a figure, but please trust me that we're spending as effectively as we can to achieve our results."

A hand in the back went up and before Yarmouth could call on her a woman stood up and began her question. She was dressed in a blue smock and looked as if she could have come directly from a lab. Her gray hair was gathered loosely in a bun that had come partially undone. She wore half-glasses over which she peered out uncertainly at Yarmouth. She was visibly agitated, and her voice boomed much louder than was necessary.

"I was at the preview of the... commercials. And frankly, I was shocked. Here you talk about stature and prestige, of 'positioning,' as it's been called. I fail to see how a rip-off of Sam & Dave helps position us as a leading institution. It just seemed shameless and in bad taste. And that student who claimed he came here because it was as good... no, he suggested it was even better than Harvard. Does that student even exist? Is he a real person?" She sat down, her face red with exertion.

"So, in sum, you're asking about the quality of our advertising. The firm that we are using is one of the most respected in its field. They have worked with dozens of universities and have a great track record in producing results for their clients."

The woman shook her head emphatically. "You're missing my point. I'm asking specifically about the content of the advertising. *In your opinion*, is it tasteful? And is it truthful? After watching the commercials, I came away with an uneasy feeling about their impact and the message they were trying to convey."

Yarmouth began pacing again. "Well, in matters of taste, I don't claim to have the final word. But I found the Sam and Dave spot fun, surprising, and definitely attention-grabbing. People will remember it. Who knows, it might even spur a revival of their music, which I happen to like a lot.

"As for the student. We did employ a model." I heard a whooshing sound in the room, a collective sucking-in of breath. "I was assured that the story, in effect a composite of student interviews, was indeed accurate. But we chose to use an actor to enhance the impact of the spot. Delivering words effectively, with the right intonation and emotion, is not something your average college student — or anyone, for that matter — can do. As for the ethics of using an actor, I don't think it's any different than when you watch a car commercial. Are all those people real car buyers? Are they that excited? Obviously not. The standards of 'real' are lower in those circumstances. I think most viewers know that. So I don't have a problem with using an actor."

"So you're saying you approved the content and approach in all the commercials?" someone shouted out.

"Indeed, I did. When I had doubts I consulted my key staff. When there were policy questions, I even called a couple of the trustees. And of course there was my executive consultant, my wife. There was not a great difference of opinion on going forward with these spots as produced, I might add.

"You also were raising questions, if I'm right, about the dignity and tone of the ads, whether they are appropriate for the university." Yarmouth paused and licked his lips. He reached for a bottle of water at the lectern. "I understand that this is not the way we would talk to one another, as colleagues and scholars, about the university. This is not the way I talk with other university presidents; this is not the manner in which you communicate with family and friends, I'd venture to guess.

"But these commercials are for a different audience and with a different purpose. If we're going to reach our target audience — of prospective students and their parents, of opinion-makers and their associates — we have to compete for their attention. That requires us to do some things that, perhaps, we would not do otherwise.

"But the truth is, these techniques work. And taking the high road, as we might call it, the road we've taken in the past, well, it doesn't work. It won't get us where we want to go, much as we might prefer it."

There was an uneasy silence in the room. Yarmouth scanned the assembled senators and he gradually resumed his confident, friendly mien.

"Of course, there is another way to look at this." A professor dressed in an outfit that could only be called professorial, complete with tweed jacket and Van Dyck beard, rose to his feet in stages. He looked to be about seventy-five. His voice was gravelly and uneven; I had to strain to hear him.

"What might that be?" Yarmouth said.

"If we choose to live by the sword, to use a common metaphor, then we will be condemned to die by the sword."

"I'm not sure I follow you." Yarmouth looked puzzled.

"If we enter a space normally dominated by commercial goods, then we in effect are becoming another commercial good. Like automobiles or soaps. There is really not a great difference between those items in the same mass consumption category. So the commercial space has to emphasize minute differences, or even to invent differences where none exist."

I realized I was listening to a voice of the Faculty Dissident Blog. Maybe *the* voice.

"You weren't in the room when the consultants gave the sales presentation, were you?" Yarmouth responded. "This is pretty much their description of what they do."

"I would give them credit for a degree of honesty, if nothing else. However, once you enter the commercial sphere, you can never escape. It is my belief that our major institutions, including but not limited to universities, do themselves irreparable harm by making this choice."

"How so?" asked Yarmouth. He was scrunching his eyebrows together with a look of concentration on his face.

The dissident, who was standing near the back of the room, now had the attention of the entire senate. People swiveled in their narrow chairs to look at him.

"Essentially, you have chosen to prioritize appearance over reality. It is a short jump to go from dipping your toe in the commercial pond to becoming a creature of the market. In fact, the path really goes just one way. Decisions, key decisions about the future of the institution, will no longer be judged according to actual merit but by how they will be perceived by... what did you call them? Oh yes, our 'target audiences.' As if we were shooting bullets or arrows at them, when our actual weapon is the use — or in this case, I would assert, the misuse — of language.

"I would argue that there are other standards worth upholding that are not reflected in the market. Indeed, most of the people in this room, I'd be willing to say, have chosen this career because of those standards. I don't want to come across as too pompous. But as a faculty member, some pomposity is my right. So let me name a few of those transcendent values: the search for truth. Vigorous debate. The transmission of these methods of inquiry from one generation to the next. Perhaps paramount is the love of learning. I'll stop there. I'm sure you are familiar with these values.

"I look around this room and realize it is primarily composed of people of my generation, who came of age in the 1960s and 70s. I ask you to think back to the time when you made your own choice to go on for a doctorate and pursue an academic career. What motivated you? If you thought about values, and I'll bet most of you did, what were those values that resonated to your core and caused you to choose a profession that has some rewards but overall is a bit of a bother?

"It's not an easy question to answer definitively. And it's probably not something to which we have devoted a great deal of time after we made our commitment to life in the academy.

"But I'm guessing that, in your introspective moments, perhaps when you are asked to serve as a mentor for an especially bright undergrad or grad student, those values — dedication to the search for truth, the importance of critical thinking in all spheres of life, the centrality of those values in our life, and our conviction of their essential importance to the future of our civilization, all these things by which we live — you think about them and you suddenly, perhaps surprisingly, find yourself passionate about them once again, as you were when you began your career. You may even, in an unguarded moment, wax eloquent about what drew you to the academy.

"Think about the world you thought you were entering. Now think about how that world is likely to be altered by the growing pressure to choose — and it is a choice — to turn higher education into simply another commodity. And make no mistake about it. We are being drawn along this path, even if we think this is simply a pet project of a few people in Main Central.

"Now President Yarmouth, I freely admit that I am a voice crying in the wilderness. It could well be that the course on which you are embarked is the only course possible, that we really don't have any other choice.

"As for me, I'm not quite willing to accept that. No, let me carry it a step further. I would be willing to toss my sabots into the gears of the commercial machine, because it is not the world in which I would choose to live. And it may well be that my symbolic cry of dissent would be as ineffective as those of long-ago workers in the newly-automated textile factories. But I don't feel I have any choice." He stood, mute, looking around the room, nodded to Yarmouth, and took his seat.

Yarmouth's mouth flapped but nothing came out. He began to form a reply, thought better of it, and shook his head.

"Well," said the chairman of the senate. "We've gone well over time on this fascinating subject. I want to thank President Yarmouth for spending part of his afternoon with us. And I'm sure we will hear more about this subject in the future."

Yarmouth appeared to stumble a bit from the platform and left hurriedly, accompanied by a phalanx of VPs.

Later that afternoon I visited the dissident blog. The earlier message had gone viral, at least in the university context. The likes now approached a thousand.

An hour later I received a query from Shelley Strong, wondering if anyone in the administration was willing to be quoted in her story, responding to the statements on the dissident blog. I passed it upstairs but was pretty sure no one would touch it. I had this feeling that Yarmouth was probably still as gobsmacked as he had appeared at the senate grilling.

Shelley's story, filed that evening and trimmed to about four inches in the print edition, simply said, "Calls to President Yarmouth and other high-ranking administrators were not returned."

It was highly likely, in any case, that Yarmouth could easily weather the squall by ignoring it. After all, the dissident's criticism was pretty hifalutin' stuff for general consumption even among faculty.

The matter had been raised and discussed. End of story, in all likelihood.

Faculty senates in general should not be mistaken for the equivalent of the legislative branch of government. Although in medieval times they actually were the locus of power in universities, now they held a largely symbolic role. They seldom operated as a check on the power of the president and had a fairly narrow range of issues that they were willing to pursue. Its members worked hard to avoid confrontation with the president, knowing that when push came to shove they were going to lose on most issues. The senate contained its fair share of grandstanding faculty, but one function of the senate was to let them vent without actually affecting anything.

The protests were likely greeted with a big yawn. I saw no signs that anyone was about to pull the plug on Yarmouth's plans for re-shaping the university's image.

CHAPTER THIRTEEN

On the way to work two days later I got a text from Andrea. The university's response to the public records request had arrived. She would wait until I came by to open the envelope. Although my passion for the Ronson mystery had cooled after meeting with Symonds, I felt an urgency to close the loop. There was probably nothing in the contract that would constitute a smoking gun — for me or especially for law enforcement. I could try to interview more of those who had been laid off, but I had come around to agreeing with Symonds that those events were too long ago to constitute a viable motive. And what he said about people in the administration who wanted Ronson gone also rang true: they might talk big, but when it came to action they were usually nowhere to be found. Neither Kingston nor Cody possessed the physical attributes for murder. And without allies, neither one of them could gain after-hours access to Main Central.

On my way to Andrea's, I was driving through an intersection when a streaking black SUV came at me from the left, seemingly out of nowhere. I slammed on the brakes and jerked the steering wheel to my right as hard as I could. I could feel the momentum tip my car as it made a 90-degree turn, the tires screeching on the pavement. The other car was close to my window and still hadn't slowed much. It scraped me not far from the driver's seat, the sound of metal against metal shrieking in my ears. I felt my door deflect inward against my hip. I was too busy trying to maneuver out of this tight spot for my life to flash before my eyes, but part of me detached from the experience and observed my desperate maneuvers. I pumped the brake and turned the wheel as hard as I could.

My right front wheel jumped the curb, traveling halfway to the sidewalk before I could bring the car to a complete stop. I was jostled but unhurt thanks to the seat belt. It was damn lucky that there were no other cars in the intersection or that there hadn't been any obstacles near that corner. As I was hyperventilating I saw the SUV scream by, accelerating down the narrow residential street. After getting out of the car, settling myself down and making sure my car could still drive — it now had a big dent in the door to complement the scratches — I took a few deep breaths and restarted the engine. My hands were still shaking and I drove around for a while, just to calm myself down. This was too coincidental to be a random event. I was starting to feel pretty smart about curtailing my investigation. My only concern was how I was going to get that message to my pursuers.

When I finally arrived at Andrea's, she kissed me and presented me with the manila envelope.

"So this could be it, the final chapter," I said.

"Whatcha mean, final?"

"I've pretty much decided to shut things down after this, babe. The police are convinced it was an accident — maybe a strange one, but an accident nonetheless, and I don't have enough hard evidence to change their minds. All I've come up with is a lot of circumstantial shit that doesn't amount to much."

"And what about the fact that we're being watched, not to mentioned threatened?" Andrea asked. I blanched slightly, trying to conceal my still-simmering discomfort. "Doesn't that mean you're onto something?"

"Hey, I'm not saying there wasn't a crime. I'm pretty sure there was, otherwise why would someone take an interest in what I've been doing? To tell the truth, it's got me more than a little spooked. But the police likely can't do anything about that, either, because there's almost nothing with which to pursue an investigation. Whoever is doing this is good, better than I am. If I can't convince the police to reactivate the case, there's little chance that I can bring the criminals to justice."

"Whatever you say, hun. But I thought you did a pretty good job with the minimal resources you have. And I think you were onto something, wherever it might lead."

She led me to her dining room table. She had cooked a meal, and judging by the table settings, with several courses. She had dimmed the lights and even put out candles.

"What's this?"

"Hey, I had a sudden urge for romance. I think we both earned it. Don't knock it, it may not happen again anytime soon." She turned to the pots steaming and sizzling in the kitchen. "Let's call it a thank you dinner, for including me in your treasure hunt."

"Well, I can't tell you how much I've appreciated the opportunity to share ideas with someone who wasn't a fellow inmate in the asylum." I came up behind her while she stirred the pots and put my arms around her waist. "Thanks for humoring me, even if at the end of the day I fall short of my goal."

"You never know what you might find in that envelope. It could open a whole new chapter. But that's for later tonight. I want the meal to have a proper reception." She uncorked the wine.

Later that evening, as we got ready for bed, I tore open the envelope. It contained a formal cover note citing the provisions of the law concerning release of public information. The response noted that the employment agreement was enclosed and that there were no known amendments. There were also no written performance reviews — I hadn't really expected any. The cover note cited the second request, for correspondence, and that this request was more complicated and would take longer to process, with no deadline mentioned — pretty much what I expected.

I flipped through the agreement, dense with legalese. This was not going to be casual late night reading.

I reached to turn off the bedside lamp. And I was out like the light.

*　*　*

I spent part of my morning at work with the door closed, poring over the agreement. It was written in such a way as to anticipate every circumstance that would compel him to relinquish his title. He pretty much had to face incarceration for a felony to give up his safety net.

And what a safety net it was. A tenured position in the department of computer science at his highest average salary as vice president. He could be assigned to teach no more than two classes a year (I could imagine the chorus of professors there adding, "As if!") and would have all the perquisites and rights of any other tenured faculty member. The contents of the agreement were intended to remain secret so long as he was alive.

To say it was a generous package was an understatement. This guy really had negotiated a golden ticket.

All the people who had been party to the agreement and were conversant with the details had either died, retired or left the university. Anyone who found themselves bound by its language would have resented its lopsided nature. But the provisions which were sure to cause rancor were unlikely to induce homicidal fury in anyone, as far as I could determine. I sighed and put the document to one side.

I called Andrea and gave her the news. "It is what it is, and if that's the last chapter of your investigation so be it. You fought the good fight and have nothing to be ashamed of.

"Just remember, buster, you said that you owed me for submitting the request, regardless of the outcome. So one day soon I'll give you a full accounting of your debt. I promise that it will involve no public humiliation. What happens in private, well, I haven't figured that out yet."

"No blood."

"Of course not. Don't be silly. But as for degradation and pain..."

"Hey, don't push it. I feel degraded enough already, having squandered so much time on this."

"Just stay tuned." I meandered through a meaningless Friday, keeping a low profile.

Monday arrived too soon. There was the usual flow of email traffic from the weekend, but nothing interesting concerning the re-branding project, no real diversions of any kind. I kept my nose to the grindstone, triaging potential news stories to the appropriate staff member, renewing my visits to the office cubicles, passing out attaboys (or girls) to staff for work well done, casually interrupting colleagues to ask about their life here and elsewhere, mercilessly satirizing our bosses and other institutional follies, joking with Stella and Fran. The usual good-boss behavior that I had relinquished when I became preoccupied by Ronson.

When I took a break around lunchtime, I went outside and noticed a traffic jam around Main Central of carts and wheeled boxes, and a big van in back. I asked Stella what was going on.

"It's the long-awaited move-in by human resources. They're taking over Ronson's space, his suite and the surrounding areas. They'd been promised that location for as long as I can remember.

"It's been quite a saga. About four months ago, they had been told the move was imminent. Don't know by whom. So they began packing up their files and personal effects. I was informed this wasn't the first time they had been instructed to prepare for the move. There had been false starts dating back at least a year. The HR staff had already mapped out how they would reconfigure the space and related decisions. Then they got word, again, that the move was off, at least for the time being. Apparently 'the move is imminent' had become a big joke in HR; they had been teased too much for anyone to take it seriously any more. But this time, at the advice of the veep, they've been living out of boxes.

"Their staff were scattered all over campus, and they wasted a lot of time trying to bring people together for meetings and discussions. It wasn't easy, with meeting rooms at a premium. There was general agreement among the campus space mavens that consolidating their offices was a good idea."

"Ronson's office, even if subdivided, seems like a pretty small space to fight over," I said.

"Haven't you looked at the area around his suite? It's actually pretty extensive. At its height, IT had quite an empire. It's been empty for a long time. Except for himself. All of his minions got canned or moved elsewhere. The last one was his assistant. There have been a bunch of empty offices up there, and he was right in the middle of them. The epitome of a bottleneck."

"Where was Ronson slated to go?" I asked as one of the movers came by with a PC on a cart. "Useless as he was, he had to be somewhere."

"Yeah, that seemed to be the hangup. I heard rumors of various scenarios, all of which would cause him to be relocated outside of Main Central. And several times everything appeared to be decided, from what I was told. But then, at the last minute, the move would be called off. I can tell you, the VP of Human Resources is mighty relieved this is finally happening. It had become a huge embarrassment for her."

I was more than a little curious to know if there was any reference to office space in Ronson's contract. I scanned it until I came across this passage:

> During his employment at the university in any capacity, whether as vice president and/or a tenured faculty member, he will always have exclusive use of the office assigned to him as vice president in the building known as Main Central. This space will be relinquished only by mutual consent of Mr. Ronson and the President.

It was funny, this heightened concern over space. As crazy as it seemed, space obsession was baked into academic culture. The size of an office, its location, its views — these kinds of things were of great concern to people who tried to measure at what level they were in the pecking order.

Clark Kerr, legendary president of the University of California in the 1960s, had half-joked that universities were composed of faculty entrepreneurs "held together by a common grievance over parking." But with the mandatory reductions in single occupancy vehicles on campus, parking wars had been supplanted by fights over space for offices, labs and classrooms. It was not unusual for faculty members who were being lured from other universities to demand a certain number of square feet of office and lab space as part of the package.

So it was scarcely surprising that Ronson insisted on maintaining his fancy office in perpetuity. It probably raised fewer eyebrows than other clauses of his contract.

I was unsurprised when I received a call later that morning from one of the assistant vice presidents in human resources, suggesting that we "might" want to write an article for the campus news highlighting their move. I know what they wanted: one of those 250 word puff pieces, with an appropriately dull photo of people carting their belongings into a new space. It was supposed to be all about the improved services we could expect from this consolidated unit. I wanted to gag, but instead I agreed to handle it myself. No reason for anyone else to be diverted from actual news for this. It wasn't offensive enough to raise a big stink; no one actually expected their services to be improved by the move.

I wandered up to the fourth floor to see the activity firsthand and gather quotes from my new neighbors. I had never spent much time up there and was too preoccupied when Stella and I explored Ronson's office to realize that most of the south half of the floor was vacant.

Now there seemed to be at least two dozen people moving in. Naturally, the vice president was taking Ronson's fancy office with the territorial views, and her minions were busy directing the maintenance people. HR staff were dressed in casual clothes suitable for hauling supplies and office equipment. There was a buzz as people moved in and organized their new digs.

I wandered down the hallway, poking my head in and welcoming to the building some people that I knew, when I was brought to a dead halt by the sight of a striking woman — well over six feet tall with long, braided platinum blond hair, dressed in jeans and a short-sleeve shirt. Her upper body showed the tone of a well-conditioned athlete. With her muscular shoulders and striking figure, she made me think of Amazon, Valkyrie, or Wonder Woman.

She was standing about two feet from a wall, trying to center a photo, her back to me. I stopped and admired her efforts.

"Think that's level?" Apparently, the woman had eyes in the back of her head. I moved a couple of steps into the office, responding to what I took to be an implied invitation. "A little lower on the left," I ventured.

She turned and shot me a glance. She had a strong, prominent chin and sea foam eyes. She frowned, cocked an eyebrow, glanced at the photo, touched the left side and moved it down a hair.

"Perfect," I said.

She put her hands on her hips, skeptically looking me over from head to toe.

She smiled slowly. And nodded slightly.

"I didn't mean to intrude," I said. "I was just walking by and… saw you. I work downstairs in the news office." I was trying to figure out if I should extend a hand and formally introduce myself, but it didn't appear this conversation was going in the meet-and-greet direction. More like the what-the-hell-brought-you-here and how-quickly-can-you-leave mode. Nonetheless, I stood my ground, challenging her to throw me out, or to take the path of least resistance and make polite conversation. After an inordinately long pause she chose the latter. She looked at my reporter's notebook.

"No quotes," she said. "I'm not authorized."

I nodded and put it away.

"I'm new here," she said, without moving toward me or making any overt gesture of friendliness. "Pretty new. Started about four months ago." She stood back, still eying the photo. Upon closer examination, I saw it looked like an army platoon.

"Were you in the military?"

She nodded. "Special forces. Actually, special forces support. Grew up as an Army brat. Always wanted to be a Green Beret or Navy SEAL. Something that would challenge me, that had an edge. I wanted to follow in my dad's footsteps but also to exceed whatever expectations he had, especially for a daughter."

"I heard they didn't accept women in special forces, that those changes were still pending."

She turned around to face me. Her frown had softened. She was wearing an orange-red lipstick that contrasted sharply with her fair complexion. She nodded. "Women weren't allowed in combat roles with the forces when I signed up. When I enlisted, the recruitment officer told me there was momentum to lift the ban. Said there was strong sentiment at the top for experimenting with mixed units, as they called them. He even shared a speech from someone way up the chain of command. It was all about how being special forces was not about doing push-ups, it was about using your brain. Forces members needed to work as a team, trust one another, and be ready to adapt quickly to critical situations. So, gender wasn't all that important in the future that he envisioned. I signed up because of that speech."

"How did that work out?"

She leaned against the corner of her desk and gestured for me to sit in the only available chair as she warmed to her subject.

"To say I was disappointed in the military — not my fellow soldiers, but the hierarchy — was an understatement. After my training, eager to put my life on the line for my country, I was angry about being given a desk job. Hard to see it as anything other than their version of women's work. Oh, they gave us all kinds of excuses. The general was speaking out of turn when he made those remarks, they told me. But coming from the recruiting officer, that speech was a promise to me. That they broke." She rubbed her ropy forearms reflexively.

"So this is your first civilian job?"

She nodded. "Since high school. I was in ROTC in college. I was surprised that a special forces background would qualify me for a position in human resources at a university. But I've always believed I can do most anything."

"Mind telling me about how you managed to land the position? It does strike me as a bit unusual." I had a comical vision of her at HR staff meetings with a bunch of bookish, smallish, conservative bureaucrats.

"No problemo. I saw the listing for an employment specialist online and filled out the app, trying my best to figure out how my experience applied to the position. I was a whiz at logistics and thought that might be my selling point. I looked at a few websites to figure out what a human resources person in a university actually does and tailored my resumé accordingly. Then I was called for an interview."

"What was that like?"

"A little crazy. I'd studied up on issues in HR. Talked with friends who had MBAs. Did some mock interviews with hypothetical situations thrown at me."

"Who interviewed you?"

"The veep. Morgan Francis." She lowered her voice to a stage whisper and glanced at the door. "She's a real piece of work. Tough as nails. If she was thirty years younger she would've been beside me in military training, and would have pushed even harder than I did for a combat assignment. Very goal-directed, results-oriented. She would do whatever it took to get her way in situations that really mattered to her. We hit it off great."

This wasn't the reputation she had in the bureaucracy. Rather than being any kind of facilitator, she had been nicknamed "Dr. No" for her inflexible attitude regarding rules and regulations around employment.

"What did she ask in the interview?"

"She asked me mostly about my training, not much about HR. Which caught me off-balance, even though it made the interview a piece of cake. She wanted to know about my physical fitness, my ability to react to different stressful situations and improvise. My motivation. My sense of mission. I figured there was no way this was ever going to work. And then, to my surprise, she called with a job offer."

"What area did she assign you to?"

"My official area is special projects. I'm not authorized to say any more than that. But so far, everything I've been assigned has fallen within my skill set." Her expression was wide-eyed and open but it was clear this subject was off limits.

"Well, I bet you're glad to finally be moving. You know the story of the delay?"

She laughed. "Of course. It affected me big time. They had picked out this office for me when I started. But they explained that 'it wasn't yet available,' even though I could walk by and see it was as empty as a spent shell. Instead, I was located about a half-mile away in a rented building. Grade B real estate. Crappy, cheap furniture that would break if you looked at it wrong. Windows about to fall out of their frames. Bathrooms that only occasionally worked. I had more comfortable spaces on base in Afghanistan."

"That bad."

I heard footsteps in the hallway. The Viking looked past me, nodded, and then continued. "That bad. Electricity would go out periodically for no reason. I got to know the physical plant people really well. There wasn't much they could do except to inform the landlord. The landlord was evidently trying to make a quick buck and didn't want to invest in the building, which was slated for demolition."

"I can imagine you were eager to get outta there."

She rummaged in one of the moving boxes. "Yeah, you could say that. And the more I learned about the cause of the situation, the angrier I got. It was just fuckin' stupid. If we had a fuck-up like that in the forces we'd know how to deal with him. We heard from the top that the move was all settled and we'd begin to pack up the boxes. Then, in the middle of packing, word came down that the move was off. We were pretty sure Ronson had somehow torpedoed the plans. It was beyond aggravating. And the veep made it clear..." Her voice trailed off. She put a few frames on the desk and looked around the office, probably for a hammer and hooks.

"Welcome to the wonderful world of higher education. Everything takes longer than you think it should. I'm sometimes amazed that anything gets done. The bureaucracy... well, I'm sure you encountered bureaucrats in the Army. But I'd put ours up against anyone in their ability to turn simple situations into ones of immense complexity."

She located the hammer and began testing out locations for her mementos, talking at me over her shoulder. "In special forces, we were away from the bureaucrats, at least at my level. I'm sure there was plenty of politicking among the mucky-mucks. But you give guys a bunch of MK 17s, a SCAR long barrel, submachine guns, grenade launchers, recoilless antitank weapons... and things start to happen. You can hold them back for a while, maybe, but eventually those babies get used. Even in logistics, there was only so much sitting around that we would take. And everyone knew it. Here..." she shook her head and sighed. "Here, they could use a little more of that 'can't wait' attitude."

"Well, finally your time came. You were lucky. You might have waited years."

"Uh, I don't think so." She just smiled. It was clear she had exhausted her supply of small talk. "Before you go, maybe you could help me with these," she gestured to a couple of frames.

"Sure."

She picked up one and held it next to the wall. "What about here?"

"About six inches to the right and down a bit."

"Now?"

"Exactly."

She drove a nail into the wall with one blow and hung what looked like a cartoon. "I just love this one. A gift from one of my buds. I'll never forget Lance. He was a hell of a leader. Didn't take shit from anybody. If there was a way to get things done, he was your guy, as long as you weren't particularly squeamish about how he accomplished his objectives. His reputation preceded him everywhere he went, so people would just get out of his way. Bad things could happen if you didn't."

The cartoon was in black and white. The scene was in an office, with filing cabinets and a computer. A man was standing in front of a desk, arms in the military "at ease" position, hands clasped behind his back. Seated at the desk was an older fellow, clearly the higher ranking official. There was only one object on the desk, a handgun, with the grip near the boss, who was addressing the man in front of him. Underneath the cartoon was a single sentence in quotes:

"Williams, we've concluded that under our current rules we can't fire you, so we've decided to kill you."

I looked up at her. She was standing with her hands on her hips.

"Pretty funny, huh? But definitely not *Stars and Stripes* material."

"Uh, sure. But pretty dark. Especially in an HR office."

"I guess. I never thought of it as dark." I noticed she would stare but hardly blink. Maybe something she picked up in training. She was calm in the way a coiled snake is calm.

"I shouldn't be giving you unsolicited advice, I suppose."

She just nodded. "I haven't been here long, but what drew me was the VP. She's given me a lot of latitude to get things done on her behalf. She doesn't ask about the details, only the results." She folded her fingers together and stretched both hands in front of her. "I think she's actually two people, one in disguise. There's the careful, buttoned-down bureaucrat that most people see in public. But there's also the tough, no-nonsense woman of action who can make things happen even if it requires some unusual steps. I work for the second one.

"It took me a while to realize that she hired me to be, what would you call it, her 'fixer.' I get rid of obstacles. No questions asked. I couldn't ask for a better job description outside of the forces." She had the hammer in her right hand and was flipping it in the air, always catching it by the handle.

"I never thought of the university as a place for people of action."

"It isn't, actually, which is why I'm probably a short-timer. I'm an adrenaline junkie. I realize that I am unlikely to find many opportunities to test my limits." She paused, stopped tossing the hammer and looked me in the eyes, a sly grin spreading over her face.

"Oh, maybe I'll get *one* more shot here, if things go my way."

I was suddenly feeling very uncomfortable. I rose from the chair. "Well, I gotta be going. If you keep your picture out of the paper and your name off the police blotter, you may never see me again. Unless of course you win a Nobel prize."

She stood up to her full height and gave me a cockeyed salute. "That will be just fine with me, sir. Hooah!"

Did she actually threaten me? I sure felt like I had been threatened. What did she mean about having one more shot?

Seldom had I encountered anyone who seemed to be a perfect mismatch for the position they held. HR was known as a conservative, rule-driven unit. Its employees were selected for their ability to keep the university out of legal trouble and otherwise be pretty much invisible. They weren't exactly a fount of action. In many ways, this woman seemed the mirror image of everything the organization stood for.

What could Morgan Francis, the VP, have been thinking when she hired her? And that cartoon. Wait until one of her colleagues sees that on her wall. I was pretty sure it would be back in the moving box within twenty-four hours.

There must have been more to her hiring than she had told me. I filed it away as just another of those inexplicable things about working here that I'd never understand. Just another mystery, albeit a minor one. I wrote my puff piece about the move, suppressing my gag reflex, and sent it upstairs for a once-over before publishing it online.

* * *

That evening, I was making polite dinner conversation with Andrea as we shared Thai takeout and mentioned my strange encounter, minus the veiled threat. She responded with more than casual interest.

"And tell me again why you stopped in front of her door," she asked, jabbing a mouthful of green curry pork.

"She looked interesting. Striking. As I said, she was like a Viking." I picked up a spoonful of Tom Yum Gung, the enhanced version of Thai shrimp soup, and inhaled it. I felt my sinuses clear.

But Andrea wasn't done with the subject.

"Hmmmm."

"What?" I looked up.

"Just that."

"What?"

"Would she have been as interesting if she was, oh, short and less 'fit'? And something other than blonde?"

I put down my spoon. "What are you suggesting?"

Andrea pointed with her chopsticks. "It's just men. And blondes. Even you. I can't say I'm surprised."

"No no no, you misunderstand. It was the whole scene, and being blonde was the least of it. This bodybuilder type in the building that houses top administrators. It just seemed unusual. Out of place."

"Uh huh. And explain to me again what she was hired to do."

"Truth is, I have no idea. All she told me was special projects, which could cover a multitude of sins. Then she claimed she wasn't authorized to talk about it. As if what she was doing was classified."

The conversation seemed to flag. Andrea appeared lost in thought: she was seldom this quiet, and it made me curious, perhaps even a bit apprehensive, about what would come next.

A few minutes later, Andrea put down her chopsticks emphatically and grinned at me.

"Now I see why you decided to shut down your investigation. You're really not very good at following the bouncing ball, are you?" I saw her lick her lips with playful delight. She loved to tease me.

I accidentally splashed some broth on my shirt. Damn, that stuff was hard to remove.

"What'd I do? I'm sorry, I don't follow you."

"Do I need to draw you a picture?" she sighed dramatically. I was confused; I actually did need a picture. "OK. I'll lead you through this. Ready?"

"I can hardly wait."

"You meet an individual. This...Viking, let's call her for lack of a better word, especially since you never got her name. Another smart move, dear. The Viking was hired by Human Resources without any particular background or skills that match the jobs in that division. And she's hired with a vague job title that could mean anything. Following so far?"

"Yes."

"Very good. Wish I had a chalk board! Anyhow, let's look at this Viking's skills, and see if that suggests anything about why she was hired. Let's make a list of her skills. I'll start: quick reactions. Your turn."

"Stealth."

"Very good. Team player."

"Improvisation under pressure."

"Very good! How about knowledge of weapons?"

"OK, but actually, it's not just arms training, but about knowing the right tool for the job, so to speak."

"Excellent! But aren't we missing something obvious?"

"Smarts."

"True. But what's a well-known characteristic of special forces? I'd say an essential part of their mission."

"She's trained to kill."

"But not just kill. Any grunt with a weapon or hand-to-hand combat training could kill someone." Andrea was tapping her foot impatiently.

I paused. Where was she headed? Then it dawned on me. It was like a lightning bolt.

"Oh no," I said, catching her drift. "You want me to say targeted assassination? You mean you think she was hired as a contract killer? An assassin? Seriously?"

"Why not? It's no crazier than the theories you were considering earlier."

"But why? Why would the HR veep want to kill Ronson?"

Andrea looked exasperated. "What were you telling me about Ronson's contract?"

"You mean the provision about a permanent office in Main Central? So Ronson was killed over his office space?"

Andrea laughed. "It does sound kinda silly when you put it that way. But you were the one who pointed out, and maybe you were exaggerating, how important the issue of space is to status at the university and how vicious the battles are. Not to mention all this other stuff, the accumulation of bad blood between Ronson and various people in the administration. This was just the final straw, when he started jerking people around. Powerful, impatient people."

I shook my head in disbelief. "It's hard for me to believe."

"So tell me, Sherlock, assuming you believe her story, do you have another explanation for why this woman was hired and what she's supposed to be doing? If you do, then I'll withdraw my theory."

"That sounds like a challenge," I said. "And here I thought my investigating career was over."

"Maybe, maybe not. I'm saying that you should give it one last try. With my full support, as if that was ever in question."

"Let's assume for a moment I accept your challenge. How would you suggest I test your theory?"

Andrea put her hands on the edge of the table and leaned back. "How the hell should I know? You're the rumpled reporter with a nose for news. You figure it out."

CHAPTER FOURTEEN

I didn't sleep well. I kept replaying my conversation with the Viking. And my restless brain kept coming up with questions:

— Did the HR vice president advertise a job looking for a hired killer or did she just land on the idea when the Viking applied?

— Do people really kill others over office space? Is the HR veep that kind of person?

— What had the Viking been suggesting when she said she might have "one more shot" at testing her limits?

— Was the HR vice president paying for this on a university budget?

The fact was, Morgan Francis had hired someone in human resources who had no relevant qualifications. Her training included how to perform stealth operations. And executions. She was expert at covering her tracks. Probably far better than our cops were at investigating.

But I just couldn't wrap my mind around the logic. This was happening... because of lust over office space?

As I tossed and turned, I thought about why someone would commit a violent crime. One thing I knew was that we underestimate the role irrationality plays in our decisions. I had seen this as a reporter but also in the halls of academe. We systematically give ourselves far too much credit for being rational creatures. In fact, we are rational only intermittently. Worse yet, we frequently act on impulse while convincing ourselves that our actions are the product of dispassionate deliberation.

The Ronson case wouldn't be the first time someone had followed a logical argument to its illogical conclusion. Why couldn't that happen at a university, and why couldn't it involve a fight over office space?

After being ready to abandon my investigation, I was convinced that Andrea's theory had a certain perverse logic. That meant I had to find some way to confirm or deny it.

Thinking back to the day just after the crime, the Viking bore more than a passing resemblance to the "graduate student" who had stood giggling near where the body had landed. So I'd been targeted for special handling from the beginning, from the moment I doubted the official explanation. This casual meeting was followed by the keying of my car, the tailgating incident, my hacked computer and the meeting earlier today. That meeting, it seemed to me, was no more a chance encounter than our first; if I hadn't found my way into her office on my own, I'm pretty sure I would have been directed there. All of this culminated in a pretty explicit threat that my fate could be the same as Ronson's.

There was no way I could confront the head of HR with this information. She'd simply laugh at me. She had conducted the job interview by herself, so only two people knew precisely what went on there. I was certain the Viking would tell me no more about her real job. I figured our next meeting would be a lot less pleasant.

Anything that might befall me in the future was subject to the "goal-oriented, results-directed" dictum from Morgan Francis and her eager, combat-trained "fixer." I woke the next morning from my restless, unsettling evening much the worse for wear. Andrea's explanation stuck with me like a sharp stone in my shoe.

I dragged myself to work, waving at Fern as I walked past in a daze. She half-opened her mouth, realized it was better not to waste words, and stuck out her tongue at me.

I sat at my desk, head in hands, trying to focus. My thoughts were scattered. I was like a dog chasing a car. But now that I had caught it (or nearly so), what was I to do?

Word got around that I looked out of it, hung over, depressed, dejected, maybe suicidal. Nearly my entire staff poked their head in the door, innocently and cheerfully, asking how I was doing. I was warmed by their concern. I was going to have to regroup and move forward. But I was haunted by the Viking's threat and the immensity of the challenge I faced.

I thanked my colleagues without sharing any of the details of my struggle.

Stella was last. She assumed that reaching the end of my investigation had caused my malaise. She shook her head, jutted out her chin, and proclaimed, "It's not so bad, and it's going to get better. You can count on it."

I thanked her and finally shut my door.

Then I picked up the phone and called Leigh Lambert, the Woman Who Knows Everyone. I explained to Leigh about my meeting with the Viking and all that had come before and asked what she thought.

"Whoa! And I thought we were just joking around about Ronson's fall. This puts it in a whole new light."

"That's what I thought. As it is, there's not much that I can do with this information. Too many missing pieces. I need another insider to help me with this crazy theory."

"Give me some time to think it over. I don't have a ready answer, but I like a challenge."

While waiting for Leigh, I decided to try Stella. I brought her into my office.

"You have pretty good access to parts of the HR database, don't you?" I asked her.

"Some. Not everything. What do you need?"

"Well, I met this woman…"

She cocked an eyebrow.

"Nonono. I'll explain this to you later. Maybe. For now, can you just do me a favor and see if you can find her? That's all I need, her name and work record. She was hired in HR a few months ago, working on special projects for the VP. Probably has a title like employment specialist or maybe assistant to the vice president. Can you take a look for me, please?"

Stella peered out at me over the top of her glasses and sighed. "I thought you'd concluded your investigation."

"I had. I thought. Just this one last thing, Stella, please."

"Only if you promise to tell me what's going on. At the appropriate time, of course."

"Of course."

A few hours later she came back.

"No luck."

"No?"

"No. I was able to look up recent hires in HR, and there's no one even close to that description. Nobody in all of human resources. No assistant or administrative assistant or consultant to the vice president. In fact, no one has been hired in central human resources in the past six months that bears any resemblance to that description."

"Huh. What if the person were a contract worker. Would that be there somewhere?"

"'Fraid so. I'm coming up empty. Maybe if I had more information…"

"I'll see what I can get for you."

Not surprising. Covering her tracks. Well, this was easy enough to fix.

I sauntered upstairs, figuring by now there might be a nameplate on the door.

There was indeed a nameplate: Alexandra Olivet, assistant to the vice president. Voilá! I stuck my head in, figuring I'd say hello again, even if that involved pushing my luck.

But the person behind the desk was petite with short, dark hair and glasses. There was no picture of a platoon or anything like that on the wall. Just family photos, vacation scenes and one art print.

"Can I help you?" I must've looked a sight, gaping at her and the office's changed interior.

"Uh, maybe. When I was by here yesterday, there was another woman moving into this office. There must've been a change in plans."

"Yes?"

"She was very tall, about six feet. Platinum blonde braids. Extremely fit. Ex-military. She had photos of her training buddies on the wall, right over here," I pointed. "And a black and white cartoon, over there."

Alexandra, if that's who it was, stood behind her desk, shifting her weight from one foot to another and studiously avoiding a glance in my direction. "I… wish I could help you. I really do. But I've never met anyone who meets that description. I was assigned this space when the move was planned. So there must be some confusion. Maybe the woman you claim you saw," she finally looked at me, "is located elsewhere on the floor. But if she works for HR, I think I would know her. It's part of my job, as Ms. Francis's assistant, to keep track of things like that."

"She was a pretty recent hire. Working directly for the vice president and assigned to special projects."

She nervously moved some papers around her desk and her words came haltingly. "All the appointments in our unit are approved by the vice president and I process the paperwork. Employees typically come to my office to sign forms or submit other documents. And we haven't had any recent hires in that area."

"Not even contract workers?"

"We typically don't use contract workers. I'm sure you can figure out why. Maybe this person was just playing a joke. Maybe she worked for one of the moving companies. I really can't explain."

"This is odd. Very odd. I work a few floors below, in the public information office, and I came up here, to this very office, and had a conversation with the woman I described. She was in the midst of unpacking boxes and settling in."

Alexandra began walking toward me. "I really don't know what to tell you. Feel free to look in the offices down the hall. But I'm certain you won't find anyone who matches that description in our unit." She gently escorted me out and shut the door. I heard the tumbler turn in the lock.

Later that day I heard from Leigh Lambert.

"Sorry, I have bad news."

"Well, I'm not surprised." I knew it was a long shot, but I was disappointed nonetheless.

"I have a big rolodex, and it includes people who can be helpful to me in one way or another. And I hate to say this, but I've never found anyone in Human Resources who was the least bit helpful. So whatever whiffs of something rotten that you're smelling, you'll need to track down the source through other means. And I wish I knew how. Sorry."

"That's OK, Leigh." I hung up the phone with a sinking feeling. So close, yet so far.

★ ★ ★

That day, just before closing time, Stella poked her head in the office to see how I was doing. One look at my face convinced her of the answer.

"Look," she said, taking an uninvited seat. "It's not so bad. You realized from the beginning, didn't you, that putting all the pieces together to reveal a different pattern was a tall order? I mean, the police aren't completely incompetent."

I held my lips together, gritted my teeth and shook my head. "There's been further developments. Serious business, I think. Got time for a confidential story?"

"You kidding?" She made herself comfortable, stretched out her legs and removed her glasses, letting them dangle by the lanyard, her hands crossed in front of her.

I told her about my encounter with the Viking, the mystery woman whose information was conspicuous by its absence from the employee database and now even from the hallway where her office had been.

"Geez." Stella wiped her glasses on her flannel shirt. "Geez. I'm speechless."

"I'm this close to figuring out the whole, sordid mess, I think. But I have no idea what to do next."

"I wish I could say I have an answer." And she left, shaking her head.

It was a long couple of days, trudging back into the routine. My work life was as flat as Kansas. The emotions were pretty much sucked out of me. I figured I had to put the Ronson story on the shelf, unless and until I could figure out how to unmask the actual killer, who by now was probably in a different state if not a different country.

A few days later, on a dark, wet winter afternoon, as I was preparing to leave, Stella stopped me. "Do you have a few minutes? I have someone I'd like you to meet."

"Sure, whatever."

Stella's breath was coming in gasps. Either she'd been walking fast or was experiencing another asthma attack. "Look, I can't promise that this is going to solve any of your problems, but it's the best I can offer. I hope it's of some value."

She directed me to a small conference room across the hall. Inside was a woman I'd seen occasionally around Main Central but had never talked with, any more than a desultory hello.

"Mr. Woodsen, I'd like you to meet Yodit," she said. "Yodit has worked the night shift for Custodial Services for how long?"

"Two years now," she said in a soft, lilting accent. "Two years of night shift. Sector 3A. Main Central, too. I am here, this building, two years now. Not every night here." I recall someone telling me that Yodit was from Eritrea. She was tall and dark, wearing heavy blue eye shadow and a colorful head scarf. The rest of her outfit was a university-issued scrubs-like mustard-color suit.

"Yodit has a few minutes before her shift begins," Stella said. "I thought you might have some questions for her. I'll leave you two alone. Just close and lock the door when you're through." The door closed with a soft click.

Yodit crossed and uncrossed her legs. Her eyes were downcast and she fidgeted in her chair.

I sighed. Stella was trying to be helpful, bless her heart. I thought that she was grasping at straws, but out of respect and affection for her I decided to play along. I was as direct as possible, wasting little of Yodit's time.

"Thank you for talking with me," I began.

"Is nothing," she looked up, smiled slightly, then looked away.

"Yodit, I want to ask you about one particular evening when you may have been in this building."

"So sorry, I don't have work calendar with me. Cannot tell which day."

"That's all right. I want you to think back about three weeks ago."

Yodit nodded slowly. "Hard remember."

"I know. But maybe you'll remember something. When you are working in Main Central, what time do you usually start here?"

"Not always same time. Usually, am on building ten o'clock, sometimes later. Almost not early."

"OK. Very good. But when you are in Main Central, do you see other people? Other people who work in the building?"

Yodit shook her head. "I work by self. No other workers here."

"Yes. But do you see administrators, office workers in the building?"

She looked up. "Nobody on building except me. Empty offices. Always empty, by self."

Well that was that, end of story. I smiled grimly at Yodit and prepared to leave.

"Oh, I think more. Wrong. I see someone, one night. Just one, I think. Very late. At top. Up high in building."

"How long ago?"

"Hard remember. No have date. I think this season, this fall, I know. Long time. I surprise her. We both surprise. A little scared me."

"You saw someone? A woman?"

"Yes. I see a woman there. Here. One time."

"Do you remember what she looked like? Can you describe her?"

Yodit looked up, wet her lips and glanced around the room, trying to grasp the right words. "Saw few minutes only. Long time."

"I understand. Was she a big woman or small? Tall?" Yodit looked puzzled. I lifted my arm as high as I could. "Or short?" I brought it down to table level.

"Big," she almost whispered. "Very big. Tall."

"Do you remember anything else about her? What about the color of her hair? Was it dark, like yours, or light?"

Yodit sat with her head down, a look of concentration on her face. "I try remember. Not long. I surprise her and she smile. Yes. Light." She smiled at me.

"Light?"

"Hair. White. Long. Behind back. Like this." She made braiding motions with her hands.

A shiver of excitement shot through my body. "A tall woman with blonde — white — hair in braids?"

"Yes. I see her on Main Central one night. She smile. I smile and go back at work. Is all." She made a palms-up gesture.

"Ah, one thing more. Her lips. Very red. More red than a fire engine, I think. Pretty smile, teeth pretty. Very big. And how you say…" she made a fist.

"Muscles. Good muscles."

Yodit smiled. "Yes. Big muscles. Woman with big muscles."

"Yodit, this is very helpful. Is there anything else you remember from that night? Anything else with that woman or anyone else in the building?"

She paused and drummed her fingers. "Same as all day. Maybe I see one office window open. Sometimes is so."

"Do you remember where the window was? Which side of the building? Which floor?"

Yodit shook her head. "No, long time. Maybe same night. Window open is… common, word is right?"

"Yes, common. Windows open is common."

"Ah, big window. Big as I am." Yodit looked down again. "Is all I remember. Nothing more." She looked at me and smiled. "Am sorry nothing more."

"No, this is good. You have helped a lot. Thank you for your time."

I opened the door for Yodit and sat back down at the conference table.

This was the closest I was going to get to the truth without a formal investigation and the weight of legal authority behind me.

I could see only one possible alternative. I needed to line up every scrap of information I had in preparation for a crazy, wild leap.

I was going right to the top.

CHAPTER FIFTEEN

This was a risky proposition. By custom and protocol I was prohibited from making an appointment directly with the president. If I did try, it wasn't at all clear that I would be granted an audience. My supervisors would probably be notified. And then there would be consequences.

But I was sure that a murder had occurred and also who did it and why. No one else at the university, including the cops, was going to listen to my story. This was a kind of "Hail Mary," but I had to give it the old college try, especially since I was an employee of the old college. At least for now.

One tiny advantage I did have was knowing Yarmouth's private email. There was a public account, one that customarily followed those broadcast email messages to the campus containing the obligatory line, "But I want to know what you think." That account was screened by any number of people who would pass on only a few of the most important or humorous messages to Yarmouth.

There could be one or more screeners in his office even for the private account, but that was my best chance.

Dear President Yarmouth:

I am taking the liberty of contacting you directly on a matter of the utmost importance, one literally of life and death. For that reason, I would urge you not to share this message with anyone. I am writing to request a private meeting with you at your earliest convenience.

I know that you are not used to receiving messages like this, and the truth is I never expected I would be writing one. But what I have to report to you is a grave matter, one that requires your urgent attention.

I let it fly and crossed my fingers. About thirty minutes later I received a response, ostensibly from Yarmouth's personal tablet.

Mr. Woodsen:
I am willing to meet with you, although I hope what you need to tell me does not match the level of alarm in your note. You should be hearing from my scheduler shortly.

The earliest appointment was two days hence. In the meantime, I'd be cooling my heels and rehearsing my remarks. I dusted off my suit, selected the least offensive member of my six-tie collection, and marched into the president's suite early in the morning, before the working day had actually begun. It was tastefully decorated with iconic images of the campus and action photos of the various sports teams. It was also the only wood-paneled suite in all of Main Central, salvaged and refurbished from bygone days. Everyone there spoke in hushed tones, and the phone was already ringing persistently.

I knew his assistant, who nodded, smiled, and put her finger to her lips as she ended another phone conversation. "He'll be able to see you in a minute. Would you like something to drink?"

Asking for Scotch was probably a nonstarter. What I really needed was a paper towel to wipe the perspiration from my hands. But I settled for water which was delivered with a small napkin. I took one of the armchairs near the receptionist.

The wait was short. Yarmouth came out to greet me with a handshake, his white sleeves rolled up to his elbows and his tie swinging. He waved me into the office and shut the door.

He directed me to a small couch while he sat in a wing chair. There was a glass coffee table at the center of what could be called a conversation area, complete with picture books of the campus.

"Your message really got my attention." He leaned forward, his hands clasped around one knee.

"I should probably begin by saying I'm not crazy. I can verify, or at least justify, every statement I'm about to make."

"OK, OK."

"I say that only because what I'm about to tell you is going to strain the bounds of credulity." I took a deep breath. "I believe a murder was committed on this campus. Specifically, I have evidence that Jeremy Ronson, the former vice president for IT, was killed. In essence, it was a contract killing motivated at least in part by one of the provisions of his employment agreement."

He whistled, then nodded slowly. "I assume there's more to the story."

I swallowed hard. "Morgan Francis hired someone a few months ago who had extensive elite military training. But no background whatsoever in human resources. She was hired allegedly to work on special projects for the vice president. But there is no evidence that her employment went through regular channels. And she seems to have mysteriously disappeared."

"I'm going to need something more than your say-so if you expect me to take this seriously. I'm sure you understand that."

"Of course. First, there is Ronson's employment agreement. It had many unusual conditions, such as granting him a tenured faculty position if he ever lost his administrative post."

Yarmouth nodded. "I'm all too aware of that. I wish I could have a conversation with my predecessors about their poor judgment."

"It seems the agreement had another provision, seemingly a minor one, that allowed Ronson to keep his office in Main Central, and perhaps the entire suite of surrounding offices, in perpetuity."

"No one ever mentioned that to me."

"It's not something most people paid attention to. But I know the people in HR, and especially Morgan Francis, were acutely aware. Mostly because they coveted the space. In fact, they had been officially assigned the space and were prepared to move several times, only to have the decision reversed at the last minute, apparently because of Ronson's intransigence. Francis was frustrated. And angry."

Yarmouth sat back and folded his arms. "So what you're telling me is that one of my vice presidents commissioned a hit, by a trained killer, on another one of the vice presidents? And that the cause of this hit was *office space*? And you expect me to take that seriously."

"Look, I know it sounds unbelievable."

"Sure does."

"After Ronson's death, when the HR move was finally underway, I had a chance conversation with the woman who was hired by Francis. Her previous employment was with special forces. She had all the training necessary for clandestine operations, for pulling off a crime in a way that would make it look like an accident. And since our conversation, she seems to have disappeared."

Yarmouth folded his arms in a gesture of skepticism. "How convenient."

"But I have reason to believe that she was in the building the evening that Ronson died. To the best of my knowledge, she was the only other person in the building at that time." I decided to shield Yodit.

"Also, I was able to determine that the stacks of paper in Ronson's office, which were on virtually every horizontal surface, had been disturbed. The disturbances described a pathway leading from his desk to the window from which he was pushed. I believe Ronson was surprised and overpowered by his assailant, dragged to the window and thrown out. The assassin tried to cover her tracks but she did not restore order to the papers.

"Of course, Vice President Francis is going to deny that this happened or that she had any role if it did happen. And the woman I met, who was hired to dispose of Ronson, also would surely deny under direct questioning what she hinted at in our conversation. If we can even locate her."

Yarmouth looked annoyed. He swallowed with an audible gulp and sat up straight, his eyes unblinking. He shook his head slowly.

I went out on an even narrower limb. "I also think, if it hasn't already been destroyed, that somewhere there's an email thread that explains why Ronson was in his office after hours, something that was highly unusual for him, and that this email will point to Francis or her confederate. Or maybe there was a series of phone calls, I'm not sure. They lured him to stay beyond his normal departure time under some pretext.

"I've pursued this as far as I can on my own, without any kind of official authority. I know that our police are unwilling to reopen the case. I've pretty much worn out my welcome with them. Which is what brought me to you."

Yarmouth yawned and scratched his chin. He seemed unperturbed. "Let me ask you, why did you pursue this in the first place? After all, you don't have any investigative or law enforcement training, do you? What made you think there was a crime?"

"I was called to the scene when the... incident occurred. Later, when the cause of death was announced I left my office, which is in this building, and stood at the scene, looking up at the fourth floor window, wondering how someone could fall accidentally. Someone who was sober and in their right mind. It just seemed so unlikely. I wasn't convinced that his death was accidental.

"Later, I was able to examine his office. To me, the office showed signs of disturbance, of things being out of order. There's no way to prove it now, but I'm pretty sure someone else was in that office with him that evening. Someone with key card access to the building after hours, or someone who was already there before the building was locked. How they maneuvered Ronson to the window, I can't say for sure. But the woman I met was powerful and well trained."

"I see. So what do you think I should do?" He took off his glasses, put them on the coffee table in front of him, and massaged the bridge of his nose. "It isn't as if I have any license to investigate things like this either. I may be president, but tracking down leads for a possible murder isn't exactly in my job description. Especially when the police have decided otherwise." He put his glasses back on. "And that's assuming I buy your line of reasoning, which you must admit seems pretty far-fetched."

"Look, I'm in no position to advise you. I've spent a fair amount of my own time looking into this, talking to people and doing what research I could. I would agree that my evidence is incomplete but not flimsy. I find it convincing. And I received some pretty explicit threats which make me think I'm on the right track."

Yarmouth stood up and clasped his hands behind his back, pacing toward his desk, then away, in measured strides. "All I need right now is for word to leak out that I'm pursuing some half-baked theory, with all due respect, concerning the murder of a high-ranking university official to secure his office space. Office space!

"I'm already taking significant heat from the faculty for this branding initiative. But my trustees and several vice presidents are adamant that we need to do more to strengthen the institution's image.

"Then there's a pressure group, also led by some trustees, who claim there will be no future for this university without a substantial commitment to online education, and they'd like to see something happen yesterday. Harvard and MIT did it, so why not us? It would help to differentiate us from every other public university and it also could address a need, because of our highly restrictive admission standards. But our esteemed faculty senate regards initiatives like this as a faculty prerogative, and their reluctance reduces progress to the pace of a three-legged tortoise.

"To add to our problems, we have a legislature that would just love to micro-manage this institution, convinced that they can make it more efficient, when in most years they can't even complete the public's business by their self-imposed deadline. Yet they feel no compunction about criticizing how we use the paltry resources they provide to us."

I tried to look sympathetic but wasn't even sure which facial muscles to employ in that pose. I was seeing first-hand how decisions were reached, how priorities were decided.

"There are days when this job is fun, but today isn't one of them. Actually, not this month or even most of this year." He began pacing faster, waving his arms. "The faculty loves to complain but never offers constructive ideas in response to proposals with which they take issue. They figure their job is to be a de facto veto group, and they wield that veto pretty effectively on occasion.

"We're living in a confusing time. I actually have some sympathy with the faculty dissident who spoke at the senate meeting. You were there, weren't you? But even he allowed that ancient institutions such as universities are being pushed to change in fundamental ways, whether we like it or not.

"We're gradually abandoning the ivory tower, and some would describe our destination as rolling in the mud. Not only is everything becoming commercial, but it's also becoming partisan. Education used to be a widely accepted societal value. Now it's becoming a bone of contention among competing ideologies. If we try to maintain our position above the fray we're going to be attacked by all sides. Or at least I will. There's no virtue in being even-handed in times like these."

He nodded. "Sorry to digress. But this is just one more thing, and with all respect not the most important thing, that is on my plate."

He resumed his seat, pushed at his sleeves and grabbed for a note pad.

"I'm going to assume, for the sake of argument, that this might be what they call a 'black swan' event. One that's extremely unlikely, but if it did happen would be the cause for a major scandal." He scribbled on the pad.

"I could summon Morgan Francis to my office and ask her point blank. But what good would that do? She's going to cop to a crime? Not likely. Hey, I spend twenty minutes with you and begin talking like Philip Marlowe.

"So one hope might be to get the hit-lady to talk, if we can find her. How likely is that? Not very. Or… we could take this case downtown and someone," he looked at me meaningfully, "could file a complaint. Then get the pros to decide if this is worth investigating." He looked at me questioningly.

"I think that's the best alternative, for you to file a complaint with the city cops. By the way, what is this hit lady's name?"

"She didn't say."

"Oh joy. An anonymous maybe hit woman. Just perfect." Yarmouth stood up, signaling an end to the interview.

He reached to shake my hand. "I believe the best course of action would be for you to file a complaint with the city PD naming this woman, a Jane Doe I think they call it, as a murder suspect. If the city police do investigate and I'm deposed, I can say truthfully that we don't have the background or experience to investigate so I sent you to them."

"That makes some sense. But I thought you should know about this anyhow. Even if you choose to stay above the fray."

He shot me a look that suggested he didn't appreciate my characterization of his response. Then he shrugged. "I'd say thank you, but I'm sure you'd know I didn't mean it." So the ball was back in my court. I had to decide whether to contact the downtown cops with my information or just drop the whole thing.

That afternoon Fran put a call through from Trencher. "What took you so long?" I asked, my voice dripping with sarcasm. I was pretty sure he'd learned of my meeting.

"What?"

"I was expecting this call a few hours ago."

"I've been kinda busy. You and I need to talk."

This would not be fun. I had scarcely walked in to Trencher's office when he lit into me.

"What the hell did you think you were doing?"

I settled into a chair, trying to stay cool. "I assume you mean my meeting with Yarmouth."

"Damn right. We have protocols here. You don't just go scheduling private meetings with the president on your own. I want to know what you were thinking. You must've known this was a violation of protocol and would bring big trouble."

I had thought through my response. "It was a private matter. Not related to anything going on in your office or my office." I was counting on Yarmouth not revealing the details of the meeting. This gave me a card in the hole. Not an ace, but maybe a face card. If Trencher thought that my conversation might have involved a whistleblower issue, he would tread lightly, lest he step over the legal guardrails put in place by state law, which prohibited threatening people who report corruption in state agencies. And by some definitions the Ronson incident could conceivably qualify.

"Still. I thought we had a relationship in which there was a modicum of trust. Anything you shared with the president you could have shared with me, without risk of exposure or recrimination. You should have known that."

"I regarded the matter as highly sensitive. One of those 'for your ears only' moments with the president. I wasn't planning this. It just happened. It was something I couldn't drop, but neither was there a logical way to pursue it through normal channels." I was waiting for him to ask me a substantive question about the subject at hand. But he deflected.

He adjusted his vest and fiddled with his tie. "You know that Yarmouth thinks your nuts. I'm sure that wasn't the outcome you had hoped for. But he thinks his head of public information is a lunatic. I don't know what you told him, I didn't press him for details, but he thinks you have lost touch with reality. 'Delusional' was the word that he used. What the hell? I'm not going to ask you what you were talking about. I'm willing to accept your explanation, that this was a highly sensitive conversation. But how do we move forward as a unit, and indeed as a university, when the president has lost confidence in one of the key players on his communications team?"

This was news to me. Not the part about being thought crazy, but being identified as a key player.

"Honestly, I don't know. Let me give this some thought."

Trencher turned back to his keyboard. "I don't really have anything else to say. Except that I'm disappointed. Really disappointed."

I found my way to the door and walked meditatively down the stairs. Despite being about as angry as I'd ever seen him, Trencher apparently wasn't going to fire me. He wasn't about to act when he thought I might have something really nasty to spill in public, whether it was protected by statute or not. But whatever trust had existed between us (we had always behaved like sparring partners defending against a sucker punch) was surely gone. I needed to figure out how much I cared about that.

I'd been putting one foot ahead of the other in tracking down clues about Ronson's death. But now I was hit smack in the face with the question of what did I want to do, not just tomorrow but in the future? What was my own personal endgame here? What was my bottom line?

I went through the rest of the day in a kind of fog. That evening, I updated Andrea on my meeting with Trencher. I had called her earlier with the details of my conversation with Yarmouth. She listened, wide-eyed, without interruption.

After a long while, she responded. "Know what I think? Call me paranoid, or whatever the word is. But I think the conspiracy is wider than we thought."

"Wider how?"

"How surprised was the president when you met with him?"

"I'm not sure how to answer that."

"Think back."

"He seemed more annoyed than anything. Just one more problem for him to confront."

Andrea pointed both index fingers at me. "Exactly."

"Exactly what?"

"He's part of it. Don't you see? The space issue was just one more straw. They had so many reasons for wanting to get rid of Ronson. He had negotiated golden handcuffs that embarrassed everyone in the administration. He was incompetent. He was a jerk. He was going to be an ongoing liability.

"No one in computer science wanted him on their faculty. He was being pigheaded and obstructive when it came to giving up his old office. His presence, day after day, was affecting the morale of everyone whose path he crossed and reflected poorly on the president's management skills. Maybe he'd go public with the details of the financial scandal and the university's lax oversight, although that was old news. Maybe he had even more dirty linen in his goodie sack, like evidence of wrongdoing within the president's cabinet, or even worse stuff.

"Who knows? He had access to a lot of sensitive information through the computer system. He'd probably accumulated all kinds of shit over the years to give himself additional insurance. Put it all together. The outcome begins to make sense."

"Well, I suppose that's one way to look at it."

"How else can you look at it? These guys are thick as thieves. They're not going to investigate themselves. Why do you think the police dropped it like a hot potato? And now, they'd probably like you to go away, too. Whatever implications that might carry."

"I don't know. I'm completely at sea here. Totally lost." I shook my head. "I need to sleep on this. Figure out what's next. If I go to the cops downtown, what are they likely to make of the mess? All I can give them is unsubstantiated information and rumor. And what happens to me if I do? Yarmouth made no offer of protecting me if I proceeded. And just to add a bit of spice, that Viking is still out there."

I slept fitfully. In lieu of actual sleep I tried to breathe deeply to calm my thumping heart and surging blood pressure. In those quiet hours just before dawn I had an epiphany. Just after sunrise I gently poked Andrea.

"How do you feel about Hawaii?"

She rubbed her eyes. "What?"

"I'm done. No more conspiracies. No more university. No more media. No more bureaucracy. I've had it. The only way to disentangle myself from this is to get out. Now."

She sat up in bed. "You're serious."

"I've never been more serious."

"How soon?"

"The end of the week, if there are flights open."

"That's quick, hun."

"I'd go sooner if I could wrap things up faster. But that gives me ample time to clean out my office, say goodbye to a few people, tie up some loose ends. You up for it?"

Andrea climbed out of bed, stretching. "Not like there's anything pressing that's keeping me here. They won't miss me at the restaurant. I've saved up some money…"

"Don't worry about that. I think I'm about to get lucky."

That morning, I put on my suit again and marched directly up to Yarmouth's office. I winked at his receptionist, who was just hanging up her coat.

"Is he in?"

"Yes, but… do you have an appointment?"

"No, but I'm pretty sure he'll see me." I breezed past her desk and opened his door before she could catch her breath.

"Hi there."

Yarmouth looked up from his desk, barricaded behind stacks of papers.

"You again."

"Me again. And for the last time."

"That's the best news I've had for a while."

"I've decided I'm not going to the downtown cops. You knew that's what I'd conclude, not that it matters much. I couldn't show them any more than I'd showed you. But that's not all. I'm here to propose a deal."

Yarmouth paused his pen in mid-air and sat back in his chair.

"I'm waiting."

"A six-month severance package."

"For you?"

"Yes. Of course for me."

"So sorry to see you go," he deadpanned.

"I just decided I've had my bellyful of this place. But I didn't want to go until I'd received some lovely parting gifts."

He smiled. "A couple of things. Three, actually. First, you should knock before entering. Quite impolite. Second, why are you bringing this curious offer to me? And third, why should I take it seriously?" He put his elbows on his desk and made a cradle for his head with his hands.

"I'm sure you recall our discussion. I don't know how much of what I said was new to you. Maybe all of it. Maybe none of it. This much I do know: the past few weeks have not been an hallucination. The conversations, the evidence I have is real. It wouldn't stand up in court. But I have a feeling that someone with better skills than I could uncover a lot more, given the head start I could provide."

Yarmouth's expression froze.

"Mr. President, what we're dealing with here are perceptions. As your branding team could tell you, if you can generate enough smoke you can convince lots of people that there's a fire. Doesn't matter whether there is one or not.

"Just imagine for a moment that a story like this goes viral on social media. Or an enterprising reporter such as Shelley Strong gets interested. People love a good conspiratorial yarn. Who knows? It might even help flush out other conspirators, and the whole story of what happened goes public. No telling who would be collateral damage in a case like this. It would be ugly for sure.

"So the question before you now is, do you want to put out a small fire, or risk a four-alarm blaze?"

Yarmouth was making some notes as I talked. "I appreciate your candor. Another way of looking at this is, do I succumb to a preposterous and extortive threat made of tissue paper, or do I call your bluff?"

I scribbled my contact information on a piece of paper at the corner of his desk. "You've already seen all of my cards. You can send your answer here. Naturally, this is all confidential, unlike our previous conversation."

He laughed. "Oh, that."

"I'll give you a day to wrestle with your conscience. Or whatever you do before deciding whether to buy people off. I'm sure I'm not the first."

Yarmouth pasted a tight-lipped smile on his face. Hate to play poker with him. And then I left.

I went down to my office, penned a brief resignation note to Trencher, got some cartons out of storage and began throwing things in. It didn't take long for Stella to get the scent.

"What the fuck?" she said, hands on hips at my door.

I extended my hand. "It's been a pleasure. But all good things must come to an end. And the other ones, too."

"What the fuck?" she repeated.

"I wish I could explain. Not sure I fully understand it myself. But it's time. This is the precise moment for a change."

"What about Ronson?"

"He's dead. Hadn't you heard?" Not even a grunt. "Seriously, I would send him a thank you note, if I believed in communicating with the dead. He's given me a lot, much more after his demise than he ever could as a living human. I feel as if a cloud has been lifted."

"So, did someone off the guy?"

"Honestly, I don't know. I'd say the odds are better than fifty/fifty. I've taken this as far as I can. It's time to let someone else pick up the torch, if they're so inclined. I never wanted to be the leader of a one-man band."

She looked disappointed. Crestfallen.

"Hey, can you do me a favor? Gather the staff together."

It was abrupt, surely too abrupt, and I could see the shock and dismay on their faces. I didn't give them any of the details; just that I felt an overwhelming urge to make a dramatic change in my life, in both my job and my residence.

Fran in particular seemed to disapprove of my decision: she kept shaking her head. There was a lot of hand-wringing followed by hand-shaking and hugs. I declined the offer of a send-off event, pleading the urgency of my travel plans. In truth, I loved these folks and was sure I'd break down and tell them the truth, my truth, if I let my guard down even a little. And that wouldn't do any of us any good.

People stopped by my office throughout the day, expressing their feelings and wishing me well. It was also clear that my colleagues weren't buying my explanation. They were very up front in noting that "seeking other opportunities" was a common euphemism to cover a variety of sins. I had to assure them, repeatedly, that I hadn't been fired or forced out.

My conversation with Gina Gertsch, our engineering reporter, was typical. "I'm still not buying your story," she said. "You may have reasons for not telling us the truth, but since we're going to be here and you'll be gone I think you owe us a more detailed explanation. People don't just pick up and leave from a job they've had for a decade."

"Gina, you may not want to believe it, but I just reached a point where I'd had enough. This place is no better, and no worse, than a lot of places you could chose to work. There are many good things about being here, and as you know there are also some bad things, as well as some strange things. I just couldn't see myself continuing to work here any longer. I still have the luxury of making that choice. I'm at a point in my life where a change like this is still possible — no dependents and no debts. I figured it was now or never."

She looked unconvinced but didn't press the issue.

As I was clearing out my desk I wondered whether Stella was going to share the sordid story with the staff after my departure. That was her business now.

Word of my decision spread quickly on campus and my inbox was full of WTFs and well wishes. Delores Sert's note was among the funniest and most touching:

Tell me it's a lie! But not like those lies we are fed daily that pass as "aspirational truths."

I'll miss exchanging psychic messages with you at staff meeting. You have the most acute antennae of anyone I've encountered.

Your humor always helped me keep perspective on this job. I'll miss that most of all.

I don't know what they did to make you leave, and I'm pretty sure I don't want to know. But please keep in touch so I can live vicariously through your adventures, which I'm sure will be many and varied.

Happy trails. Keep the wind at your back.

There was no email or call from Trencher. Nor from Ganas. My metamorphosis from person to unperson had occurred quickly in some quarters.

As I filled the final box with personal effects, Fran knocked.

"So, you're really going to abandon us? Throw us to the wolves?"

"Fran, the wolves were already at the door. Hell, they're wandering around inside the house, paws up on the counter. I was just guarding a few of the more valuable things, like you. And the rest of the staff. But they were going to get there sooner or later. You know that."

She sniffed. "I still think you should take us with you."

"Pick your own time and place. When I first entered the world of work, I thought choosing a job was all about values. Finding an organization that would allow me to live out my beliefs. I had the innocence and arrogance to think of work as a career. As I've grown older and acquired more seasoning, I've learned better. Lately, I've found myself recalling a stanza from a poem I memorized in high school:

Olaf (upon what were once knees)
does almost ceaselessly repeat
'there is some shit I will not eat.'"

"A bit overly-dramatic, I'd say," Fran responded. "And really badly out of context. Cummings was describing pretty much the opposite of what you're doing. The poem was about suffering for your values. Olaf was a conscientious objector who was tortured for his beliefs. He didn't take the next available plane to paradise."

"Interesting point. The poem, as I read it, also is a commentary on the limits of human tolerance for bullshit, the idea of drawing a line, categorically saying there are some things that person simply cannot do. I know that the current situation isn't up there with subverting democracy or throwing the World Series. Still…

"I've decided it's time for a break. Not just a pause but a complete change. I admit a few years from now I might regret this. And I know you're convinced that this isn't the optimal way to handle the situation. But maybe it's the least bad alternative. Come see me in a few years and I'll tell you if it was the right decision or not."

"I'll hold you to that."

* * *

Hapuna Beach. A gentle breeze over the pure, smooth sand. A cool drink. Andrea. Life is good.

"Sure beats working," I said to her, watching youngsters frolicking in the surf with their little dog.

"You gotta stop saying that. Although it's true."

"I kinda like this living off the grid with luxury. Fresh fish nearby, little solar powered house on a road to nowhere. No TV, no Internet. As little touch with the outside world as possible."

Andrea lifted herself from the beach chaise to flip over. "How long you think we can do this? Without getting bored, I mean."

"At least until the money runs out, if not longer."

She took off her shades and squinted up at me. "Don't you wonder in the least how it all came out? If anyone was called to account for what happened? Or how close we came to nailing it?"

"I like your use of the 'we.'"

"Hey, I did my part!"

"Indeed. Without you I'd still be wandering around in the grass below Main Central."

A long pause.

"You know, the whole experience is receding quickly in my rearview mirror, like my car was going a hundred miles an hour. I'm surprised how easy it was to disentangle. I have very limited curiosity about affairs back there. Maybe it's selfish, but I prefer to live in the present, here."

"Speaking of which, I have a hankering for one of those Three Frogs killah tacos," she said.

I roused myself from the chair and got into my saoris. "Your wish is my command. Besides, I could use some of that great Kahlua pork and a guava smoothie."

"Don't get lost or find any dead bodies."

I snapped my towel in her general direction. "You know how funny you are? Not at all."

Acknowledgements

Thanks to my family, for putting up with my roller coaster moods as I worked through the creation of my first novel. I'm happy we all survived. Ben and Vivi, my son and daughter-in-law, have been supportive and encouraging throughout the process. My wife Kathy has always been there, especially to remind me that there is more to life than fiction.

My friend and colleague Nancy Wick provided valuable editing assistance and encouragement when I finished the draft and didn't really know what I had. The novel is better for her efforts.

Aldo Chan is a great designer. Just look at that cover. Valerie Blassey, my Web guru, provided the sturdy bones for my online presence. Photographer Karen Orders made me look better, and younger, than I really am.

A big shout-out to my old gang at NINFO, who put up with my wry observations and jokey approach to management with equanimity and the occasional guffaw. To everyone else at that institution: You're so vain you probably think this is about you.

Finally, I raise my glass in salute to bureaucrats everywhere, who are forced to live daily with the endemic absurdities they confront while laboring in one of society's major institutions, either public or private. Hang in there. And always remember: It's not your life, it's just a job.

About the Author

Robert Roseth was raised in the Chicago area and moved to Seattle in 1977. He holds a bachelor's degree from MIT in political science and a master's degree in journalism from the University of Missouri. He worked at the University of Washington from 1977 to 2015, starting as a science writer and becoming director of the Office of News and Information in 1984. *Ivy is a Weed* is his first novel.

Find out more, including tips for book clubs and how to become a subscriber, at https://robertroseth.com/

Email: robertmroseth@gmail.com

Review *Ivy is a Weed*

If you liked this book, please post your comments at your favorite review site. Thank you!

CPSIA information can be obtained
at www.ICGtesting.com
Printed in the USA
FSHW011548280520
70528FS